MAJOR

MAUREEN CHILD

First Published in Great Britain 2016
By Mills & Boon, an imprint of HarperCollins*Publishers*
1 London Bridge Street, London, SE1 9GF

A Touch Of Persuasion, Terms Of Engagement and *An Outrageous Proposal* were first published in Great Britain by Harlequin (UK) Limited.

ISBN: 978-0-263-92057-4

05-0316

Our policy is to use papers that are natural, renewable and recyclable products and made from wood grown in sustainable forests.The logging and manufacturing processes conform to the legal environmental regulations of the country of origin.

Printed and bound in Spain
by CPI, Barcelona

A TOUCH OF PERSUASION

BY
JANICE MAYNARD

For Deener,
Your energy, enthusiasm and *joie de vivre* challenge
the rest of us to embrace life more fully!
I am glad you are my friend!

Janice Maynard came to writing early in life. When her short story *The Princess and the Robbers* won a red ribbon in her third-grade school arts fair, Janice was hooked. She holds a BA from Emory and Henry College and an MA from East Tennessee State University. In 2002 Janice left a fifteen-year career as an elementary teacher to pursue writing full-time. Her first love is creating sexy, character-driven, contemporary romance. She has written for Kensington and NAL, and now is so very happy to also be part of the Harlequin family—a lifelong dream, by the way!

Janice and her husband live in beautiful east Tennessee in the shadow of the Great Smoky Mountains. She loves to travel and enjoys using those experiences as settings for books.

Hearing from readers is one of the best perks of the job! Visit her website at www.janicemaynard.com or e-mail her at JESM13@aol.com. And of course, don't forget Facebook (www.facebook.com/JaniceMaynardReader Page). Find her on Twitter at www.twitter.com/Janice Maynard and visit all the men of Wolff Mountain at www.wolffmountain.com.

One

Kieran stood on the front porch of the small, daffodil-yellow house and fisted his hands at his hips. In the distance, the sounds of a lawn mower mingled with childish shouts and laughter. The Santa Monica neighborhood where he had finally tracked down Olivia's address was firmly, pleasantly middle class.

He told himself not to jump to conclusions.

The article he'd clipped from one of his father's newspapers crackled in his pocket like the warning rattle of a venomous snake. He didn't need to take it out for a second read. The words were emblazoned in his brain.

Oscar winners Javier and Lolita Delgado threw a lavish party for their only grandchild's fifth birthday. The power couple, two of the few remaining MGM "Hollywood royals," commanded an A-list crowd that included a who's who of movie magic. Little "Cammie," the star of the show, enjoyed pony rides, inflatables and a lavish afternoon buffet that stopped just short of caviar. The child's mother, Olivia Delgado, stayed out of the limelight as is her custom, but was seen occasionally in the company of rising film star Jeremy Vargas.

Like a dog worrying a bone, his brain circled back to the stunning possibility. The timing was right. But that didn't mean he and Olivia had produced a child.

Anger, searing and unexpected, filled his chest, choking him with confusion and inexplicable remorse. He'd done his best to eradicate memories of Olivia. Their time together had been brief but spectacular. He'd loved her with a young man's reckless passion.

It couldn't be true, could it?

Though it wasn't his style to postpone confrontation, he extracted the damning blurb one more time and studied the grainy black-and-white photo. The child's face was in shadow, but he knew her family all too well.

Did Kieran have a daughter?

His hands trembled. He'd been home from the Far East less than seventy-two hours. Jet lag threatened to drag him under. Things hadn't ended well with Olivia, but surely she wouldn't have kept such a thing from him.

The shocking discovery in his father's office set all of Kieran's plans awry. Instead of enjoying a long overdue reunion with his extended family on their remote mountaintop in the Virginia Blue Ridge, he had said hello and goodbye with dizzying speed and hopped on another plane, this time to California.

Though he'd be loath to admit it, he was jittery and panicked. With a muttered curse, he reached out and jabbed the bell.

When the door swung open, he squared his shoulders and smiled grimly. "Hello, Olivia."

The woman facing him could have been a movie star

herself. She was quietly beautiful; a sweeter, gentler version of her mother's exotic, Latin looks. Warm, sun-kissed skin. A fall of mahogany hair. And huge brown eyes that at the moment were staring at him aghast.

He probably should be ashamed that he felt a jolt of satisfaction when she went white. The urge to hurt her was unsettling. "May I come in?"

She wet her lips with her tongue, a pulse throbbing visibly at the side of her neck. "Why are you here?" Her voice cracked, though she was clearly trying hard to appear unconcerned.

"I thought we could catch up…for old times' sake. Six years is a long span."

She didn't give an inch. Her hand clenched the edge of the door, and her body language shouted a resounding *no.* "I'm working," she said stiffly. "Now's not a good time."

He might have been amused by her futile attempt at resistance if he hadn't been so tightly wound. Her generous breasts filled out the front of a white scooped-neck top. It was almost impossible not to stare. Any healthy man between the ages of sixteen and seventy would be drawn to the lush sexuality of a body that, if anything, was more pulse-stopping than ever.

He pushed his way in, inexorably but gently. "Perhaps not for you. I happen to think it's a damn good time."

She stepped back instinctively as he moved past her into a neat, pleasantly furnished living room. Though it was warm and charming, not an item was out of place. No toys, no puzzles, no evidence of a child.

On the far wall, built-in bookcases housed a plethora of volumes ranging from popular fiction to history and art appreciation. Olivia had been a phenomenally intelligent student, an overachiever who possessed the unusual combination of creativity and solid business sense.

A single framed picture caught his eye. As he crossed the room for a closer look, he recognized the background. Olivia had written her graduate thesis about the life and work of famed children's author and illustrator Beatrix Potter. On one memorable weekend, Olivia had dragged Kieran with her to England's Lake District. After touring the house and grounds where the beloved character Peter Rabbit was born, Kieran had booked a room at a charming, romantic B and B.

Remembering the incredible, erotic days and nights he and Olivia had shared on a fluffy, down-filled mattress tightened his gut and made his sex stir. Had he ever felt that way since?

He'd tried so damned hard to forget her, to fulfill his duty as a Wolff son. A million times he had questioned the decisions he made back then. Leaving her without a word. Ending an affair that was too new…too fragile.

But he had ached for her. God, he had ached. For Olivia…elegant, funny, beautiful Olivia…with a body that could make a man weep for joy or pray that time stood still.

He shoved aside the arousing memory. There was a strong chance that this woman had perpetrated an unforgivable deception. He refused to let his good sense be impaired by nostalgia. And let's face it…this meeting should be taking place on neutral ground. Because without witnesses, there was a good chance he was going to wring Olivia's neck.

Again, he studied the photo. Olivia stood, smiling for the camera, holding the hand of a young child. Kieran's world shifted on its axis. He lost the ability to breathe. My God. The kid was a Wolff. No one could doubt it. The wide-spaced eyes, the wary expression, the uptilted chin.

He whirled to face his betrayer. "Where is she?" he asked hoarsely. "Where's my daughter?"

Two

Olivia called upon every parentally bestowed dramatic gene she possessed to appear mildly confused. "Your daughter?"

The man facing her scowled. "Don't screw with me, Olivia. I'm not in the mood." She saw his throat work. "I want to see her. Now."

Without waiting for an invitation, he bounded up the nearby stairs, Olivia scurrying in his wake with her heart pounding. She'd known on some level that this day would come. But in her mind, she'd always thought that *she* would be the one orchestrating the reunion.

Kieran Wolff had been her first and only lover. Back then she'd been a shy, lonely, bookish girl with her head in the clouds. He had shown her a world of intimate pleasures. And then he had disappeared.

Any guilt she was feeling about the current situation evaporated in a rush of remembered confusion and pain.

On the landing he paused, then strode through the open door of what was unmistakably a little girl's bedroom. A Disney princess canopy bed…huge movie posters from a variety of animated children's films…a pair of ballet slippers dangling from a hook on the door.

For a moment, Olivia was reluctantly moved by the anguish on his face, but she firmed her resolve. "I repeat the question. What are you doing here, *Kevin?*"

A dull flush of color rose from the neck of his open-collared shirt. Short-cropped hair a shade darker than hers feathered to a halt at his nape. He was dressed like a contemporary Indiana Jones, looking as if he might be ready to take off on his next adventure. Which was exactly why, among other reasons, she had never contacted him.

He faced her, his gaze an impossible-to-decipher mélange of emotions. "So you know who I am." It was more of a statement than a question.

She shrugged. "I do now. A few years ago I hired a private investigator to find out the truth about Kevin Wade. Imagine my surprise when I learned that no such man existed. At least not the one I knew."

"There were reasons, Olivia."

"I'm sure there were. But those reasons mean less than nothing to me at this point. I need you to leave my house before I call the police."

Her futile threat rolled off him unnoticed. He was intensely masculine, in control, his tall lanky frame lean and muscular without an ounce of fat. Amber eyes narrowed. "Maybe *I'll* call the police and discuss charges of kidnapping."

"Don't do this," she whispered, her throat tight and her eyes burning. "Not after all this time. Please." The entreaty was forced between numb lips. She owed him nothing. But he could destroy her life.

"Where is the child?" His unequivocal tone brooked no opposition.

"She's traveling with her grandparents in Europe." Not for anything would Olivia reveal the fact that Cammie's flight wasn't departing LAX for several hours.

"Tell me she's mine. Admit it." He grasped her shoulders and shook her, his hands warm, but firm. "No lies, Olivia."

She was close enough to smell him, to remember with painful clarity the warm scent of his skin after lovemaking. Her stomach quivered. At one time she had believed she would wake up beside this man for the rest of her life. Now, in retrospect, she winced for the naive, foolish innocent she had been.

In high heels she could have met him eye to eye, but barefoot, wearing nothing but shorts and a casual top, she was at a distinct disadvantage. She pushed hard against his broad chest. "Let me go, you Neanderthal. You have no right to come here and push me around."

He released her abruptly. "I want the truth, damn it. Tell me."

"You wouldn't know the truth if it bit you in the ass. Go home, *Kevin Wade*."

Her deliberate taunt increased the fury bracketing his mouth with lines of stress. "We need to talk," he said as he glanced at his watch. "I have a conference call I can't miss in thirty minutes, so you have a choice. Tonight at my hotel. Or tomorrow in a room with two lawyers. Your call. But the way I'm feeling, a public forum might be the best option."

The sinking sensation in her belly told her that he would not give up easily. "I don't have anything to say to you," she said, her bravado forced at best.

He stared her down, his piercing golden eyes seeming to probe right through her to get at the truth. "Then I'll do all the talking."

Olivia watched, stunned, while he departed as quickly as he had come. She trailed after him, ready to slam the front door at the earliest opportunity, forcefully closing the door to the past. He paused on the porch. "I'll send a driver for you at six," he said bluntly. "Don't be late."

When he drove away, her legs gave out beneath her. She sank into a chair, her whole body shaking. Dear God. What was she going to do? She was a terrible liar, but she dared not tell him the truth. Kieran Wolff—she still had trouble thinking of him by that name—was not the laughing young man she remembered from their graduate days at Oxford.

His skin was deeply tanned, and sun lines at the corners of his eyes gave testament to the hours he now spent outdoors. He was as lethal and predatory as the sleek cats that inhabited the jungles he frequented. The man who helped dig wells in remote villages and who built and rebuilt bridges and buildings in war-torn countries was hard as glass.

She shuddered, remembering the implacable demand in his gaze. Would she be able to withstand his interrogation?

But there were more immediate details to address. Picking up the phone, she dialed the mother of Cammie's favorite playmate. The two families' backyards adjoined, and Cammie was spending part of the afternoon with her friend. Olivia had been terrified that Cammie would come home while Kieran was in the house.

Twenty minutes later, Olivia watched her daughter labor over a thank-you picture for her grandparents. Despite Olivia's reservations about the recent birthday party, the worst that had happened to her precocious offspring was the almost inevitable spilled punch on a five-hundred-dollar party dress…and a sunburned nose.

The dress had been a gift from Lolita. Olivia warned her mother that the exquisite frock was highly inappropriate for a child's birthday party. But as always, Lolo, as she liked to be called by her granddaughter, ignored Olivia's wishes and bought the dress, anyway.

Cammie frowned at a smudge in the corner of the drawing. "I need some more paper," she said, close to pouting. "This one's all messed up."

"It's fine, sweetheart. You've done a great job." At five, Cammie was already a perfectionist. Olivia worried about her intensity.

"I have to start over."

Sensing a full-blown tantrum in the offing, Olivia sighed and produced another sheet of clean white paper. Sometimes it was easier to avoid confrontation, especially over something so minor. Did all single mothers worry that they were ruining their children forever?

If Cammie had a father in her life, would she be less highly strung? More able to take things in stride?

Olivia's stomach pitched. She wouldn't think of Kieran right now. Not until Cammie was safely away.

She would miss her baby while Cammie was gone. The hours of reading storybooks. The fun baking experiments. The leisurely walks around the neighborhood in the evenings. The silly bathtub bubble fights. They were a family of two. A completely normal family.

Was she trying to convince herself or someone else?

She desperately wanted for Cammie the emotional security Olivia had never known as a child. The simple pleasure of hugs and homework. Of kisses and kites.

Olivia had been raised for the most part by a series of well-meaning nannies and tutors. She had learned early on that expensive Parisian dolls were supposed to make up for long absences during which her parents ignored her. The stereotypical poor little rich kid. With a closet full of expensive and often inappropriate toys, and a bruised heart.

Olivia remembered her own childish tantrums when her parents didn't bring presents she wanted. Thinking back on her egocentric younger self made her wince. Thank heavens she had outgrown that phase.

Maturity and a sense of perspective enabled her to be glad that her parents were far more invested in Cammie's life than they had ever been in their own daughter's. Perhaps grandparenthood had changed them.

Olivia's determination to live a solidly middle class life baffled Lolita and Javier, and they did their best to thwart her at every turn, genuinely convinced that money was meant to be spent.

The weekend party was an example of the lifestyle Olivia had tried so hard to escape. It wasn't good for a child to understand that she could have anything she wanted. Even if Olivia died penniless—and that wasn't likely—Cammie stood to inherit millions of dollars from her grandparents.

Money spoiled people. Olivia knew that firsthand. Growing up in Hollywood was a lesson in overindulgence and narcissism.

Cammie finally smiled, satisfied with her second attempt. "I wish Lolo had a refrigerator. My friend Aya, at preschool, says her nana hangs stuff on the front of the refrigerator."

Olivia smiled at her daughter's bent head. *Lolo* owned several refrigerators, all in different kitchens spread from L.A. to New York to Paris. But it was doubtful she ever opened one, much less decorated any of them with Cammie's artwork. Lolita Delgado had "people" to deal with that. In fact, she had an entourage to handle every detail of her tempestuous life.

"Lolo will love your drawing, Cammie, and so will Jojo." Olivia's father, Javier, wasn't crazy about his nickname, but he doted on his granddaughter, probably—in addition to the ties of blood—because she gave him what he craved the most. Unrestrained adoration.

Cammie bounced to her feet. "I'm gonna get my backpack. They'll be here in a minute."

"Slow down, baby...." But it was too late. Cammie ran at her usual pace up the stairs, determined to be ready and waiting by the door when the limo arrived. Olivia's parents were taking Cammie to Euro Disney for a few days in conjunction with a film award they were both receiving in Florence.

Olivia had argued that the trip was too much on the heels of the over-the-top birthday party, but in the end she had been unable to hold out against Cammie's beseeching eyes and tight hugs. The two adults and one child, when teamed against Olivia, made a formidable opponent.

Cammie reappeared, backpack in hand. Olivia had her suitcase ready. "Promise me you'll be good for your grandparents."

Cammie rolled her eyes in a manner far too advanced for her years. "You always say that."

"And I always mean it."

The doorbell rang. Cammie's screech nearly peeled the paint from the walls. "Bye, Mommy."

Olivia followed her out to the car. In the flurry of activity over getting one excited five-year-old settled in the vehicle, Lolita and Javier managed to appear both pleased and sophisticated as they absorbed their granddaughter's enthusiasm.

Olivia gave her mother a hug, careful not to rumple her vintage Chanel suit. "Please don't spoil her." For one fleeting second, Olivia wanted to share the truth about Kieran with her parents. To beg for guidance. She had never divulged a single detail about her daughter's parentage to anyone.

But the moment passed when Javier bussed his daughter's cheek with a wide grin. "It's what we do best, Olivia."

The house was silent in the aftermath of the exodus. Without the distraction of Cammie, the evening with Kieran loomed menacingly. Olivia wandered from room to room, too restless to work. Cammie would be going to kindergarten very soon. Olivia had mixed emotions about the prospect. She knew that her highly intelligent daughter would thrive in an academic environment and that the socialization skills she acquired with children her own age would be very important.

But it had been just the two of them for so long.

And now Kieran seemed poised to upset the apple cart.

When Olivia felt her eyes sting, she made a concerted effort to shake off the maudlin mood. Life was good. Her days were filled with family, a job she adored and a cadre of close, trusted friends. Kieran wasn't part of the package. And she was glad. She had made the right choice in protecting Cammie from his selfishness.

And she would continue to do so.

The remainder of the day was a total loss. She had a series of watercolors due for her book publisher in less than two weeks, but putting the finishing touches on the last picture in the set was more than she could handle today. She loved her work as a children's illustrator, and it gave her flexibility to spend lots of time with Cammie.

But the concentration required for her best efforts was beyond her right now. Instead, she prowled her small house, unable to stem the tide of memories.

They had met as expatriate grad students at a traditional English country house party hosted by mutual friends. With only six weeks of the term left, each knew the relationship had a preordained end. But in Olivia's case, with stars in her eyes and a heart that was head-over-heels in lust with the handsome, charismatic Kevin Wade, she'd spun fairy tales of continuing their affair back in the U.S.

It hadn't quite turned out that way. During the final days of exam week, "Kevin" had simply disappeared with nothing more than a brief note to say goodbye. Thinking about that terrible time made Olivia's stomach churn with nausea. Her fledgling love had morphed into hate, and she'd done her best to turn her back on any memory of the boy who broke her heart. And fathered her child.

After a quick shower, she stared at her reflection in the mirror. Even if Olivia wanted to follow in her mother's footsteps, she would never have stood a chance in Hollywood. She was twenty pounds too heavy, and though today's pool of actresses was more diverse, many directors still preferred willowy blondes. Olivia was neither.

By the time the limo pulled up in front of her house, Olivia was a wreck. But since birth, she'd been taught "the show must go on" mantra, and to the world, Olivia Delgado was unflappable. For six years, she had spun lies to protect her daughter, to make a life so unexceptionable that the tabloids had long since left her alone.

An unwed mother in Hollywood was boring news. As long as no one discovered the father was a Wolff.

Tonight Olivia would be no less discreet.

She had dressed to play a part. Confident and chic were the qualities she planned to convey with her taupe linen tank dress and coral sandals. Though she had not inherited an iota of her parents' love for acting, she had inevitably learned from them along the way what it meant to present a serene face to the world, no matter if your life was in ruins.

Kieran Wolff's hotel was tucked away in a quiet back street of Santa Monica. Exclusive, discreet and no doubt wildly expensive, it catered to those whose utmost wish was privacy. The manager, himself, actually escorted Olivia to the fifth floor suite.

After that, she was left to stand alone at the door. Instead of knocking, she took a few seconds to contemplate fleeing the country. Cammie was everything to her, and the prospect of losing her child was impossible to imagine.

But such thoughts were defeatist. Though she might not be able to go toe-to-toe with the Wolff empire when it came to bank accounts, Olivia did have considerable financial means at her disposal. In a legal battle, she could hold her own. And judges often sided with a mother, particularly in this situation.

She had no notion of what awaited her on the other side of the door, but she wouldn't go down without a fight. Kieran Wolff didn't deserve to be a father. And if it came to that, she would tell him so.

Deliberately taking a moment to shore up her nerve, she rapped sharply at the door and took a deep breath.

Kieran had worn a trail in the carpet by the time his reluctant guest arrived. When he yanked open the door and saw her standing in the vestibule, his gut pitched and tightened. God, she was gorgeous. Every male hormone he possessed stood up and saluted. A man would have to be almost dead not to respond to her inherent sexuality.

Like the pin-up girls of the 1940s, with legs that went on forever, breasts that were real and plenty of feminine curves right where they should be, Olivia Delgado was a vivid, honey-skinned fantasy.

But today wasn't about appeasing the hunger in his gut, even if he *had* been celibate during a recent, hellacious foray into the wilds of Thailand. Bugs, abysmal weather and local politics had complicated his life enormously. He'd been more than ready to return to central Virginia and reconnect with his family. Not that he ever stayed very long, but still…that closely guarded mountain in the Blue Ridge was the only place he called home.

With an effort, he recalled his wayward thoughts. "Come in, Olivia. I've ordered dinner. It should be delivered any moment now."

She slipped past him in a cloud of Chanel No. 5, making him wonder if she had worn the evocative scent on purpose. In the old days, she had often come to his bed wearing nothing but a long strand of pearls and that same perfume.

He waited for her to be seated on the love seat and then took an armchair for himself a few feet away. In the intervening hours, he'd rehearsed how this would go. Having her here, on somewhat public turf, seemed like a good idea. He was determined to keep his cool, no matter the provocation.

They faced off in silence for at least a minute. When he realized she wasn't going to crack, he sighed. "Surely you can't deny it, Olivia. You were a virgin when we met. I can do the math. Your daughter is mine."

Her eyes flashed. "My daughter is none of your business. You may have introduced me to sex, but there have been plenty of men since."

"Liar. Name one."

Her jaw dropped. "Um…"

He chuckled, feeling the first hint of amusement he'd had since he saw the article about the party. Olivia might look like a woman of immense sophistication and experience, but he'd bet his last dime that she was still the sweet, down-to-earth girl he'd known back at university, completely unaware of her stunning beauty.

"Show me her birth certificate."

Her chin lifted. "Don't be ridiculous. I don't carry it around in my purse."

"But you probably have it at the house, right? In order to register her for kindergarten?"

She nibbled her bottom lip. "Well, I…"

Thank God she was a lousy liar. "Whose name is on the birth certificate, Olivia? You might as well tell me. You know I can find out."

Suddenly she looked neither sweet nor innocent. "Kevin Wade. Is that what you wanted to hear?"

The sharp pain in his chest took his breath away. "Kevin Wade…"

"Exactly. So you can see that no judge would think you have any rights in this instance at all." Her eyes were cold, and even that realization was painful. The Olivia he had known smiled constantly, her joie de vivre captivating and so very seductive.

Now her demeanor was icy.

"You put my name on her birth certificate," he croaked. It kept coming back to that. Kevin Wade was a father. Kieran had a daughter.

"Correction," she said with a flat intonation that disguised any emotion. "In the hospital, when I gave birth to my daughter, I listed a fictional name for her father. It had nothing to do with you."

He clamped down on his frustration, acknowledging that he was getting nowhere with this approach. Unable to sit any longer, he sprang to his feet and paced, pausing at the windows to look out at the ocean in the far distance. One summer he had lived for six weeks on a houseboat in Bali. It was the freest he had ever felt, the most relaxed.

Too bad life wasn't always so easy.

Olivia continued to sit in stubborn silence, so he kept his back to her. "When you hired an investigator, what did you find out about me?"

After several seconds of silence, she spoke. "That your

real name is Kieran Wolff. You lost your mother and aunt to a violent abduction and shooting when you were small. Your father and uncle raised you and your siblings and cousins in seclusion, because they were afraid of another kidnapping attempt."

He faced her, brooding. "Will you listen to my side of the story?" he asked quietly.

Olivia's hands were clenched together in her lap, her posture so rigid she seemed in danger of shattering into a million pieces. Though she hid it well, he could sense her agitation. At one time he had been attuned to her every thought and desire.

He swallowed, painfully aware that a king-size bed lay just on the other side of the door. The intensity of the desire he felt for her was shocking. As was the need for her to understand and forgive him. He was culpable for his sins in the past, no doubt about it. But that didn't excuse Olivia for hiding the existence of his child, his blood.

"Will you listen?" he asked again.

She nodded slowly, eyes downcast.

With a prayer for patience, he crossed the expanse of expensive carpet to sit beside her, hip to hip. She froze, inching back into her corner.

"Look at me, Olivia." He took her chin in his hand with a gentle grasp, lifting it until her gaze met his. "I'm not the enemy," he swore. "All I need is for you to be honest with me. And I'll try my damnedest to do the same."

Her chocolate-brown eyes were shiny with tears, but she blinked them back, giving him a second terse nod. He tucked a stray strand of hair behind her ear and forced himself to release her. Touching her was a luxury he couldn't afford at the moment.

"Okay, then." He was more a man of action than of words. But if he was fighting for his daughter, he would use any means necessary, even if that meant revealing truths he'd rather not expose.

He leaned forward, elbows on his knees, and dropped his head in his hands. "You were important to me, Olivia."

A slight *humph* was her only response. Was that skepticism or denial or maybe both?

"It's true," he insisted. "I'd been with a lot of girls before I met you, but you were different."

Dead silence.

"You made me laugh even when I wanted you so badly, I ached. I never meant to hurt you. But I had made a vow to my father."

"Of course you had."

She could give lessons in sarcasm.

"Sneer if you like, but the vow was real. My brothers and cousins and I swore to my father and my uncle that if they would let us go off to college without bodyguards, we would use assumed names and never tell *anyone* who we really were."

"So it was okay to sleep with me, but you couldn't share with me something as simple as the truth about your real name. Charming."

This time it was Olivia who jumped to her feet and paced. He sat back and stared at her, tracking the gentle sway of her hips as she crisscrossed the room. "I was going to tell you," he insisted. "But I had to get my father's permission. And before I could do that, he had a heart attack. That's when I left England so suddenly."

She wrapped her arms around her waist. "Leaving behind a lovely eight-word note. *Dear Olivia, I have to go home. Sorry.*"

He winced. "I was in a hurry."

"Do you have any clue at all how humiliated I was when I went to the Dean's office to beg for information about you and was told that Kevin Wade was no longer enrolled? And they were not allowed to give out any information as to your whereabouts because of privacy rules? God, I was embarrassed. And then I was mad at myself for being such a credulous fool."

"You weren't a fool," he said automatically, mentally replaying her words and for the first time realizing what he had put her through. "I'm sorry."

She kicked the leg of the coffee table, revealing a hint of her mother's flamboyant temper. "Sorry doesn't explain why suddenly neither your cell phone nor your email address worked when I tried to reach you."

"They were school accounts. My exams were over. I knew I wasn't coming back, so I let them go inactive, because I thought it was the easiest way to make a clean break."

"If you're trying to make a case for yourself, you're failing miserably."

"I never wanted to hurt you," he insisted.

"They call them clichés for a reason." The careful veil she'd kept over her emotions had shredded, and now he was privy to the pure, clean burn of her anger.

"Things were crazy at home," he said wearily. "I stayed at the hospital round-the-clock for a week. Then when Dad was released, he was extremely depressed. My brother Jacob and I had to entertain him, read to him, listen to music with him. I barely had a thought to myself."

She nodded slowly. "I get it, Kieran." He watched her frown as she rolled the last word on her tongue. "I was a temporary girlfriend. Too bad I was so naive. I didn't realize for a few weeks that I had been dumped. I kept making excuses for you, believing—despite the evidence to the contrary— that we shared something special."

"We did, damn it."

"But not special enough for you to pick up the phone and make a call. And you had to know I was back home in California. Yet you didn't even bother. I should thank you, really. That experience taught me a lot. I grew up fast. You were a horny young man. I was easy pickings. So if that's all, I'm out of here. I absolve you of any guilt."

Fortunately for Kieran, the arrival of dinner halted Olivia's headlong progress to the door. She was forced to cool her heels while the waiter rolled a small table in front of the picture window and smiled as Kieran tipped him generously. When the man departed, the amazing smells wafting from the collection of covered dishes won Olivia over, despite Kieran's botched attempts to deal with their past.

Neither of them spoke a word for fifteen minutes as they devoured grilled swordfish with mango salsa and spinach salad.

Kieran realized he'd gotten off track. They were supposed to be talking about why Olivia had hidden the existence of his daughter. Instead, Kieran had ended up in a defensive position. Time for a new game plan.

He ate a couple of bites of melon sorbet, wiped his mouth with a snowy linen napkin and leaned back in his chair. "I may have been a jerk," he said bluntly, "but that doesn't explain why you never told me I had a daughter. Your turn in the hot seat, Olivia."

Three

Olivia choked on a sliced almond and had to wash it down with a long gulp of water. The Wolff family was far more powerful than even Olivia's world-famous parents. If the truth came out, she knew the Wolff patriarchs might help Kieran take Cammie. And she couldn't allow that. "You don't have a daughter," she said calmly, her voice hoarse from coughing. Hearing Kieran's explanation of why he had left England so suddenly had done nothing to alleviate her fears. "I do."

Kieran scowled. Any attempts he might have made to appease her were derailed by his obvious dislike of having his wishes thwarted. "I'll lock you in here with me if I have to," he said, daring her to challenge his ability to do so.

"And how would that solve anything?"

Suddenly her cell phone rang. With a wince for the unfortunate timing, she stood up. "Excuse me. I need to take this."

Kieran made no move to give her privacy, so she turned her back on him and moved to the far side of the room. Tapping the screen of her phone to answer, she smiled. “Hey, sweetheart. Are you in New York?”

The brief conversation ended with Olivia’s mother on the other end promising to make Cammie sleep on the flight over to Paris. Olivia’s daughter had flown internationally several times, but she wasn’t so blasé about jet travel that she would simply nod off. Olivia had packed several of the child’s bedtime books in her carry-on, hoping that a semi-familiar routine would do the trick.

When Olivia hung up and turned around, Kieran was scowling. “I thought you said she was in Europe.”

She shrugged. “That’s their ultimate destination.”

“So this morning when I came to your house, where was she?”

“At the neighbor’s.”

“Damn you, Olivia.”

It was her turn to frown in exasperation. “What would you have done if I had told you, Kieran? Made a dramatic run through the yard calling her name? My daughter is now traveling with her grandparents. That’s all you need to know.”

“When will they be back?”

“A week…ten days… My mother isn’t crazy about abiding by schedules.”

His scowl blackened. “Tell me she’s my daughter.”

Her stomach flipped once, hard, but she held on to her composure by a thread. “Go to hell.”

Abruptly he shoved back his chair and went to the mini bar to pour himself a Scotch, downing the contents with one quick toss of his head. His throat was tanned like the rest of him, and the tantalizing glimpse of his chest at the opening of his shirt struck Olivia as unbearably erotic.

Sensing her own foray into the quicksand of nostalgia, she attacked. "If you want to have children someday, you should probably work on those alcoholic tendencies."

"I'm not an alcoholic, though God knows you could drive a man to drink." He ran a hand through his hair, rumpling it into disarray. She saw for the first time that he was exhausted, probably running on nothing but adrenaline.

"You don't even own a house," she blurted out.

Confusion etched his face. "Excuse me?"

"A house," she reiterated. "Most people who want a family start with a house and a white picket fence. All you do is travel the globe. What are you afraid of? Getting stuck in one place for too long?"

Her random shot hit its mark.

"Maybe," he muttered, his expression bleak. "My brothers have been begging me to come home for a long time now. But I'm not sure I know how."

"Then I think you should leave," she said calmly. "Get back on a plane and go save the world. No one needs you here."

"You didn't used to be so callous." His expression was sober. Regretful. And his cat eyes watched her every move as if he were stalking prey.

"I'm simply being realistic. Even if I *had* given birth to a child that was yours, what makes you think you have what it takes to be a father? Parenting is about being *present.* That's not really your forte, now is it?"

She heard the cruel words tumbling from her lips and couldn't stop them. If she could drive him away in anger, he would go and leave Olivia to raise her daughter in peace.

"I'm here now," he said quietly, his control making her ashamed of her outburst. "Cammie is my daughter, I want to get to know her."

Olivia's heart stopped. Hearing him say her daughter's

name did something odd to her heart. "How exactly do you mean that?"

"Let me stay here with you for a little while."

"Absolutely not." She shivered, imagining his big body in her guest bed…a few feet down the hall from hers.

"Then I want the two of you to come to Wolff Mountain with me for the summer and meet my family. This afternoon I talked to the CEO of my foundation, Bridge to the Future. He's lining up people to take my place until early September."

"Thank you for the invitation," she said politely. "But we can't. Perhaps some other time." *When hell freezes over.* If she let Cammie go anywhere near the Wolff family compound, Olivia stood a chance of never seeing her daughter again. Kieran's relatives made up a tight familial unit, and if they got wind that another wolf had been born into the pack, Olivia feared that her status as Cammie's mother would carry little weight.

He shoved his hands in his pockets. "At the risk of sounding like one of your father's action hero characters, I'm warning you. We can do this the easy way or the hard way. I can get a court order for a DNA sample."

Olivia shivered inwardly as she felt her options narrowing. She could buy some time by stonewalling, but ultimately, the Wolff would prevail. "My daughter and I have lives, Kieran. It's unrealistic of you to expect us to visit strangers for no other reason than your sudden odd conviction that you are a daddy."

"Your work is portable. Cammie doesn't start school until the fall. I'll make a deal with you. I won't claim her as mine…. I won't even tell my family what I know to be true. But in exchange, you agree to let me see her as much as possible in the next few weeks."

"She's not yours." The words were beginning to sound weak, even to her ears.

He came toward her. The silent intensity of his stare was hypnotic. When they were almost touching, chest to chest, he put his hands on her shoulders, the warmth of his touch searing her skin even through a layer of fabric. "Don't be afraid of me, Olivia."

His mouth moved over hers, light as a whisper, teasing, coaxing. The fact that her knees lost their starch should have made her angry, but there was no room for negative emotion in that moment. For no other reason than pleasure, her lips moved under his. Seeking. Responding.

He made an inarticulate murmur that encompassed surprise and masculine satisfaction. Then the kiss deepened.

His leg moved between her thighs as he drew her closer. "You haven't changed," he said roughly. "I've dreamed about you over the years. On nights when I couldn't sleep. And remembered you just like this. God, you're sweet."

She felt the press of his heavy erection against her belly, and everything inside her went liquid with drugged delight. How long had it been? How long? No longer a responsible mother, she was once again a giddy young woman, desperate for her lover's touch.

Unbidden, the memories came flooding back….

"You're a virgin?"

Kevin's shock worried her. Surely he wouldn't abandon her now. Not when they were naked and tangled in her bed. "Does it matter? I want this, Kevin. I really do. I want you."

He sat up beside her, magnificently nude, his expression troubled. "I haven't ever done it with a virgin. You're twenty-two, Olivia. For God's sake. I had no idea."

With a confidence that surprised her, she laid a hand on his hard, hairy thigh, her fingertips almost brushing his thick penis. "I told you I had led a sheltered life. Why do you think I wanted to cross an ocean to finish my schooling? I'm tired of living in a cocoon. Make love to me, Kevin. Please."

His hunger, coupled with her entreaty, defeated him. Groaning like a man tormented on a rack, he moved between her legs once more, his erect shaft nudging eagerly at her entrance. Braced on his forearms, he leaned down to kiss her...hard. "I know I'll hurt you. I'm sorry."

"No apology needed," she whispered, sensing the momentous turning point in her life. "I need this. I need you."

He pushed forward an inch, and she braced instinctively against the sharp sting of pain.

"Easy," he whispered, his beautiful eyes alight with tenderness. "Relax, Olivia."

She tried to do as he asked, but he was fully aroused, and she was so tight. His whole big body trembled violently, and she wanted to cry at the beauty of it. Another inch. Another gasped cry to be swallowed up in his wild kiss.

She felt torn asunder, violated, but in the best possible way. Never again would her body be hers. Kevin claimed it, claimed her.

When he was fully seated, tears rolled silently down her cheeks, wetting her hair, sliding into her ears.

He rested his forehead on hers. "Was it that bad?" he asked, clearly striving for humor, but unable to hide his distress over what had transpired.

"Try moving," she said breathlessly. "I think I can handle it."

"Holy hell." His discomfiture almost elicited a giggle, but when he followed her naive suggestion, humor fled. Slowly, inexorably, her untried body learned his rhythm. Deep inside her a tiny flame flickered to life.

She moaned, arching her back and driving him deeper on a down thrust. It was easier now, and far more exciting.

Her long legs wrapped around his waist. Skin damp with exertion, they devoured each other, desperately trying to get closer still.

Kevin went rigid and cursed, closing his eyes and groaning as he climaxed inside her. She was taking the pill, and he had been tested recently, so no condom came between them.

As he slumped on top of her, she wrinkled her nose in disappointment. She had been so close to something spectacular. But the feeling faded. Taking its place was a warmth and satisfaction that she had been able to give him pleasure.

He rolled to his side. "Did you come?"

She nibbled her lip. Would it hurt to lie? It wasn't a habit she wanted to start. "Not exactly. But I know it takes practice. Don't worry about it...really."

He chuckled, yawning and stretching. "For a novice, you're pretty damned wonderful. Hold still, baby, and let's finish this."

Without ceremony, he put his hand between her legs and touched her. She flinched, still not quite comfortable with this level of intimacy, and also feeling tender and sore. His fingers were gentle, finding a certain spot and rubbing lightly. Her hips came off the bed.

"Um, Kevin?"

"What, honey?"

"You don't have to do this. To tell you the truth, I'm feeling sort of embarrassed."

"Why?" The strum of his fingers picked up tempo.

"Well, you're...um...finished, and it's a little weird now." Her voice caught in her throat. "That's enough. I feel good. Really."

He entered her with two fingers and bit the side of her neck. "How about now?"

Her shriek could have peeled paint off the walls, but she

was too far gone to care. The attention she gave herself now and again when the lights were out barely held a candle to this maelstrom. Kevin gave no quarter, stroking her firmly until her orgasm crested, exploded and winnowed away, leaving her spent in his arms.

She cried again.

He made fun of her with gentle humor.

Then they turned out the lights and spent their first night together, wrapped in each other's arms.

Kieran cupped her breast with his hand, and just like that, Olivia was fully in the present. What shocked her back to reality was the incredible realization that she was a hairsbreadth away from letting him have her again. No protest. No discussion. Simply mindless pleasure.

And while that may have been okay six years ago, now she had a daughter to think about. Sexual reminiscing with Kieran Wolff was not only self-destructive and stupid, but also detrimental to her role as a parent.

"Enough," she said hoarsely, tearing herself from his embrace and warding him off with a hand when he would have dragged her back for another kiss. "I mean it," she said. "We're not doing this. You can't seduce me into agreeing to your terms."

"Give us both more credit than that, Olivia. What happened just now proves that we've always had chemistry… and still do."

"If you're expecting to pick up where we left off, you're destined for disappointment."

"Is that so? From what I could tell, what just happened was a two-way street."

"It's late," she said abruptly. "I have to go."

He crossed his arms over his chest and leaned a hip against the back of the sofa, his eyes narrowed. From the look of him, no one would guess that sixty seconds ago he'd been kissing her senseless. "You can't run from me, Olivia. Closing your eyes and thinking about Kansas is a child's game. I want some answers."

Her phone chimed to signal a text, and she pulled it from her pocket, glancing at it automatically. Her mother's words chilled her blood.

Kieran touched her shoulder as she sank to a seat. "What is it? What's wrong?"

"The flight was delayed. My mother has a stalker fan, and he showed up at the airport."

He squatted beside her, his mere presence lending comfort. "What happened?"

"When he tried to burst through a checkpoint, calling her name, TSA arrested him."

He frowned. "I don't like the thought of Cammie being exposed to something like that."

"First of all, my parents take security very seriously, and second of all, this is none of your business. I'm her mother. It's up to me to keep her safe."

From his vantage point crouched at her side, their gazes collided. "You don't have to do this alone anymore," he said quietly, the words like a vow. "Any child with my blood running in her veins has the protection of the entire Wolff clan at her back."

She swallowed hard, near tears, missing her daughter and feeling out of her depth. "A child is not a belonging. She's her own person. Even if she *is* only five."

"You think I don't know that? I was a year younger than she is now when my mother was killed." He sprang to his feet, pacing once more. "My brother Gareth was the only one of us really old enough to understand and remember the details, but I lived it, and those terrible days are buried somewhere in my psyche…the confusion, the loneliness, the knowledge that my world was never going to be the same.

No child should lose a parent, Olivia, even if she thinks she has only one."

Guilt reached inside her chest and squeezed hard. Kieran Wolff had hurt her badly. Did she have the right to make her daughter vulnerable to his undeniable charm? Conversely, was she wrong to deny her child a father, even an absentee one? The same questions had haunted her for half a decade.

Her head ached. "We'll visit for a long weekend," she said, her voice tight. "As soon as Cammie gets back from Europe. But that's all it will be. All it will ever be. And if you break your word to me, I'll take her away and never speak to you again."

His lips quirked in a half smile. "Mama Bear protecting her cub. I like seeing you in this maternal role, Olivia. It suits you."

She gathered her purse and the light sweater she'd brought with her. "No one and nothing in this world means more to me than Cammie. And you'd do well to remember that. Good night, Kieran. Pleasant dreams."

He followed her to the door, having the temerity to press another hard kiss to her lips before allowing her to leave. "I'll dream," he said, brushing her cheek with the back of a hand. "But I have a feeling that pleasant won't be the right word for it."

Four

Kieran had never liked waiting. The ten days that elapsed between his confrontation with Olivia and her arrival at Wolff Mountain were interminable. Every moment of every day he imagined a dozen excuses she could make to keep from showing up.

As an adolescent he'd imagined the walls of the monstrous house closing in on him, as if he were trapped in a castle dungeon. Even now, his homecoming was tainted with confusion. Mostly he felt the agitation of being stuck in one place. He liked the freedom of the open road.

But if he were honest with himself, he had to admit that Wolff Mountain drew him home time and again despite his conflicted feelings about its past...his past.

Having his brothers close went a long way toward passing the time. They shared meals at the "big house," and Kieran was introduced to Gracie, Gareth's new wife.

Kieran's older brother was happier than Kieran had seen him in years, and it was clear that he adored his bride.

In the mornings, Kieran hiked the mountain trails with Gareth, and after lunch every day, he helped Jacob add on a new room to the doc's already state-of-the-art clinic. Kieran welcomed the physical exertion. Only by pushing himself to the point of exhaustion was he able to sleep at night. And even then he dreamed… God, he dreamed.

Olivia…in his bed, beneath him, her fabulous mane of hair spread across the pillows like a river of molten chocolate shot with gold. Her honey smooth skin bare-ass naked, waiting for him to touch every inch of it with his lips, his tongue, his ragged breath…

He'd dreamed of her before… At least in the beginning. When he first lost her. But the pain of doing so had ultimately led him to pretend she didn't exist. It was the only way he had survived.

But now, knowing that he and Olivia would soon be sharing a roof, the chains he'd used to bind up his memories shattered. He'd taken more cold showers in the past week than he had as a hormone-driven teen. And in the darkest hours of the night, he wondered with no small amount of guilt if he was using his own daughter as leverage to spend more time with the woman he'd never been able to forget.

Olivia wasn't coming here to be his lover. She'd made that crystal clear. Her single concession was to allow Cammie a visit. And that was only because Kieran threatened court proceedings.

He still felt bad about that, but Olivia's stubbornness infuriated him. Why couldn't she just admit that in the short time they were together, they created a life? He knew the truth in his gut, but he needed Olivia to be honest…to tell him face-to-face. Until he heard her say the words out loud, he wouldn't be satisfied.

With Cammie as his child, everything changed. It meant that when he was laboring in some godforsaken corner of the world, he could dream about returning home to someone who was his, a child who would love him and hug his neck.

Kieran's family loved him, but coming home to Wolff Mountain was painful. So painful, in fact, that he made it back to the States only a couple of times a year. No matter how hard he tried, the memories of his mother, though vague and indistinct, permeated the air here. And those same memories reminded him of how helpless he had felt when she died.

Seeing his father and uncle and brothers and cousins crying had left an indelible mark on an impressionable four-year-old. Until then, he'd believed that men never cried, especially not his big, gruff daddy. Kieran had been confused, and fearful, and so desperate to make everything better.

The day of the funeral he pretended to take a nap while the adults were gone. While the nanny was on the phone with her boyfriend, Kieran slipped into his mother's bedroom and ransacked the large walk-in closet that housed her clothes. He tugged at the hems of blouses and dresses and evening gowns, ripping them from the hangers and piling them up haphazardly until he had a small mountain.

The fabrics smelled like her. With tears streaming down his face, he climbed atop his makeshift bed, curled into a ball of misery and fell asleep, his thumb tucked in his mouth.

Kieran inhaled sharply, realizing that he had allowed himself the bittersweet, two-edged sword of memory. That's why he came home so seldom. In another hemisphere he could pretend that his life was normal. That it had always been normal.

Returning to Wolff Mountain always pulled the Band-Aid off a wound that had never healed cleanly. He remembered being discovered on that terrible funeral day and escorted out of his parents' bedroom. No one chastised him. No one took him to task for what he had done. But three days later when he worked up the courage to once again sneak into his mother's closet, every trace of her was gone… as if she had never existed. Even the hangers had been removed.

That day he'd cried again, huddled in a ball in the corner of the bare closet. And this time, there was no comfort to be found. His world had shredded around him, leaving nothing but uncertainty and bleakness. He hated the stomach-hollowing feelings and the sensation of doom.

No child should ever have to feel abandoned, and sadly, Kieran and his brothers had been emotional orphans when their father fell apart in the wake of Laura Wolff's death. It took Victor Wolff literally years to recover, and by then, the damage was done. The boys loved their father, but they had become closed off to softer emotions.

Kieran cursed and kicked at a pile of loose gravel in the driveway. *Was* Cammie his daughter? A tiny shred of doubt remained. He found it almost impossible to believe that Olivia had gone from his bed to another man's so quickly. But he had hurt her badly…and she might have done it out of spite.

The girl in the photograph at Olivia's house looked like a Wolff, though that might be wishful thinking on Kieran's part. And as for the Kevin Wade on the birth certificate, well… Olivia might have done that to preserve her privacy. Using the name of a man who didn't exist to protect her rights as a mother.

But God help him, if Olivia had lied…if she had kept him

from his own flesh and blood, there was going to be hell to pay.

His cell phone beeped with a text from the front gate guard at the foot of the mountain. Olivia's car had arrived.

She had flatly refused Wolff transportation, either the private jet or a ride from the airport. Her independence made a statement that said Kieran was unnecessary. It would be his pleasure to show her how wrong she was.

When a modest rental vehicle pulled into sight, he felt his heart race, not only at the prospect of seeing Olivia, but at the realization that he might be, for the first time, coming face-to-face with his progeny.

The car slid to a halt and Olivia stepped out. Before she could come around and help with the passenger door, it was flung open from the inside, and a small, slender girl hopped into view. She had brown hair pulled back into pigtails and wore a wary expression as she surveyed her surroundings. Though Kieran didn't move, she spotted him immediately. Try as he might, Kieran could see no hint that she resembled his family. She looked like a kid. That's all. A little kid.

She slipped her hand into Olivia's. "It's like Cinderella's castle. Do we get to sleep here?"

"For a few nights."

Kieran wondered if Olivia was intimidated by the size and scope of the house. She had grown up as the only child of famous, wealthy parents, but this structure—part fortress, part fairy tale—was beyond imagination for most people. All it was missing was gargoyles on the parapets. With turrets and battlements and thick, gray stone walls, it should have looked unwelcoming, but somehow, it suited this wild mountaintop.

"Who's that, Mommy?"

Kieran stepped forward, but before he could speak,

Olivia gave Kieran a warning look. "His name is Kieran. He's a friend of mine. But you can call him Mr. Wolff."

"She'd better call me Kieran to avoid confusion, because she's going to be meeting a lot of Mr. Wolffs."

Olivia's lips tightened, but she didn't argue.

Kieran knelt beside Cammie. "We're glad to have you and your mommy here for a visit. Would you like to see the horses?" He took a punch to the chest when he realized the child's eyes were the same color as his own, dark amber with flecks of gold and brown.

He glanced up at Olivia, his heart in his throat. *Tell me,* his gaze signaled furiously.

Olivia didn't give an inch. "I think it would be best if Cammie and I rested for a while. It was a long, tiring flight and we're beat."

"But, Mommy," Cammie wailed. "I love horses."

Kieran straightened. "Surely a quick trip to the stables wouldn't hurt. And after that you'll nap with no argument, right, Cammie?"

The child was smart enough to know when a deal was worth taking. "Okay," she said, the resignation in her voice oddly adult. She slipped her hand into Kieran's. "C'mon, before she changes her mind."

Olivia followed behind the pair of them, realizing with chagrin that she would have been better served letting Kieran stay with them in California. On his turf, already Olivia felt at a disadvantage. And she hadn't missed Kieran's poleaxed look when he saw her daughter's eye color. It was unusual to say the least. And a dead giveaway when it came to parentage.

Behind the massive house stood an immaculate barn with adjoining stables. Inside the latter, the smell of hay mingled not unpleasantly with the odor of warm horseflesh.

Kieran led Cammie past the stalls of mighty stallions to

an enclosure where a pretty brown-and-white pony stood contentedly munching hay. He handed Cammie a few apple chunks from a nearby bin. "Hold out your hand with the fingers flat, like this."

She obeyed instantly, her small face alight with glee as the pony approached cautiously and scooped up the food with a delicate swipe of its lips. "Mommy, look," she cried. "It likes me."

Kieran put a hand on her shoulder. "Her name is Sunshine, and you can ride her as long as you're here."

"Now?" Cammie asked, practically bouncing on her feet. "Please, Mommy."

Over her head, the two adults' gazes met, Olivia's filled with frustration, Kieran's bland. "Later," Olivia said firmly. "We have plenty of time."

She had been afraid that she would have to meet a phalanx of Kieran's relatives while she was still rumpled and road weary, but he led them to a quiet, peaceful wing of the house where the windows were thrown open to embrace the warm, early summer breezes.

"This will be your room, Olivia." Kieran paused to indicate a lovely suite decorated in shades of celadon and pale buttercup. "And through here…" He passed through a connecting door to another room clearly meant for a child. "This is yours, Cammie."

Olivia saw her daughter's eyes grow wide. The furnishings had been made to resemble a tree house, with the sleep space atop a small pedestal accessed by rope netting, which coincidentally made any possibility of falling out of bed harmless.

Cammie kicked off her shoes and scampered up the rope apron like the monkey she was. "Look at me," she cried. "This is awesome. Thank you, Kieran."

Soon she was oblivious to the adults as she explored the

tree trunk bookcase, the two massive toy chests shaped like daisies and the enormous fish tank.

Olivia drew Kieran aside. “Are you insane?” she asked, her low whisper incredulous. “This must have cost a fortune. And for three nights? You can’t buy my compliance, Kieran. Nor hers.”

“The money isn’t an issue,” he said quietly, a small smile on his face as he watched Cammie scoot from one wonder to the next. “I wanted my daughter to feel at home here.”

“She’s not your daughter.” The denial was automatic, but lacked conviction.

Kieran barely noticed. “She’s smart, isn’t she?”

“Oh, yes. Talking in full sentences before she was two. Reading at three and a half. Learning how to use my laptop almost a year ago. I can barely keep up with her.”

“A child needs two parents, Olivia.” He wasn’t looking at her, but the words sounded like a threat.

“You grew up with only one,” she shot back. “And you’ve done all right.”

He half turned and she could see the riot of emotions in his eyes. “I wouldn’t wish my childhood on anyone,” he said. The blunt words were harsh and ragged with grief.

Shame choked her and she laid a hand on his arm. “I’m so sorry, Kieran. I really am.”

He took her wrist in his hand, bringing it up to his mouth and brushing a kiss across her knuckles. “Tonight. When she’s asleep. We’ll talk in my suite. One of the housekeepers can babysit and make sure she’s okay.” His grip tightened. “This isn’t optional, Olivia.”

Once again she was thrown by the way he mingled tenderness with masculine authority. Kieran wasn’t a man who could be “handled.” He expected to be obeyed, and it incensed her. But at the same time, she knew she dared not cross him and risk having him blurt out the truth to

Cammie. That she had a father. A flesh and blood man who wanted to know her and be part of her life. What kind of mother would Olivia be if she stood in the way of that?

What else did Kieran want? Was this weekend visit going to appease him? Would he sue for joint custody? Or perhaps at the urging of his paranoid father, would he insist on full custody and try to lock Cammie up here in the castle until she was old enough to escape?

That's essentially what Kieran and his brothers had experienced. They had been hidden away from the world until they were allowed to go away to school with aliases.

Olivia couldn't live like that. And she certainly didn't want her daughter to endure such isolation. So she had no choice but to convince Kieran that being a father was too much for him to handle.

He left them finally, and Olivia and Cammie fell into an exhausted sleep, both of them in Olivia's bed. For a five-year-old, even with a private playground at her disposal, sometimes the most comfortable place to be was curled up in Mommy's arms.

Shadows filled the room when they awoke. Someone had slid a note under the door indicating that dinner would be at seven. As Olivia and Cammie washed up and changed clothes, a smiling young maid brought by a tray of grapes, cheese and crackers.

Olivia blessed whoever had the foresight to be so thoughtful. When Cammie got hungry, she got cranky, and her resultant attitude could be unpredictable.

Fortunately Cammie was on her best behavior that evening. And it helped that the whole Wolff clan was not in residence. Only Kieran's father, Victor, Kieran's brothers, Gareth and Jacob, and the newest member of the family, Gareth's wife, Gracie, were seated around the large mahogany dining table when Olivia and Cammie walked into the room.

Olivia put a hand on her daughter's thin shoulder. "Sorry if we're late. We took a wrong turn in the third floor hallway."

Victor Wolff, one of the clan's two patriarchs, lumbered to his feet, chuckling at Olivia's lame joke. "Quite understandable. No problem. We're just getting ready for the soup course." His gaze landed on Cammie and stayed there, full of avid interest. "Welcome to the mountain, ladies. Kieran rarely brings such lovely guests."

"Thank you, sir." Olivia took a seat, and settled Cammie beside her, surprised to find that she was nervous as hell. It certainly wasn't the formal dinner that had her baffled. She'd conquered dining etiquette as a child. No, it was the barely veiled speculation in the eyes of everyone at the table when they looked at Olivia and Cammie.

Only Kieran seemed oblivious to the undercurrents in the room. After digging into his pan-fried trout, caught in one of the streams on the property, he waved a fork at his father. "So tell me, Dad...what big projects do you and Uncle Vincent have lined up for the summer?"

He sat to the left of Olivia, and in an aside, he said, "My dad always likes to keep things humming here on the mountain. One year he repainted the entire house. Took the workmen six weeks and untold gallons of paint. Another time he added a bowling alley in the basement."

She smiled, hyperaware of Kieran's warm thigh so close to her own. "I imagine with a place this size there is always something that needs your attention."

Victor nodded. "Indeed. But this time I'm branching out. I've decided to plant a portion of the back of the mountain in Christmas trees."

Cammie's face lit up, her attention momentarily diverted

from her macaroni and cheese. "I *love* Christmas. My mama covers the whole house with decorations."

Victor smiled at her. "How old are you, young lady?"

"Five," she said casually, returning her attention to her meal.

Victor honed in on Olivia then. "My son hasn't told us much about you, Olivia. Have you known each other very long?"

The food she had eaten congealed into a knot in her stomach. She had been dreading just such a line of questioning. It took all she had to answer in a matter-of-fact voice. "We met when Kieran and I were doing graduate work at Oxford. You were taken ill soon after that, and he and I lost touch."

"I see." Olivia was very much afraid that he *did* see.

Her phone buzzed in the pocket of her skirt. Javier and Lolita tended to worry when she and Cammie were out of their reach, and they called often to check in. Since there was a lull before dessert, she smiled at the group in general and said, "Excuse me, please."

When she returned a few moments later, Kieran jumped up to move out her chair. He leaned over as he seated her, whispering in her ear, "What's wrong? You're pale as a ghost."

She wanted to hold on to him for comfort, and that scared her. So she swallowed her dismay and produced a smile. "Everything's fine. That was my mother checking up on us."

Kieran frowned, obviously unconvinced. "Olivia's parents are Javier and Lolita Delgado."

A rippled murmur swept the table. Gareth Wolff lifted an eyebrow. "I remember seeing her in *Fly by Night* when I was sixteen. She's amazing."

Jacob joined in the verbal applause. "And I'll never forget

when your dad played his first big role in *Vigilante Justice*. I thought he was the coolest dude ever."

Hearing Kieran's reserved brothers speak so enthusiastically about her parents made Olivia realize anew how much the older couple was beloved around the world. As their daughter, she saw them in a different light, but she understood the admiration and passion they generated in audiences.

Unfortunately not all of it was positive.

Biting her lip, she decided to share her unease. "My mother has a stalker fan who has been causing some problems. She just told me that he has hacked into her private email account and started sending her weird messages."

All four Wolff males wore matching expressions of ferocity. "Like what?" Kieran demanded, sliding an arm across the back of her chair.

Olivia slanted a worried glance at her daughter, but Cammie was engrossed in playing with a kitten that had wandered into the dining room. Olivia lowered her voice, anyway. "He's threatening violence. To my mother and to the people she holds dear. I could tell my mother is really spooked."

"It's a good thing you're here," Victor boomed, his florid face indignant. "How long are you staying?"

"Just until Monday."

Kieran brushed her arm with his fingertips. "I could only get her to agree to a three-night visit, but I'm hoping to change her mind." In front of God and everyone at the table, he leaned in and kissed her gently on the lips.

Olivia stiffened and turned red with mortification. Kieran's family only grinned.

Victor signaled an end to the dinner by rising unsteadily to his feet. "Well, keep us posted. I'd be happy to help in any way I can."

Gracie moved around the table and gave her brother-in-law a hug. "Nice of you to bring some estrogen to this male enclave." She smiled at Olivia. "I hear you're a children's book illustrator. I'd love to pick your brain about that if you have time. I'm a painter."

"I'd be happy to," Olivia said. "But at the moment, I need to get Cammie ready for bed. When we cross time zones, it's tough to keep her routine intact."

Kieran took her arm as they left the dining room. "Remember," he said. "My suite. Don't make me hunt you down."

She shivered, looking into his eyes for any sign of weakness. But there was none. His gaze was steady, confident, implacable. Her time of reckoning was nigh.

Cammie was irritable and uncooperative, perhaps picking up on Olivia's unsettled mood. It was close to ten o'clock when the child finally went to sleep in her tree house bed.

One of the older housekeepers took a seat in front of the television in Olivia's sitting room and promised to be vigilant in keeping an eye and ear out for Cammie. Olivia knew that her daughter rarely woke up after falling asleep, so she had no real reason to procrastinate any longer.

She slipped into the bathroom and changed out of the dress she had worn to dinner. Instead, she opted for soft, well-worn jeans and a light cashmere pullover sweater in pale mauve. Her mass of hair seemed unruly, so she swept it up in a thick ponytail.

The woman in the mirror had big eyes and a troubled expression. She'd been waiting for six years to face what was coming. But knowing the day had finally arrived made it no easier.

Somehow she had to prevent Kieran from seeing how much she still responded to him sexually. Giving him that advantage would weaken her, and she couldn't afford that… not when Cammie's life and well-being were at stake.

Kieran's suite of rooms was across the hall from hers. Was the arrangement designed to let him see more of his daughter or to remind Olivia that she could no longer hide from him?

She wiped damp palms on her jeans and knocked.

Five

Kieran had wondered if she would come. It wouldn't have surprised him if she had used jet lag or some other excuse to postpone this meeting, yet here she was. In casual clothes and with her hair pulled back, she seemed scarcely old enough to be the mother of a five-year-old child. "Come in," he said, feeling his muscles clench as she slipped past him. "Would you like some wine?"

"Yes," she said, her voice husky and low. "White, please."

He handed her a glass of the zinfandel he remember she liked and motioned for her to be seated. His suite, like the one he had chosen for her, included a bedroom, a lavish bath and this sitting room.

Olivia perched primly on a comfy chair, her knees together, ankles and feet aligned. Her curvy ass filled out the jeans she wore in a mouth-drying way. And that sweater. Jesus. Had she dressed this way deliberately to throw him off track?

Kieran remained standing, finishing his drink and setting the glass aside. "Cammie is mine," he said slowly, still stunned by the notion. "Without a doubt. But you told me six years ago that you were taking the pill."

She grimaced. "I was. But one morning I forgot to take it, and I found it lying by the sink when I got ready for bed that night. I swallowed it down right away, but obviously the damage was already done."

"Hmm." He was itchy, nervous, unsettled as hell. Tiptoeing through a minefield, that's what this was. He cleared his throat. "We're done with dancing around this, Olivia. I need to hear you say it. Tell me that Cammie is my daughter."

When she remained stubbornly silent, he sighed. "Do you want to know the real reason I didn't contact you after I left England?"

Shock flashed across her face, and she nodded cautiously, looking at him as if waiting for bad news from a doctor.

He ran both hands through his hair, searching for the right words. "After we had been together for a couple of weeks, you began telling me stories from your childhood... about what it was like to be the daughter of world famous celebrities. How there were always bodyguards and races to avoid paparazzi. You said you hated the isolation and never being able to play at a friend's house. You told me you weren't allowed to go to school, but instead, had private tutors. Do you remember saying all that?"

She nodded, frowning. "Of course."

"Well, what I couldn't tell you was that your story mirrored my own in many ways. We both suffered growing up, and I understood completely your feelings of being trapped, of wanting to fly the coop. You said on more than one occasion that all you wanted out of life was to be normal. To raise any children you might have like regular people."

Grimacing, she took a sip of wine. "You really listened."

"I did. And that's why I never called. It's not ego talking when I say that I knew you were falling in love with me. I felt the same way. You weren't like any girl I had ever dated, and I wanted you so badly I couldn't think straight half the time."

"You never said anything."

"I thought you'd be able to tell how I felt when we were making love. And I didn't want to bare my soul when you knew me as Kevin Wade. If I told you I loved you, I wanted you to know I was Kieran."

"And when your father had his heart attack?"

"It shook me. The night before I had called him and asked permission to tell you the truth. He was terribly upset, and the next morning I got the call that he'd been taken to the hospital. It felt like I had caused the heart attack, and maybe I did."

"So you decided before you ever left England that we were over?"

"If I'm being honest…yes. I knew I could never give you what you needed, and I didn't want to hurt you. My family is not normal. So it seemed kinder in the long run to end things before we both got in too deep. No matter how far I try to run from it, I'll always be a Wolff, and the money will always make me and those I love a target. You have this dream of being a PTA mom and having a white picket fence. There's not a place for me in that scenario."

He thought his explanation would make her feel better. Instead, she looked furious.

"What gives you the right to make decisions for me, to map out my life?" she said angrily. "I had nothing but lies to go on, Kevin Wade. You're an arrogant ass." Her eyes flashed fire at him and her chest heaved.

How the hell did he become the bad guy, when he was

only trying to protect her from hurt? "Tell me that Cammie is mine," he demanded through clenched teeth.

Her lustrous eyes were wounded, her lips pale where she had pressed them together so hard. "Your sperm may have generated her life, but Cammie is *my* daughter."

His heart caught in his throat and he sank onto the sofa, not for the world willing to admit that his knees had gone weak. "So you're admitting we made a baby?"

Olivia's face softened, and she came to sit beside him. Not touching but close. "Of course we did. Have you *looked* at her?"

Fury built in his belly. "How could you keep her from me for five long years? Damn it, Olivia. Do you have any idea what I've missed?" He vaulted to his feet, unable to bear her presence so close. He didn't know whether to kiss her in gratitude for giving him a child or to strangle her for her deception.

He was shaking all over, and the weakness and turmoil he experienced infuriated him. Grief for the time he would never recoup mingled with wonder that a part of him lay asleep in a nearby room.

"When can we tell her?"

Olivia went white. "It's not the kind of thing you blurt out. Maybe you should get to know her first."

"In three days?" He was incredulous that she didn't understand his urgency. "Guess again. I'm keeping her here this summer."

"You can't."

"Oh, yes," he said in dead earnest. "I can and I will. Both of you will move in here for the duration."

"You can't order me," she whispered, anguish marking her face.

He shrugged. "I'm not being unreasonable. Your work

can be done anywhere. She's not in school yet. If you don't agree, I'll take you to court. I know plenty of judges who frown on parents who kidnap their own kids."

"I didn't kidnap her. That's a terrible thing to say."

"You kept her existence a secret from her father. Semantics, Olivia. I'm calling the shots now."

"You're bluffing."

He felt a tingle of sympathy for her distress, but only that. She'd do well to understand that he fought for what was his. "It wouldn't be such a terrible thing, would it? To spend time here on the mountain?"

Clearly unconvinced, she frowned stubbornly as she stood up and crossed the room to stand nose to nose with him. "I can't turn my life upside down overnight. You're a bully."

He grinned, feeling suddenly lighthearted and free. A daddy. He was a daddy.

Olivia cocked her head. "What's so funny?"

"You. Me. Life in general."

"I don't see any humor in this situation at all," she huffed.

He scooped her up, lifting her until his belt buckle pressed into her stomach. Her arms went around his neck. "Thank you, Olivia, for giving me Cammie." He kissed her nose.

"She's not a *thing* to give. But you're welcome."

He slid his lips across hers, tasting the flavors of the coffee and lemon pie she had consumed earlier. "One summer," he coaxed.

"One weekend," she countered.

He palmed her ass, pulling her into his thrusting erection. The clothes separating them were a frustration. So he set her on her feet and began undressing her.

Olivia went beet-red and batted at his hands. "What do

you think you're doing?" she sputtered. "Sex won't make me change my mind."

"The decision's already made." He groaned aloud as he peeled away her sweater and revealed a mauve demi-bra barely concealing its bounty. "Sweet heaven. Please don't stop me, Olivia. I need you more than my next breath." His body was one huge ache that concentrated in his hard erection.

Her eyelids fluttered shut as her shoulders rose and fell in a deep sigh. He removed the remainder of her clothing posthaste. The well-washed jeans, the socks and shoes, the scanty bra and, finally, the lacy thong.

Was it possible that he had forgotten how gorgeous she was? Full breasts with light brown centers topped a narrow waist and hourglass hips. He must have been insane six years ago. How had he left her?

He weighed both her breasts in his hands. "Look at me, Olivia."

She opened her eyes and what he saw there humbled him. Sadness, resignation, need. "This won't solve anything, Kieran."

He nodded, refusing to let the future taint the moment. "Then don't think. Just let me make you feel."

A bleak smile lifted the corners of her lips. "Do you think you're that irresistible? You have a bad habit of wanting to run the show."

"I'll work on my failings," he promised, ready to agree to anything as long as she stayed in this room with him for the next half hour.

"What makes you think I'll be lured into your bed given our history?"

"It's *because* of our history that I believe it. We could never keep our hands off each other, and you know it."

"I won't have Cammie be hurt or confused by any relationship we might initiate."

"Of course not. This is no one's business but ours."

"Someone might come in," she said, nibbling her bottom lip.

"I locked the door, I swear."

"And the housekeeper?"

"I told her you'd be back no later than eleven-thirty."

Her face flamed again. "Oh, my God, Kieran. Don't you think she knows we're across the hall having sex?"

"We're *not* having sex," he pointed out ruefully.

"You know what I mean."

His hands moved to her waist, petting her, soothing her. "She thinks we went for a walk in the moonlight. And she's a romantic soul. Quit worrying."

For one interminable heartbeat he thought Olivia would refuse him. But finally she nodded as if coming to some unknown decision. Her hands went to his belt buckle. "If we have a curfew, I suppose we'd better not waste any time."

"I agree," he said fervently, batting her hands away and ripping off his clothing in two quick swipes as he toed off his shoes.

Her eyes rounded in a gratifying way as she took stock of his considerably aroused state. "I seem to have forgotten a few things about you," she said, cupping him in her hands.

He sucked in a breath between clenched teeth. "I'm on a hair trigger, Olivia. It's been a while. Maybe you shouldn't touch me."

"There you go again, bossing me around." She dropped to her knees on the plush carpet and licked him daintily.

The shock of it ricocheted through his body like streaks of fire. He cursed, gripping her head, and with one snap of his wrist breaking the band that held her ponytail in place.

That fabulous hair tumbled across her cheeks, around his straining penis. The eroticism of the image sent him over the edge, and he came with a ragged shout.

They collapsed to the floor and Olivia lay beside him, a small, pensive smile on her face.

He rubbed his eyes with the heels of his hands. "Was that meant to prove something?"

"Maybe. I'm not a kid anymore, Kieran. I'm a woman, and I've been running my life for six years without your help."

"But you have to admit that when we do things together, the results are pretty spectacular."

"Is that a sexual reference?"

"Could be, but in this case I was talking about Cammie."

She curled into him, hooking one long, slender leg over his thigh. "I can't argue with that."

He stroked her hair. "We don't have to be adversaries."

"As long as you understand that you can't ride roughshod over my feelings and opinions. And we don't have to be a couple."

"Fair enough."

She touched him intimately. "If you're trying to manipulate me with sex, it won't work."

His erection flexed and thickened. "Understood."

"Then I think we're on the same page."

He stood and pulled her to her feet. "Bed this time," he grunted, reduced to one syllable words. He lifted her into his arms and deposited her in the center of his large mattress. The old Olivia would have pulled a sheet over herself immediately, but this more mature version lifted one knee, propped her head on her hand and smiled.

It was the smile of a woman learning her own power. Kieran was not immune. He sprawled beside her and entertained himself by relearning every curve and dip of her feminine body.

Olivia melted for him, her soft gasps and tiny cries filling him with determination to pleasure her as she had never been pleasured before. He brought her to the brink with his hands and then moved between her legs. At the last moment he remembered the need for a condom. He wasn't taking any chances this time.

Not that he considered Cammie a mistake, but because he needed to learn how to be a father. One child was enough for the moment.

He sheathed himself in the latex and positioned the head of his penis against Olivia's warm, moist flesh. She was pink and perfect, her sex swollen where he had teased her.

Her eyes were shut. "Look at me," he insisted. When she obeyed, he drove into her, eliciting groans from both of them. Her body squeezed him, begged him not to leave. Panting, he withdrew and surged deep again. "We're good this way," he muttered. "So damn good."

The truth of the statement tormented him.

He was not a family man. After a lifetime of living caged up, he needed the freedom he found in anonymous villages on the other side of the world. Olivia was important to him, and Cammie was part of him, flesh and blood.

But what did it matter when he was condemned to be alone? Loving meant loss, and he'd had his share of that.

Olivia's sultry smile was drowsy. "Does it have to end?"

Even the question was enough to send heat streaking down his spine, sparking into his balls and rushing through the part of him that longed for release. His jaw clenched, the muscles in his neck corded and he shouted half in relief, half in awe when his body shuddered in the throes of a climax that left him weak.

Dimly he was aware that Olivia joined him at the end.

Panting, half addled from the scalding deluge of release, he rolled to his back, dragging her on top of him, their bodies still joined.

"Stay the night." The words were muffled as he buried his face in her cleavage.

"I can't," she said, disentangling their limbs and rolling to sit on the side of the bed.

"I could come to your room."

Her body stilled, her back to him. "No."

As he watched, only momentarily sated, she dressed rapidly and finger-combed her hair. He frowned, already missing the feel of her in his arms. "Dismiss the housekeeper and come back. We could set an alarm so you'll be in your room by morning."

"I have responsibilities," she said, not meeting his gaze.

"And that precludes meeting your needs as a woman?"

She stopped at the door and faced him across the room. In her eyes he saw regret and resolution. "I can't afford to get involved with you again. Sharing a daughter will be hard enough. Let's view tonight as one for Auld Lang Syne and put it behind us."

"I'm not a fan of that plan. It wouldn't hurt for Cammie to see us getting along."

"We can be civil without starting something we can't finish. I'm here for a very short time. And unlike you, I don't happen to see recreational sex as an appropriate lifestyle."

Now he was pissed. "Who said anything about recreational sex?"

He strode to where she stood backed up against the door and got in her face. "I'm attracted to you, Olivia Delgado. I like you. And as of today, I know we share a child. Any intimacies we indulge in are far from casual."

She licked her lips, her eyes huge. "You're bullying me again," she whispered.

Damn it. He was hard. And hungry. And mad as hell that she seemed to see him as some kind of a lowlife. He backed up two feet and crossed his arms over his chest. "You have more power than you think. But I won't be pushed away."

She reached behind her for the knob and opened the door. Since he was buck naked, and knowing that one of the housekeepers sat just across the hall, he didn't have a prayer of stopping her.

But his chest was tight when he closed the door and banged his forehead against the unforgiving wood. She was making him crazy. Two steps forward…one step back. Perhaps it was time for a change of plan. He would get to know his daughter, and in the meantime, maybe Olivia would acknowledge the fire that burned between them and return to his bed on her own.

Six

A strange house. Odd night sounds. And dreams that were riddled with images of Kieran Wolff. No wonder Olivia slept poorly. She had no more defenses against him now than she had as a naive university student. All he had to do was crook his little finger and she fell into his arms without protest.

It was infuriating and humbling and, if she were honest, exciting. Her days since Cammie was born had been pleasant. And the white-picket-fence life she had so deliberately created was good. Really good. But what woman—still two years shy of thirty—should be willing to settle for that?

Kieran's recent intrusion into her life was a jolt of adrenaline. Now she was scared and aroused and worried and challenged, but she wasn't bored.

Finally, at 4:00 a.m., she fell into a deep sleep, only to be awakened at the crack of dawn when Cammie crawled into bed with her. Crossing three time zones was not an easy adjustment for a child.

Olivia yawned. "Good morning, sweetheart."

"What are we going to do today?" Cammie snuggled close, her small, warm body a comfort Olivia never tired of.

"I think Kieran wants to hang out with us. Is that okay?"

In the semidark, her daughter's face was hard to read. "Yep. I like him."

That was it. Four short words. But hearing her daughter's vote of confidence relieved at least some of Olivia's concern.

Olivia dozed off again. When she woke, Cammie was gone, and light streamed into the room. Good Lord. She was a sweet kid, but mischievous at times. Olivia stumbled from her bed and rushed through the connecting passageway to Cammie's whimsical bedroom. She stopped short when she realized that Cammie was sprawled on the floor on her stomach alongside Kieran, who was aligned in a similar position.

Both of them were playing with an expensive model train set. A small black engine *choo-chooed* its way around a figure-eight track. Seeing the two of them side by side wrenched something inside her chest and brought hot tears to her eyes. She blinked them back, refusing to dwell on what might have been.

Kieran looked up, his gaze raking her from head to toe, taking in the flimsy silk nightie that ended above her knees, her thinly covered breasts, her tousled hair. "Rough night, Olivia?"

His bland intonation was meant to bait.

"Slept like a baby," she said, glaring at him when she thought her daughter wouldn't see. Kieran looked delicious…clear-eyed and dressed casually in jeans and an old faded yellow oxford shirt with the sleeves rolled up. His big masculine feet were bare, and Olivia discovered that there was no part of him that didn't make her heart beat faster.

He motioned to a nearby tray. "Cook sent up fresh scones and homemade blackberry jam. And there's a carafe of coffee."

Cammie had barely acknowledged her mother's presence, too caught up in the new entertainment. Olivia shifted her feet, reluctant to parade in front of her host to get a much-needed cup of caffeine. The awkward silence grew.

Kieran took pity on her. "Go take a shower if you want to. I'll pour you some coffee and set it on the nightstand. Okay?"

"Thanks," she muttered, escaping to the privacy of her room. In twenty minutes she had showered and changed into trim khakis and a turquoise peasant shirt that left one shoulder bare. She hadn't needed to wash her hair this morning, so she brushed it vigorously and left one swathe to lie over the exposed skin.

The coffee awaited as promised. She drank it rapidly and went in search of a second cup. What she saw stunned her. Cammie, often shy around strangers, sat in Kieran's lap in a sunshine-yellow rocker as he read to her from an Eric Carle book.

The two of them looked up with identical expressions of inquiry. Cammie's typical smile danced across her face. "You look pretty, Mommy. Kieran's going to take us to the attic."

Olivia glanced down ruefully at her fairly expensive outfit. "Do I need to change?"

Kieran laid the book aside and shook his head. "The Wolff attic is more of a carefully maintained museum than a dusty hiding place. You'll be fine."

While Cammie took another turn with the train, Kieran spoke, sotto voce to Olivia. "She's right. You look lovely."

He brushed a kiss across her cheek. "I wanted you when I woke up this morning."

The gravelly statement sent goose bumps up and down her arms. She glanced at Cammie, but the child was oblivious to the adult's tension. "You shouldn't say things like that. Not here. Not now."

He shrugged, unrepentant, and suddenly she saw the source of Cammie's mischievous grin. Circling Olivia's waist with one arm, he pulled her close and whispered in her ear, his hot breath tickling sensitive skin. "If you had stayed in my bed last night, neither of us would have gotten any rest. Remember the evening after the Coldplay concert? We didn't sleep that night at all."

His naughty reminiscence was deliberate. In a hotel room high above the streets of London, they had fallen onto the luxurious bed, drunk on each other and the evening of evocative music. Again and again he had taken her, until she was sore and finally had to beg off.

The resultant apology and intimate sponge bath had almost broken his control and hers.

"Stop it," she hissed. "That was a lifetime ago. We're different people."

"Perhaps. But I don't think so." He bit gently at her earlobe, half turned so Cammie couldn't see his naughty caress. "You make me ache, Olivia. Tell me you feel the same."

She broke free of his embrace. "Cammie, are you ready for the attic?"

Kieran grimaced inwardly, realizing that he had already strayed from his plan. As long as he pushed, Olivia would run. Only time would tell if another tack would woo her in the right direction.

As they climbed the attic stairs, Cammie slipped her little hand into his with a natural trust that cut him off at the knees. Frankly it scared him spitless. What did he know about raising a kid? He'd been too young when his mother died to have many memories of her. And when his father imploded into a near breakdown, the only familial support Kieran had known was from his uncle, his two brothers and his cousins, all of whom were grieving as much or more than he was.

He halted Cammie at the top of the stairs. "Hold on, poppet. Let me get the switch." It had been years since he had been up here, but the cavernous space hadn't changed much. Polished hardwood floors, elegant enough for any ballroom, were illuminated with old-fashioned wall sconces as well as pure crystalline sunbeams from a central etched glass skylight. Almost thirty years of junk lay heaped in piles across the broad expanse.

Olivia's face lit up. "This is amazing…like a storybook. Oh, Kieran. You were so lucky to grow up here."

Though her comment hit a raw nerve, he realized that she meant it. Seeing the phenomenal house through a newcomer's eyes made him admit, if only to himself, that not all his memories were unpleasant. How many hours had he and Gareth and Jacob and their cousins whiled away up here on rainy days? The adults had left them alone as long as they didn't create a ruckus, and there was many a time when the attic had become Narnia, or a Civil War battlefield, or even a Star Wars landscape.

He cleared his throat. "It's a wonderful place to play," he said quietly, caught up in the web of memory. Across the room he spotted what he'd been looking for—a large red carton. He dragged it into an empty spot and grinned at Cammie. "This was my favorite toy."

"I remember having some of these." Olivia squatted down beside them and soon, the Lincoln Logs were transformed into barns and bridges and roads.

Kieran ruffled Cammie's hair. "You're good at building things," he said softly, still struggling to believe that she was his.

"Mommy says I get that from my daddy."

His gut froze. "Your daddy?"

"Uh-huh. He lives on the other side of the world, so we don't get to see him."

Kieran couldn't look at Olivia. He stumbled to his feet. "Be right back," he said hoarsely. He made a beeline for the stairs, loped down them and closed himself in the nearest room, which happened to be the library. His throat was so tight it was painful, and his head pounded. Closing his eyes and fisting his hands at his temples, he fought back the tsunami of emotion that had hit him unawares.

A child's simple statement. *We don't get to see him....* How many times had Olivia talked to Cammie about her absentee father? And how many times had a small child wondered why her daddy didn't care enough to show up?

His stomach churned with nausea. If he had known, things would have been different. Damn Olivia.

As he stood, rigid, holding himself together by sheer will, an unpalatable truth bubbled to the surface. He *did* live on the other side of the world. He'd logged more hours in the air than he'd spent in the States in the past five years. What would he have done if Olivia had found him and told him the truth?

His lies to her in England had been the genesis of an impossible Gordian knot. One bad decision led to another until now Kieran had a daughter he didn't know, Olivia was afraid to trust him and Kieran himself didn't have a clue what to do about the future.

When he thought he could breathe again, he returned to the attic. Cammie had lost interest in the Lincoln Logs, and she and Olivia were now playing with a pile of dress-up clothes. Cammie pirouetted, wearing a magenta tutu that had once belonged to Kieran's cousin Annalise. "Look at me," she insisted, wobbling as she tried to stand up in toe shoes.

Kieran stopped short of the two females, not trusting himself at the moment to behave rationally. "Very nice," he croaked.

Olivia looked at him with a gaze that telegraphed inquiry and concern. "You okay?" she mouthed, studying him in a way that made him want to hide. He didn't need or want her sympathy. She was the one who had stripped him of a father's rights.

He nodded tersely. "I'll leave you two up here to play for a while. I have some business calls to make."

Olivia watched the tall, lean man leave, her heart hurting for him. In hindsight, she wondered if she and Kieran might have had a chance if he hadn't lied about who he was, and if she had been able to get past her anger and righteous indignation long enough to notify him that she was having his baby.

It was all water under the bridge now. The past couldn't be rewritten.

She and Cammie were on their own for most of the afternoon, despite Kieran's insistence that he wanted to get to know his daughter. After lunch and a nap, Olivia took her daughter outside to explore the mountaintop. They found Gareth's woodworking shop, and Cammie made friends with the basset hound, Fenton.

On this beautiful early summer day, Wolff Mountain was twenty degrees cooler than down in the valley, and Olivia fell in love with the peace and tranquility found in towering trees, singing birds and gentle breezes.

She and Cammie ran into Victor Wolff on the way back to the house. He was slightly stoop-shouldered, and his almost bald head glistened with sweat. From what Olivia had gleaned from the private investigator and from a variety of internet sources, Victor had been a decade and a half older than his short-lived bride…which meant he must now be banging on the door of seventy.

The old man stared at Cammie with an expression that made Olivia's heart pound with anxiety. He shot a glance at Olivia. "The child has beautiful eyes. Very unusual."

Olivia held her ground, battling an atavistic need to tuck her baby under her wing. "Yes, she may grow up to be a beauty like my mother."

Cammie had no interest in adult conversation. She started picking flowers and dancing among the swaying fronds of a large weeping willow that cast a broad patch of shade. Victor's eyes followed her wistfully. "I may die before I get to see any grandchildren. Gareth is the only one of my sons who is married, and he and Gracie have decided to wait a bit to start their family."

"Are you ill?" Olivia asked bluntly.

He shook his head, still tracking the child's movements. "A bad heart. If I watch what I eat and remember to exercise, my son, the doc, says I probably have a few thousand more miles under the hood."

"But you don't believe him?"

"None of us knows how many days we have on this earth."

"I'm sorry about your wife, Mr. Wolff. I can't imagine how hard that must have been losing her so young."

He shrugged. "We argued that day. Before she left to go shopping. She wanted to let the boys take piano lessons and I thought it was a sissy endeavor. I told her so in no uncertain terms."

"And then she died."

"Yes." He aged before her eyes. "I've made a lot of mistakes in my life, Olivia."

"We all do, sir."

"Perhaps. But I almost ruined my sons, keeping them locked up like prisoners. My brother, Vincent, was the same. Six children between us, vulnerable little babies. I was terrified, you know. My brother and I both were."

"That's understandable." She began to feel a reluctant sympathy for the frail patriarch.

Suddenly his eyes shot fire at her, and the metamorphosis was so unexpected that Olivia actually took a step backward. "Kieran's a good boy. It's not his fault that the memories here keep him away."

"We all have our own demons to face," Olivia said. "But children shouldn't have to suffer for our mistakes."

"Are you talking about me or about you?"

His candor caught her off guard. "I suppose it could be either," she said slowly. "But know this, Mr. Wolff. I will do anything to protect my daughter."

He actually chuckled, a rusty sound that seemed to surprise him as much as it did her. "I like you, Olivia. Too bad I didn't have a daughter to take after my dear Laura."

Olivia couldn't think of a response to that, so she held her peace, walking beside Kieran's father as the three of them made their way back to the house.

Seven

Kieran saw the three of them approach the house. He was watching from an upstairs window. Part of him resented the fact that his father was sharing time with Olivia and Cammie, something Kieran had intended as the primary focus of the weekend. But anger boiled in his veins, and he was afraid that if he snapped and confronted Olivia in Cammie's presence, the child would be frightened.

Still, it was time for a showdown, and since nothing appeared to mitigate the harshness of the rage that gripped him, Olivia had better beware.

Dinner was an awkward affair with only the four of them. Jacob had been called way unexpectedly, and Gareth and Gracie were still in the honeymoon phase of their marriage, enjoying time together at home alone.

Cammie behaved beautifully at the overly formal table, conversing easily with Kieran and smiling shyly when Victor Wolff addressed her. Olivia was pale and quiet, perhaps sensing that a storm was brewing. The courses passed slowly. At last, Victor pushed back from the table. "I'll leave you young people to it. If you'll excuse an old man, I'm going upstairs to put on my slippers and sit by the fire."

Cammie wrinkled her nose as he left. "A fire? That's silly. It's summertime."

Kieran smiled, loving how bright she was, how aware of her surroundings. "You're right about that, little one. But my father has his eccentricities, and we all adjust."

"X cin…" She gave up trying to replicate the difficult word.

Olivia leaned over to remove crumbs from her daughter's chin with a napkin. "It means that Mr. Wolff has lived a long time and he sometimes does strange things."

"Like when Jojo puts hot sauce on his ice cream."

Olivia grinned. "Something like that."

Kieran saw himself suddenly as if from a distance, sitting at a table with his lover and their child. Anyone peering in the window would see a family, a unit of three. A mundane but extraordinarily wonderful relationship built on love, not lies.

But appearances were deceiving.

So abruptly that Olivia frowned, he stood up and tossed his napkin on the table. "Why don't I tuck Cammie in tonight? Is that okay with you, Olivia?"

He saw the refusal ready to tumble automatically from her lips, but she stopped and inhaled sharply, her hands clenching the edge of the table. "I suppose that would be fine. What do you think, Cammie?"

"Sure. Let's go, Kieran. Do you have any boats to play with in your bathtub?"

After they were gone, the silence resonated. Olivia realized that she was inconveniencing the waitstaff as long as she sat at the table, so she got up, as well. There were so many rooms in the huge house, it was easy to get lost. Not wanting to be too far away from Cammie, she found a staircase that led to the second floor and walked toward her suite. When she could hear laughter and splashing from the bathroom, she paused in the sitting room to call her mother.

Lolita's well-modulated voice answered on the first ring. "Hello, darling. How's the visit with your school friend?"

Olivia might possibly have fudged a bit on the details of her trip. "Going well. But I'm worried about you and Dad. Anything else from your psycho fan?"

"Don't be so cruel, Olivia. Men can't help falling in love with me. It's the characters on the screen, of course, but I play them so well, they seem genuine and warm, especially to someone who has already experienced a disconnect with reality. We should have compassion for the poor soul who is obsessed with me."

Olivia's mother had no problem with self-esteem. But her nonchalance seemed shortsighted. Olivia might have been even more worried were it not for the fact that Javier Delgado took his responsibilities as a husband very seriously. He was narcissistic to a fault, but he did love his tempestuous wife, and he had the bodyguards and manpower to prove it.

"Still, Mom, please be vigilant. Don't let down your guard."

"It's a tempest in a teapot, Olivia. Just a sad man wanting attention. Quit worrying."

"Has he sent more emails?"

"A few. The police are monitoring my computer."

"What did the notes say?"

"More of the same. Threats to me and the people I love. But you and Cammie are in a safe place for now, and your father and I are well taken care of. Everything's fine."

The conversation ended with Olivia feeling no less concerned than she had been earlier. As much as she hated to admit it, her parents would always be targets because of their celebrity and their wealth. Which was exactly why Olivia had struggled so hard to make a home for herself and her daughter away from the limelight that surrounded Lolita and Javier. Even letting Cammie travel with her grandparents was a leap of faith, but Olivia wanted the three of them to be close, so she bit her tongue and prayed when necessary.

The noise of Cammie's bedtime rituals moved from the bathroom to the bedroom. Olivia walked through the door in time to see Kieran tuck his daughter into the raised bed, giving her a kiss in the process. "My turn," she said.

Feeling awkward beneath Kieran's steady gaze, she hugged Cammie and tucked the covers close. "Sweet dreams."

Cammie's eyes were already drooping. "Nite, Mommy. Nite, Kieran." The two adults stepped into the hall. Kieran's expression was brooding, none of the lightheartedness he'd exhibited in Cammie's presence remaining. "Put some other shoes on," he said. "We're going for a walk."

Kieran saw on her face that she recognized the blunt command for what it was.

She frowned. "When you have a child, you can't waltz away whenever you want. She's too small to be left alone."

"I'm not stupid, Olivia." Her patronizing words irritated him. "Jacob returned a little while ago. Cook is fixing him some leftovers. He's bringing a stack of medical journals with him and has promised to sit up here until we get back."

"I don't know why we have to leave the house."

"Because it's a beautiful night and because I don't think you want to risk having our conversation overheard."

That shut her up. He was in a mood to brook no opposition, and the sooner he stated his piece, the better.

About the time Jacob appeared upstairs, Olivia returned wearing athletic shoes as instructed. She had changed into jeans and a long-sleeve shirt in deference to the chill of the late hour. Even in summer, nights on the mountain were cool.

They chatted briefly with Jacob, and then Kieran cocked his head toward the door. “Let’s go.”

Outside, Olivia stopped short. “You haven’t told me where we’re going.”

“To the top of the mountain.”

“I thought we *were* on top.”

“The house sits on a saddle of fairly level land, but at either end of the property, the peak splits into two outcroppings. One has been turned into a helipad. We’re headed to the other.”

She followed him in silence as he strode off into the darkness, deliberately keeping up an ambitious pace. If she ended up exhausted and out of breath, perhaps she wouldn’t be able to argue with him.

When the trail angled sharply upward, she called out his name. “Kieran, stop. I need to rest.”

He paused there in the woods and looked at her across the space of several feet. Her face was a pale blur in the darkness. The sound of her breathing indicated exertion.

“Can we go now?” He was determined not to show her any consideration tonight. Nothing would dissuade him from his course of judgment.

She nodded.

He spun on his heel and pressed on. They were three miles from the house when the final ascent began. “Take my hand,” he said gruffly, not willing to place her in any actual danger.

The touch of her slender fingers in his elicited emotions that were at odds with his general mood of condemnation.

He pushed back the softer feelings and concentrated on his need for retribution.

Clambering over rocks and thick roots, they made their way slowly upward. At last, breaking out of the trees, they were treated to a vista of the heavens that included an unmistakable Milky Way and stars that numbered in the millions.

Despite his black mood, the scene humbled him as it always did. Every trip home he made this pilgrimage at least once. To the right, a single large boulder with a flat top worn down by millennia of wind and rain offered a seat. He drew her to sit with him. Only feet away, just in front them, the mountain plunged into a steep, seemingly endless ravine.

Olivia perched beside him, their hips touching. "Are you planning to throw me off?" she asked, daring to tease him.

"Don't tempt me."

"It's a good thing I'm not afraid of heights."

"We'll come back in the daylight sometime. You can see for miles from up here."

They sat in silence for long minutes. Perhaps this had been a mistake. The wild, secluded beauty of this remote mountain was chipping away at his discontent. Occasionally the breeze teased his nostrils with Olivia's scent. All around them nocturnal creatures went about their business. Barred owls hooted nearby, their mournful sound punctuating the night.

Olivia sat quietly, her arms wrapped around her.

He rested his elbows on his knees, staring out into the inky darkness. "You committed an unpardonable sin against me, Olivia. Robbing me of my daughter—" His voice broke, and he had to take a deep, shuddering breath before he could continue. "Nothing can excuse that…no provocation, no set of circumstances."

"I'm sorry you missed seeing her grow from a baby into a funny, smart girl."

"But that's not really an apology, is it? You'd do the same thing again."

"The father of my child was a liar who abandoned me without warning or explanation. And later, when I did discover the truth, I found out what kind of man you are. An eternal Peter Pan, always searching for Neverland. Never quite able to settle down to reality."

"You think you have me all figured out."

"It's not that hard. All I have to do is look at the stamps on your passport."

"Traveling the world is not a crime."

"No, but it's an inherently selfish lifestyle. I'll admit that your work is important, but those bridges you build have also created unseen walls. You've never had to answer to anyone but yourself. And you like it that way."

The grain of truth in her bald assessment stung. "I might have made different choices had I known about Cammie."

"Doubtful. You were hardly equipped to care for a baby. And by your own admission, you've returned to Wolff Mountain barely a handful of times in six years. You may feel like the wronged party in this situation, Kieran, but from where I'm standing, both of our lives played out as they had to—separate…unrelated."

He couldn't let go of the sick regret twisting his insides with the knowledge that he had never been allowed to hold his infant child. "You call me selfish, Olivia, but you like playing God, controlling all the shots. That hardly makes you an admirable character in this scenario."

"I did what was necessary to survive."

"Lucky for you, your parents had money."

"Yes."

"Because, otherwise, you'd have been forced to come

crawling to me, and that would have eaten away at your pride."

"I would never have come to you for money."

He pounded his fists on his knees. "Damn you. Do you know how arrogant you sound?"

"Me? Arrogant?" Her voice rose. "That's rich. You wrote the book, Kieran. All you do is throw your weight around. I won't apologize for protecting my daughter from an absentee father."

"Military families deal with long absences all the time and their children survive."

"That's true. But those kids suffer. Sometimes they cry themselves to sleep at night wishing with all their hearts that their mommy or daddy was there to tuck them in. It's a tough life."

"But you never gave us a chance to see if we could make it work."

"You had sex with me for six weeks and never told me your real identity. What in God's name makes you think I would have put myself out there to be slapped down again? You hurt me, Kieran…badly. And when I found out a baby was on the way, it was all I could do to hold things together. If you had at least contacted me, who knows what might have happened. But you didn't. So forget the postmortems. What's done is done."

"I want to tell her I'm her father."

"No."

"I have legal rights."

"And you have plane tickets to Timbuktu at the end of the summer. Telling her would be cruel. Can't you see that?"

"She needs me. A girl should have a daddy to spoil her and teach her how to ride a bike."

"And you'll do that via Skype? Is that what you had in mind?"

"God, you're cold."

"What I am is a realist. We're not talking about how much Cammie needs *you.* This is really about you needing *her,* isn't it? And if you'll stop and think about it, the mature thing to do would be to walk away before she gets hurt."

"I want her to stay for the whole summer."

"She would fall in love with you and then be crushed when it was over. Absolutely not."

"We're getting nowhere with this," he groused. "It's a circular argument. I have a proposition. My cousin Annalise is returning tomorrow. She's great with children, and Cammie will love her. I have to make an overnight trip the following morning to New York to meet with a charitable board about the September project. I want you to come with me and we'll see if we can work this thing out."

"There's nothing to work out."

"Let me put it this way…either you agree to go to New York and hash things out on neutral ground, or I tell Cammie the truth when she wakes up in the morning."

"You can't."

"Try and stop me." He was beyond pleasantries, fighting for his life, his future.

Olivia leaped to her feet and he grabbed for her wrist. "Be careful, damn it. You're too close to the edge of the cliff."

She struggled instinctively, and then froze when his words sank in. "Take me back to the house." Unmistakable tears thickened her voice.

He stood up and backed them both from the precipice. "Don't make this so hard, Olivia," he murmured, sliding his hands down her arms. "We're her parents. Together. I don't want to fight with you."

"But you want to torture me."

"Not that, either." Her nearness affected him predictably.

"I want to make love to you, but I don't have a death wish, so I suggest we get off this ledge."

He steered her down the winding, narrow path until they were once again cloaked in the pungent forest of fir and pine. When he halted and slid his hands beneath her hair to tilt her face toward his for a kiss, she didn't protest. But her lips were unmoving.

His thumbs stroked her cheeks, wiping away dampness. "You have to trust me, Olivia." He could feel the tremors in her body as he pulled her closer. "I won't hurt Cammie. I won't hurt you." He said it almost like a vow, but as the words left his lips, he realized the truth of them.

Traditional or not, Olivia and Cammie were his family… as much or more than Gareth, Jacob and Victor. He would protect them with every fiber of his being, to the death if necessary. If he could make Olivia understand how deep his feelings ran, how desperately he wanted to take care of both the women in his life, perhaps she would be more inclined to believe his sincerity and his resolve.

With aching slowness he claimed her mouth, tasting her, nipping at her tongue. At last, her arms circled his neck and her sweet lips dueled with his. There was less tenderness tonight, more unrestrained passion. Frustration and conflict segued into ragged hunger and rough caresses.

He jerked her shirt over her head and fumbled with the bra, dragging it down her arms and tossing it away haphazardly. Red-hot desire hazed his vision, and he trembled as if he had a fever.

Her lush breasts took on gooseflesh in the night air, and her nipples pebbled into small, hard stones. He took them in his mouth, one after the other, and suckled her, dragging on her tender flesh with his mouth and plumping her breasts with worshipful hands.

Olivia moaned, a sound that went straight to his groin

and sent scalding heat to scorch him alive. He ripped at her jeans, shoving them down her hips only enough to touch her between her legs. She was damp and ready for him.

Freeing his own eager sex, he fumbled in his pants pocket for a condom, rolled it on and then lifted her and braced her against the nearest tree. It was animalistic and raw and absolutely necessary.

With a grunt of determination, he thrust up and into her warm, hot passage. The sensation of being caressed by wet silk made him groan aloud. "I can't get enough of you," he said, the words muffled against her neck. "God, you make me burn."

After that, conversation evaporated in the white-hot conflagration of his drive to completion. Olivia's fingernails bit into his shoulders as she clung to him in desperation. He gripped her ass and lifted her high, angling his hips to fill her more deeply.

She cried out and trembled, heart pounding against his as she climaxed wildly, her inner muscles milking him. Her release triggered his. Keeping his hands under her ass to protect her from painful contact with the tree, he thrust recklessly, not caring if his hands suffered in the process. Nothing could have separated him from her in that moment.

She kissed him softly, and the simple caress was his undoing. Shaking, breathing hoarsely, he came with a rapid fire punch of his hips, feeling his strength drain away as he reached the end.

Legs embarrassingly weak, he went down, rolling onto his back in a sea of pine needles, settling Olivia on top of him as they both recovered. "Stay the summer," he begged.

She put her hand on his lips. "Stop. Let it go for now. I'll travel to New York with you. That's two more nights, total. After that, Cammie and I have to go home. I have a project to finish, and she has play dates scheduled with friends. We have a life, Kieran. But I'll consider returning later in the summer for a visit. Don't push me on this."

It was hard to be angry when she laid on top of him, every voluptuous inch of her his for the taking. Lazily he rubbed her firm, generous ass. She was the most intensely *female* woman he had ever known. As though her entire body was created for the purpose of male fantasy.

His erection was already perking up, but he had only brought one condom. Bad mistake. Instead of feeding his own hungry obsession, he reached between them and touched the tiny bud of nerves that made her quiver and pant. Deliberately he brought her to the brink again. She tried to fight him, but her body defeated her.

"Come for me, baby," he urged, relishing the feel of her dew on his fingers. He might ache, unappeased, for hours, but it was worth it to hear her call his name as she spiraled into bliss and then slumped onto his chest.

Eight

Olivia wanted to remain in the dark. Deep in the woods, she could pretend that she wasn't scared of repeating mistakes that should have been far behind her.

She wasn't lying to Kieran when she said she didn't want Cammie falling in love with him only to experience a child's broken heart when he left. But that was only half the truth.

Olivia couldn't, shouldn't, wouldn't fall in love with him again, either, and that's what was bound to happen if she remained on Wolff Mountain for the summer. Though she'd die rather than admit it, Kieran *was* irresistible. Look how she'd tumbled into his arms with barely a protest. Only physical distance could protect her. In New York, she planned to make her position clear.

Neutral ground, Kieran had said. The proposition sounded sensible on the surface. But Olivia had been to

New York several times, and she knew that with the right man, the city would be magical.

She could always make celibacy a condition of the trip, but that would be self-deceptive in the extreme. She *wanted* Kieran…looked forward to spending an uninterrupted night in his arms. And by reminding herself that when it was done, it was done, she could protect her heart.

Maybe in August she and Cammie would make one final quick trip for Kieran to see his daughter. Then he'd fly out across the globe, and she and Cammie could get back to their normal lives.

Why did that thought have to hurt so much?

Olivia had grown up in chaos, being dragged around to movie sets all over the world, hiding in her bedroom when her flamboyant parents indulged in one of their theatrical shouting matches. All she had ever wanted was a peaceful, normal existence to raise her child. And if she looked seriously, surely there was some nice guy out there who would want to marry her and add to the family.

Try as she might, such a picture never came into focus.

Kieran held her hand as they made their way back to the house. Their feet made scarcely a sound as they walked.

Her fingers clung to his, wishing she had the right to be with him like this forever. He was a loving man, and an honorable one, despite his youthful misjudgments. He loved his family, and he was clearly on his way to loving Cammie, as well.

But ultimately he saw Wolff Mountain as a trap, one that had robbed him of his childhood. And though he might visit from time to time, he was never going to settle in one place.

They entered through the back of the house, treading quietly in deference to sleeping servants. When they entered the room where Jacob kept watch, he stood up and stretched. "I was about to give up on you."

Kieran grimaced. “Sorry. The time got away from me. It’s a beautiful night.”

Jacob’s gaze settled on Olivia. He was a quiet, intense man, and his piercing eyes, like the X-ray machines he used, seemed to see right through her. “You need to watch out for my brother,” he joked. “We used to call him the ‘were-Wolff,’ because he loved roaming the woods at night.”

She blushed, feeling as if Jacob could see exactly what she and Kieran had been up to. “I enjoyed the walk,” she said. Her red cheeks were probably a dead giveaway, but she kept her expression noncommittal.

In the wake of Jacob’s departure, an awkward silence bloomed. Kieran’s jaw was rigid, and hunger still tightened the planes of his face. “Will you come to my room?” he asked.

She shook her head, backing away. “I need to get some sleep. Cammie will be up early. Good night.”

Hcr rctrcat was cmbarrassing to say thc lcast, but shc needed distance. His masculinity dragged her in, demanding a response, and for tonight, she needed to regroup and figure out how to protect her vulnerable heart.

Late the following morning Kieran’s cousin Annalise arrived. She blew in on a burst of wind and rain, her laughter contagious and her genuine welcome hard to resist.

“So glad to meet you both,” she said, squatting in Prada pumps to hug Cammie.

She was tall, dark-headed and gorgeous. And when she looked at Cammie, she was clearly shocked.

Olivia squirmed under her assessing gaze, but refused to be lured into saying something she would regret. “How was the family vacation?”

Annalise hugged her cousins, as well. Kieran and Jacob had showed up to eat lunch with her before going back to their construction project at Jacob's clinic. Gareth had gone home to see Gracie. "Daddy and the boys are still fishing in Wyoming, but I reached my fill of tying lures and fighting mosquitoes. Plus, I had to get home to see Kieran. It's like a sighting of the Loch Ness monster. You don't want to miss it."

"Very funny." Kieran suffered her teasing with an easy grin, slinging an arm around her shoulders as they walked to the dining room. "Admit it, brat. You just had to come home and meet my guests."

She wrinkled her classically beautiful nose. "You got me." She gave Olivia a rueful glance. "It's a well-known failing of mine," she said, patting Cammie's head as she seated herself at the table. "Whenever we were little, the guys tortured me by pretending to have secrets I wasn't privy to. I'd badger them unmercifully, until half the time they admitted that they had made it all up."

"It must have been hard being the only girl."

"You have no idea." She paused, expression concerned. "Where's Uncle Victor?"

"He had a rough night," Jacob said. "But he hopes to be with us for dinner."

Over a lunch of cold salads and fresh fruit, Olivia watched Annalise interact with her family. There were three more males not present, the brothers Annalise spoke of, as well as Vincent Wolff, who was Victor's twin. Clearly Annalise was close to Kieran and Jacob. She teased and kidded them with open affection.

The six young cousins had been raised in isolation in this huge house after the violent deaths of their mothers. It was no wonder they had formed a bond. Tragedy had marked this family and shaped its face.

When the meal was concluded, the men were itching to get back to work. Annalise turned to Olivia, her face alight with enthusiasm. "Why don't we go swim in Gareth and Gracie's pool?"

"A pool?" Olivia looked askance at the window where lightning flashed and water rolled down the panes.

"Indoors, silly." Annalise laughed.

Kieran frowned. "Does Cammie know how to swim?"

"We're from southern California. Of course she does." Olivia noted Kieran's response, as did Annalise. He had reacted with a parent's automatic concern. Olivia wondered how long it would be before someone in Kieran's family came right out and demanded to know if Cammie was a Wolff.

The pool was amazing. Built to resemble a natural tropical lake, it featured a waterfall, twittering parakeets and water that was heated just enough to be luxuriously comfortable.

Cammie loved it. She swam like a fish, and soon she was all over the pool. Gracie joined them soon after they arrived. The small redhead had a quiet smile and a look of contentment about her that Olivia envied.

At one point, Annalise threw back her head and laughed in delight. "I *love* having women here," she exclaimed, beaming in her gold bikini that seemed more suited to sunbathing at a resort on the French Riviera rather than actually getting wet.

Gracie nodded. "Me, too. After our honeymoon, Annalise was gone, and I have to confess that I was lonely sometimes for girl talk."

"How long have you two been married?" Olivia asked.

"Less than two months. I'm still getting used to this amazing house."

Gareth's Western-themed home was spectacular, though not as large as Wolff Castle, of course. And Olivia had glimpsed Jacob's more modern house through the trees. She frowned. "Why has Kieran never built his own place?"

Annalise shrugged. "Doesn't need one. He's here less than a dozen nights during the year. Two days at Christmas if we're lucky. Other than that, he's always on the go. The constraints of our situation were hard on all of us kids growing up, but Kieran chafed at them more than anyone. At the first opportunity, he struck out for freedom and has never really looked back. You can't cage a man who wants to roam."

Was that pity Olivia saw in Annalise's eyes? Olivia hoped not. It was bad enough for Olivia to acknowledge to herself that a future with Kieran was impossible. She didn't want or need anyone's commiseration, no matter how well meant.

When Gracie hopped out of the pool to dry off and get back to her painting, Olivia spoke quietly to Annalise, all the while keeping tabs on Cammie's high energy stunts. "Kieran has asked me to go to New York with him overnight. He thought you wouldn't mind keeping Cammie. Did he volunteer you too freely?"

"Of course not." Annalise straightened one of the flimsy triangles of her bathing suit top. Though she was the complete antithesis of Olivia's mother in looks, she possessed the same star quality. A woman no one, particularly no man, could resist. She smiled. "Cammie is a delight, and I'd be happy to look after her."

Standing next to her, waist deep in silky water, Olivia felt frumpy and large, though Kieran certainly seemed to have no complaints about her less than reed-thin figure. His appreciation for her…assets was flattering.

She signed inwardly. "Just one night, and we won't be late the following day, because Cammie and I will have to catch the red-eye back to the West Coast. That reminds me, I need to shift our tickets one day later."

"Why don't you take the family jet? Did Kieran not offer?"

"He has. Several times. But I prefer to make my own travel arrangements."

"Because you don't want to feel beholden to him?"

"It's not that. I've tried to raise Cammie away from the over-the-top lifestyle my parents enjoy."

"How's that workin' out for you?"

Olivia shook her head ruefully. "Sometimes I think it's a losing battle."

"So you didn't like growing up with all the bells and whistles?"

"I liked the toys and activities as much as the next kid. But I had friends whose parents were what I thought of as *normal.* Nine-to-five jobs, cookouts on the weekend. T-ball games. That wasn't part of my life, and I wanted it for Cammie."

"Sometimes we don't appreciate what's in our own backyard. There's something to be said for not having to worry constantly about money. And there's also the satisfaction that comes from helping people less fortunate. Our family has never wanted for anything, but I like to think we aren't spoiled. Our fathers instilled in us a sense of responsibility, *noblesse oblige,* if you will."

"If I can do as much for Cammie, I'll be happy."

Annalise twisted the ends of her long hair and squeezed out water. "She's a great kid, already. For a single mom, you've done a great job. It can't have been easy."

Here it comes. Olivia braced herself, waiting for Annalise to demand an explanation of Cammie's parentage. But the other woman merely smiled.

"Thank you," Olivia said awkwardly. She followed Annalise out of the pool and began drying off.

"If you ever need a friendly ear, I'm here." For once, the bubbly personality shifted to reveal a deep vein of seriousness. Her eyes, like Jacob's, seemed to see all.

"I appreciate that." For a moment, Olivia was tempted. She wanted to share with another female the fears and heartaches that came with being Kieran's lover, with bearing his child. But Annalise was Kieran's cousin, part of his family. Olivia had not even allowed Kieran to claim his daughter yet, so it would be unethical at the very least to share their secret.

She wrapped a towel around her waist and stretched out on a lounge chair to watch Cammie play. Annalise did the same. From speakers tucked away somewhere in the foliage, pleasant music played. Olivia yawned, ruefully aware that her unsettled sleep had everything to do with Kieran. When she wasn't actually with him, she was dreaming about him. What did that say about her subconscious desires?

Annalise's long legs were tanned and toned, making Olivia realize it had been some time since she herself had hit the gym. It was tough with a child. An older woman in Olivia's neighborhood came most mornings for several hours to watch Cammie so Olivia could work. Cammie still napped in the afternoons, and after that it was time to fix dinner, play games and enjoy bath time.

The routine worked well for them, and Olivia wasn't willing to leave her child with an evening babysitter to go work out. Perhaps after Cammie started kindergarten it would be easier.

Cammie did a handstand in the shallow end, making sure both women were watching. They clapped and cheered her success.

Olivia grinned, pleased that her daughter was enjoying

this visit. “Cammie found one of your old ballet costumes in the attic. I hope it was okay for her to play with it.”

“Of course.” Annalise yawned, leaning back her head and closing her eyes. “Tomorrow I’ll show her my secret trove of Barbie dolls. I had to keep them hidden or the boys would pop off their heads.”

“That’s terrible.” But Olivia chuckled in spite of herself.

Annalise lifted one eyelid, her expression morose. “Don’t get me started.”

Nine

Olivia and Kieran left for New York at first light. Though Olivia had worried about abandoning Cammie, it was clear the child was having the time of her life. Victor Wolff doted on her. Jacob promised her a tour of his clinic and a lollipop, and Gareth and Gracie had sent up a note inviting Cammie to swim again.

And then there was Annalise. She and Cammie had bonded like long lost sisters. If anything, Cammie was the more sensible of the two. Annalise had planned out a twenty-four-hour agenda of fun that would be impossible to fulfill, but she delighted in making Cammie laugh at her antics.

Kieran and Olivia said their goodbyes and departed via helicopter to a small airstrip near Charlottesville. There, the Wolff family jet sat waiting, its brilliant white fuselage gleaming in the sunlight. Though Olivia was well accustomed to luxury and pampering, the level of wealth enjoyed by Kieran and his clan far surpassed anything she had experienced.

Fortunately she had packed liberally in preparation for her trip to Wolff Mountain. Knowing nothing of Kieran's family or what to expect socially, she had gladly paid for extra bags so her wardrobe and Cammie's would cover all eventualities. Which meant that she had plenty of choices for this impromptu New York trip.

Inside the plane, a handsome male attendant offered Olivia her pick of beverages along with a midmorning snack, in case her breakfast had been inadequate. She declined the fruit parfait with murmured thanks. Her earlier meal had been more than generous. Victor Wolff's current chef had once served in the White House, and with three full-time cooks to assist him, the menu offerings were varied and delicious.

Kieran grabbed a bag of cashews and went forward to chat with the pilot. As Olivia fastened her seat belt in preparation for takeoff, she had time to appreciate her plush seat. It was more of an armchair, really. She stretched her legs and felt a little frisson of excitement wend its way through her veins.

Rarely did she take time all to herself for something as frivolous as a vacation. Tending to a rambunctious child, even when she and Cammie traveled with Lolita and Javier, generally meant little downtime.

Closing her eyes with a smile of contentment, she let her mind drift. It was a shock when she felt a warm hand settle on her shoulder. When she looked up, Kieran grinned at her, his expression more lighthearted than she had seen him at any time since their university days.

He sat down in the seat adjacent to hers and clicked his belt. "Are you a good flier, or one of the white-knuckled types?"

"I love it," she said simply. "How about you?"

"It gets me from A to B quickly, and for someone in my line of work, that's the main thing. But I also love the freedom and the sense of adventure. I've never lost that. Don't guess I ever will."

Olivia's heart sank. This Kieran, chomping at the bit to take off, was the man who circumnavigated the globe. She could see in his body language the expectation, the energy.

The day dimmed suddenly and her anticipation of the trip palled. It was painful to see the evidence of what she had only surmised. Her lover, the father of her child, was a road warrior, an adventurer. He would never be content to live inside Olivia's mythical white picket fence.

Soon, the noise of takeoff overrode the possibility of conversation. Olivia closed her eyes again and pretended to sleep. Her emotions were too close to the surface. She could fall in love with him again so easily. Not with the nostalgic reminiscence of a young woman's rosy fantasy, but in a solid, real way. How could she not? He was caring and honorable. With Cammie, he showed a gentle side that ripped at Olivia's heart.

Kieran loved his daughter, even knowing as little of her as he did. He was committed to being her dad. Only Olivia's fears and reservations stood in the way. That and her determination to protect herself from the pain of losing him again. The devastation six years ago still rippled inside her, waiting to be resurrected. Terrifying in its power.

As Kieran spoke to the attendant, Olivia studied his profile. Classic nose, sculpted chin. Straight teeth that flashed white in a tanned face when he smiled. His body was fit and healthy; his long limbs and broad shoulders were a pleasing package of masculine perfection.

Her mouth dried and her thighs tightened as she remembered last night's lovemaking. When they were together, he made her feel like the most important, most desirable woman in the world. His frank hunger and sensual demands called to the essence of her femininity.

Though she was well capable of taking care of herself, she enjoyed his protectiveness, his innate gentlemanly core of behavior. In a crisis, Kieran Wolff would be a rock.

At one time, being his wife had been her dream. Now she knew that even if he put his name on a piece of paper, the dream would end in pain and frustration. Olivia knew herself. She needed a lover who would be there on the ordinary days and not just in the midst of an emergency.

Kieran could handle the crises. No doubt about that. But Olivia was pretty sure that he would just as soon not have to deal with the mundane aspects of family life.

Taking out the trash, paying bills, mowing the grass. Ordinary husbands and fathers did those things.

Too bad Kieran Wolff was not ordinary. And too bad that *ordinary* was what Olivia had always wanted.

To Olivia's surprise, she actually slept. Kieran woke her in time to peek out the nearest window and see the Statue of Liberty as they flew past. Soon, the landing gear deployed, the pilot set them down with a tiny bump and it was time to go.

A limousine awaited them on the tarmac.

In no time at all, Kieran and Olivia were speeding toward the city amidst a maze of taxicabs. He took her hand, surprising her. As he lifted it to his lips for a kiss, he smiled lazily. "We're going to drop you downtown. Do you mind entertaining yourself for a couple of hours while I get this meeting out of the way?"

"Of course not, but I…"

"What?"

She bit her lip. "I owe you an apology. I thought this *business trip* was only an excuse to get me alone."

They were sitting so close, she could inhale the aftershave he had used that morning. In a severely tailored charcoal-gray suit with a pale blue shirt and matching tie, he looked nothing like the man she had come to know. If he had reminded her of Indiana Jones before, now he looked more like a character from Wall Street. She wasn't sure she liked the transformation.

He tugged her closer, one strong arm encircling her waist as he claimed her mouth with an aggressive kiss. When she was breathless, her heart pounding, he released her and sat back. "Sucking up to the fat cats is a necessary evil for the work I do."

"What do you mean?"

"I'm meeting this morning with the heirs of a wealthy socialite. The dead mother wanted to fund a variety of charitable works around the world. But her charming children thought the ten million she left each of them was an insult, so they went to court. Fortunately the judge couldn't be bought and he upheld the will. Unfortunately for me, the kids sit on the foundation board, so I have to deal with their greedy, petulant demands to get what I need for my next project."

"The one in September?"

He nodded. "We're going to design and build an orphanage in the Sudan. A variety of church agencies will do the staffing and oversee operations."

"Isn't it dangerous there?"

He shrugged. "Have you looked around the Big Apple? You can get killed crossing the street."

Before Olivia could respond, the car pulled up in front of a row of small, and obviously expensive, designer shops. She wrinkled her nose. "I'd really rather go to Macy's, the original on 34th Street. You know…from the movie. Is that too far out of our way?"

"No. But I thought given your Hollywood roots you'd enjoy the upscale shopping."

She shrugged. "I'm really more of a Macy's kind of gal."

"Whatever you say." The ride to midtown didn't take long. When Kieran hopped out to open Olivia's door and escort her to the sidewalk, he tucked a stray hair behind her ear, his gaze filled with something she wanted to believe was more than affection. "Here's my card with all my numbers. Have fun," he said softly, brushing a kiss across her lips.

Her arms wanted to cling, to beg him to stay. She forced herself to back up. "Go to your meeting. I'll be fine."

He winced when a cacophony of horns protested the illegally parked limo. "I'll call you when we're done."

Kieran tolerated the meeting with less than his customary patience. The "awful offspring," as he had nicknamed them in his mind, were no more difficult than usual, but today he was in no frame of mind to placate them. All he could think about was getting Olivia back to a hotel room and spending twenty-four hours in bed.

It was a great fantasy, but, of course, the gentlemanly thing to do would be to show her a good time out on the town first. Even that would be fun with Olivia.

And then there was the issue of Cammie. Once he made his case for claiming his rights as a father, would the mood be ruined? He wasn't sure where Olivia stood at the moment. Sometimes it seemed as if she was ready for him to tell Cammie the truth. But on other occasions, she bowed up, determined that Kieran was not father material.

To further strain his mood, the meeting ran long. At twelve-thirty, he finally stood and excused himself. The major business had been completed. All that was left was the minutiae that didn't require his presence.

He called downstairs, and the limo was waiting when he strode out into the sunshine. Unfortunately the lunch hour rush had traffic backed up in all directions. When they finally reached Macy's, after sending Olivia a text that they were on the way, Kieran's head was pounding from hunger and tension.

Olivia jumped in quickly, all smiles. A lot of women would be bitching about his late arrival. Instead, she seemed happy to see him. Kieran reacted to her greeting automatically, but inside, he dealt with a stunning realization. He had become addicted to her smile. In fact, he couldn't imagine going a day without seeing that look on her face.

The knowledge shook him. Since the death of his mother and his father's involuntary emotional abandonment, Kieran had never really allowed himself to *need* anyone. He prided himself on being self-sufficient, a lone Wolff.

He took Olivia's hand in his, clearing his throat to speak. "I know several great restaurants where we can have lunch. Do you have a preference?"

She patted the large shopping bag at her feet. "When your meeting ran late, I picked up several things at the gourmet shop around the corner. I thought we could have a picnic in Central Park. What do you think?"

Suddenly the irritations of the past several hours rolled away. "Sounds perfect." He gave the driver a few directions, and soon they were hopping out in front of the Metropolitan Museum of Art. As they crossed Fifth Avenue and entered the park, he took Olivia's heavy bag. "Good Lord. What all did you buy?"

She laughed, shoving her hair out of her face as the wind whipped it carelessly. Her beautiful creamy skin glowed in the sunlight, revealing not a flaw or an imperfection. He suspected that Olivia, growing up as she had in the shadow of her outrageous mother, had no clue that she was equally stunning. It would be his job and his pleasure to convince her.

With no blanket to stretch on the grass, they instead sat on a bench overlooking the lake, in a patch of shade that lent dappled shadows to their alfresco feast. Olivia wore a white sundress scattered with yellow-and-orange sunflowers. When she took off her small sweater, Kieran's food stuck in his throat.

Her body was like a centerfold's, curvaceous, even voluptuous. With her sienna hair and chocolate eyes, she reminded him of a young Sophia Loren. The dress was not particularly immodest, but the crisscrossed vee of the neckline was hard-pressed to contain her full breasts. He imagined licking his way from her collarbone down each rich slope, and his body hardened painfully, visualizing what it would be like to peel back the cloth and reveal pert nipples.

Nestled against the cleavage was a yellow diamond pendant that he remembered from their university days. Her parents had given it to her for her twenty-first birthday. Olivia had been loath to wear the expensive bauble on a daily basis, but he had lobbied for enjoying the gift and not worrying about losing it.

He tore his gaze from her charms and guzzled his Perrier, wishing fervently that they had dined in a more private locale. All around them life ebbed and flowed…the dog walkers, the teenage lovers, the nannies pushing expensive strollers. Seeing the babies made him frown.

How *would* he have reacted if Olivia had let him know she was pregnant? Back then, he'd been full of piss and vinegar, chomping at the bit to make a name for himself in the world, especially a world that had nothing to do with the Wolff empire. Parenthood wasn't even on his radar.

As soon as Victor recovered from the heart attack that had brought Kieran home from Oxford, Kieran had hit the road, determined to explore the globe despite his father's concerns about safety. Where Kieran went, no one knew or cared who he was. He waded through rice paddies, canoed down rivers of sludge in mosquito-infested jungles, hiked soaring peaks where the air was so thin a man gasped to breathe.

And every mile took him farther and farther away from the mountain that had been his prison, albeit a luxurious one. He'd kept in touch via the occasional email and phone call, learning that Gareth and Jacob were acting out their own rebellions. As far as the civilized world knew, Kieran Wolff had ceased to exist.

Gradually his nomadic existence with no purpose began to pall. His first project had come about almost by accident. He'd been in Bangladesh during a monsoon, and the resultant water damage had left a huge cleanup effort. Kieran had pitched in to rebuild bridges that connected remote villages to the help they so desperately needed.

After that, he'd found his architectural skills in demand from place to place. He used to joke that he was a cross between Johnny Appleseed and Frank Lloyd Wright. His work gave him a sense of peace and fulfillment, something he'd never been able to find at home.

But what if he had known about Cammie?

The question buzzed in his brain like an annoying gadfly.

Olivia brushed bread crumbs off her skirt and stretched out her legs, crossing them at the ankles. Her toenails were painted a deep coral that matched her dress. Kieran wanted desperately to kiss each delicately arched, perfect foot.

God knows he'd never been a fetishist, but somehow, Olivia was turning everything he thought he knew about himself on its ear. She made him ache and sweat and laugh all in the space of a single conversation. How had he ever made the decision to leave her six years ago?

The answer was easy. For once in his life, he'd done the mature thing. When Olivia talked back then, he had listened. Hearing about how much she hated the unsettled childhood she had experienced and how badly she wanted to settle down and be *normal* made him realize he had to give her up before either of them got in too deep.

The Wolffs were not a normal family.

But his altruistic decision had, in the end, caused Olivia even more pain. She believed he didn't want her. Surely she couldn't doubt that now. He needed the summer to prove to her that he had wanted her back then and he wanted her still.

Cammie's existence changed everything. Kieran and Olivia *were* involved. Only time would tell how deeply.

He sighed inwardly, wondering if such a thing as salvation existed. He was more than happy to pay atonement, but Olivia had to accept his offering. "What now?" he asked abruptly. "A Broadway matinee? A harbor tour? More shopping?"

Olivia half turned to face him, her face shadowed with worry. "We can't ignore the elephant in the room. You brought me here to hash out our situation. We might as well deal with that, and maybe then I'll be able to enjoy the rest of the day."

He shrugged, stretching his arms along the back of the bench and staring out across the water. "You know my position. I want you to stay for the entire summer, and I want to tell Cammie that I'm her dad."

Olivia nibbled her bottom lip, hands twisting in her lap. "I have work to finish, Kieran. I need to get back to my studio."

"Tell me about that," he said, wanting to know everything concerning her life, what made her tick. He'd been impressed with her talent for whimsical watercolors when they first met, and he'd recognized an ambition and drive for perfection that mirrored his own.

"I illustrate children's stories for two publishers here in New York. It's a flexible job, which means I can be there for Cammie when she needs me. One of my last books was nominated for an award."

"You've done well, then."

She nodded. "I never wanted to live off my parents. I like my independence and the security of knowing I'm providing for my daughter."

"So why can't you work on the mountain?"

"It's not as easy as that, Kieran. I have paints and papers and supplies. And besides…"

"Yes?" He had a feeling he wasn't going to like this one.

"I haven't changed my mind about what your leaving would do to Cammie. She sees you as a buddy now, but it would be so much worse if you were her father. I haven't told you this, because I didn't want to cause you pain, but she has always begged me for a daddy, ever since she was old enough to know that she was supposed to have two parents and not just me. If we told her the truth, she would jump to the conclusion that you were going to come back to California and live with us."

The image of his baby daughter begging for a daddy haunted him. Regret sat like a boulder on his chest. "So that's your final word?"

She stared at him, solemn, wary. "Are you going to take me to court?"

He stood up and turned away from her, afraid of what she might see on his face. "Oh, hell. Of course not." Impotence and rage tore at him, but what made it worse was that he had no target for his anger.

Olivia joined him, wrapping an arm around his waist and laying her head on his shoulder. "Don't be mad…please. I'm trying to do what's best. Maybe not for you or for me, but for Cammie."

He tugged her close with his left arm, still staring at boaters on the lake that sparkled like diamonds in the sun. "I'm not mad," he said gruffly.

"Let me go home tomorrow," she said. "I'll finish my project. Cammie and I have some fun summer activities planned. Then in August we'll come back for another visit before you have to leave for the Sudan."

He thought of all the long, lonely weeks that stretched between now and then. "Will you promise to think about letting me tell her who I really am?"

Her body stiffened in his embrace and finally relaxed. "I'll think about it," she said softly.

"That's all I ask." He wanted more…so much more. But for now he would bide his time.

Ten

Olivia felt terrible. Kieran was being firm, but reasonable, and she was the one refusing to compromise. But how could she? Nothing Kieran suggested had any basis in reality.

At least they had solved the question of whether or not she and Cammie would go home. Olivia badly needed physical distance to recoup her equilibrium. If she stayed with Kieran much longer, she would end up agreeing to anything solely to see his smile and to feel his body wrapped around hers.

He had shed his suit jacket in the limo earlier, and had rolled up his shirtsleeves. To the casual observer he was a big city businessman taking a lunch break in the midst of a busy day. But Olivia knew better. Like a chameleon, he had assumed the camouflage that enabled him to get what he wanted.

Kieran Wolff might appear civilized at the moment, but in reality, he was a man's man—steel-cored, physically honed, mentally sharp. Olivia had no doubt that he could accomplish anything he put his mind to…which didn't bode well for her ability to hold out against his wishes in the long run. He might very well be planning to wear down her resistance by any means necessary…including intimacy.

She had little defense against him, though she'd tried to keep her distance. Men could have sex for the sake of sex. Why couldn't women? If Olivia kept her head, she could enjoy the time with Kieran but not let her good sense be swayed by his magnetism.

Two choices, both risky. Leave and take Cammie away, provoking Kieran's anger and possible vengeance. Or stay, and keep her heart intact by regarding any sexual relationship as temporary and recreational.

She gulped inwardly. There was no doubt that she and Kieran were going to end up in bed together before the day was out. Not because he was going to lure her there, but because she wanted him desperately. One more day. Surely she could keep her messy emotions at bay for one more day. And then a brief visit in August. After that, Kieran would be safely on the other side of the world, and there would be no chance of Olivia doing something embarrassing like going down on her knees and begging him to stay and love her *and* her daughter.

He released her and gathered up their lunch debris, tossing it in a nearby receptacle. "Have you ever taken a carriage ride in the park?" he asked.

"No. But I'd rather do that at night, I think."

"Okay. Then what shall we do now? Anything you want. I'm at your disposal."

"How about we check into our hotel and not waste any more time?"

Her boldness shocked him. Heck, she shocked herself. It was almost amusing to see the slack-jawed surprise on

Kieran's face. Almost, but not quite. Limbs trembling and stomach doing flips, she awaited his answer.

Kieran stood there in the sunlight, gorgeous as a big jungle cat, and equally dangerous. "Are you serious?"

She approached him slowly, her feet having a hard time making the steps. "Completely. I want to be with you for as much time as we have. I want to sleep in your bed and wake up beside you. I want it all."

All constituted a heck of a lot in her book, surely more than he was willing or able to give. But he would think she was referring to sex, and that was okay. No reason for him to know that she was so much in love with him that the thought of returning to California was an actual pain in her chest.

He took her wrist and reeled her in, snaking an arm behind her waist and pulling her against his chest. "You're going to get me arrested," he muttered, his mouth moving over hers with sensual intent. "I'm not sure I can resist taking you here…now." He dragged her off the path near a clump of trees. Privacy was still not an option, but at least they weren't smack in the middle of the walkway.

His erection thrust between them, full, hard, seeking.

Her knees went weak, and if he hadn't been supporting her, she might have melted to the ground in a puddle of need. No one was paying any attention to them. But this game was dangerous. "Isn't the hotel close?" she panted.

"Not close enough." He bit her bottom lip and pulled it into his mouth, sucking until she shuddered. She wanted to climb inside his clothes, rip them from his body.

"Call the car," she begged.

He smelled of starched cotton and warm male skin. His hands cupped her ass. "I could tell the driver to circle the city…over and over and over. Have you ever made love in a limo, Olivia?"

Dizzy, needing oxygen, she leaned into him. "No. Have you?"

"Never had the pleasure. But damned if I couldn't be persuaded right about now."

She whimpered when he pulled away and barked an order into his cell phone. The planes of his face were taut, his eyes glittering with arousal. "C'mon. He's picking us up in five minutes."

Hand in hand, they walked rapidly. His breathing was audible and as choppy as her own.

Unfortunately the car ride from the edge of the park to the Carlyle was long enough for only one heated kiss. Suddenly a uniformed gentleman was opening Olivia's door and they were engulfed in the bustle of check-in. Twenty minutes later, in a luxurious suite that was blessedly quiet and totally private, Kieran faced her, arms folded across his chest. "Take off your dress."

The blunt command, combined with the intensity of his regard made her thighs quiver and her sex dampen. Never contemplating refusal, she shed the tiny shrug sweater and reached behind her for the zipper. When she stepped out of the dress and tossed it on a chair, she saw his eyes widen and his Adam's apple bob up and down.

The dress didn't require a bra, so she stood facing him in nothing but a lacy red thong and high heels. Her generous breasts were firm and high. The urge to cover them with her hands was there, but she resisted, wanting to please him.

His whispered curse was barely audible. She saw his fists clench at his hips. "Walk toward me."

The distance between her and the door where he stood was considerable, more so because she was naked and he was eyeing her like a condemned man who hadn't seen a woman in months.

When she was halfway across the room, he held out a hand. "Stop. Turn around. Take down your hair."

She had tucked it up in a loose chignon during lunch when the heat of the day made the weight of her long hair uncomfortable. Now she reached for the pins and removed them, dropping them into a cut glass dish on the coffee table. Deliberately she ran a hand through the masses of heavy, silky strands and shook her head.

When she was done, she looked at him over her shoulder through lowered lashes. "Does this meet with your approval, Mr. Wolff?"

His jaw firmed. "Are you sassing me, Olivia?"

"Would I do that?" Her eyes widened dramatically.

"Face me. Touch your breasts."

They were playing a game of chicken, and Kieran had just upped the stakes. Olivia felt her throat and cheeks flush, but she reversed her position and hesitantly placed her hands on her chest. Her voice was gone, locked down by the giant lump in her throat.

"I said *touch* them. Put your fingers on your nipples."

Good Lord. She licked her lips, dizzy and desperate for his touch. Feeling awkward but aroused, she did as he demanded, feeling her sensitive flesh bud and tighten as she stroked herself. The sensation was incredible, pleasuring herself as Kieran watched with a hooded gaze.

"Beautiful." He breathed the word like a prayer, the three syllables almost inaudible.

When her skin became too sensitive to continue, her hands dropped to her sides.

Kieran didn't move. How did he do it? She was so hungry for him, her whole body trembled.

But he wasn't finished. His gaze blazing with his heat, he narrowed his eyes. "Go to the bedroom. Don't look back. Lie down on the bed on your stomach."

She flinched in momentary fear. But it was a gut reaction. Kieran would never hurt her or make her uncomfortable. This was all about pleasure. His and hers.

Turning away from him was difficult. She knew he watched her, hawklike, as she walked slowly toward the doorway that led into the rest of the suite. Once, she stumbled, but she finally made it into the bedroom. For a moment, she stood in indecision. Was she supposed to turn back the covers?

The bedding was expensive and ornate. Making a rapid decision, she folded back the top layers and lay, facedown, on the smooth crisp sheet. Her heartbeat sounded loud and irregular in her ears. Her arms were by her sides. Ten seconds passed. She raised her arms over her head.

What did he want? What were his plans?

Moments later she heard the sound of his footsteps on the carpet. Nearby a rustle and then the rasp of a zipper. A soft clink when the belt buckle slid free. The sounds of a man undressing.

An activity that was at once commonplace and yet deeply erotic, particularly when the woman in his bed was not allowed to witness the disrobing. She imagined his long, muscular limbs, narrow hips, jutting arousal.

The bed shuddered when he put a knee beside her hip and joined her on the mattress. Without warning, he took her two wrists and bound them together with what felt like his necktie. She struggled instinctively. He paid her no mind.

The silk fabric tightened, and then she felt him lean down as he whispered in her ear. "You're at my mercy now. Everything I ask of you, you'll do, and in exchange, I'll make you burn."

"Kieran..." The word ended on a cry as he ran his tongue around the shell of her ear and winnowed his fingers through her hair. With a slow, steady touch, he massaged her scalp. His fingertips skated to her nape, the back of her ear. Her whole body craved his attention, but he was set on a course that was drugging, slow and steady.

Gradually, almost imperceptibly, he moved south, digging his thumbs into the tense muscles of her neck and shoulders. Her spine caught his focus. He ran his tongue the length of it and then rubbed gently on either side.

At her ass, he made a sound, a cross between a groan and a curse. Quivering, helpless, she felt him plump the cheeks, trace the cleft, reach beneath her and brush the part of her that ached the most.

When she spread her legs, begging wordlessly, he chuckled and abandoned the ground he had barely conquered. "Patience, Olivia."

She felt his hands beneath her hips, lifting her, turning her. Now she could see him, and the sight took her breath and shredded it. His broad chest was tanned and rippled with muscle. An arrow of fine, dark hair traced the midline, all the way down to where his shaft reared proudly against his abdomen.

His erection was thick and long, and a drop of moisture glistened on the tip. "Please," she begged without pride. "Please don't make us wait."

"Waiting is half the fun. I want you crazed when I finally take you, so lost to reason that nothing exists but you and me and this bed."

It was as if he were a hypnotist. Her body responded to his words atavistically, ceding control without a qualm. But by the look on his face, *his* control was more fragile than he was willing to admit. His jaw was tight. The dark flush of color staining his cheeks made him look wild and uncivilized…a man close to the edge.

He bent over her, no part of his body touching hers except

his lips. "I love your mouth," he said, tracing the soft flesh with his tongue and sliding through to taste her.

She tried to link her bound wrists over his head to trap him close, but he moved away, using one big hand to pin hers to the mattress. "Naughty, naughty," he teased.

Suddenly very serious, he kept his gaze locked on hers as he slid his free hand down her stomach and between her thighs. Two large fingers entered her, testing her readiness. Her hips came off the bed, her heartbeat racing as sweat beaded her forehead.

He never looked away and neither could she. All the secrets of a man's desires were there in his eyes if she could only translate them. Was this all he wanted from her? Dare she hope he needed more?

Stroking lazily, he turned interrogator. "Tell me about the men in your life, Olivia. Who has benefitted from what I taught you back in England?"

His finger brushed her clitoris and she gasped. "None of your damned business, Wolff man. I haven't quizzed you about your women in every port."

Back and forth. Back and forth. That brazen fingertip brought her closer and closer to the edge. "There haven't been that many," he said slowly, looking at his hand's mischief and not her face. "I work long hours when I'm overseas. Not much time for play."

"But a man like you can't go without sex for long. Back in university you wanted it twice a day, three times if we were lucky."

"That's because I was obsessed with you."

The blunt confession gave wings to her heart. But she reined in her excitement. The pertinent word in that sentence was in the past tense. *Was.* Kieran had been a horny young adult male. And Olivia had fallen into his bed like the proverbial ripe peach.

As a fully mature man, he was no less sexually primed, but he'd had any number of women since he left England so suddenly. And even now, being with Olivia was probably more about expedience and availability than any deep-seated obsession.

Kieran's early experiences in life had clearly stunted his ability to express deep emotion. He was a passionate man, but she doubted whether he was capable of true romantic love. That would mean putting a female first in his life, and she had seen no sign of such willingness in his behavior.

He clearly *wanted* her, but for Olivia, that would never be enough.

His hand moved, and she gave up analyzing the situation. Today was about physical pleasure. Her heart was safely locked away.

Kieran released her wrists. Sliding far down in the bed, he used his hands to widen the vee of her legs. When she felt his hot breath on her thighs, she tensed in panic. They had never explored this kind of intimacy when she was younger. "No, wait..." she blurted out. "I don't like this."

"How do you know?" he asked, a lazy smile tilting the corners of his mouth.

"Seriously, Kieran." She pushed at his shoulder. "I mean it. Stop."

He reared up, all humor erased from his face. "I'll stop. If you insist. But it would give me great pleasure to do this with you."

She nibbled her lower lip, caught between unease and cautious interest. "What if I can't come, because I'm too self-conscious?" Blurting out what she was thinking wasn't something she planned, but he might as well know the truth.

"Relax, Olivia. It's not an exam you have to study for. I want to make you happy. That's all. You don't have to do a thing."

Her hand fell to the sheet. "Well, I…"

Anticipating her consent, he resumed his earlier position. She felt the softness of his hair on her leg, jerked briefly as his hot breath feathered over her belly. "You're beautiful," he murmured.

She closed her eyes, arching her back at the first gentle pass of his tongue. When she moaned, helpless in the grip of shivering sensation that spread in warm ripples throughout her lower body, he repeated the motion. The sensation was indescribable. Like a warm, electric shock that built and built until she called out his name in a frenzy of need. "Kieran. Oh, God. Kieran."

His muffled response was neither decipherable nor important. She was lost, caught up in a whirlwind that slammed into her, dragged her over the edge of a perfect climax and dropped her helpless into his embrace.

When she recovered, he had moved up beside her and was leaning on an elbow watching her with a totally masculine satisfaction. "Still don't like it?" he asked drolly. One eyebrow lifted in a questioning stance.

She tried to corral her ragged breathing. "Don't brag."

He placed his hand, palm opened flat, on her belly. "Watching you come like that ranks as the highlight of my year."

"The year's only halfway done," she quipped, trying not to let him see how completely undone she was. "Too early to tell." She put her hand on top of his and laced their fingers together.

"Don't be so modest. I'm sure they heard you in Brooklyn."

"Kieran!" Mortification washed over her and she rolled to her side, bending her knee and resting her leg across his hairy thighs. They were hard and corded with muscle. His deep tan extended everywhere except for a narrow band of white at his hips and the tops of his thighs.

She imagined him, laboring out beneath a blazing tropical sun, shirtless, wearing only cargo shorts and boots. Did he ever get lonely always living among strangers? The question hovered on her lips, but she knew it was self-serving. Obviously his lifestyle suited him. Otherwise, he would have come home long ago.

He lifted her without warning and settled her astride his hips. His hunger unappeased, he flexed and grew at least another centimeter beneath her fascinated gaze. She put both hands on him, measuring the length and breadth.

Hard steel pulsed beneath his velvet skin. Even if she had been with a dozen lovers in the interim, she couldn't imagine that any of them would have been as beautiful in body and spirit as Kieran Wolff. Perhaps such a virile man might balk at the feminine adjective, but Olivia chose not to retract it, even in her own private discourse.

Kieran's body was perfect. Even the smattering of scars that were part and parcel of the hard physical labor he performed only served to make his physique more interesting.

She saw him reach for a condom, and her heartbeat accelerated.

Extending his hand, he challenged her. "Will you do the honors?"

Eleven

Kieran waited, amused and impatient, as Olivia fumbled with the condom. The earnest intent on her face filled him with tenderness and another feeling not so easy to diagnose. He brushed aside the unfamiliar emotion and concentrated on the physical.

While she labored, he played with her breasts displayed so temptingly in front of his face. He tweaked a nipple, noticing with interest that his gentle pinch washed her face with color. A similar firm caress on the other breast deepened the crimson.

Olivia finished her task, her face damp with perspiration. "There. All set."

He tested the fit and nodded. "Good thing I brought a dozen."

"A dozen?"

The strangled squeak in her voice made him chuckle despite the fact that the skin on his penis was tight enough to cause every vein to bulge. He'd been in this state, in varying degrees, for over an hour now. In fact, he might set some kind of damned record for extended foreplay.

Not that he hadn't enjoyed himself immensely. God, she was sweet. And hot as a firecracker. Though she probably didn't see it in herself, she was one of the most innately sensual women he had ever met.

With his hand, he positioned himself. "You ready, honey?"

Her eyelids were at half-mast, her lips swollen from his kisses. The skin at her throat bore the marks of his passion, and her nipples puckered as if begging for his kisses. He leaned up and obliged, just as he thrust as hard as he could manage into her welcoming heat.

Their foreheads actually bumped together.

"Hell," he said ruefully, the pain giving him a moment's respite from total insanity. "Rub my head." His hands were clenched on her curvy ass, and he had no plans to let go.

She kissed his forehead. "Poor baby."

Her innocent motion seated him more deeply. "Hold still," he said through clenched teeth. "Damn it, I'm about to come."

"Isn't that the object of this exercise?"

He groaned, caught between incredulous laughter and the imminent explosion in his loins. Had any woman ever made him experience both in such measure? His heart caught, and he buried his face in her neck, panting, trying to stay the course. "You're killing me."

Reaching behind her, she found his sac and delicately played with him. It was like being hit by a lightning bolt. He lost control of himself, of her, of the entire flippin' situation.

Pumping his hips wildly, he thrust upward again and again, deaf, blind, mute…except for the caveman grunts that were all he could manage. Olivia clung to his shoulders as he fell to his back. Her breasts glided across his face, sweet-smelling, soft and warm.

God, he never wanted to stop. He wanted to mark her as his, to stake a claim. She found his lips and kissed him. That was all it took. He shot so hard that his balls pulled up, a vise tightened around his forehead and he saw nothing but blackness and yellow sparks for long, agonizing seconds.

At last, he lay spent, Olivia draped over him like a weary nymph.

"Good God in heaven."

She nodded, her breasts smashed against his heaving chest, her cheek resting atop his thundering heart. "I hope you're in good shape. I'd hate to have to call the concierge for the number of the closest cardiac center."

He stroked her ass, deciding he might never move. "You're something else, Olivia Delgado."

One eyelid lifted and then fluttered shut. "Mmm…"

"Don't go to sleep on me."

"Is that literally or metaphorically?"

Given her current posture, it was a fair question. "Either, I suppose." He yawned and stretched. "Any idea what time it is?"

"Do we care?"

"I may not have been entirely truthful." When she stiffened in his arms, he could have kicked himself for his unfortunate phraseology. "I promised we could do this for twenty-four hours, but I think I'm going to need sustenance."

"Room service?"

He patted her butt. "I was thinking of something a bit more upscale. After all, we *are* in the greatest city in the world. We should go somewhere incredibly expensive and over-the-top."

"And you know such a spot?" She slid off him, sat up and clutched the sheet to her chest.

Her sudden modesty was baffling. But then again, he never claimed to understand women. "I've heard Jacob talk about a place he likes."

"Jacob, the strong silent doctor? Somehow I thought he was above us mere mortals who need to eat."

"Jacob has his weaknesses. New York style cheesecake, for one. He's usually here in the city for medical conferences every year or so. In fact, he did a consult at Lenox Hill Hospital last Christmas."

"He's scary smart, isn't he?"

Kieran grinned. "Oh, yeah. Perfect score on the SATs. Four years of college in two and a half." He paused, and cocked his head. "Do we have to talk about my brother any longer, or can I interest you in a shower?"

"I'll race you."

He was treated to a delicious view of Olivia's backside as she dropped her only covering and darted into the bathroom. When he followed her, she was already hidden from view, water running. "Room for two?" he asked, stepping in without an invitation.

When Olivia sputtered with maidenly affront, he grinned. "I'll take that as a yes."

Olivia discovered that even a man who slept in grass huts and swallowed the occasional disgusting, edible bug could drum up romance if he put his mind to it, starting with a tuxedo that appeared as if by magic, delivered by a uniformed bellman.

When Kieran strode out of the bedroom clad in crisp black and white, fumbling with a bow tie, her breathing hitched. He was gorgeous. No other word to describe him.

"Help me with this damned thing," he said. "They're a necessary evil, but I'm out of practice."

She stood behind him and wrapped her arms around his neck, deftly folding the fabric into the desired configuration. "Out of practice?" She nipped his earlobe with her teeth. "I don't think so."

He turned and scooped her off her feet, twirling her in a circle before setting her back down. "I love reviews from satisfied customers."

"Customer? Good grief. Am I going to get a bill for services rendered?"

"I haven't decided yet. This afternoon was only my warm-up. I'll have to let you know."

He slid his hands beneath her hair and steadied her head while he dove deep for a hungry, forceful kiss.

On tiptoe, Olivia clung to his forearms and tried not to get the vapors. Kieran Wolff was like hundred-proof whiskey: guaranteed to go straight to a woman's head.

The night was clear and relatively cool so they decided to walk. The restaurant Kieran had chosen was only a couple of blocks away on a side street around the corner from East 76th.

He didn't hold her hand. But he did wrap an arm around her shoulders and tuck her close to his side. She felt warm and cherished, and for the span of an evening's stroll, she allowed herself to knit cobwebby dreams about happily ever afters.

When they arrived, Olivia paused on the sidewalk. "Do you mind if I call Cammie? She'll be in bed by the time we finish dinner."

"Of course not."

Olivia took her cell phone from her purse and punched in the contact info she'd saved for the Wolff house. An employee answered, and seconds later, Cammie's excited voice came on the line.

"Hi, Mommy. Me and Annalise are dressing up for dinner."

"Oh?" She grinned at her daughter's enthusiasm.

"We're going to be..." A muffled conversation ensued to the side and then Cammie said loudly, "...flappers."

"That sounds fun. Will you ask Annalise to take a picture for me?"

"Yes, ma'am. May I speak to Kieran now?"

Olivia hesitated, taken aback. Usually Cammie chattered away forever on such a phone call. "Sure," she said, handing her cell toward Kieran. "She wants to talk to you."

He blinked, and then smiled, barely masking his pleased surprise. But he hit the button for speakerphone, a thoughtful gesture that made Olivia ashamed of her odd jealousy. "Hey there, ladybug. What's happenin'?"

"I got to play with your wooden submarine today," Cammie said. "It's way cool, and Annalise tried to torpedo me a bunch of times, but I got out of the way."

Kieran laughed out loud. "Tomorrow morning, ask her to show you the secret tunnel. It's a little spooky, but a brave girl like you will like it."

Suddenly the line went silent, but in the background they could hear Cammie's excited squeal.

Annalise picked up the call. "How are you lovebirds getting along in New York?"

Kieran's lips quirked. He gave Olivia a rueful smile. "Behave, brat," he told his cousin firmly. "We're fine. Should be home by lunch tomorrow. I'll bring you a dozen bagels if you're nice to me."

"Oooh...bagels. Big spender."

Olivia giggled. "I can do better than that, Annalise.

Thanks again for keeping Cammie. Give her a kiss and hug for me."

They all said their goodbyes, and Kieran took Olivia's arm. "Ready to eat?"

She nodded, relieved to know that Cammie was happy and content. "I'm starving."

Patrice's was delightful, with snowy linen tablecloths, fresh bouquets of Dutch iris and freesias, and a modest string ensemble tucked away in a far corner. Even the lighting was perfect.

Olivia sank onto a velvet-covered banquette and leaned back with a sigh of appreciation. "Order for me," she said. "I'm in the mood to be surprised."

Kieran wondered how surprised Olivia would be if he were honest about his intentions. After dinner, he planned to hustle her back to the room and hold her captive there until they were forced to check out the following morning. He'd let her sleep…occasionally. But the sand in his hourglass was running out rapidly, so he didn't plan to waste a minute.

As they'd entered the restaurant earlier, practically every head had turned, the women's faces reflecting envy, and the men's expressions frankly lustful. Olivia was oblivious. How could she not recognize the impact she made? He'd never met a woman more genuinely modest and unselfconscious, especially not one with Olivia's stunning beauty.

The dress she wore tonight was deceptively simple…a slender column of deep burgundy with a halter neck and a back that plunged to the base of her spine. Her hair was pinned on top of her head in one of those messy knots women managed to create. The only accessory she had chosen to wear was a pair of dangling earrings comprised of tiny ruby and jet beads.

He knew her body intimately, and he was pretty certain she was wearing nothing beneath the sinuous fabric that clung to her body like a second skin.

A waiter interrupted Kieran's musings. By the time their order was placed, the sommelier appeared to offer a wine selection. Kieran perused the extensive list. "We'll have champagne," he said. "To celebrate." He indicated a choice near the top of the price list.

Olivia propped her chin on one hand and gazed at him curiously. "What are we celebrating?"

"How amazing you look in that dress."

His sincere compliment flustered her. She straightened and fidgeted, looking at their fellow diners. "Thank you."

"I mean it," he said. "You outshine your mother any day."

"Oh, please," she huffed. "I could stand to lose a few pounds, my mouth is too wide and my chest is too big."

He burst out laughing.

"What?" she cried.

"You really have no clue, do you?"

"I'm not sure what you mean." She played with her silverware, refusing to meet his gaze.

"First of all, my naive chick, as far as a man is concerned, there's no such thing as a chest that's too big. God in his infinite wisdom created breasts in all shapes and sizes, and yours are a work of art."

Her head snapped up at that, a small frown between her brows. But she didn't speak.

"Second of all," he continued, "just because your mother is petite and thin doesn't make her more beautiful than you. The camera may love the way she looks, but you are fabulous just the way you are. You're incredibly feminine and knock-'em-dead gorgeous. Every man in this room wishes he were sitting in my chair."

Her cheeks went pink. "You're a tall-tale raconteur, but thank you. That's very sweet."

He threw up his hands. "I give up. But know this, Olivia Delgado. I wouldn't change a thing about you." As the words left his mouth, he understood just how true they were. She was his ideal woman. And if he were in the market for a wife, he'd have to look no farther.

But he wasn't…in the market, that is. He was a man destined to travel alone. Despite that reality, he hoped to forge a bond with Cammie this summer that could withstand the long separations. He might not be the best dad in the world, but he would ensure that his daughter knew her father loved her.

Over a meal of stuffed quail and apple-chestnut dressing, they conversed lazily. Though he drank guardedly, the wine went to his head, and all he could think about was getting Olivia naked again. She, on the other hand, seemed content to enjoy the formal, drawn-out dinner.

Finally the final bite of dessert was consumed, the last cup of coffee sipped. Kieran summoned the waiter, asked for their check and waited, fingers drumming on the tablecloth, for Olivia to return from a trip to the ladies' room.

As he watched her make her way between the carefully orchestrated maze of tables, someone reached out a hand to stop her. Olivia's face lit up, and the next thing Kieran knew, his lover was being kissed enthusiastically on the mouth by a tall, handsome man in a dark suit.

Feeling his temper rise, Kieran got to his feet. Olivia didn't even look his way. Now she was hugging the mystery guy and patting his cheek. The waiter had the temerity to block Kieran's field of view for a few seconds as he provided the bill. Kieran scribbled his name with leashed impatience on the credit card slip and started toward the couple on the far side of the room.

"Olivia?"

She stayed where she was, only now the fellow had his arm around her waist. By the look of things, Olivia's admirer was dining alone. And in the meantime, trolling for other men's girlfriends?

Kieran tamped down his annoyance. "Am I missing the party?" he asked, not managing entirely to squelch his pique.

She reached for his hand. "Come meet someone, Kieran. This is my dear friend, Jeremy Vargas. We've known each other forever. We used to be in school together on the MGM lot. He's here in New York rehearsing for a stint in a Broadway play…during a brief lull between shooting a string of great movies. Jeremy, this is Kieran Wolff, my…" She stumbled, licked her lips and trailed off.

"Olivia and I are seeing each other." Kieran shook the man's hand, taking in the firm grip and easy smile that said Jeremy Vargas was confident and in no way threatened by Kieran's glower. "Nice to meet you," Kieran said, lying through his teeth.

Vargas might be a stage name, because Jeremy didn't appear to have a drop of Latino blood. He was the quintessential Hollywood golden boy, blond hair, blue eyes and a killer smile.

Olivia recovered and beamed her approval back and forth between the two of them.

Jeremy continued to embrace Olivia. "It's a pleasure, Kieran. You've snagged a great girl."

"A great *woman.*" Was he the only one who noticed the note of over-familiarity in Jeremy's voice? And did Jeremy know about Cammie?

Olivia finally freed herself from the other man's proprietary hold and stood beside Kieran. "I wish we'd known you were here. We could have shared a meal."

Like hell. Kieran suddenly remembered where he had heard Vargas's name. He was mentioned in the article about Cammie's birthday party…as Olivia's date.

Intellectually Kieran knew that Olivia hadn't been a nun for the past five years. She was a passionate, gloriously beautiful woman. But seeing with his own eyes that other men weren't blind to her beauty put a sour taste in Kieran's mouth.

One day soon, when Olivia was ready to expand her white picket fence, perhaps with a second baby on the way, she wouldn't have any trouble finding men to line up for the role of husband and father.

Kieran brooded on the way back to the hotel. Damn Jeremy and his inopportune arrival. "Have you and Vargas dated?" he asked abruptly, tormented by the fact that she had an entire life apart from him.

"He's like a brother." The blunt response shut him up. After that, Olivia was mostly silent. Kieran wasn't sure if she was sleepy from too much champagne or if she was remembering all the reasons she wanted to keep him at arm's length.

In their hotel room, he paced, stripping off his jacket and tie, and swallowing a glass of ice water, hoping it would cool him down. Olivia removed her earrings. When that innocent tableau turned his sex to stone, he knew he was in trouble.

He cleared his throat. "Are you ready for bed?"

Twelve

Olivia dropped the earrings on the table. "For bed or for sex?" She met his gaze squarely, no pretense, no games. Her big brown eyes were rich and dark, masking her secrets.

"I want to make love to you." The words ripped his throat raw. He'd never said them to any woman.

Her face softened as if she read his inner turmoil. "I don't expect you to change for me, Kieran. You are who you are. I am who I am. We're two people who met at the wrong time and the wrong place. But we created a child and we have to put her first."

When he stood rigid, torn between honesty and seduction, she came to him and held out her hand. "Let's have tonight. Tomorrow will take care of itself."

He allowed himself to be persuaded. There was no choice, really. If he didn't have Olivia one more time, he would die, incinerated by the fire of his own reckless passion.

This time, he vowed to give her tenderness. He'd been

rough with her earlier, rough and earthy and carnal. What she deserved was a man who would worship at her feet.

He dropped to his knees, heart in his throat. Encircling her hips with his arms, he laid his head against her belly. She had carried his child, her lovely body rounded and large with the fruit of their desire. God, how he wished he had been with her, had been able to see her flesh expand and grow in lush, fertile beauty.

Her swollen breasts had nursed their baby. If life had played out differently, Kieran would have been there to watch. To be a part of something wonderful and new.

Regret was a futile emotion, one he'd learned a long time ago to push down into a dark, unacknowledged corner of his gut. The only important thing was the here and now. He lived for the moment…*in* the moment.

Olivia trembled in his embrace.

She stroked his hair. The light caress covered his skin in gooseflesh. What he felt for her hurt, reminding him of a dimly remembered anguish from his childhood. Women were soft and warm and wonderful. But loving them meant vulnerability. A man could not afford to let down his guard.

Without speaking, he snuggled her navel with his tongue, wetting the fabric of her dress. Carefully he bunched the cloth in his hands and lifted the long, slim skirt until he could see what had tantalized him all evening. A wispy pair of black lace panties, a thong, which explained why he'd thought she might be naked.

Despite his vow of gentleness, he gripped the thin bands at either side of her ass and ripped the fragile undergarment. It fell away, exposing her intimate feminine flesh.

Her smooth, honey-skinned thighs were scented with the distinctive perfume he'd come to recognize as her favorite.

Olivia tugged at his hair. "You're embarrassing me," she whispered. "Quit staring."

He stood abruptly and scooped her into his arms. "Whatever the lady wants." As he strode with her into the bedroom, Olivia nestled her head against his shoulder. The trust implicit in her posture dinged his conscience. He had failed her once before. This time he had to do what was right. He wanted the world to know he was Cammie's father, but if Olivia truly believed that was a mistake, Kieran might be forced to humble his pride and step back.

Retreat had never been his style. But for Olivia, he would try.

Beside the bed he stood her on her feet and, without ceremony, removed her dress. She stepped out of her shoes and put her cheek to his chest, hands on his shoulders. "Thank you for bringing me to New York," she whispered. "I think we needed this…for closure. I didn't want bad feelings between us."

He ignored her comments that intimated a swift and unwelcome end to their physical relationship. "Let me love you," he said hoarsely, the "L" word rolling more easily from his lips this time. "Lie down, Olivia."

Stripping off his clothes, he joined her on the bed. When she held up her arms, he couldn't decide if the smile on her face was a lover's welcome or the erotic coaxing of a siren, luring a man to doom.

Foreplay wasn't even an option. That had gone up in smoke during a four-course dinner with Olivia sitting across from him wearing a dress designed to turn a man's brain to mush. He found a condom, rolled it on and moved between her legs.

Their eyes met. As he entered her slowly, her lashes widened. Her breath caught. Her throat and upper chest flushed with color. He put his forehead to hers, filled with a maelstrom of inexplicable urges.

Half a millennium ago, he would have slain dragons for

her, might even have used his travels to bring home chests of gold and jewels. But Olivia didn't want the knight on the white charger. She was looking for a more stable fellow, perhaps the village miller or the town carpenter.

If Kieran truly wanted to make her happy, he would head out on his next crusade and leave her to build a life between the castle walls. Without him.

The room was silent save for their mingled breathing. He moved in her so slowly that her body seemed to clasp him and squeeze on every stroke. It was heaven and hell. Giving a man what he hadn't known he needed and in the next breath reminding him that the gift had an expiration date.

He braced most of his weight on his arms, but his hips pressed against hers, pinning her to the mattress. Her hair, fanned across the pillows, made an erotic picture that seared into his brain, never to be forgotten.

As he picked up the tempo, her legs came around his waist. Lifting up into his strokes, she arched her back and took what she wanted. Sensual and sweet, she looked like the girl he had first met on a rainy Saturday in the English countryside. She'd been alone, away from the hustle and bustle of an overcrowded house party, standing in the lane beneath a giant black umbrella, fumbling with a map and muttering mild imprecations beneath her breath.

Why hadn't he recognized what had landed in the palm of his hand for one brief spring? The vibrant, fragile butterfly that had been his relationship with Olivia….

How had he been so foolish as to crush those wings by his abrupt departure?

She touched his forehead, rubbing at the unconscious frown that had gathered between his brows. "You'll always be my first love," she said, gasping as he thrust deep. "No matter what happens next."

First love. Was that his only role? That and sperm provider?

Gentleness fled, chased away by frustration and self-directed anger. Damn the past. What about the future?

His body betrayed him then, slamming into hers with a violence that shook the bed. Olivia cried out as she climaxed, her eyes closed, her hands fisted in the sheets.

He felt his own orgasm breathing hot flames down his neck and tried to battle it back. But it was too late. Molten lava turned him inside out, gave birth to a shout of exultation laced with surrender, and trailed away, leaving a dark, inexplicable confusion.

Easing onto his back, he tried to corral his breathing. Olivia lay unmoving beside him, her chest rising and falling rapidly.

"We should get married," he said, the words coming from out of nowhere and surprising him as much as they apparently did Olivia.

Her body jerked, and she stiffened. "What? Why?"

Because I love you madly and can't imagine living my life without you. Any version of that response would have been acceptable to Olivia. But Kieran hadn't read the same script.

He ran a hand over his face and sighed. "It would be good for Cammie, I think. Assuming you're eventually going to tell her that I'm her father. If you and I were married, all the times I'm gone, she would have the security of knowing that we're a family."

"That won't make her miss you less."

"Maybe not. But she would know that I'm coming home to her eventually."

Eventually. Olivia hated that word. And she hated the fact that her stupid heart threw her under the bus again and again. Kieran wasn't in love with her. He felt *something* for her…affection, maybe…and a sense of duty. But that was never going to be enough. Not when Olivia wanted to give him every bit of her passion and devotion.

Kieran didn't need her. They weren't a couple.

"I don't like the idea," she said flatly. "I deserve to have a man in my life who loves me and can't live without me. What you're describing would be dishonest. Children are more intuitive than you realize. She would know the truth. I promised to think about you and Cammie. Give me time. Let me go home. In August I'll give you your answer."

He didn't respond, and to her chagrin, she realized that he had fallen asleep. Disheartened, she turned her back to him, and did the same.

When she woke up, Kieran wasn't in the bed beside her. A whiff of aftershave lingered in the air, so she surmised that he had risen early to shower. Perhaps after their awkward conversation the night before, he'd had no inclination to initiate any early-morning fooling around.

She leaned up on an elbow to look at the clock. Still plenty of time before their scheduled flight. The jet would be on standby, ready to go at their convenience. But Kieran had promised Annalise that he and Olivia would be back by lunchtime, so Olivia needed to get dressed.

When she appeared in the sitting room thirty minutes later, Kieran stood in front of the window, hands behind his back, looking down at the quiet street below.

He turned to face her, his expression grave. "Where's your cell phone?" he asked.

She grimaced. "I forgot to charge it last night. The battery's probably dead."

"Sit down, Olivia." He came to join her on the sofa, taking her hands in his and studying her face, his eyes filled with compassion. "Your parents have been trying to reach you. They finally called the house to relay a message, and Father contacted me."

Her heart thudded with fear. "What's wrong?"

"I need you to be brave," he said. "We'll get through this."

"Oh, my God…was there an accident?" Her blood turned to ice in her veins.

"Not that. They're fine."

"Then what?"

She actually saw on his face the struggle to choose a correct phrase. And Kieran's loss of words scared her more than anything had in a long, long time. "Just tell me," she croaked. "I can take it."

His thumbs rubbed absently over the backs of her hands, the repetitive motion not at all soothing given that his expression was torn and troubled. "Your mother's psycho stalker fire-bombed your house last night. It burned to the ground. Everything is gone."

She saw his lips moving, but the roaring in her ears drowned it out. Her eyes closed as hysteria welled in her chest. "No. You're wrong," she said, batting his hands away when he tried to hold her. "That's not possible. Cammie's baby album is there…and my paintings. All her toys…" Agony clogged her throat, exacerbated by the way Kieran looked at her. It couldn't be true.

"Take me there," she said. "Take me now. I want to see it." She was shaking all over, and the last words came out on a cry of pain.

Kieran took her shoulders and dragged her close, ignoring her wildly flailing fists, stroking her hair. "Hush, baby," he said. "I'm right here. It's going to be okay."

She cried in broken, gasping, wretched sobs that hurt her chest. A great, yawning chasm opened up at her feet, and she was terrified that she was going to fall into the depths and never claw her way back to the top. Again and again she repeated his words in her head. *Everything is gone.*

It seemed impossible and at the same time terrifyingly real.

She clung to Kieran, unashamed. Nothing else made sense. Time lost all meaning.

When the tears ran out, she lay limp in his embrace, her breathing ragged. "Did they catch him?" For some reason, that was the first question that popped into her brain.

"Not yet. But they will. He knew you weren't at home. The police profiler doesn't think he really wants to hurt anyone. This was a bid for attention."

"What about my parents?"

"They're surrounded by a twenty-four-hour security detail. The authorities think you and Cammie need to stay where you are until the man is in custody."

The irony didn't escape her. Kieran was getting exactly what he wanted. More time with his daughter.

She jerked out of his arms, wiping her cheeks with the heels of her hands. "I have to see my house. If you won't take me, I'll go on my own."

"Of course I'll take you," he said, frustration replacing his solicitous tone. "But I think it's a bad idea. There's nothing there. You don't want to see it, believe me."

"I don't *want* to," she said bleakly. "I have to."

Kieran didn't know it was possible to hurt so badly for another human being. Standing beside Olivia a few hours later, giving her all the support he was able to in light of her mercurial mood, he watched as she surveyed what was left of her property. They'd made the trip via jet in record time, though sadly, there was no reason to hurry.

Yellow police tape cordoned off the area. Curious neighbors gawked, but kept a respectful distance. Olivia had already been questioned by police personnel as well as the chief fire marshal.

The house had literally burned to the ground, leaving nothing but a smoldering mass of debris. On a bright, sunny California afternoon, the evidence marking a violent act seemed even worse.

Olivia wrapped her arms around her waist, face paper-white, eyes haunted. "At least we weren't at home," she said.

"They think the man was watching the house…that he knew when you packed up and left."

Her bottom lip trembled. "Cammie was supposed to grow up here. I always felt so safe," she whispered. "Our little haven away from the world. But there's no hiding, is there?" She gasped on a hiccupping sob.

Kieran didn't bother to answer the rhetorical question. The difficult truth was one he'd learned at the tender age of four, a painful, vivid lesson that had marked the course of his subsequent life.

Rage filled him at the senseless destruction. Rage and an impotent guilt. A man was supposed to protect his family. Now, more than ever, he understood his father's actions. Though occasionally misguided, Victor Wolff and his brother, Vincent, had taken the necessary steps to protect what was theirs, to make sure their children were safe.

Losing their wives, having them murdered in cold blood, had been the catalyst for founding a sanctuary at Wolff Mountain. And now, thank God, Kieran would be able to keep Olivia and Cammie there, cocooned from further danger, until the dangerous fire-bomber was apprehended.

The thought that the man might track Olivia and Cammie to the mountain made Kieran's blood run cold.

Unexpectedly a uniformed investigator approached them, gingerly holding a small item that was apparently hot to the touch. He tipped his hat briefly in a polite salute and extended his hand toward Olivia. "I found this…thought you might want it. Be careful. It's still warm."

He ducked back under the tape and quickly returned to his job, perhaps not comfortable with tears. Kieran didn't think Olivia even realized she was crying. But slow, wet trickles made tracks down her cheeks.

She looked down at the silver object in her hand, and the shaking she'd finally brought under control began anew.

Kieran put his arm around her, holding her close.

When Olivia looked up at him, her wet lashes were spiky. "It's the baby rattle I bought for her when she was born. I had it engraved."

He glanced at the spot where she had rubbed away the soot to reveal a shiny patch. *To Cammie with love from Mommy and Daddy.* Throat tight, he shot her a questioning glance.

"I didn't want her to think that her father didn't care."

He should have been angry, faced anew with the proof that Olivia had hidden his existence. But he couldn't drum up any negative emotion, not with the mother of his child looking as if she might shatter into a million tiny pieces.

Not only that, but he ached from the certainty that his own mistakes had brought them to this tragic point. "Let's go," he said gruffly. "We need to get home to Cammie."

Even with the convenience of a private jet, crossing from the East Coast to the West Coast and back in one day was no easy feat. Jacob had called a pharmacy in Olivia's neighborhood and ordered a light sedative. Once on the plane, Kieran insisted she swallow it with a glass of milk and a handful of saltines.

So far he hadn't managed to persuade her to eat a morsel of food. Olivia was operating on nothing more than adrenaline and sheer will. He settled her in a seat and reclined it to the sleeping position. The steward furnished a pillow and blankets. Olivia was asleep before the wheels left the tarmac.

After takeoff, Kieran unfastened his seat belt and crouched beside her, brushing the hair from her face with a gentle touch. One of her hands was tucked under her cheek. Her eyelashes fanned in crescents over the dark smudges beneath her eyes.

As he watched the almost imperceptible rise and fall of her breasts, he felt a painful pressure in his own chest. *He loved her.* Body and soul. What he had tried to cut off at the root half a dozen years ago had regenerated in the warmth and sunshine of Olivia's return to his life.

And the knowledge that they shared a daughter….

He stood abruptly and strode up to the cockpit, unable to deal with the rush of emotion. It made him dizzy and sick and terrified. What if he lost one of them…or both? It didn't have to be some tragic circumstance. Olivia might simply take Cammie and walk away. After all, she had turned down his marriage proposal without so much a blink.

Kieran stepped through the curtain, legs weak. "Captain, how's the weather looking up ahead?" Idle chitchat wouldn't distract him for long from his dark thoughts, but sitting beside Olivia was torture.

Olivia fought the nightmares. At long last, her heart pounding and her skin clammy with sweat, she surfaced from a drugged sleep. It took several interminable seconds for her to identify her surroundings…and then to remember why she was on a plane.

A shaky sob worked its way up her throat, but she choked it back, sitting up to rub her eyes. Thousands of people around the world had lost their homes this year alone, during floods and tornados and hurricanes. Olivia had been knocked down. But the crying was over. She had Cammie. She had her health. And she had financial resources.

She would be fine. But in truth, the prospect of starting over was daunting.

Kieran appeared suddenly from the front of the plane. His shirt was rumpled. He hadn't shaved. And there were deep grooves etched into his forehead and at the sides of his mouth. Lines she could swear weren't there yesterday.

Exhaustion shrouded him, decimating his usual energy. Seeing Kieran made her wonder how bad she must look. He didn't give her the opportunity to find out. He took his seat and fastened the belt. "We're landing shortly."

She raised her seat and folded the blankets, handing them and the pillow to the steward with a murmured thanks. "How long was I out?"

He shrugged. "You slept across five states, give or take a few. But don't worry…you didn't miss much. It was mostly clouds."

For a wry attempt at humor, it wasn't bad, especially given the circumstances. She summoned a weak smile, her face aching with the effort. "Thank you, Kieran." She reached across the small space dividing them and took his hand in hers. "Thank you for going with me."

The sound of the flaps being deployed and the whine of the engines powering down made conversation difficult. Kieran stared down at their linked fingers. "You going to be okay?" He played with the small cameo ring on her right hand.

She nodded, unable to speak. Clinging to him and never letting go was very appealing. Either that or asking the pilot to fly them to Antarctica.

Thinking about what lay ahead scared her. How do you tell a five-year-old that the only home she has ever known is gone?

Kieran's grasp tightened on her hand. "What is it?" he asked. "What are you thinking?"

"Cammie," she said simply. "How am I ever going to tell Cammie?"

Thirteen

In the end, they did it together. Annalise had bathed Cammie and fed her and tucked her into clean pajamas. They were reading a book when Olivia and Kieran finally made their way upstairs to the bedroom that Kieran had so carefully picked out for his daughter.

The child's face lit up when she saw them. "Mommy! Kieran! I missed you. Did you bring me a present?"

Annalise excused herself quietly, pausing only to give Olivia a quick hug as she left the room. The gentle gesture of compassion tested Olivia's tear-free resolve.

Kieran scooped Cammie up in his arms and held her tight. On his face, Olivia saw her own sadness and thankfulness. Things could have been so much worse.

The three of them sat together on a cushioned window seat overlooking the mountainside in the gathering dusk. Kieran gazed at Olivia over the five-year-old's head, telegraphing a question. *You ready?*

She shook her head, putting her fist to her mouth. *You do it,* she signaled. If she tried to explain, she might burst into tears, and she didn't want to scare her child.

Kieran rested his chin on Cammie's head for a long moment, and then pulled back when she wiggled. "Something bad has happened, sweetheart. I need you to be brave when I tell you this."

Every ounce of childish glee melted away to be replaced by an oddly adult expression of anxiety. "What is it?"

Olivia saw the muscles in his throat work, and knew how unfair she was being to make him do her dirty work. He had to know the impending news would hurt their daughter. But like parents wincing in empathy for an uncomprehending infant about to get vaccinations, she and Kieran had no choice but to tell Cammie the awful truth.

"There was a fire at your house in California," he said slowly, choosing his words with care.

Cammie's eyes rounded. "Did Mommy leave the iron on?"

In spite of everything, Olivia wanted to giggle. "No, baby."

Kieran's sober expression softened. "A bad man made a fire and it got out of control."

"Is Princess Boots okay?"

At Kieran's baffled look, Olivia jumped in. "Kitty is still with Mrs. Capella. Remember?"

"Oh, yeah." She frowned, scrunching up her nose and eyes in concentration. "So we have to stay here for a while?"

Kieran nodded slowly. "If that's okay with your mom."

Olivia nodded, her eyes wet. Clearly Cammie didn't understand the import of what had happened…at least not yet. She was only five. Time enough for upsetting revelations as she asked questions in the coming weeks.

Cammie wiggled off Kieran's knee. "I'm glad Bun-Bun

was here with me." Bun-Bun was the much-loved stuffed animal without which Cammie couldn't sleep. Perhaps in Cammie's eyes, that was enough.

Kieran ruffled her hair. "I'm glad, too. Time for bed, big girl. Your mommy and I have been flying all day, and we're beat."

As they tucked her in, Cammie yawned and surveyed them sleepily. She studied Kieran's face. "Are you my mommy's boyfriend?"

Olivia choked. "Where did you hear about boyfriends?"

"Mrs. Capella says that her daughter is getting a dee-vors because she has a boyfriend *and* a husband. You don't have a husband, so I thought Kieran might be your boyfriend."

The two adults held back their laughter with heroic effort. Kieran's face was red when he said, "Your mommy and I are friends. And we both love you very much. Now go to sleep, and tomorrow, we'll all do something fun together."

Outside in the hall, they collapsed against the wall, laughing uncontrollably until at last they both wheezed and gasped and braced their hands against the Chinese silk wallpaper. Olivia knew the moment of hilarity was a cleansing response to the day's tragedy.

Trust a child to restore a sense of balance to life.

Olivia wiped her eyes. "Thank you," she said. "For telling her. You were perfect."

He put the back of his hand to her hot cheek. "Far from perfect. But I love that little girl."

What happened next was inevitable. In shared grief and exhaustion, they came together, heart to heart, breath mingling with breath. Kieran held her as if she might break, his embrace gentle, his body warm and solid and comforting.

They kissed carefully, as if for the first time. She came so close to blurting out her love, laying it at his feet in gratitude. It would be unfair to burden him with her feelings when he had done so much for her already.

Gradually tenderness heated to passion. She felt him tremble as her hands roved his back.

He sighed, hugging her so tightly her ribs protested. "I need to stay with you tonight, Olivia. To make sure you're okay. Please."

How could she deny what she wanted so badly? "Yes."

He kissed her again, covering her face with light, almost-not-there brushes of his lips. "But first I'm going to feed you."

Food? Her awakening arousal protested. She wrapped her arms around his neck and pressed closer. Sex offered oblivion. Forgetfulness. That was all she wanted and needed right now.

He broke free and stepped back, breathing heavily. "Go get cleaned up. Put on a nightgown. I'll consult with the chef and bring up a tray."

"I'm not hungry," she grumbled. The thought of food made nausea churn in her stomach.

"Doesn't matter." His mien was more drill sergeant than lover. "You have to eat."

She followed his initial direction and stepped into the shower. Beneath the hot, pelting spray, she had to admit that Kieran was right. The water was cleansing in more ways than one. If a few more tears were shed amidst the soapy rivulets swirling down the drain, no one was the wiser.

Though her body ached, her breasts felt heavy and full as she washed them. Imagining Kieran's hands on her sensitive flesh brought a different kind of healing. And she trembled anew with fear for the future. Not for lack of housing. That was minor in the grand scheme of things.

Saying goodbye to Kieran when she went home to start over would make today's events mere shadows of pain. How would she live without him in her life? She had been doing it for six long years. Cammie had filled her days with joy and purpose.

But now Olivia wanted more. She wanted and needed the man she'd fallen in love with during an idyllic semester in Oxford, England.

After drying off and dressing in her favorite silk peignoir of coffee satin and cream lace, she checked on Cammie. Her little girl was sleeping peacefully, but a forbidden thumb was in her mouth, a habit Olivia thought they had defeated a long time ago.

Was the childish comfort technique a sign that Cammie was more affected by the news of the fire than she had seemed?

Olivia removed the thumb without waking her and rearranged the covers. "I love you," she whispered, kissing Cammie's cheek and inhaling the wonderful combined scents of shampoo and graham crackers from her bedtime snack.

When she returned to her bedroom via the connecting door, Kieran was already there…and in the process of setting a large silver tray on a low table in front of the settee. His eyes warmed as he turned and saw her. With heated regard he swept his gaze from her bare toes, up her body to her freshly washed hair. She'd shampooed it three times, convinced that the smell of smoke still lingered.

He held out a hand. "Come. Eat with me."

The massive fireplace normally sat empty in the summertime, hidden behind a large arrangement of fresh flowers. Kieran had removed the vase and stacked logs and kindling, which were now burning brightly.

She cocked her head, her gaze drawn to the warmth of the crackling blaze. "Isn't this extravagant?"

He shrugged, looking like a mischievous boy. "I had to

crank down the AC ten degrees, but I like the ambience. You deserve extravagance after the day you've had."

"The food looks amazing." She joined him on the small sofa, feeling oddly shy considering the activities they'd indulged in the past couple of days. Her stomach rumbled loudly. "I could get used to having a chef on call."

Kieran uncovered a silver salver. "Nothing too heavy... roasted chicken, lemon-infused rice and fresh kale from the garden." He waved at a smaller dish. "And a surprise for dessert if you clean your plate."

They ate in companionable silence, both of them starved. With the warmth from the fire and a full tummy, Olivia's lids grew heavy. At last she sat back, unable to eat another bite. "That was delicious," she said. "And I'm not just raving because I was so hungry."

Kieran poured two cups of fragrant coffee, handing her one. "I'm glad you enjoyed it." Leaning forward, he removed the top of the mystery dish and uncovered a bowl of sugared dates. "Now for your treat." He picked up one piece of fruit and held it to her lips. "Try this."

As she opened her mouth automatically, Kieran tucked the sugary sweet between her lips. She bit off a piece and without thinking, licked the crystals that clung to his fingertips. He froze, his eyes heating with arousal and his breathing growing harsh. "Have another."

The room was heavy with unspoken desire, hers... his. The fire played a mesmerizing symphony of pop and crackle. Three times he fed her, and three times she sucked his fingertips into her mouth to clean them.

Kieran cracked first. He stood up and strode to the window, throwing up the sash and letting in a rush of cool night air. "Bloody stupid idea having a fire," he muttered. He took off his shirt, exposing a chest that made Olivia's toes curl.

He was all hard planes and rippling muscle.

"I like it," she protested, removing the negligee that topped her barely there gown.

His eyes grew wide. "I am not going to have sex with you tonight. You don't need that."

"Don't tell me what I need."

She lowered the tiny straps of the satin garment and let it slither over her hips and fall to the carpet. "*You* haven't had dessert," she pointed out.

The front of his trousers lifted noticeably. His torso gleamed damp in the soft lamplight. Hooded eyes tracked her every movement. "I wanted to comfort you tonight…to hold you in case you had bad dreams."

"Perhaps if you *entertain* me, my dreams won't be bad at all."

He shoved his hands in the pockets of his pants, frowning. "I think you may still be in shock. You should get a good night's sleep."

Though his mouth spoke prosaic words, his body told a different story. His entire frame was rigid, the cloth of his trousers barely containing his thrusting shaft.

She walked right up to him, buck naked, her toes curling in the soft, luxurious carpet beneath their feet. Now the tips of her breasts brushed his bare rib cage.

"Stop." He inhaled sharply, groaning as she laid her cheek against his shoulder.

"We're just getting started," she murmured. Insinuating one of her thighs between his legs, she rubbed up against him like a cat.

Kieran was a strong man, but he was only a man. How in the hell could he cosset her when she was hell-bent on seducing him? He gave up the fight, because losing was better than anything he had planned. Cupping her firm butt in his palms, he pulled her closer still. "Did anyone ever tell you you're stubborn?"

She went up on tiptoe to kiss his chin. "All the time."

"The door?"

"I locked it. We'll hear her if she stirs…but she won't."

"I'll leave before morning." He wouldn't confuse Cammie, not with so much at stake.

"That's a whole seven hours from now," Olivia said, her nimble fingers attacking his belt buckle. "I can think of a few ways to fill the time."

The ornate mantel clock marked off the minutes and hours as Kieran devoted himself to entertaining Olivia. She tried rushing the game, but he was on to her tricks. With one hand, he manacled her wrists over her head, and at the same time trapped her legs with his thigh.

Her chest heaved, eyes flashing in annoyance. "I want to touch you."

The agitation of her breathing made her breasts quiver. The sight of those magnificent heaving bosoms mesmerized him for a split second. He cleared his throat. "Not yet."

"When?"

"After I've finished with you."

Eyes rounded, she gazed up at him. "That sounds ominous."

"I promise you'll enjoy every second."

Her eyes fluttered shut. A tiny sigh of anticipation slipped from her pursed lips and filled him with purpose. Tonight was for Olivia alone.

Flipping her to her stomach and sitting astride her thighs, he reached for a bottle of lotion on the nightstand and squeezed a generous amount into his hand. Warming the thick liquid between his palms, he gazed down at her. Those narrow shoulders had carried a heavy burden for the past six years, a burden that he should have been sharing.

The knowledge was a sharp pang in his belly. Deliberately he placed his hands on her upper back and began a deep massage. Olivia moaned and settled more deeply into the mattress, her body boneless and limp.

In his younger, wilder days, he'd once had the good fortune to spend a three-day vacation with a sexy Indonesian masseuse. She'd taught Kieran a thing or two about the human body and how to relax. Dredging up those pleasant memories, he applied himself to making Olivia feel pampered, hopefully draining away the stresses of their long, emotionally fraught day.

Touching her was a penance. If his hands shook, surely she didn't notice. He was tormented by the notion that Olivia and Cammie might have been in the house when it went up in a ball of flame. Nothing he could have done would have saved them if he had been on the other side of the world. Olivia could have died, and Kieran would not have known for weeks, months.

He'd been living without her for a long time. How was it that the possibility of her death, and his daughter's, as well, turned his stomach to stone?

He finished at last and brushed her cheek with a fingertip. "Olivia?" Though *her* muscles were warm and loose, he was strung tightly enough to snap. "Olivia?"

A gentle snore was his only answer.

Incredulous, frustrated, but oddly proud that he had lulled her into slumber, he slid down into the bed beside her, condemned to a painful night. Her nude body snuggled into his even in sleep, her bottom coming to rest against his rock-hard erection. He contemplated giving himself relief, but he didn't want to wake her.

He closed his eyes. The covers suffocated him. Willing himself to breathe slowly, he used the deep inhale and exhale technique he knew would eventually coax sleep.

Arms tight around Olivia, he yawned and pressed his cheek to her back.

As the moments passed, he gained control and a sense of perspective. Contentment washed over him with the unexpected advent of a gentle summer rain. This house had held nothing for him in the past but pain and duty. He'd never known real happiness here. All he ever wanted to do in the midst of his rare visits was to escape.

Even spending time with his family had not blunted the hurtful memories that in his mind hung over the massive house as a shroud.

Gareth had built a home here, as had Jacob. Why were they able to get past the tragedy when Kieran couldn't? Was he weaker than his brothers? Kieran and Annalise were the youngest of all six of the cousins when they lost their mothers. Did that make a difference? Annalise hadn't settled down on the mountain, either.

But unlike Kieran, she was filled with light and a happiness that was almost palpable. Her soul wasn't scarred by what had happened.

He allowed himself for one wary second to reach for the memories of his mother. A scent. A fleeting visual. The sound of her gentle laugh. She danced in his memory, hand in hand with her little son, twirling him around in a dizzying circle. Then the image faded. It was all he had…all he would ever have.

This was the point at which he usually surrendered to the urge to flee, a knee-jerk reaction to pain so strong it brought a toughened man to the brink of despair.

As he lay there in the darkness, dry-eyed, he realized with stunned certainty that the pain was gone. Obliterated. In the depth of the night, he heard his mother's whisper. *Be happy, Kieran. For me....*

Did she know about Olivia and Cammie? Was she somewhere up there in heaven, grieving because she couldn't meet her granddaughter?

He closed his eyes, throat tight with emotion, grateful that no one was around to see his weakness. Had his mother really counseled him to be happy? Was it even possible? Did he have it in him to let go and simply live again?

Existing from job to job, tent to tent, was the perfect camouflage for a man who was empty inside. He never stopped moving long enough for anyone to realize…to care.

Olivia murmured his name in her sleep. He stroked her hair, curling a mass of it around his hand and holding it in his fist as if by doing so, this unprecedented feeling of peace might last.

She felt perfect in his arms.

But he was an imperfect man.

Could he change for her? For his daughter?

Fourteen

When Olivia awoke, she was alone. The pillow beside hers bore the imprint of Kieran's head, but the bed was empty. She knew he had to leave her…it made sense. But her heart grieved.

Outside her window, dawn had barely arrived; the treetops no more than shadowy sentinels, though birdsong filled the early-morning air. She yawned and stretched, wondering how long it would be before Cammie bounded into the room with her usual burst of energy.

It was too soon to call Lolita and Javier. They were on Pacific Time, still the middle of the night in California.

Had the police made an arrest? Was her mother's stalker continuing to lurk in the shadows of their lives?

Itchy and restless, Olivia climbed out of bed, feeling the aches and pains of an old woman. The benefits of Kieran's selfless massage evaporated in a rush of uncertainty that tightened her neck muscles. It had been only a short time since the fire, but already, waiting for an end to the drama was unbearable. She longed to go home, but she had nowhere to call her own anymore.

The truth was ugly and inescapable.

By the time she finished her shower, Cammie was up and demanding breakfast. To Olivia's surprise, Victor awaited them in the formal dining room.

"Good morning, sir," she said, sitting stiffly in a chair and giving Cammie a visual warning to behave. Cammie needed little urging. She was too busy digging into a plateful of small pancakes shaped like bears and fir trees.

The old man had an empty plate in front of him, but it bore the evidence of bacon and eggs. He nursed coffee in a china cup that looked far too fragile for his big hands. Like his sons, he was a large man, but his hair had faded away to little tufts of white over his ears, and his florid skin spoke of unhealthy habits.

His portly figure and piercing eyes were intimidating to say the least.

Olivia ate without speaking, all the while making sure Cammie was not poised to launch into one of her stream of consciousness chattering sessions.

The meal was silent and uncomfortable.

When Olivia had swallowed as many bites as she could manage of an omelet and crisp toast, she shoved her plate aside. "We'll get out of your hair," she said, biting her lip when she realized that Cammie was still finishing up.

Victor Wolff raised one beetling eyebrow. "So soon? I've arranged for the sous chef to make cookies with Cammie so you and I can talk, Olivia. Is that okay with you, little one?"

Cammie looked up, a drizzle of sticky syrup coating one side of her chin. Her mouth was too full for speech, but she nodded enthusiastically.

Unease slithered down Olivia's spine. "Where is Kieran?" she asked, needing reinforcements before a confrontation with her host.

Victor shrugged. "He and Gareth and Jacob took off at first light for Charlottesville, something about buying a new Jeep."

"It takes three men to purchase a vehicle?"

"My boys are close. And they seldom have the opportunity to spend time together as a trio."

A pleasant young woman appeared from the direction of the kitchen, introducing herself as LeeAnn. Olivia watched, helpless, as Cammie's face lit up. She took her new friend's hand, and the two of them disappeared, leaving Olivia to face Victor alone.

He stood up. "We'll go to my study," he said, allowing Olivia no opportunity to refuse.

Trailing in his wake, she pondered his intent. There was little time to formulate a plan of rebuttal for whatever was about to transpire. Victor's private sanctum was on the main floor, as was the kitchen.

The room was like something out of a movie. Heavy hunter-green drapes flanked mullioned windows that sparkled as if they were cleaned every night by an army of elves…and perhaps they were. The thick folds of velvet picked up and accentuated the intricate design in an antique Persian rug that covered a large expanse of the hardwood floor.

Victor motioned to a wing chair opposite his dark mahogany desk. "Have a seat."

Feeling a bit too much like a wayward schoolchild, Olivia sat, hands in lap, and waited. She wasn't intentionally silent, but in truth, she could not think of a single subject, other than the weather, with which to counter Victor's liegelike summons.

He frowned at her. "When are you going to tell me I have a grandchild?"

Nothing like a direct attack to catch the unwary off guard. Olivia bit her lip, stalling for time. "Is that why you asked me to come in here? Did you wait for your son to leave so you could ambush me?"

Guilt landed briefly on his heavy features before disappearing. "You're impertinent."

"I mean no disrespect, but I won't be bullied."

They tiptoed around the subject that couldn't be broached. Not yet. Not without Kieran's participation.

Victor harrumphed and sat back in his chair, swiveling from side to side just enough to make Olivia dizzy. Despite his bluster, or maybe because of it, she suddenly saw that he was afraid. Of what? she wondered.

After tapping an empty pipe on the blotter, he put it to his lips and took a lengthy draw, perhaps using the scent of tobacco long past to satisfy an urge. "Ask him to stay," he commanded. "Ask Kieran to stay. He'll do it for you. I know he will. He's never before brought a woman to Wolff Mountain. You're special to him."

Her heart sank. "Sorry to burst your bubble, Mr. Wolff, but you're wrong."

"Call me Victor. And I'm seldom wrong. What makes you so sure that I am now?"

Time to bury her pride. Taking a deep, painful breath, she gave him the unvarnished truth. "He offered to marry me in order to give Cammie security. A family on paper. But he wasn't offering to stay. That wasn't part of the package. He's leaving for the Sudan in September. Nothing has changed."

Before her eyes, the old man aged a decade, his brown-spotted hands trembling before he gripped the arms of the chair to steady them. "Damn it. This is his home. He needs to settle down…."

His words trailed off in impotence. He wasn't the first parent to rue a son's choices, and he wouldn't be the last.

Olivia sighed. "I've never had any illusions about Kieran. He's a wonderful man, but more than anyone I've ever known, he needs to wander. It's a lifestyle well suited to a single man."

"And if he has a family?"

"If he has a family, it wasn't by choice." Her words were blunt. Said as much to remind herself of the truth as they were to make the truth clear to a desperate father. "He'll continue to come back from time to time if you don't harass him. That's probably the most you can hope for."

Victor glared at her. "In my day women knew how to use sex to get what they wanted from a man."

Olivia's face flamed. Aghast at his gall, she gaped at him. "Are you actually suggesting that I try to manipulate your son with intimacy?"

"Any fool, even an old one, can see the fireworks between you two. Make the boy crazy. Reel him in. Don't worry about being so damned politically correct."

"Forgive me if I don't want a man I have to coerce into loving me."

"Who said anything about love? Once he parks his boots, he'll figure out that you and Cammie are good for him."

"Like prunes and brussels sprouts? No, thank you. I deserve a man who will love me and my child and put us first."

"Then fight for the boy, damn it."

Olivia stood up, beyond finished with the circuitous conversation. "I appreciate your hospitality, Mr. Wolff, but my relationship with Kieran is none of your business. I wish I could give you what you want."

He waved a hand as if dismissing her stilted words. "Any

news about your house…or the stalker? I'm sorry about that, by the way. Must have been a damned shock."

"Nothing yet. I'll call my parents when it gets a little later." His compassion touched her in spite of their adversarial meeting.

"You're always welcome on Wolff Mountain. I give you my word." His rheumy eyes glittered with tears.

Her throat tightened. This magnificent house was part of Cammie's birthright. Whatever transpired between Kieran and Olivia, that relationship would never change. Victor Wolff was Cammie's grandfather.

"Thank you," she said softly. "I'll bring her to visit when I can."

He nodded, a single tear streaking down his leathery cheek. "See that you do, Olivia Delgado. See that you do."

She escaped Victor's study, and after checking on Cammie who was still elbow-deep in cookie dough, Olivia retrieved her cell phone from the bedroom and began making a necessary string of phone calls. The insurance adjuster, of course. And the neighbor to check on the cat.

That second call meant answering a host of questions. Mrs. Capella was a dear, but a notorious gossip. No doubt she'd be preening on the block since she had direct contact with Olivia.

Finally, when it was a decent hour to roust her night-owl parents out of bed, Olivia dialed their number.

Lolita's sleep-thickened voice answered. "You do realize that a woman my age needs her beauty sleep," she complained.

"You're gorgeous, Mother…with or without sleep." The implied request for flattery was received and acknowledged. "Are you and Daddy okay?"

Javier Delgado picked up the conversation. "She went

to make coffee. We're fine, baby. Are you and my granddaughter staying put?"

"Yes." But not for long. She had another phone call to make that would set things in motion. Unfortunately every minute spent with Kieran made the inevitable parting that much harder. It was time to break free.

"Why didn't you tell us you were flying out here yesterday?"

Her father's pique made her feel guilty. "You said on the phone that Mom had gone to bed with a sedative. I didn't want her to see my house. Not yet. We both know she doesn't handle crises well."

"We'll get the bastard who did this."

Javier often spoke like a movie character. But his vehemence made Olivia smile. "I know. I just called to say I love you and to tell you to be very careful. This man is obsessed with Mother. No one knows what he'll try next."

"Not to worry, my love. The house is surrounded with so much firepower, I feel like we're hiding out at the Alamo."

"That standoff didn't end well, Daddy."

"No. But it was a hell of a role." Javier had played Davy Crockett once upon a time, and could still produce a creditable southern accent.

She wiped her cheek, surprised to realize she was crying. Her parents were eccentric and self-centered and prone to overdramatization in every situation, but she loved them dearly. "I'll call again soon," she promised. "Keep me posted."

When she hung up, she gnawed her lip, worried that her mother wouldn't take the threat seriously, despite the fire. Olivia was sure that a part of Lolita felt flattered that a fan cared enough to be irrational.

The three Wolff men were not back by lunchtime. Cammie pouted, missing Kieran's attentions. Olivia felt much the same, but without the luxury of acting like a five-year-old. For the next several hours, Cammie was fractious and inconsolable. Refusing to nap, she sulked around her wonderful bedroom until Olivia was at her wit's end. Was all this bad behavior a result of last night's news? Would it help if Olivia coaxed her daughter into talking about the fire? Or would that make things worse?

It was far too hot to play outside. Huge thunderclouds built on the western horizon, and the sticky, oppressive heat shimmered in waves, obscuring the usual, far flung vistas.

When Cammie finally succumbed to a fitful sleep, it was after four o'clock. Olivia fell into a chair exhausted. It was always a mistake to let her offspring nap this late in the day. It meant Cammie wouldn't want to go to bed at her normal bedtime, and battle would inevitably ensue.

But the child was clearly in need of rest. Olivia wasn't about to wake her up, even for dinner. They could always raid the kitchen later.

At six-thirty, Olivia dressed in a salmon voile sundress that she had not yet worn. The filmy layers were cool, and the color flattered her skin tones. No bra was required. Her breathing quickened as she pictured Kieran's reaction later when they were alone.

She owed him something for last night. After her insistence that they make love, she had flaked out on him in no time. Had he been terribly disappointed?

No matter. They had time for one last metaphorical dance. Then Olivia would go home. Kieran was who he was. He wouldn't change. And Olivia couldn't bruise her heart any longer hoping for a different outcome. After running a brush through her hair, she clipped it up in a loose chignon. Dangling crystal earrings added a note of formality to her appearance. If she had to play verbal badminton with Victor Wolff again, she needed all the armor she could muster.

Poor Cammie looked like an urchin when Olivia checked on her. She had shed her shorts and top and was wearing an old T-shirt Kieran had given her that said, Girls Rule, Boys Drool.

Grinning wryly, Olivia picked up the monitor and tucked it in the pocket of her full skirt. When Cammie awoke, it would be easy to hear her. The child usually demanded a snack before her eyes were open. More like her grandmother than her mother, she didn't waken easily.

Olivia descended the stairs to the main floor, stopping short when Kieran came striding toward her. Something was different about him, but she couldn't pinpoint it. There was almost a spring in his step.

He gave her a broad grin. "Hello, beautiful. Did you miss me?"

Fifteen

Kieran had thoroughly enjoyed the day with his brothers. Catching up on each others' lives, sharing stupid inside jokes from their adolescent years…all of it had been comfortable and familiar and pretty damned wonderful. There'd been nothing touchy feely or emotionally intrusive. But Gareth and Jacob, by their behavior and conversation, had made it clear how glad they were to have him home.

Even in the midst of a testosterone fest, though, Kieran had missed his girls. He hugged Olivia now, inhaling her scent with a deep, cleansing breath.

She pulled back and smiled at him. "Yes. We missed you. In fact, Cammie was a spoiled brat today. Not having you here to entertain her was not fun."

"Where is she now?"

"Taking a late nap." She pulled the monitor from her pocket. "I'll hear her when she wakes up."

"Do you think she was acting out because of what we told her last night?"

"I thought about that. But she never mentioned the fire."

"What have you heard from California?"

"Nothing much. The man is still on the loose. Mom and Dad are fine…holed up with a phalanx of security guards."

He squeezed her hand. "And how about you?"

"I'm fine."

Her words weren't all that convincing. The shadows smudged beneath her eyes accentuated her pallor. He had a feeling that she was running on nothing more than adrenaline and determination. Olivia was strong, very strong. But losing a home was a blow to anyone.

He put his arm around her as they walked to the dining room. "We'll do whatever needs to be done," he said quietly. "Try not to worry."

Gareth had lingered, and Gracie joined them for dinner. With Jacob and Annalise present, as well, it was a lively meal. Annalise's siblings and father were due back to the mountain in another week.

Surprisingly it was quiet Jacob who pressed Olivia for details. "When they catch the guy, what will you do?"

She took a sip of her wine and winced. "As soon as that happens, Cammie and I will head home…. I mean…"

Kieran's hand tightened on hers beneath the tablecloth.

She took a breath. "Cammie and I will stay with my parents, I suppose, until we decide what to do…whether to rebuild in the same place or closer to my mom and dad. I haven't really had time to think it through."

"Speaking of Cammie, I thought she'd be awake by now," Kieran said. He watched as she pulled the monitor from her pocket, listened a moment and shook it. He frowned. "What's wrong?"

"I think the batteries are dead."

Olivia's look of consternation mirrored his own gut feeling of trouble. "I'll go get her," he said. "Stay and eat your dinner."

But he'd barely had time to stand up when Cammie appeared in the doorway—sucking her thumb, wearing an old T-shirt. Her hair was sleep tousled. Relief flooded him, along with amusement. "Hi, sweetheart. You ready for some dinner?"

She surveyed the assemblage at the table, her small face solemn. "I forgot Bun-Bun. He wants to eat with us." Turning back, she ran out of the room.

"Put your clothes on," Olivia called after her.

Kieran sat back down. "Don't hassle her. As kids we showed up at meals in all varieties of threadbare shirts and jeans."

Victor chuckled. "Not for lack of trying on my part. Vincent and I did our best to impart rules of etiquette, but rarely did they stick. It was a household of hellions back in those days."

"Not me." Annalise's smile was smug. "Somebody had to have some couth around here."

The men hooted. Gareth grinned, his arm stretched out along the back of his wife's chair. "You were a goody two-shoes. But what Dad and Uncle Vincent didn't know was that you came home from playing in the woods just as nasty as the rest of us. Unfortunately you had this feminine knack for turning grubby Cinderella into an infuriating, sanctimonious princess in the blink of an eye. Made us mad as hell."

In the burst of laughter that followed, Kieran leaned toward Olivia. "Should I go get Cammie?"

She shook her head. "Not in the mood she's in. I'll deal with it. Just don't eat my dessert," she added as she went to retrieve her daughter.

Kieran had finished his meal and was having a second

glass of wine when Olivia rushed back into the room, panic written all over her face.

"She's not upstairs. I can't find her. She's gone."

He grabbed her shoulders, easing her into a chair before she fainted on him. Her skin had gone milk-white. "Don't jump to conclusions, honey. She probably got turned around and lost her way down a hall somewhere. You know how this house is."

"Cammie has a perfect sense of direction." Olivia gazed up at him, clutching his sleeve. "She never gets lost. Something's wrong."

Terror ripped at his chest, but he fought it back. There had to be a simple explanation.

Everyone at the table was on their feet in an instant, Victor included.

Kieran sucked in a breath and barked out orders. "Gareth, you and Gracie take the yard and your house. She loves the dog and the pool. Jacob, search this floor with Father. Olivia and I will start with the second floor and work our way up. Annalise, question the staff. When each of you finishes, come back. Does everyone have a cell phone? Call if you locate her."

The next half hour was a nightmare. They tore the house apart, from basement to attic. Cammie was nowhere to be found.

When the search parties met, empty-handed, Olivia broke down finally, sobbing so hard Kieran feared she would make herself ill. Holding her close, he breathed hope into her, shoring her up with only his will. Deep in his gut, her anguish was his own.

She sank onto a sofa, her eyes haunted. "That man has her. I know it. He said he was going to hurt the people my mother loves, and my mother adores Cammie."

Kieran's hands fisted. "How would he even know how to find you here?"

"The police said he's been watching my house. You came there. He must have figured out who you were."

"I was in a rental car."

"But you gave your real name?"

"Yes." Dear God in heaven…

Jacob spoke, his words carefully neutral. "We at least have to consider the possibility."

Olivia bowed her head. "There are no fences," she said dully. "Only the one at the front gate. Anyone could walk in."

Victor shook his head. "It would be a fool's mission. We have four hundred acres."

"Gracie made it up here," Gareth pointed out, his face troubled. His new wife had once upon a time sneaked onto the property to confront Gareth on her father's behalf.

"But Gracie didn't try to get into the main house, kidnap a child and leave again." Kieran's fierce shout cowed no one. In the faces of the people he loved, he saw compassion, concern and his own bubbling fear.

Olivia gathered her composure with a visible, superhuman effort, her chest heaving as tremors threatened to rattle her bones. "Do we call the police?"

A momentary silence fell over the room. The Wolff family had suffered terribly at the hands of the press over the years. Privacy was practically inscribed on the family crest. And for Lolita and Javier, this kind of publicity was not desirable, either. The tabloids would have a field day.

Kieran squatted in front of Olivia. "We'll do whatever you want. You're her mother." He took her hands in his, trying to warm the icy skin. She was close to being in shock, and he was damn glad Jacob was on hand.

"It will take them a long time to get here, won't it?" The words were barely a whisper, spoken through bloodless lips.

Everyone nodded. Victor's breathing was harsh and labored. "The nearest law enforcement is forty-five to fifty minutes away."

Olivia shook free of Kieran's solicitous grasp and stood up. "We'll give it an hour, then…before we make a call."

Gareth spoke up, pacing restlessly. "I scouted the perimeter of the house. No sign of forced entry, no footprints, nothing to indicate an intruder. But that doesn't mean anything. Psychopaths are often brilliant. He would try to cover his tracks."

A blinding flash of lightning lit up the room in which they all stood as a simultaneous crack of thunder roared across the mountaintop and rattled glass in the windows.

Kieran made a decision. "If he has her, he'll use one of the trails. It would be too hard to travel through the underbrush. I'm going to walk the closest sections to look for signs that anyone has passed by recently. I'll start with the north and the east since that portion of the property is nearest a road."

Jacob nodded. "Gareth and I will take the west and south quadrants."

"I'm going with you." Olivia in her dainty, feminine dress held her stance as aggressively as a bulldog.

"It's too dangerous," Kieran said through clenched teeth. "Trust me."

"I do trust you," she said. "But that's my baby out in the storm."

He eyed her low-heeled sandals. They were flimsy at best, but the clock was ticking. She was close to collapse, and the knowledge that he had not been able to protect her or his daughter flailed him like a whip. "Fine," he ground out, his anger self-directed. "Suit yourself. Let's move out."

Olivia stumbled behind Kieran, trying to keep up with his loping stride. She knew he was angry with her, but she couldn't stay inside the house and wait. She couldn't. Not when Cammie was terrified of storms.

Who had her? What was his intent? Ransom? Kieran's mother had been murdered in just such a situation. Was Kieran thinking of Laura Wolff right now? Did fear turn his limbs to jelly as it did Olivia's?

All around them lightning danced. Rain poured from the skies relentlessly, drenching Olivia to the skin and blinding her. Kieran called to Cammie again and again, until his voice was hoarse and exhausted.

There were at least a dozen trails crisscrossing the mountaintop. None of them showed a single sign that anyone had walked them recently. But the rain was rapidly turning everything to mud, so even if there had been shreds of cloth or remnants of footprints, they would soon be eradicated completely.

In a clearing, Kieran stopped abruptly. During a brief flash of illumination, Olivia saw anguish and grief on his face. But when she touched his arm, his expression morphed into determination.

Had she imagined his emotion?

He strode on, giving her no choice but to follow.

When they finally met up with Jacob and Gareth, the four adults looked for signs of hope in each others' faces. Huddled against the wind, they wordlessly acknowledged the truth. If an intruder had taken Cammie out in this storm, the chances of finding her were slim to none.

Stumbling back into the house with the others, Olivia struggled not to collapse in hysteria. Annalise and Gracie had prepared hot coffee. Olivia grasped a warm mug, trying to still the trembling that threatened to drag her under.

Annalise tugged her out of the foyer into a side chamber.

"I brought down dry clothes. You need to change immediately. It won't help Cammie if you make yourself sick."

With clumsy fingers, Olivia tried to do as she was asked. But her coordination was shot. Annalise took over, dealing with zippers and buttons. She stripped Olivia all the way down to her bare skin and then bundled her up quickly in dry underwear, a fleecy sweatshirt and jeans.

When they returned to the front of the house, the men were huddled together, their clothing still dripping onto the marble floor. Gareth turned his eyes to the ceiling, his body rigid with concentration.

Suddenly he swung around and pinned Annalise with a laserlike gaze. "Did you take Cammie to the secret tunnel?"

Annalise nodded. "I showed her where it was, but we didn't go in. The whole thing is probably full of spiders and mice. Ick. No child would want to get in there."

Kieran's expression was bleak. "I did. When I was just her age."

For a moment, the silence was stunned and uncomfortable. Olivia knew he was telling them that the secret tunnel was where he used to hide to grieve his mother.

En masse, they started up the stairs. Second floor, third floor, attic.

Olivia was confused. "But we've searched all this," she cried. "Several times."

"Over here," Kieran said, already crossing the attic to a portion of the wall where a frieze of carved flowers decorated a protruding section that looked like it was concealing ductwork. But it suddenly dawned on Olivia that the vents for the heat and air system were on the opposite side of the room.

Kieran pressed on a rose. Nothing happened. He glanced over his shoulder at Annalise. "Do you remember which one?"

She shrugged unhappily. "I never actually got it to open. All I did was tell Cammie how it worked in theory. I didn't think she paid attention to what I was saying."

Kieran pressed and punched until his knuckles were raw.

Annalise shoved him aside. "For Pete's sake. Move, you big lug."

Delicately, skimming her fingertips over the rough surface as if she were reading Braille, she searched for the mechanism. With a little click and a whir, the wheels engaged and the door swung open. It was only four feet high.

The seven adults gasped in unison. Annalise had not been wrong. The corners of the gaping opening were laced with spiderwebs. And the interior of the space was pitch-black, the single lightbulb long since burned out.

But lying curled up on the floor was Cammie, fast asleep. Her dirty face was streaked where tears had run through layers of dust. Her little fingernails were caked with grime from scratching at the inside of the door.

Kieran crouched and scooped her into his arms. "Wake up, baby. I'm here. Your daddy is here."

Olivia touched her daughter's soft cheek. "Wake up, Cammie. Please."

The child's lashes fluttered and lifted, causing her to blink against the sudden advent of bright light into her dark prison. "I got locked in," she complained, her arms around Kieran's neck. "Annalise never explained how to get out."

The indignant glare she shot Kieran's cousin might have made them all laugh had not each one been choking back emotion.

Olivia smoothed her daughter's rumpled hair, hoping it was spider free. "Why did you hide, sweetheart? We thought you were coming down for dinner, but when you went to get Bun-Bun you never came back."

Cammie's lower lip trembled. "When I woke up and went down to the dining room, I heard you say that when they catch the bad man you're gonna take me back to California. I want to stay here, Mommy. With Kieran. And you, too. I like it here."

"But, honey…"

Victor touched her arm in warning, silently pointing her attention to Kieran's face. Olivia's once incognito lover had nothing to hide now. His love and his pride were laid bare for all to see. He looked down at Cammie in his arms like a man who had finally found the treasure he'd spent a lifetime looking for.

Before Olivia could say another word, Kieran pulled her close, drawing the three of them into a tight hug. Saying a litany of thank-you prayers, she put her head on his shoulder and wept tears of gratitude.

When Cammie finally struggled to get down, demanding food, Olivia realized that the others had crept silently away, leaving this odd family of three to a reunion. Cammie faced off against her parents, arms akimbo. "You said you're my daddy," she accused, pointing at Kieran with an imperious finger. "I heard you."

Olivia saw him struggle for words. She knew he hadn't meant to betray her trust without her consent. The declaration had tumbled out, straight from his heart in the heat of the moment.

"Cammie, I…" He ran his hands through his hair, glancing in desperation at Olivia.

She stepped forward, squatting to look her daughter in the face. "He *is* your daddy, my sweet little jelly bean."

Cammie's eyes rounded. "Why didn't you tell me when we got here?"

It was a fair question. Cammie's hurt and confusion were exactly what Olivia had been hoping to avoid. Speaking slowly, choosing her words carefully, Olivia explained, "Kieran didn't know he was your daddy until I told him. When you were born, I didn't know where he was, because he works on the other side of the world."

"Did you look for him?"

Another zinger.

"I was busy taking care of you. I loved you very much and I was very happy to be your mommy."

Cammie stared at Kieran, Bun-Bun dangling from one fist, dragging the floor. "Do you want to be my daddy?"

Her innocence and vulnerability would have shredded a heart far more hardened than Kieran's. He blinked once. "I *am* your daddy," he said forcefully, crouching beside her. "But even if I weren't, I would want to be. Because I think you are the most special little girl in the whole wide world… and I love you."

Olivia knew the words were torn from his throat. He was not a man to say them lightly. When Cammie threw herself against his chest and his arms closed around her, Kieran's expression was painfully open, his raw and bleeding heart on display.

She had to look away, feeling anew the guilt of her decision to keep father and daughter apart.

The past couldn't be undone. Now all the three of them could do was move forward.

Kieran scooped Cammie up and stood with her, gazing at Olivia with an inscrutable expression. "Let's get our little chick some food," he said quietly.

Without ceremony, they made their way downstairs to Olivia's suite of rooms. One call to the kitchen netted them a child's feast of chicken fingers, peanut butter crackers, cooked apples and chocolate cake for dessert.

Olivia and Kieran sat side by side, not touching, as they watched their daughter devour an astounding amount of food given her small size. When she was satisfied, she wiped her mouth with her hand, yawning.

Suddenly her face brightened. "If our other house is gone, this can be my new bedroom. Forever."

Olivia felt Kieran tense. She gnawed her lip. "Kieran and I are going to talk about that," she said, wishing this conversation had been preceded by some kind of well-thought-out plan.

He had no such qualms. "It's your bedroom forever. Definitely. No matter what happens."

"You can stay here for the rest of the summer," Olivia conceded, knowing she had little choice at this point. "But Lolo and Jojo live in California…and you'll be starting kindergarten soon. We have lots to think about."

Kieran shot her a sharp glance, but didn't interrupt.

Puzzlement etched the features that already bore the stamp of the Wolff clan, emphasizing Cammie's resemblance to Annalise. "What does that mean?"

Kieran stood. "Grown-up stuff, poppet. Let's get you in a bath. You smell like a skunk."

With Cammie giggling in delight, the two of them disappeared into the bathroom, leaving Olivia to sit alone with her troubled thoughts.

Sixteen

Kieran brooded out on the terrace, reluctant to go back inside and face the inquisition from his family about why he'd had a daughter for five years and had never told them about her.

Cammie. His daughter. Even now the words sounded unfamiliar, and yet somehow right.

The storm had passed, and the summer sky was lit with scores of stars. The night was peaceful and serene in the aftermath of the tempest.

His own situation was not so calm. For his entire adult life, he'd had no one to worry about but himself. That thought drew him up short. It wasn't exactly true. He'd worried about his father plenty, especially after the heart attack that had brought Kieran home from university and caused him to leave Olivia behind.

Kieran had spent many a night praying for his father's recovery…wondering bleakly if Olivia had found some cocky English chap to pick up where Kieran had left off.

But as the months passed, once Kieran had made the choice to set out on the open road, he'd been remarkably self-centered. Okay, maybe not selfish exactly. He was kind, and his work was important to the people it benefited. But all in all, nothing had mattered to him but the next dot on the map and how soon he'd be on his way there.

Now, he stood at a new crossroads…one that a GPS couldn't locate on any grid. He had a daughter…and a lover…and a mountain that was calling him home. Normally he'd be chomping at the bit to pack his duffel bag and head out for parts unknown. Usually his passport was in his back pocket, ready for the next stamp.

But now, inexplicably, the thought of leaving at the end of the summer was unbearable.

He strode back into the house, eager to see Olivia, ready to make plans, to map out a course of action.

His father met him in the hallway. "There's a fellow at the front gate by the name of Jeremy Vargas. The guard wants to know whether to send him up or not."

Kieran frowned, wishing he could say no. "Let him in," he said.

Victor put a hand on his arm. "When you're ready, we'd all like to hear about you and Olivia and Cammie." He winced. "Olivia is the one you wanted to tell the truth to… back in Oxford."

It was a statement, not a question. "Yes."

"But I had a heart attack and you left her." His face twisted. "God, I'm sorry, son."

"It wasn't your fault."

"Why did she never let you know you had a daughter?"

"Because she thought my name was Kevin Wade, and when she found out I'd been lying to her…when she learned my true identity, she didn't think I deserved or needed to know."

Victor's head bowed. "Son of a bitch…" The expletive held little heat. The old man was defeated, worn down.

"Don't sweat it, Dad. It's all water under the bridge. We'll get through this."

The front door opened, and in walked Jeremy Vargas. Kieran introduced his father, then Victor excused himself. The two men faced off in the foyer.

"Why are you here?" Kieran asked bluntly, in no mood to play the welcoming host.

A lazy smile lifted the corners of a mouth that had kissed a variety of big name actresses. "Olivia called me after the fire. I'm to escort her home."

"The hell you say." Fury ignited deep in Kieran's belly. Caveman instincts kicked in. No one was leaving this house without his consent.

Olivia descended the stairs at that moment, wearing dark jeans and an emerald-green tank top. Her feet were bare. The smile she sent Jeremy's way was sweet, uncomplicated. Kieran had never received such a smile from her, and that pissed him off.

God, she was beautiful. Already it seemed like years since he had made love to her. He wanted to scoop her up and kiss her senseless. Or maybe kiss some sense into her.

He glared. "You never said anything about Vargas coming."

Her gaze was cool. "I wasn't sure how quickly he could get here. I didn't really expect him until tomorrow."

Jeremy stood in silence, allowing the two of them to duel with words and unspoken innuendo.

"I thought we agreed that you weren't leaving…not until your mother's stalker is in custody."

"Cammie will stay here. The two of you will have the

time you asked for to get to know each other better. I'll be able to deal with all the details about the fire and not have to worry about her."

Kieran ground his teeth. "May I speak with you in private?"

She shook her head. "We've said enough, I think. Once I've had some time to figure out my plans about what to do next, we can talk about custody arrangements."

She was shutting him out. Drawing a line in the sand. To hell with that. If she thought Kieran would agree to let her run the show, she was in for a big surprise.

"And when are you planning to leave?" He folded his arms across his chest.

"In the morning when I'm sure Cammie is okay." She turned to Jeremy. "I'll go check with Kieran's father and see if it's okay for you to spend the night. Thanks for coming, Jeremy."

In the wake of her departure, the silence lengthened. Jeremy stood, hands in his pockets, with an enigmatic smile on his handsome face.

Kieran wanted to punch him hard enough to rearrange those perfect features. He stared at the unwelcome intruder. "What's the deal with you and Olivia?"

Jeremy shrugged. "No comment."

"I don't like you, Vargas. Not one damn bit."

The smile deepened.

"You're in love with her."

Jeremy shrugged. "I *love* her. And I've known her long enough to realize you were the one who screwed over her life. I don't plan to let you do it again."

"Sanctimonious bastard." Kieran simmered, his fists itching for a brawl. But it had been years since he and his brothers had settled their differences with a fight. And

Victor would frown on bloodshed in his foyer. "You have no say in what goes on between Olivia and me."

"We'll see. But I'll be keeping an eye on you, Wolff. So watch your step."

The next morning, Olivia hugged Cammie so tightly the child finally wiggled free with a protest. Olivia brushed her daughter's wispy bangs with a fingertip. "You're sure you want to stay? You don't have to."

Cammie made a face. "I'll miss you, Mommy. Tell Lolo and Jojo I love them." Before Olivia could snag another kiss, Cammie was gone, running off to play with Gareth's dog.

Kieran stared at her, face impassive. She'd heard him knock on her door last night. But she had locked it. She was pretty sure he was going to propose marriage again, and that would have shattered her brittle heart. Everything was out in the open now. Cammie was Kieran's daughter…a Wolff who had been welcomed into the pack with open arms. His family loved her and had a lot of years to make up for.

This would be the longest time Olivia had ever been separated from her daughter. Leaving her this way was agony. But not even for Cammie's sake could Olivia linger. If Kieran continued to press for marriage as a practical solution, she might eventually cave to his persuasions. And that would be disastrous.

Olivia couldn't bear to play the dutiful wife, tucked away on Wolff Mountain like Rapunzel in her tower, waiting for her prince to come home. Not without love.

She handed her carry-on to Jeremy who was loading their belongings into his rental car. Turning back one last time, she went up on tiptoe and kissed Kieran's cheek. "Goodbye," she said quietly. "Look after our girl. I'll be in touch."

As Jeremy headed the car down the mountain, tears

trickled down Olivia's cheeks. He handed her a tissue. "Why don't you put him out of his misery? You love him."

"He doesn't love me. He's attracted to me, and he loves the fact that we share a daughter, but I can't live with that."

"So it's better to live without him?"

"Infinitely. I did it for five years and it wasn't so bad."

"But now you've been in his bed. You've shared things with him you've never shared with anyone else."

"How do you know?"

"Because I know *you,*" he said simply, shooting her a sideways glance. "You've had maybe ten dates in the last five years, and a couple of those were premieres with me, which doesn't really count."

"It's hard being a single mom. A lot of men aren't interested in raising another man's child."

"That's not it. Most guys I know would fall all over themselves to be with you, even if you had a dozen rug rats. You're smart and funny and sweet and flat-out gorgeous."

She sniffled, wiping her nose and sighing loudly. "You're good for my ego, sweet Jeremy."

He waited for the massive front gate to slide open before steering the car through and aiming for the airport. "I call 'em as I see 'em, and I think you should decide what or who you want, and then fight for your future."

"That's funny. Victor Wolff gave me a variation of the same advice."

"Maybe you should take your head out of the sand and listen."

Olivia spent three weeks in California. The first seven days were filled with meetings and planning and insurance questions. Not only that, but she had to finish up her illustrations and overnight them to her publisher, a task that made her feel lighter once it was done. Fortunately she always carried her originals with her in a sturdy folio. Much had been destroyed in the fire, but not her latest work.

Week two brought the arrest of Lolita's stalker, a sad, lonely man with definite mental issues. After that came the really difficult decisions, such as Olivia giving the go-ahead to raze the remnants of her property in order to sell the lot.

Jeremy stood with her the day the bulldozers came. He held her hand, and she cried as the last of her "normal" life was lifted and dumped into rubbish bins.

She stared at the destruction, remembering Cammie's first Christmas…the marks on the kitchen wall that measured her height. The big, fuzzy leopard-print throw that they snuggled beneath together to watch cartoons on Saturday mornings.

"All I ever wanted was to have a regular family."

Jeremy's childhood and adolescence were as tumultuous as hers. He understood exactly what her dreams were and why. Which made the shock all the bigger when he turned on her.

"Quit being such a drama queen," he said, squeezing her shoulders. "Unless you're willing to admit you're more like your mother than you realize. You lost your house, and yeah, that's a bitch. But look what you've gained. A daddy for Cammie. Relatives who love you. And a new home if you're willing to think outside the box."

"Except for my time in school, I've never lived anywhere but California."

"Me, either. But it turns out, I love New York City. And I think you love Wolff Mountain. You've damn sure talked about it nonstop for the last two and a half weeks."

"What about my parents?"

"Your folks are a hell of a long way from needing a nursing home. They have their own life with all its crazy excitement. And we have these things called jets now that fly cross-country. Don't you think it's time for you to have everything you want?"

"I'm scared, Jeremy. He hurt me so badly the last time."

"You were a kid. Now you're a grown woman. And besides, he knows I'll kick his ass if he's mean to you."

They both laughed, arm in arm, feeling the warmth of a southern California sun. It was a long way to the Blue Ridge Mountains of Virginia.

Turning her back on what was but would never be again, Olivia walked back across the street, Jeremy at her side. As they paused, looking at each other over the top of the car, she grinned at him. "We've got to find you a nice woman, Jeremy Vargas."

He chuckled, sliding into the car and turning the ignition. "I like being single," he said. "Let's concentrate on you for now."

Seventeen

Olivia's return to Wolff Mountain was anticlimactic. The big house was virtually empty save for the staff who went about their work so unobtrusively that it seemed as if phantoms ran the place. The head housekeeper welcomed Olivia politely and was able to explain the whereabouts of almost everyone.

Annalise and Victor had taken Cammie to Charlottesville to buy her new clothes for school. Jacob was working in his lab. Gareth and Gracie were repainting a room at their house.

Only Kieran's activities were a mystery. Supposedly he was still on the mountain, but no one had seen him since breakfast.

Olivia freshened up in her suite and changed into casual clothes, glad to be alone for the moment. Her composure was in shreds. She had returned to Wolff Mountain for a brief visit because she missed her daughter terribly, and because she and Kieran needed to talk about custody arrangements. Cammie had been told her mother would stay a week. Olivia was not sure she could hold out that long. Returning to the mountain gave new life to her regrets.

She had pondered Jeremy's advice about fighting for what she wanted. And if she had believed it was possible to win, she would have. But she was a realist. The situation was beyond compromise. She and Kieran were too different. End of story.

All she needed now was closure. It would help if Kieran would go ahead and fly away. Then maybe her heart could finally accept that the two of them were never meant to be.

Olivia grimaced at the state of Cammie's room. Apparently without her mother around, she had forgotten every one of Olivia's lectures about keeping her toys and things tidy.

The housekeeper hovered in the doorway, bringing an armload of fresh towels. "Sorry about the mess, ma'am. But Mr. Kieran said that if I cleaned up after the little one, she'd never learn responsibility."

Surprised and impressed, Olivia nodded. "He's right. I'll have a chat with her at bedtime tonight."

"She's still a baby."

"Yes. But not too young to learn how to be neater."

The older woman smiled and excused herself, leaving Olivia to wander the halls, familiarizing herself once again with the sights and sounds and smells of the "castle." Kieran and his brothers called it that when they wanted to tease their father, but the description wasn't far off.

At last, she gave up on finding anyone to talk to and decided to take a walk. When Cammie came back, there would be little time for quiet reflection. It was a perfect summer afternoon, the moist air heavy with expectation. A day for dreaming…a day when time seemed to stand still.

Passing the turn to Gareth's house, Olivia wandered on, across the back of the property and deeper into the woods where the forest was cool and shady and the wind whispered secrets.

She needed to talk to Kieran about their future as a blended family. And it should be done in private. Which likely meant she'd have to wait until after dinner. Contact between the two of them had been virtually nonexistent since she left. Cammie got on the phone most evenings and Annalise always chatted when Olivia called. But Kieran was mysteriously unavailable whenever Olivia asked about him.

She had no clue as to his state of mind. And no idea what he expected of her.

Thinking about the intimacies they had shared made her face flame, even though she was alone. For three weeks she'd had trouble sleeping, tormented by memories of Kieran's lovemaking. In his arms, she'd felt complete…content.

As if she had conjured him out of thin air, he appeared suddenly, pushing aside a low-hanging branch of maple, ducking beneath it and stopping a few feet away. Hungrily she looked her fill. His shoulders were still as broad, his dark eyes as wary and unreadable as ever. Ripped, faded jeans covered the lower half of his body, but his torso was bare.

A faint sheen of sweat covered his chest.

He leaned against a tree, his indolent pose at odds with the intensity of his gaze. "You're back."

"Yes." She nodded, as if he might not have understood the word.

"Is Vargas with you?"

"Jeremy? No." Frowning, she wondered why he asked. "How are things with Cammie?"

His expression softened, making him look younger, happier. "She's great. We've been fishing, hiking… I taught her how to play checkers."

"Sounds fun."

"You've done a great job with her, Olivia. You should be proud."

His praise made her uncomfortable. "Thank you."

Straightening, he rubbed the back of his arm across his forehead. "I could use a drink. You ready to go back to the house?"

He held out a hand, but she couldn't bring herself to touch him, afraid that she might resort to begging. It was not a pose she wanted to assume.

Kieran's face darkened when she pretended not to notice his gesture. In silence, they made their way back.

He made a beeline for the kitchen, where a pitcher of fresh-squeezed lemonade sat ready on the granite countertop, the sides of the glass container glistening with moisture.

As she watched, he poured two glasses, handing one to her. Their fingers brushed. A spark of electricity arced between them. Over the rim of his tumbler, his gaze tracked every move she made as she drank.

"I want to show you something," he said abruptly, draining his glass and putting hers in the sink, as well.

Puzzled, she followed him up the stairs all the way to the attic. One corner of the massive room had been partitioned off and a door added. Kieran ushered her inside.

She stopped, her progress halted by awe and amazement. A second enormous skylight had been cut into the roof, permitting rays of pure, brilliant sunlight to shine down on what appeared to be every art supply known to man. Brushes, canvases and easels. A top-of-the-line desk. Towels and turpentine. Palettes and paint.

Turning in a slow circle to take it all in, she said, "What is all this?"

He paced, not looking at her as he spoke. "A studio for you to use…when you're here."

Torn between confusion and despair, she touched him on the shoulder, halting his restless motion. "I don't understand."

They were so close she could see the muscles in his throat work as he swallowed. "I was hoping this could be your new home. Permanently."

Desperately she searched his face for clarification. "That's very kind of you, but I wouldn't want to impose on your family." And she needed distance to survive.

He brushed her cheek with the back of his hand. "Then marry me," he muttered. "And you'll *be* family."

Wincing, she pulled away, backing clumsily into a ladder-back chair that held an artist smock. "We've been through this," she said. "You're Cammie's father now. I've brought papers that give you shared custody. Fifty-fifty. Even if all three of us occasionally share the same roof, it isn't necessary for you and me to be married."

"It's necessary to me," he said quietly.

"I'll bring Cammie often. Every time you come home. You needn't worry that I'll try to keep her from you."

"Olivia," he said abruptly, running both hands through his hair. "For God's sake. You're not listening. I *love* you."

She bit her lip. "You want me," she corrected, not willing to be duped by her own wistful heart.

"Of course I want you. More than my next breath. These last few weeks have been hell. All I can think about is stripping you bare and sinking into you until we both die from pleasure. So yes, I do want you. But what I said was that I *love* you. Till death do us part. For eternity. Am I making myself clear?"

"You're shouting," she said, her teeth chattering with nerves. She wanted so badly for this scene they were playing out to be real, but caution held her back.

Cords stood out on his neck as he squeezed his eyes shut and pinched the bridge of his nose. "You weren't this much trouble at twenty-two."

"And you weren't Kieran Wolff. So I guess we're even." She picked up a small paintbrush and tested the sable bristles on the palm of her hand. "I'm not sure it would work."

"What?" he asked, confusion replacing annoyance.

"A long-distance relationship. Seeing each other only once or twice a year. Annalise told me your pattern. Father's Day, and sometimes Christmas. That's not much for Cammie and me to hang our hats on."

The string of curses he muttered beneath his breath was extraordinary for its variety and complexity. She was pretty sure the imprecations covered five or six languages.

He grabbed her by the shoulders and smashed his mouth to hers in a kiss that was not at all elegant, but that made her knees wobble. She tasted his desperation, her own dawning hope. Wrapping her arms around his neck, she moaned when his fingers plucked roughly at her tight nipples through the thin fabric of her blouse.

She wanted him so badly, she felt faint from need, weak with hunger.

Kieran came up for air at last, his chest heaving. She was pretty sure her fingernails had left scratch marks on his back. He stared down at her, telling her with his eyes the wild and wonderful truth. "I'm not going anywhere," he said.

"Today?" She tried to move back into her safety zone, but he had his hands at her hips, immobilizing her for the moment.

"Ever," he said flatly. "Do you believe me?"

"But what about your job?"

"I'll get someone to sub for me in September. Everything else can be passed off to other architects and engineers."

"What will you do?" This sudden about-face was mind-boggling.

He slid his hands up her waist until they landed beneath her breasts. Weighing each one with a gentle lift, he bent to kiss her again, this time with agonizing gentleness. "First of all," he said, his words slurred as he moved his mouth over the skin of her throat. "I'll build our house…and a swing set…and a corral for the pony…and—"

She put her hands over his lips. "You're serious?" It didn't seem possible. "You think you can give it up cold turkey? No more jetting round the globe? No more frequent flier miles? No more mosquito nets and hard hats?"

He bit her finger, enough to sting. "I have no reason to leave," he said simply. "Everything I want and need is here if you'll stay with me."

Tears stung her eyes. "Don't say it if you don't mean it," she begged. "I couldn't bear it if you changed your mind."

"God, Olivia. I know I kicked the shit out of your ability to trust me, but you have to believe me. If you give me another chance…if you'll make a family with me, you'll never regret it. I'm going to spend the rest of my life making you scream my name, night after night. It will be so loud, the neighbors will complain."

She laughed and hiccupped a sob at the same time. "There are no neighbors," she pointed out, caught by the image of Kieran making her cry out as she climaxed.

He scooped her up in his arms and crossed the room. "Did you notice I had the interior design team include a settee? All great artists have settees."

"Is that so people can pose for me?" She lifted her arms obediently as he undressed her with more urgency than care.

"It's so I can screw you," he panted, now working on his own clothing. His gaze was fixated on her chest. "Lie down."

She didn't have to be told twice. It was either that or melt into a puddle on the floor.

He came down between her legs, shifting her left foot to prop it on the back of their makeshift nest. His thumbs traced the folds of her sex, gathering moisture and spreading it on the head of his erection. The shaft was long and hard and throbbing with eagerness.

Kieran groaned, closing his eyes. "I love you, Olivia." Positioning himself at the mother lode, he plunged deep, wringing a cry from her and filling her so completely, she forgot to breathe. He stilled for a moment, allowing both of them to absorb the shattering pleasure.

Inside her, he flexed. She gripped handfuls of his hair as he bent to taste her breasts, one after the other, licking and suckling them until she sensed her first orgasm in the wings.

His hands moved, sliding under her bottom to lift her into his thrusts. She clung to him, dizzy and panting. "Kieran..." She didn't know what she wanted to say, what she needed him to hear.

"I'm here, honey. Always."

The vow... and the swivel of his hips that ground the base of his erection against her sweet spot sent her over the edge. The climax lasted forever, raking her body with shivers of sensation that rode the edge of pain and ecstasy.

Before she had fully recovered, he went rigid, his back arched in a rictus of release that lasted for long, shuddering seconds.

Minutes later, maybe hours, she recovered the ability to speak. "I love this settee," she muttered, licking a drop of sweat from her upper lip. The sun warmed them like a benediction. Kieran's weight was a delicious burden, his shaft still pulsing with aftershocks.

"Hell," he said, his body shaking with laughter. "I didn't wear a condom. I swear, woman. Around you I take leave of my senses."

She stroked his hair, staring up at a sky so blue it seemed to go on forever. Peace, utter and infinite, filled her heart, her mind, her soul. "I'd like to be pregnant again," she whispered, daring to dream of home and hearth with the man she loved.

Wolff Mountain was a wonderful place to grow up. And now that she'd experienced the fear generated by violence and danger, she decided that being tucked away from the world wasn't altogether a bad thing.

Kieran sat up, rubbing his eyes. "I haven't slept at all since you left. This wedding has to be soon. I want you in my bed. Every night."

"I want that, too." She bent down to rescue her bra and blouse. "Annalise strikes me as someone who would love to plan just such an occasion."

"We can set up a large tent…to keep the paparazzi at bay. Unless, of course, your parents don't mind being photographed."

She laughed. "You never know with them. My mother does love keeping count of how many times her face appears on the tabloids. She thinks they're sleazy gossip rags, but she hates being left out."

They managed to dress, but it was a slow process. Kieran kept interrupting her to nibble her rib cage, caress her bottom, bite her earlobe. Finally, completely clothed except for her shoes, she looked at him. "Do you think anyone is home yet?"

He zipped his fly. "Who knows? Why do you ask?"

She cupped him boldly, her fingers squeezing softly as

she found his sex tucked in the front of his jeans. "I'm still not sure I'm not dreaming. Maybe you could take another shot at convincing me."

By the time they ultimately made their way back downstairs, they were eager to share their news. Kieran used his cell phone to convene an audience for afternoon tea, and soon, in the large, formal living room, the entire clan was gathered, including Annalise's brothers and father.

Cammie spotted her mother and ran across the room, throwing herself into Olivia's arms. "You're back. You're back."

Olivia hugged her, feeling uneasy at being the cynosure of all eyes. "I surely am. Have you been a good girl while I was gone?"

"Yes, ma'am."

Victor stood up, his weathered face beaming. "I think some introductions are in order…and perhaps a formal announcement?" He looked inquiringly at his youngest son.

Kieran moved closer, putting his arms around Cammie and Olivia. "Six years ago, Olivia and I met each other at Oxford. But as you all know, we Wolffs attended college under false names. When I left suddenly to come home in the aftermath of Dad's heart attack, Olivia and I lost touch. But she had my baby."

Olivia wondered if she was the only one who noticed the crack in his voice.

He continued, scanning the room, his gaze landing one by one on the faces of the people who had shared tragedy with him in the past. "My traveling days are over," he said quietly. "Olivia has agreed to marry me. My next design project will be our new house here on Wolff Mountain."

The whoops and hollers that erupted rattled the rafters. Cammie and Olivia and Kieran were engulfed in a barrage of hugs and kisses and congratulations. Olivia enjoyed every moment of it. The Wolffs were not a normal family, but they were *her* family…from now on.

She managed to get their attention, and the room quieted. "Thank you all for welcoming me and for being so sweet to Cammie. This will be pretty close to a shotgun wedding as far as the time frame goes, but if Annalise is willing, I'm going to let her handle all the details."

Gracie piped up, eyes dancing. "I'll help, too. It's about time we had some girly stuff going on up on this mountain."

Everyone laughed.

Victor held out a hand, cradling a champagne flute as two young women passed around matching glasses to the crowd. Cammie's was filled with orange juice.

When everyone was served, Victor cleared his throat to quiet the rambunctious assemblage. "To Kieran…and his bride-to-be and daughter. May you always be as happy as you are today."

Glasses were raised and emptied. Kieran leaned down to kiss Cammie and then Olivia. "To my girls," he said softly. "I love you both."

Hours later, when the clock was about to strike midnight, Kieran and Olivia stood beside their daughter's bed. Olivia held his hand, her head on his shoulder. "You missed so much," she said. "I'll never be able to give that back to you."

He was quiet for long moments, his chest barely moving as he breathed. "We all walk our own road, Olivia. Yours and mine diverged at the worst possible time, but we won't ever have to worry about that again. Side by side. Day by day. We're marking a new path that will be ours alone."

"And you *do* want more children?"

He turned to face her. "Give me a dozen," he said, teeth

flashing white in the semidarkness. "We've got room to grow on this mountain. God willing, there will be plenty of cousins, too."

She went up on tiptoe and kissed him. "I knew the first day I saw you that you were the man I wanted to marry."

He scooped her into his arms, carrying her to the adjoining bedroom where half a dozen candles were lit. As he laid her on the bed, coming down beside her, he grimaced. "If I had handled things better back then, we wouldn't have wasted so much time."

She caressed his face, cupping his cheeks, rubbing her thumbs across his bottom lip. "I tried to convince myself that what we had was a fling, a college romance. But deep in my heart, I've always known you were the one. Which made it pretty difficult to go out with other guys."

"I don't want to hear about the other guys," he muttered. "Not now, anyway." He slid a hand along her thigh from her ankle to the place that readied itself for him with damp heat.

She stopped him, trapping his fingers by placing hers on top. "There were none," she said simply. "Only you."

Silence throbbed. His eyes widened, and something that was a combination of astonishment, relief, joy and humble gratitude flashed in their depths. "You're mine, Olivia. I'm yours."

As Kieran positioned himself for a thrust that would take him home, he heard a faint voice…words that faded as the one who spoke them moved into another realm. *I love you, my son. Be happy....*

Unexpected tears stung the backs of his eyes as he filled Olivia's tight passage with a surge of longing and the length of his passion.

He *was* home…and he was happy.

* * * * *

TERMS OF ENGAGEMENT

BY
ANN MAJOR

Ann Major lives in Texas with her husband of many years and is the mother of three grown children. She has a master's degree from Texas A&M at Kingsville, Texas, and is a former English teacher. She is a founding board member of the Romance Writers of America and a frequent speaker at writers' groups.

Ann loves to write—she considers her ability to do so a gift. Her hobbies include hiking in the mountains, sailing, ocean kayaking, traveling and playing the piano. But most of all, she enjoys her family. Visit her website at www.annmajor.com.

To Ted, with all my love.
And as always I must thank my editor, Stacy Boyd,
and Shana Smith, along with the entire Desire team
for their talented expertise.
I thank as well my agent, Karen Solem.

One

No good deed goes unpunished.

When would she ever learn? Kira wondered.

With her luck, never.

So, here she sat, in the office of oil billionaire Quinn Sullivan, too nervous to concentrate on her magazine as she waited to see if he would make time for a woman he probably thought of as just another adversary to be crushed in his quest for revenge.

Dreadful, arrogant man.

If he did grant her an audience, would she have any chance of changing his mind about destroying her family's company, Murray Oil, and forcing her sister Jaycee into marriage?

A man vengeful enough to hold a grudge against her father for twenty years couldn't possibly have a heart that could be swayed.

Kira Murray clenched and unclenched her hands. Then

she sat on them, twisting in her chair. When the man across from her began to stare, she told herself to quit squirming. Lowering her eyes to her magazine, she pretended to read a very boring article on supertankers.

High heels clicked rapidly on marble, causing Kira to look up in panic.

"Miss Murray, I'm so sorry. I was wrong. Mr. Sullivan *is* still here." There was surprise in his secretary's classy, soothing purr.

"In fact, he'll see you now."

"He will?" Kira squeaked. *"Now?"*

The secretary's answering smile was a brilliant white.

Kira's own mouth felt as dry as sandpaper. She actually began to shake. To hide this dreadful reaction, she jumped to her feet so fast she sent the glossy magazine to the floor, causing the man across from her to glare in annoyance.

Obviously, she'd been hoping Quinn would refuse to see her. A ridiculous wish when she'd come here for the express purpose of finally meeting him properly and having her say.

Sure, she'd run into him once, informally. It had been right after he'd announced he wanted to marry one of the Murray daughters to make his takeover of Murray Oil less hostile. Her father had suggested Jaycee, and Kira couldn't help but think he'd done so because Jaycee was his favorite and most biddable daughter. As always, Jaycee had dutifully agreed with their father's wishes, so Quinn had come to the ranch for a celebratory dinner to seal the bargain.

He'd been late. A man as rich and arrogant as he was probably thought himself entitled to run on his own schedule.

Wounded by her mother's less-than-kind assessment of her outfit when she'd first arrived—"Jeans and a torn shirt? How could you think that appropriate for meeting a man so important to this family's welfare?"—Kira had stormed out of the house. She hadn't had time to change after the crisis at her best friend's restaurant, where Kira was temporarily waiting tables while looking for a museum curator position. Since her mother always turned a deaf ear to Kira's excuses, rather than explain, Kira had decided to walk her dad's hunting spaniels while she nursed her injured feelings.

The brilliant, red sun that had been sinking fast had been in her eyes as the spaniels leaped onto the gravel driveway, dragging her in their wake. Blinded, she'd neither seen nor heard Quinn's low-slung, silver Aston Martin screaming around the curve. Slamming on his brakes, he'd veered clear of her with several feet to spare. She'd tripped over the dogs and fallen into a mud puddle.

Yipping wildly, the dogs had raced back to the house, leaving her to face Quinn on her own with cold, dirty water dripping from her chin.

Quinn had gotten out of his fancy car and stomped over in his fancy Italian loafers just as she got to her feet. For a long moment, he'd inspected every inch of her. Then, mindless of her smudged face, chattering teeth and muddy clothes, he'd pulled her against his tall, hard body, making her much too aware of his clean, male smell and hard, muscular body.

"Tell me you're okay."

He was tall and broad-shouldered, so tall he'd towered over her. His angry blue eyes had burned her; his viselike fingers had cut into her elbow. Despite his overcharged emotions, she'd liked being in his arms—liked it too much.

"Damn it, I didn't hit you, did I? Well, say something, why don't you?"

"How can I—with you yelling at me?"

"Are you okay, then?" he asked, his grip loosening, his

voice softening into a husky sound so unexpectedly beautiful she'd shivered. This time, she saw concern in his hard expression.

Had it happened then?

Oh, be honest, Kira, at least with yourself. That was the moment you formed an inappropriate crush on your sister's future fiancé, a man whose main goal in life is to destroy your family.

He'd been wearing faded jeans, a white shirt, his sleeves rolled up to his elbows. On her, jeans looked rumpled, but on him, jeans had made him ruggedly, devastatingly handsome. Over one arm, he carried a cashmere jacket.

She noted his jet-black hair and carved cheekbones with approval. Any woman would have. His skin had been darkly bronzed, and the dangerous aura of sensuality surrounding him had her sizzling.

Shaken by her fall and by the fact that *the enemy* was such an attractive, powerful man who continued to hold her close and stare down at her with blazing eyes, her breath had come in fits and starts.

"I said—*are you okay?*"

"I was fine—until you grabbed me." Her hesitant voice was tremulous…and sounded strangely shy. "You're hurting me, really hurting me!" She'd lied so he would let her go, and yet part of her hadn't wanted to be released.

His eyes narrowed suspiciously. "Sorry," he'd said, his tone harsh again.

"Who the hell are you anyway?" he'd demanded.

"Nobody important," she'd muttered.

His dark brows winged upward. "Wait…I've seen your pictures… You're the older sister. The waitress."

"Only temporarily…until I get a new job as a curator."

"Right. You were fired."

"So, you've heard Father's version. The truth is, my professional opinion wasn't as important to the museum director as I might have liked, but I was let go due to budget constraints."

"Your sister speaks highly of you."

"Sometimes I think she's the only one in this family who does."

Nodding as if he understood, he draped his jacket around her shoulders. "I've wanted to meet you." When she glanced up at him, he said, "You're shivering. The least I can do is offer you my jacket and a ride back to the house."

Her heart pounded much too fast, and she was mortified that she was covered with mud and that she found her family's enemy exciting and the prospect of wearing his jacket a thrill. Not trusting herself to spend another second with such a dangerous man, especially in the close quarters of his glamorous car, she'd shaken her head. "I'm too muddy."

"Do you think I give a damn about that? I could have killed you."

"You didn't. So let's just forget about it."

"Not possible! Now, put my jacket on before you catch your death."

Pulling his jacket around her shoulders, she turned on her heel and left him. Nothing had happened, she'd told herself as she stalked rapidly through the woods toward the house.

Nothing except the enemy she'd feared had held her and made her feel dangerously alive in a way no other man ever had.

When she'd reached the house, she'd been surprised to find him outside waiting for her as he held on to her yapping dogs. Feeling tingly and shyly thrilled as he handed her their tangled leashes, she'd used her muddy clothes again as an excuse to go home and avoid dinner, when her father would formally announce Quinn was to marry her sister.

Yes, he was set on revenge against those she loved most, but that hadn't been the reason she couldn't sit across the table from him. No, it was her crush. How could she have endured such a dinner when just to look at him made her skin heat?

For weeks after that chance meeting, her inappropriate attachment to Quinn had continued to claim her, causing her much guilt-ridden pain. She'd thought of him constantly. And more than once, before she'd returned his jacket to Jaycee, she'd worn it around her apartment, draped over her shoulders, just because his scent lingered on the soft fabric.

Now, retrieving the magazine she'd dropped, she set it carefully on the side table. Then she sucked in a deep breath. Not that it steadied her nerves.

No. Instead, her heart raced when Quinn Sullivan's secretary turned away, saying, "Follow me."

Kira swallowed. She'd put this interview off to the last possible moment—to the end of the business day—because she'd been trying to formulate a plan to confront a man as powerful and dictatorial and, yes, as dangerously sexy, as Quinn Sullivan.

But she hadn't come up with a plan. Did she ever have a plan? She'd be at a disadvantage since Sullivan planned everything down to the last detail, including taking his revenge plot up a notch by marrying Jaycee.

Kira had to sprint to keep up with the sleek, blonde secretary, whose ridiculous, four-inch, ice-pick, gold heels clicked on the polished gray marble. Did *he* make the poor girl wear such gaudy, crippling footwear?

Quinn's waiting room with its butter-soft leather couches and polished wainscoting had reeked of old money. In truth, he was nothing but a brash, bad-tempered upstart. His long hallway, decorated with paintings of vivid minimalistic splashes of color, led to what would probably prove to be an obscenely opulent office. Still, despite her wish to dislike everything about him, she admired the art and wished she could stop and study several of the pictures. They were elegant, tasteful and interesting. Had he selected them himself?

Probably not. He was an arrogant show-off.

After their one encounter, she'd researched him. It seemed he believed her father had profited excessively when he'd bought Quinn's father out of their mutually owned company. In addition, he blamed her father for his father's suicide—if suicide it had been.

Quinn, who'd known hardship after his father's death, was determined to make up for his early privations, by living rich and large. Craving glamour and the spotlight, he never attended a party without a beauty even more dazzling than his secretary on his arm.

He was a respected art collector. In various interviews he'd made it clear nobody would ever look down on him again. Not in business; not in his personal life. He was king of his kingdom.

From the internet, she'd gleaned that Quinn's bedroom had a revolving door. Apparently, a few nights' pleasuring the same woman were more than enough for him. Just when a woman might believe she meant something to him, he'd drop her and date another gorgeous blonde, who was invariably more beautiful than the one he'd jilted. There had been one woman, also blonde, who'd jilted him a year or so ago, a Cristina somebody. Not that she hadn't been quickly forgotten by the press when he'd resumed chasing more beauties as carelessly as before.

From what Kira had seen, his life was about winning,

not about caring deeply. For that purpose only, he'd surrounded himself with the mansions, the cars, the yachts, the art collections and the fair-haired beauties. She had no illusions about what his marriage to Jaycee would be like. He had no intention of being a faithful husband to Kira's beautiful, blonde sister.

Rich, handsome womanizer that he was, Kira might have pitied him for being cursed with such a dark heart—if only her precious Jaycee wasn't central in his revenge scheme.

Kira was not gifted at planning or at being confrontational, which were two big reasons why she wasn't getting ahead in her career. And Quinn was the last person on earth she wanted to confront. But the need to take care of Jaycee, as she had done since her sister's birth, was paramount.

Naturally, Kira's first step had been to beg her father to change his mind about using her sister to smooth over a business deal, but her father had been adamant about the benefits of the marriage.

Kira didn't understand the financials of Quinn's hostile takeover of Murray Oil, but her father seemed to think Quinn would make a brilliant CEO. Her parents had said that if Jaycee didn't walk down the aisle with Quinn as agreed, Quinn's terms would become far more onerous. Not to mention that the employees would resent him as an outsider. Even though Quinn's father had been a co-owner, Quinn was viewed as a man with a personal vendetta against the Murrays and Murray Oil. Ever since his father's death, rumors about his hostility toward all things Murray had been widely circulated by the press. Only if he married Jaycee would the employees believe that peace between the two families had at last been achieved and that the company would be safe in his hands.

Hence, Kira was here, to face Quinn Sullivan.

She was determined to stop him from marrying Jaycee, but how? Pausing in panic even as his secretary rushed ahead, she reminded herself that she couldn't turn back, plan or not.

Quickening her pace, Kira caught up to the efficient young woman, who was probably moving so quickly because she was as scared of the unfeeling brute as Kira was.

When his secretary pushed open Quinn's door, the deep, rich tones of the man's surprisingly beautiful voice moved through Kira like music. Her knees lost strength, and she stopped in midstep.

Oh, no, it was happening again.

She'd known from meeting him the first time that he was charismatic, but she'd counted on her newly amassed knowledge of his despicable character to protect her. His edgy baritone slid across her nerve endings, causing warm tingles in her secret, feminine places, and she knew she was as vulnerable to him as before.

Fighting not to notice that her nipples ached and that her pulse had sped up, she took a deep breath before daring a glance at the black-headed rogue. Looking very much at ease, he sat sprawled at his desk, the back of his linebacker shoulders to her as he leaned against his chair, a telephone jammed to his ear.

She couldn't, wouldn't, be attracted to this man.

On his desk she noted a silver-framed photograph of his father. With their intense blue eyes, black hair and strongly chiseled, tanned features, father and son closely resembled each other. Both, she knew, had been college athletes. Did Quinn keep the photo so close out of love or to energize him in his quest for revenge?

"I told you to buy, Habib," he ordered brusquely in that

too-beautiful voice. "What's there to talk about? Do it." He ended the call.

At least he was every bit as rude as she remembered. Deep baritone or not, it should be easy to hate him.

His secretary coughed to let him know they were at the door.

Quinn whirled around in his massive, black leather chair, scowling, but went still the instant he saw Kira.

He lifted that hard, carved chin, which surprisingly enough had the most darling dimple, and, just like that, dismissed his secretary.

His piercing, laser-blue gaze slammed into Kira full force and heated her through—just like before.

Black hair. Bronze skin. Fierce, brilliant eyes… With a single glance the man bewitched her.

When his mouth lifted at the edges, her world shifted as it had that first evening—and he hadn't even touched her.

He was as outrageously handsome as ever. Every bit as dark, tall, lean and hard, as cynical and untamed—even in his orderly office with his efficient secretary standing guard.

Still, for an instant, Kira thought she saw turbulent grief and longing mix with unexpected pleasure at the sight of her.

He remembered her.

But in a flash the light went out of his eyes, and his handsome features tightened into those of the tough, heartless man he wanted people to see.

In spite of his attempt at distance, a chord of recognition had been struck. It was as if they'd seen into each other's souls, had sensed each other's secret yearnings.

She wanted her family, who deemed her difficult and frustrating, to love and accept her for herself, as they did her sister.

He had longings that revenge and outward success had failed to satisfy. What were they? What was lacking in his disciplined, showy, materialistic life?

Was he as drawn to her as she was to him?

Impossible.

So how could he be the only man who'd ever made her feel less alone in the universe?

Hating him even more because he'd exposed needs she preferred to conceal, she tensed. He had no right to open her heart and arouse such longings.

Frowning, he cocked his dark head and studied her. "I owe you an apology for the last time we met," he drawled in that slow, mocking baritone that turned her insides to mush. "I was nervous about the takeover and the engagement and about making a good impression on you and your family. I was too harsh with you. A few inches more…and I could have killed you. I was afraid, and that made me angry."

"You owe me nothing," she said coolly.

"I don't blame you in the least for avoiding me all these weeks. I probably scared the hell out of you."

"I haven't been avoiding you. Not really," she murmured, but a telltale flush heated her neck as she thought of the family dinners she'd opted out of because she'd known he'd be there.

If only she could run now, escape him. But Jaycee needed her, so instead, she hedged. "I've been busy."

"Waitressing?"

"Yes! I'm helping out Betty, my best friend, while I interview for museum jobs. Opening a restaurant on the San Antonio River Walk was a lifetime dream of hers. She got busier faster than she expected, and she offered me a job. Since I waited tables one summer between college semesters, I've got some experience."

He smiled. "I like it that you're helping your friend

realize her dream even though your career is stalled. That's nice."

"We grew up together. Betty was our housekeeper's daughter. When we got older my mother kept hoping I'd outgrow the friendship while Daddy helped Betty get a scholarship."

"I like that you're generous and loyal." He hesitated. "Your pictures don't do you justice. Nor did my memory of you."

His blue eyes gleamed with so much appreciation her cheeks heated. "Maybe because the last time I saw you I was slathered in mud."

He smiled. "Still, being a waitress seems like a strange job for a museum curator, even if it's temporary. You did major in art history at Princeton and completed that internship at the Metropolitan Museum of Art. I believe you graduated with honors."

She had no idea how she'd done so well, but when her grades had thrilled her father, she'd worked even harder.

"Has Daddy, who by the way, has a bad habit of talking too much, told you my life history?"

For a long moment, Quinn didn't confirm her accusation or deny it.

"Well, is that where you learned these details?"

"If he talked about you, it was because I was curious and asked him."

Not good. She frowned as she imagined her parents complaining about her disappointments since Princeton during all those family dinners she'd avoided.

"Did my father tell you that I've had a hard time with a couple of museum directors because they micromanaged me?"

"Not exactly."

"I'll bet. He takes the boss's side because he's every bit

as high-handed and dictatorial. Unfortunately, one night after finishing the setup of a new show, when I was dead tired, the director started second-guessing my judgment about stuff he'd already signed off on. I made the mistake of telling him what I really thought. When there were budget cuts, you can probably guess who he let go."

"I'm sorry about that."

"I'm good at what I do. I'll find another job, but until I do, I don't see why I shouldn't help Betty. Unfortunately, my father disagrees. We frequently disagree."

"It's your life, not his."

Her thoughts exactly. Having him concur was really sort of annoying, since Quinn was supposed to be the enemy.

In the conversational lull, she noticed that his spectacular physique was elegantly clad in a dark gray suit cut to emphasize every hard sinew of his powerful body. Suddenly, she wished she'd dressed up. Then she caught herself. Why should she care about looking her best for a man she should hate, when her appearance was something she rarely thought about?

All she'd done today was scoop her long, dark hair into a ponytail that cascaded down her back. Still, when his eyes hungrily skimmed her figure, she was glad that she'd worn the loosely flowing white shirt and long red scarf over her tight jeans because the swirls of cloth hid her body.

His burning gaze, which had ignited way too many feminine hormones, rose to her face again. When he smiled as he continued to stare, she bit her bottom lip to keep from returning his smile.

Rising, he towered over her, making her feel small and feminine and lovely in ways she'd never felt lovely before. He moved toward her, seized her hand in his much larger one and shook it gently.

"I'm very glad you decided to give me a second chance."

Why did his blunt fingers have to feel so warm and hard, his touch and gaze so deliciously intimate? She snatched her hand away, causing his eyes to flash with that pain he didn't want her to see.

"That's not what this is."

"But you *were* avoiding me, weren't you?"

"I *was,*" she admitted and then instantly regretted being so truthful.

"That was a mistake—for both of us."

When he asked her if she wanted coffee or a soda or anything at all to drink, she said no and looked out the windows at the sun sinking low against the San Antonio skyline. She couldn't risk looking at him any more than necessary because her attraction seemed to be building. He would probably sense it and use it against her somehow.

With some difficulty she reminded herself that she disliked him. So, why did she still feel hot and clammy and slightly breathless, as if there were a lack of oxygen in the room?

It's called chemistry. Sexual attraction. It's irrational.

Her awareness only sharpened when he pulled out a chair for her and returned to his own. Sitting down and crossing one long leg over the other, he leaned back again. The pose should have seemed relaxed, but as he concentrated on her she could see he wasn't relaxed—he was intently assessing her.

The elegant office became eerily silent as he stared. Behind the closed doors, she felt trapped. Leaning forward, her posture grew as rigid as his was seemingly careless.

His hard, blue eyes held her motionless.

"So, to what do I owe the pleasure of your visit this afternoon…or should I say this evening?" he asked in that pleasant tone that made her tremble with excitement.

She imagined them on his megayacht, sailing silently across the vast, blue Gulf of Mexico. Her auburn hair would blow in the wind as he pulled her close and suggested they go below.

"You're my last appointment, so I can give you as much time as you want," he said, thankfully interrupting her seduction fantasy.

Her guilty heart sped up. Why had she come at such a late hour when he might not have another appointment afterward?

The sky was rapidly darkening, casting a shadow across his carved face, making him look stark and feral, adding to the danger she felt upon finding herself alone with him.

Even though her fear made her want to flee, she was far too determined to do what she had to do to give in to it.

She blurted out, "I don't want you to marry Jaycee." Oh, dear, she'd meant to lead up to this in some clever way.

He brought his blunt fingertips together in a position of prayer. When he leaned across his desk toward her, she sank lower in her own chair. "Don't you? How very strange."

"It's not strange. You can't marry her. You don't love her. You and she are too different to care for each other as a man and wife should."

His eyes darkened in a way that made him seem more alive than any man she'd ever known. "I wasn't referring to Jacinda. I was talking about you…and me and how strange that I should feel…so much—" He stopped. "When for all practical purposes we just met."

His eyes bored into hers with that piercing intensity that left her breathless. Once again she felt connected to him by some dark, forbidden, primal force.

"I never anticipated this wrinkle when I suggested a marriage with a Murray daughter," he murmured.

When his eyes slid over her body again in that devouring way, her heart raced. Her tall, slim figure wasn't appealing to most men. She'd come to believe there was nothing special about her. Could he possibly be as attracted to her as she was to him?

"You don't love her," she repeated even more shakily.

"Love? No. I don't love her. How could I? I barely know her."

"You see!"

"Your father chose her, and she agreed."

"Because she's always done everything he tells her to."

"You, however, would not have agreed so easily?" He paused. "Love does not matter to me in the least. But now I find myself curious about his choice of brides. And…even more curious about you. I want to get to know you better." His tone remained disturbingly intimate.

She remembered his revolving bedroom door and the parade of voluptuous blondes who'd passed through it. Was he so base he'd think it nothing to seduce his future wife's sister and then discard her, too?

"You've made no secret of how you feel about my father," she whispered with growing wariness. "Why marry his daughter?"

"Business. There are all these rumors in the press that I want to destroy Murray Oil, a company that once belonged to my beloved father."

"It makes perfect sense."

"No, it doesn't. I would never pay an immense amount of money for a valuable property in order to destroy it."

"But you think my father blackened your father's name and then profited after buying your father out. That's why you're so determined to destroy everything he's built, everything he loves…including Jaycee."

His lips thinned. Suddenly, his eyes were arctic. "My father built Murray Oil, not yours. Only back then it was called Sullivan and Murray Oil. Your father seized the opportunity, when my dad was down, to buy him out at five cents on the dollar."

"My father made the company what it is today."

"Well, now I'm going to take it over and improve upon it. Marriage to a Murray daughter will reassure the numerous employees that family, not a vengeful marauder, will be at the helm of the business."

"That would be a lie. You are a marauder, and you're not family."

"Not yet," he amended. "But a few Saturdays hence, if I marry Jaycee, we will be…family."

"Never. Not over my dead body!" She expelled the words in an outraged gasp.

"The thought of anything so awful happening to your delectable body is hateful to me." When he hesitated, his avid, searching expression made her warm again.

"Okay," he said. "Let's say I take you at your word. You're here to save your sister from me. And you'd die before you'd let me marry her. Is that right?"

"Essentially."

"What else would you do to stop me? Surely there is some lesser, more appealing sacrifice you'd be willing to make to inspire me to change my mind."

"I…don't know what you mean."

"Well, what if I were to agree to your proposal and forgo marriage to your lovely sister, a woman you say is so unsuited to my temperament I could never love her—I want to know what I will get in return."

"Do you always have to get something in return? You wouldn't actually be making a sacrifice."

His smile was a triumphant flash of white against his deeply tanned skin. "Always. Most decidedly. My hypothetical marriage to your sister is a business deal, after all. As a businessman, I would require compensation for letting the deal fall through."

Awful man.

His blue eyes stung her, causing the pulse in her throat to hammer frantically.

"Maybe…er…the satisfaction of doing a good deed for once in your life?" she said.

He laughed. "That's a refreshing idea if ever I heard one, and from a very charming woman—but, like most humans, I'm driven by the desire to avoid pain and pursue pleasure."

"And to think—I imagined you to be primarily driven by greed. Well, I don't have any money."

"I don't want your money."

"What do you want, then?"

"I think you know," he said silkily, leaning closer. "*You. You* interest me…quite a lot. I believe we could give each other immense pleasure…under the right circumstances."

The unavoidable heat in his eyes caused an unwanted shock wave of fiery prickles to spread through her body. She'd seriously underestimated the risk of confronting this man.

"In fact, I think we both knew what we wanted the moment we looked at each other today," he said.

He wanted her.

And even though he was promised to Jaycee, he didn't have a qualm about acknowledging his impossible, unsavory need for the skinnier, plainer, older sister. Maybe the thought of bedding his future wife's sister improved upon his original idea of revenge. Or maybe he was simply a man who never denied himself a female who might amuse him, however briefly. If any of those assumptions were true, he was too horrible for words.

"I'm hungry," he continued. "Why don't we discuss your proposition over dinner," he said.

"No. I couldn't possibly. You've said more than enough to convince me of the kind of man you are."

"Who are you kidding? You were prejudiced against me before you showed up here. If I'd played the saint, you would have still thought me the devil…and yet you would have also still…been secretly attracted. And you are attracted to me. Admit it."

Stunned at his boldness, she hissed out a breath. "I'm not."

Then why was she staring at his darling dimple as if she was hypnotized by it?

He laughed. "Do you have a boyfriend?" he asked. "Or dinner plans you need to change?"

"No," she admitted before she thought.

"Good." He smiled at her as if he was genuinely pleased. "Then it's settled."

"What?"

"You and I have a dinner date."

"No!"

"What are you afraid of?" he asked in that deep, velvet tone that let her know he had much more than dinner in mind. And some part of her, God help her, wanted to rush toward him like a moth toward flame, despite her sister, despite the knowledge that he wanted to destroy her family.

Kira was shaking her head vehemently when he said, "You came here today to talk to me, to convince me to do as you ask. I'm making myself available to you."

"But?"

He gave her a slow, insolent grin. "If you want to save your sister from the Big Bad Wolf, well—here's your chance."

Two

When they turned the corner and she saw the gaily lit restaurant, Kira wished with all her heart she'd never agreed to this dinner with Quinn.

Not that he hadn't behaved like a perfect gentleman as they'd walked over together.

When she'd said she wanted to go somewhere within walking distance of his office, she'd foolishly thought she'd be safer with him on foot.

"You're not afraid to get in my car, to be alone with me, are you?" he'd teased.

"It just seems simpler…to go somewhere close," she'd hedged. "Besides, you're a busy man."

"Not too busy for what really matters."

Then he'd suggested they walk along the river. The lovely reflections in the still, brown water where ducks swam and the companionable silences they'd shared as they'd made their way along the flagstones edged by lush vegetation, restaurants and bars had been altogether too enjoyable.

She'd never made a study of predators, but she had a cat, Rudy. When on the hunt, he was purposeful, diligent and very patient. He enjoyed playing with his prey before the kill, just to make the game last longer. She couldn't help but think Quinn was doing something similar with her.

No sooner did Quinn push open the door so she could enter one of the most popular Mexican restaurants in all of San Antonio than warmth, vibrant laughter and the heavy beat of Latin music hit her.

A man, who was hurrying outside after a woman, said, "Oh, excuse us, please, miss."

Quinn reached out and put his strong arm protectively around Kira's waist, shielding her with his powerful body. Pulling her close, he tugged her to one side to let the other couple pass.

When Quinn's body brushed against hers intimately, as if they were a couple, heat washed over her as it had the afternoon when she'd been muddy and he'd pulled her into his arms. She inhaled his clean, male scent. As before, he drew her like a sexual magnet.

When she let out an excited little gasp, he smiled and pulled her even closer. "You feel much too good," he whispered.

She should run, but the March evening was cooler than she'd dressed for, causing her to instinctively cling to his hot, big-boned body and stay nestled against his welcoming warmth.

She felt the red scarf she wore around her neck tighten as if to warn her away. She yanked at it and gulped in a breath before she shoved herself free of him.

He laughed. "You're not the only one who's been stunned by our connection, you know. I like holding you as much as you like being in my arms. In fact, that's all I want to do…hold you. Does that make me evil? Or all too human because I've found a woman I have no will to resist?"

"You are too much! Why did I let you talk me into this dinner?"

"Because it was the logical thing to do, and I insisted. Because I'm very good at getting what I want. Maybe because *you* wanted to. But now I'd be quite happy to skip dinner. We could order takeout and go to my loft apartment, which isn't far, by the way. You're a curator. I'm a collector. I have several pieces that might interest you."

"I'll bet! Not a good idea."

Again he laughed.

She didn't feel any safer once they were inside the crowded, brilliantly lit establishment. The restaurant with its friendly waitstaff, strolling mariachis, delicious aromas and ceiling festooned with tiny lights and colorful banners was too festive, too conducive to lowering one's guard. It would be too easy to succumb to temptation, something she couldn't afford to do.

I'll have a taco, a glass of water. We'll talk about Jaycee, and I'll leave. What could possibly go wrong if I nip this attraction in the bud?

When told there was a thirty-minute wait, Quinn didn't seem to mind. To the contrary, he seemed pleased. "We'll wait in the bar," he said, smiling.

Then he ushered them into a large room with a high-beamed ceiling dominated by a towering carved oak bar, inspired by the baroque elegance of the hotels in nineteenth-century San Antonio.

When a young redheaded waiter bragged on the various imported tequilas available, Quinn ordered them two margaritas made of a particularly costly tequila he said he had a weakness for.

"I'd rather have sparkling water," she said, sitting up straighter, thinking she needed all her wits about her.

"As you wish," Quinn said gallantly, ordering the water as well, but she noted that he didn't cancel the second margarita.

When their drinks arrived, he lifted his margarita to his lips and licked at the salt that edged the rim. And just watching the movement of his tongue across the grit of those glimmering crystals flooded her with ridiculous heat as she imagined him licking her skin.

"I think our first dinner together calls for a toast, don't you?" he said.

Her hand moved toward her glass of sparkling water.

"The tequila really is worth a taste."

She looked into his eyes and hesitated. Almost without her knowing it, her hand moved slowly away from the icy glass of water to her chilled margarita glass.

"You won't be sorry," he promised in that silken baritone.

Toying with the slender green stem of her glass, she lifted it and then tentatively clinked it against his.

"To us," he said. "To new beginnings." He smiled benevolently, but his blue eyes were excessively brilliant.

Her first swallow of the margarita was salty, sweet and very strong. She knew she shouldn't drink any more. Then, almost at once, a pleasant warmth buzzed through her, softening her attitude toward him and weakening her willpower. Somewhere the mariachis began to play "La Paloma," a favorite love song of hers. Was it a sign?

"I'm glad you at least took a sip," he said, his gaze lingering on her lips a second too long. "It would be a pity to miss tasting something so delicious."

"You're right. It's really quite good."

"The best—all the more reason not to miss it. One can't retrace one's journey in this life. We must make the most of every moment…because once lost, those moments are gone forever."

"Indeed." Eyeing him, she sipped again. "Funny, I hadn't thought of you as a philosopher."

"You might be surprised by who I really am, if you took the trouble to get to know me."

"I doubt it."

Every muscle in his handsome face tensed. When his eyes darkened, she wondered if she'd wounded him.

No. Impossible.

Her nerves jingled, urging her to consider just one more sip of the truly delicious margarita. What could it hurt? That second sip led to a third, then another and another, each sliding down her throat more easily than the last. She hardly noticed when Quinn moved from his side of the booth to hers, and yet how could she not notice? He didn't touch her, yet it was thrilling to be so near him, to know that only their clothes separated her thigh from his, to wonder what he would do next.

His gaze never strayed from her. Focusing on her exclusively, he told her stories about his youth, about the time before his father had died. His father had played ball with him, he said, had taken him hunting and fishing, had helped him with his homework. He stayed off the grim subjects of his parents' divorce and his father's death.

"When school was out for any reason, he always took me to his office. He was determined to instill a work ethic in me."

"He sounds like the perfect father," she said wistfully. "I never seemed to be able to please mine. If he read to me, I fidgeted too much, and he would lose his place and his temper. If he took me fishing, I grew bored or hot and squirmed too much, kicking over the minnow bucket or snapping his line. Once I stood up too fast and turned the boat over."

"Maybe I won't take you fishing."

"He always wanted a son, and I didn't please Mother any better. She thought Jaycee, who loved to dress up and go to parties, was perfect. She still does. Neither of them like what I'm doing with my life."

"Well, they're not in control, are they? No one is, really. And just when we think we are, we usually get struck by a lightning bolt that shows us we're not," Quinn said in a silken tone that made her breath quicken. "Like tonight."

"What do you mean?"

"Us."

Her gaze fixed on his dimple. "Are you coming on to me?"

He laid his hand on top of hers. "Would that be so terrible?"

By the time they'd been seated at their dinner table and had ordered their meal, she'd lost all her fear of him. She was actually enjoying herself.

Usually, she dated guys who couldn't afford to take her out to eat very often, so she cooked for them in her apartment. Even though this meal was not a date, it was nice to dine in a pleasant restaurant and be served for a change.

When Quinn said how sorry he was that they hadn't met before that afternoon when he'd nearly run her down, she answered truthfully, "I thought you were marrying my sister solely to hurt all of us. I couldn't condone that."

He frowned. "And you love your sister so much, you came to my office today to try to find a way to stop me from marrying her."

"I was a fool to admit that to you."

"I think you're sweet, and I admire your honesty. You were right to come. You did me one helluva favor. I've been on the wrong course. But I don't want to talk about Jacinda. I want to talk about you."

"But will you think about…not marrying her?"

When he nodded and said, "Definitely," in a very convincing manner, she relaxed and took still another sip of her margarita with no more thoughts of how dangerous it might be for her to continue relaxing around him.

When he reached across the table and wrapped her hand in his warm, blunt fingers, the shock of his touch sent a wave of heat through her whole body. For a second, she entwined her fingers with his and clung as if he were a vital lifeline. Then, when she realized what she was doing, she wrenched her hand free.

"Why are you so afraid of me, Kira?"

"You might still marry Jaycee and ruin her life," she lied.

"Impossible, now that I've met you."

Kira's breath quickened. Dimple or not, he was still the enemy. She had to remember that.

"Do you really think I'm so callous I could marry your sister when I want you so much?"

"But what are you going to do about Jaycee?"

"I told you. She became irrelevant the minute I saw you standing inside my office this afternoon."

"She's beautiful…and *blonde*."

"Yes, but your beauty affects me more. Don't you know that?"

She shook her head. "The truth isn't in you. You only date blondes."

"Then it must be time for a change."

"I'm going to confess a secret wish. All my life I wished I was blonde…so I'd look more like the rest of my family, especially my mother and my sister. I thought maybe then I'd feel like I belonged."

"You *are* beautiful."

"A man like you would say anything..."

"I've never lied to any woman. Don't you know how incredibly lovely you are? With your shining dark eyes that show your sweet, pure soul every time you look at me and defend your sister? I feel your love for her rushing through you like liquid electricity. You're graceful. You move like a ballerina. I love the way you feel so intensely and blush when you think I might touch you."

"Like a child."

"No. Like a responsive, passionate woman. I like that... too much. And your hair...it's long and soft and shines like chestnut satin. Yet there's fire in it. I want to run my hands through it."

"But we hardly know one another. And I've hated you..."

"None of the Murrays have been favorites of mine either...but I'm beginning to see the error of my ways. And I don't think you hate me as much as you pretend."

Kira stared at him, searching his hard face for some sign that he was lying to her, seducing her as he'd seduced all those other women, saying these things because he had some dark agenda. All she saw was warmth and honesty and intense emotion. Nobody had ever looked at her with such hunger or made her feel so beautiful.

All her life she'd wanted someone to make her feel this special. It was ironic that Quinn Sullivan should be the one.

"I thought you were so bad, no...pure evil," she repeated.

His eyebrows arched. "Ouch."

If he'd been twisted in his original motives, maybe it

had been because of the grief he'd felt at losing someone he loved.

"How could I have been so wrong about you?" Even as she said it, some part of her wondered if she weren't being naive. He had dated, and jilted, all those beautiful women. He had intended to take revenge on her father and use her sister in his plan. Maybe when she'd walked into his office she'd become part of his diabolical plan, too.

"I was misguided," he said.

"I need more time to think about all this. Like I said…a mere hour or two ago I heartily disliked you. Or at least I thought I did."

"Because you didn't know me. Hell, maybe I didn't know me either…because everything is different now, since I met you."

She felt the same way. But she knew she should slow it down, reassess.

"I'm not good at picking boyfriends," she whispered.

"Their loss."

His hand closed over hers and he pressed her fingers, causing a melting sensation in her tummy. "My gain."

Her tacos came, looking and smelling delicious, but she hardly touched them. Her every sense was attuned to Quinn's carved features and his beautiful voice.

When a musician came to their table, Quinn hired him to sing several songs, including "La Paloma." While the man serenaded her, Quinn idly stroked her wrist and the length of her fingers, causing fire to shoot down her spine.

She met his eyes and felt that she had known him always, that he was already her lover, her soul mate. She was crazy to feel such things and think such thoughts about a man she barely knew, but when dinner was over, they skipped dessert.

An hour later, she sat across from him in his downtown

loft, sipping coffee while he drank brandy. In vain, she tried to act unimpressed by his art collection and sparkling views of the city. Not easy, since both were impressive.

His entrance was filled with an installation of crimson light by one of her favorite artists. The foyer was a dazzling ruby void that opened into a living room with high, white ceilings. All the rooms of his apartment held an eclectic mix of sculpture, porcelains and paintings.

Although she hadn't yet complimented his stylish home, she couldn't help but compare her small, littered apartment to his spacious one. Who was she to label him an arrogant upstart? He was a success in the international oil business and a man of impeccable taste, while she was still floundering in her career and struggling to find herself.

"I wanted to be alone with you like this the minute I saw you today," he said.

She shifted uneasily on his cream-leather sofa. Yet more evidence that he was a planner. "Well, I didn't."

"I think you did. You just couldn't let yourself believe you did."

"No," she whispered, setting down her cup. With difficulty she tried to focus on her mission. "So, what about Jaycee? You're sure that's over?"

"Finished. From the first moment I saw you."

"Without mud all over my face."

He laughed. "Actually, you got to me that day, too. Every time I dined with Jacinda and your family, I kept hoping I'd meet you again."

Even as she remembered all those dinner invitations her parents had extended and she'd declined, she couldn't believe he was telling the truth.

"I had my team research you," he said.

"Why?"

"I asked myself the same question. I think you intrigued

me…like I said, even with mud on your face. First thing tomorrow, I will break it off with Jacinda formally. Which means you've won. Does that make you happy? You have what you came for."

He was all charm, especially his warm, white smile. Like a child with a new playmate, she was happy just being with him, but she couldn't admit that to him.

He must have sensed her feelings, though, because he got up and moved silently toward her. "I feel like I've lived my whole life since my father's death alone—until you. And that's how I wanted to live—until you."

She knew it was sudden and reckless, but she felt the same way. If she wasn't careful, she would forget all that should divide them.

As if in a dream, she took his hand when he offered it and kissed his fingers with feverish devotion.

"You've made me realize how lonely I've been," he said.

"That's a very good line."

"It's the truth."

"But you are so successful, while I…"

"Look what you're doing in the interim—helping a friend to realize her dream."

"My father says I'm wasting my potential."

"You will find yourself…if you are patient." He cupped her chin and stared into her eyes. Again she felt that uncanny recognition. He was a kindred soul who knew what it was to feel lost.

"Dear God," he muttered. "Don't listen to me. I don't know a damn thing about patience. Like now… I should let you go…but I can't."

He pulled her to him and crushed her close. It wasn't long before holding her wasn't enough. He had to have her lips, her throat, her breasts. She felt the same way. Shedding her shirt, scarf and bra, she burst into flame as he kissed her. Even though she barely knew him, she could not wait another moment to belong to him.

"I'm not feeling so patient right now myself," she admitted huskily.

Do not give yourself to this man, said an inner voice. *Remember all those blondes. Remember his urge for revenge.*

Even as her emotions spiraled out of control, she knew she was no femme fatale, while he was a devastatingly attractive man. Had he said all these same wonderful things to all those other women he'd bedded? Had he done and felt all the same things, too, a thousand times before? Were nights like this routine for him, while he was the first to make her feel so thrillingly alive?

But then his mouth claimed hers again, and again, with a fierce, wild hunger that made her forget her doubts and shake and cling to him. His kisses completed her as she'd never been completed before. He was a wounded soul, and she understood his wounds. How could she feel so much when they hadn't even made love?

Lifting her into his arms, he carried her into his vast bedroom, which was bathed in silver moonlight. Over her shoulder she saw his big, black bed in the middle of an ocean of white marble and Persian carpets.

He was a driven, successful billionaire, and she was a waitress. Feeling out of her depth, her nerves returned. Not knowing what else to do, she pressed a fingertip to his lips. Gently, shyly, she traced his dimple.

Feeling her tension, he set her down. She pushed against his chest and then took a step away from him. Watching her, he said, "You can finish undressing in the bathroom if you'd prefer privacy. Or we can stop. I'll drive you to your car. Your choice."

She should have said, "I don't belong here with you,"

and accepted his gallant offer. Instead, without a word, she scampered toward the door he'd indicated. Alone in his beige marble bathroom with golden fixtures and a lovely, compelling etching by another one of her favorite artists, she barely recognized her own flushed face, tousled hair and sparkling eyes.

The radiant girl in his tall mirror *was* as beautiful as an enchanted princess. She looked expectant, excited. Maybe she did belong here with him. Maybe he was the beginning of her new life, the first correct step toward the bright future that had so long eluded her.

When she tiptoed back into the bedroom, wearing nothing but his white robe, he was in bed. She couldn't help admiring the width of his bronzed shoulders as he leaned back against several plumped pillows. She had never dated anyone half so handsome; she'd never felt anything as powerful as the glorious heady heat that suffused her entire being as his blue eyes studied her hungrily. Still, she was nervy, shaking.

"I'm no good at sex," she said. "You're probably very good… Of course you are. You're good at everything."

"Come here," he whispered.

"But…"

"Just come to me. You could not possibly delight me more. Surely you know that."

Did he really feel as much as she did?

Removing his bathrobe, she flew to him before she lost her nerve, fell into his bed and into his arms, consumed by forces beyond her control. Nothing mattered but sliding against his long body, being held close in his strong arms. Beneath the covers, his heat was delicious and welcoming as she nestled against him.

He gave her a moment to settle before he rolled on top of her. Bracing himself with his elbows against the mattress, so as not to crush her, he kissed her lips, her cheeks, her brows and then her eyelids with urgent yet featherlike strokes. Slowly, gently, each kiss was driving her mad.

"Take me," she whispered, in the grip of a fever such as she'd never experienced before. "I want you inside me. Now."

"I know," he said, laughing. "I'm as ravenous as you are. But have patience, darlin'."

"You have a funny way of showing your hunger."

"If I do what you ask, it would be over in a heartbeat. This moment, our first time together, is too special to me."

Was she special?

"We must savor it, draw it out, make it last," he said.

"Maybe I want it to be over swiftly," she begged. "Maybe this obsessive need is unbearable."

"Exquisite expectation?"

"I can't stand it."

"And I want to heighten it. Which means we're at cross-purposes."

He didn't take her. With infinite care and maddening patience he adored her with his clever mouth and skilled hands. His fevered lips skimmed across her soft skin, raising goose bumps in secret places. As she lay beneath him, he licked each nipple until it grew hard, licked her navel until he had all her nerve endings on fire for him. Then he kissed her belly and dived even lower to explore those hidden, honey-sweet lips between her legs. When she felt his tongue dart inside, she gasped and drew back.

"Relax," he whispered.

With slow, hot kisses, he made her gush. All too soon her embarrassment was gone, and she was melting, shivering, whimpering—all but begging him to give her release.

Until tonight she had been an exile in the world of love. With all other men, not that there had been that many, she had been going through the motions, playing a part, searching always for something meaningful and never finding it.

Until now, tonight, with him.

He couldn't matter this much! She couldn't let this be more than fierce, wild sex. He, the man, couldn't matter. But her building emotions told her that he did matter—in ways she'd never imagined possible before.

He took her breast in his mouth and suckled again. Then his hand entered her heated wetness, making her gasp helplessly and plead. When he stroked her, his fingers sliding against that secret flesh, she arched against his expert touch, while her breath came in hard, tortured pants.

Just when she didn't think she could bear it any longer, he dragged her beneath him and slid inside her. He was huge, massive, wonderful. Crying out, she clung to him and pushed her pelvis against his, aching for him to fill her even more deeply. *"Yes! Yes!"*

When he sank deeper, ever deeper, she moaned. For a long moment he held her and caressed her. Then he began to plunge in and out, slowly at first. Her rising pleasure carried her and shook her in sharp, hot waves, causing her to climax and scream his name.

He went crazy when she dug her nails in his shoulder. Then she came again, and again, sobbing. She had no idea how many climaxes she had before she felt his hard loins bunch as he exploded.

Afterward, sweat dripped off his brow. His whole body was flushed, burning up, and so was hers.

"Darlin' Kira," he whispered in that husky baritone that could still make her shiver even when she was spent. "Darlin' Kira."

For a long time, she lay in his arms, not speaking, feeling too weak to move any part of her body. Then he leaned over and nibbled at her bottom lip.

The second time he made love to her, he did so with a reverent gentleness that made her weep and hold on to him for a long time afterward. He'd used a condom the second time, causing her to realize belatedly that he hadn't the first time.

How could they have been so careless? She had simply been swept away. Maybe he had, too. Well, it was useless to worry about that now. Besides, she was too happy, too relaxed to care about anything except being in his arms. There was no going back.

For a long time they lay together, facing each other while they talked. He told her about his father's financial crisis and how her father had turned on him and made things worse. He spoke of his mother's extravagance and betrayal and his profound hurt that his world had fallen apart so quickly and brutally. She listened as he explained how grief, poverty and helplessness had twisted him and made him hard.

"Love made me too vulnerable, as it did my father. It was a destructive force. My father loved my mother, and it ruined him. She was greedy and extravagant," he said. "Love destroys the men in our family."

"If you don't want to love, why did you date all those women I read about?"

"I wasn't looking for love, and neither were they."

"You were just using them, then?"

"They were using me, too."

"That's so cynical."

"That's how my life has been. I loved my father so much, and I hurt so much when he died, I gave up on love. He loved my mother, and she broke his heart with her unrelenting demands. When he lost the business, she lost interest in him and began searching for a richer man."

"And did she find him?"

“Several.”

“Do you ever see her?”

“No. I was an accident she regretted, I believe. She couldn’t relate to children, and after I was grown, I had no interest in her. Love, no matter what kind, always costs too much. I do write her a monthly check, however.”

“So, my father was only part of your father’s problem.”

“But a big part. Losing ownership in Sullivan and Murray Oil made my father feel like he was less than nothing. My mother left him because of that loss. She stripped him of what little wealth and self-esteem he had left. Alone, without his company or his wife, he grew depressed. He wouldn’t eat. He couldn’t sleep. I’d hear the stairs creak as he paced at night.

“Then early one morning I heard a shot. When I called his name, he didn’t answer. I found him in the shop attached to our garage. In a pool of blood on the floor, dead. I still don’t know if it was an accident or…what I feared it was. He was gone. At first I was frightened. Then I became angry. I wanted to blame someone, to get even, to make his death right. I lived for revenge. But now that I’ve almost achieved my goal of taking back Murray Oil, it’s as if my fever’s burned out.”

“Oh, I wouldn’t say that,” she teased, touching his damp brow.

“I mean my fever for revenge, which was what kept me going.”

“So,” she asked, “what will you live for now?”

“I don’t know. I guess a lot of people just wake up in the morning and go to work, then come home at night and drink while they flip channels with their remote.”

“Not you.”

“Who’s to say? Maybe such people are lucky. At least they’re not driven by hate, as I was.”

"I can't even begin to imagine what that must have felt like for you." She'd always been driven by the need for love.

When he stared into her eyes with fierce longing, she pulled him close and ran her hands through his hair. "You are young yet. You'll find something to give your life meaning," she said.

"Well, it won't be love, because I've experienced love's dark side for too many years. I want you to know that. You are special, but I can't ever love you, no matter how good we are together. I'm no longer capable of that emotion."

"So you keep telling me," she said, pretending his words didn't hurt.

"I just want to be honest."

"Do we always know our own truths?"

"Darlin'," he whispered. "Forgive me if I sounded too harsh. It's just that...I don't want to hurt you by raising your expectations about something I'm incapable of. Other women have become unhappy because of the way I am."

"You're my family's enemy. Why would I ever want to love you?"

Wrapping her legs around him, she held him for hours, trying to comfort the boy who'd lost so much as well as the angry man who'd gained a fortune because he'd been consumed by a fierce, if misplaced, hatred.

"My father had nothing to do with your father's death," she whispered. "He didn't."

"You have your view, and I have mine," he said. "The important thing is that I don't hold you responsible for your father's sins any longer."

"Don't you?"

"No."

After that, he was silent. Soon afterward he let her go and rolled onto his side.

She lay awake for hours. Where would they go from here? He had hated her family for years. Had he really let go of all those harsh feelings? Had she deluded herself into thinking he wasn't her enemy?

What price would she pay for sleeping with a man who probably only saw her as an instrument for revenge?

Three

When Kira woke up naked in bed with Quinn, she felt unsettled and very self-conscious. Propping herself on an elbow, she watched him warily in the dim rosy half light of dawn. All her doubts returned a hundredfold.

How could she have let things go this far? How could she have risked pregnancy?

What if… No, she couldn't be that unlucky.

Besides, it did no good to regret what had happened, she reminded herself again. If she hadn't slept with him she would never have known such ecstasy was possible.

Now, at least, she knew. Even if it wasn't love, it had been so great she felt an immense tenderness well up in her in spite of her renewed doubts.

He was absurdly handsome with his thick, unruly black hair falling across his brow, with his sharp cheekbones and sculpted mouth. She'd been touched when he'd shown her his vulnerability last night. Just looking at him now was enough to make her stomach flutter with fresh desire.

She was about to stroke his hair, when, without warning, his obscenely long lashes snapped open, and he met her gaze with that directness that still startled her. Maybe because there were so many imperfections she wanted to keep hidden. In the next instant, his expression softened, disarming her.

"Good morning, darlin'." His rough, to-die-for, sexy baritone caressed her.

A jolt sizzled through her even before he reached out a bronzed hand to pull her face to his so he could kiss her lightly on the lips. Never had she wanted anyone as much as she wanted him.

"I haven't brushed my teeth," she warned.

"Neither the hell have I. I don't expect you to be perfect. I simply want you. I can't do without you. You should know that after last night."

She was amazed because she felt exactly the same. Still, with those doubts still lingering, she felt she had to protect herself by protesting.

"Last night was probably a mistake," she murmured.

"Maybe. Or maybe it's a complication, a challenge. Or a good thing. In any case, it's too late to worry about it. I want you more now than ever."

"But for how long?"

"Is anything certain?"

He kissed her hard. Before she could protest again, he rolled on top of her and was inside her, claiming her fiercely, his body piercing her to the bed, his massive erection filling her. When he rode her violently, she bucked like a wild thing, too, her doubts dissolving like mist as primal desire swept her past reason.

"I'm sorry," he said afterward. "I wanted you too much."

He had, however, at the last second, remembered to use a condom. This time, he didn't hold her tenderly or make small talk or confide sweet nothings as he had last night. In fact, he seemed hellishly annoyed at himself.

Was he already tired of her? Would there be a new blonde in his bed tonight? At the thought, a sob caught in her throat.

"You can have the master bathroom. I'll make coffee," he said tersely.

Just like that, he wanted her gone. Since she'd researched him and had known his habits, she shouldn't feel shocked or hurt. Hadn't he warned her he was incapable of feeling close to anyone? She should be grateful for the sublime sexual experience and let the rest go.

Well, she had her pride. She wasn't about to cling to him or show that she cared. But she did care. Oh, how she cared. Her family's worst enemy had quickly gained a curious hold on her heart.

Without a word, she rose and walked naked across the vast expanse of thick, white carpet, every female cell vividly aware that, bored with her though he might be, he didn't tear his eyes from her until she reached the bathroom and shut the door. Once inside she turned the lock and leaned heavily against the wall in a state of collapse.

She took a deep breath and stared at her pale, guilt-stricken reflection, so different from the glowing wanton of last night.

She'd known the kind of guy he was, in spite of his seductive words. How could she have opened herself to such a hard man? Her father's implacable enemy?

What had she done?

By the time she'd showered, brushed her hair and dressed, he was in the kitchen, looking no worse for wear.

Indeed, he seemed energized by what they had shared. Freshly showered, he wore a white shirt and crisply pressed dark slacks. He'd shaved, and his glossy black hair was combed. He looked so civilized, she felt the crazy urge to run her hands through his hair, just to muss it up and leave her mark.

The television was on, and he was watching the latest stock market report while he held his cell phone against his ear. Behind him, a freshly made pot of aromatic coffee sat on the gleaming white counter.

She was about to step inside when he flicked the remote, killing the sound of the television. She heard his voice, as sharp and hard as it had been with the caller yesterday in his office.

"Habib, business is business," he snapped. "I know I have to convince the shareholders and the public I'm some shining white knight. That's why I agreed to marry a Murray daughter and why her parents, especially her father, who wants an easy transition of power, suggested Jacinda and persuaded her to accept me. However, if the older Murray sister agrees to marry me instead, why should it matter to you or to anyone else…other than to Jacinda, who will no doubt be delighted to have her life back?"

Habib, whoever he was, must have argued, because Quinn's next response was much angrier. "Yes, I know the family history and why you consider Jacinda the preferable choice, but since nobody else knows, apparently not even Kira, it's of no consequence. So, if I've decided to marry the older sister instead of the younger, and this decision will make the shareholders and employees just as happy, why the hell should you care?"

The man must have countered again, because Quinn's low tone was even more cutting. "No, I haven't asked her yet. It's too soon. But when I do, I'll remind her that I told her yesterday I'd demand a price for freeing her sister. She'll have to pay it, that's all. She'll have no choice but to do what's best for her family and her sister. Hell, she'll do anything for their approval."

One sister or the other—and he didn't care which one. That he could speak of marrying her instead of Jaycee as a cold business deal before he'd even bothered to propose made Kira's tender heart swell with hurt and outrage. That he would use her desire for her family's love and acceptance to his own advantage was too horrible to endure.

Obviously, she was that insignificant to him. But hadn't she known that? So why did it hurt so much?

He'd said she was special. Nobody had ever made her feel so cherished before.

Thinking herself a needy, romantic fool, she shut her eyes. Unready to face him or confess what she'd overheard and how much it bothered her, Kira backed out of the kitchen and returned to the bedroom. In her present state she was incapable of acting rationally and simply demanding an explanation.

He was a planner. Her seduction must have been a calculated move. No longer could she believe he'd been swept off his feet by her as she had by him. She was skinny and plain. He'd known she desired him, and he was using that to manipulate her.

Last night, when he'd promised he'd break it off with her sister, she'd never guessed the devious manner in which he'd planned to honor that promise.

She was still struggling to process everything she'd learned, when Quinn himself strode into the bedroom looking much too arrogant, masterful and self-satisfied for her liking.

"Good, you're dressed," he said in that beautiful voice. "You look gorgeous."

Refusing to meet the warmth of his admiring gaze for fear she might believe his compliment and thereby lose her determination to escape him, she nodded.

"I made coffee."

"Smells good," she whispered, staring out the window.

"Do you have time for breakfast?"

"No!"

"Something wrong?"

If he was dishonest, why should she bother to be straight with him? "I'm fine," she said, but in a softer tone.

"Right. That must be why you seem so cool."

"Indeed?"

"And they say men are the ones who withdraw the morning aftcr."

She bit her lip to keep herself from screaming at him.

"Still, I understand," he said.

"Last night is going to take some getting used to," she said.

"For me, as well."

To that she said nothing.

"Well, the coffee's in the kitchen," he said, turning away.

Preferring to part from him without an argument, she followed him into the kitchen where he poured her a steaming cup and handed it to her.

"Do you take cream? Sugar?"

She shook her head. "We don't know the most basic things about each other, do we?"

"After last night, I'd have to disagree with you, darlin'."

She blushed in confusion. "Don't call me that."

He eyed her thoughtfully. "You really do seem upset."

She sipped from her cup, again choosing silence instead of arguing the point. Was he good at everything? Rich and strong, the coffee was to die for.

"For the record, I take mine black, very black," he said.

"Without sugar. So, we have that in common. And we have what we shared last night."

"Don't…"

"I'd say we're off to a great start."

Until I realized what you were up to, I would have agreed. She longed to claw him. Instead, she clenched her nails into her palms and chewed her lower lip mutinously.

The rosy glow from last night, when he'd made her feel so special, had faded. She felt awkward and unsure…and hurt, which was ridiculous because she'd gone into this knowing who and what he was.

Obviously, last night had been business as usual for him. Why not marry the Murray sister who'd practically thrown herself at him? Did he believe she was so smitten and desperate for affection she'd be more easily controlled?

Why had she let herself be swept away by his looks, his confidences and his suave, expert lovemaking?

Because, your stupid crush on him turned your brain to mush.

And turned her raging hormones to fire. Never had she felt so physically and spiritually in tune with anyone. She'd actually thought, at one point, that they could be soul mates.

Soul mates! It was all an illusion. You were a fool, girl, and not for the first time.

"Look, I'd really better go," she said, her tone so sharp his dark head jerked toward her.

"Right. Then I'll drive you, since you left your car downtown."

"I can call a cab."

"No! I'll drive you."

Silently, she nodded.

He led the way to stairs that went down to the elevator and garage. In silence, they sped along the freeway in his silver Aston Martin until he slowed to take the off-ramp that led to where she'd parked downtown. After that, she *had* to speak to him in order to direct him to her small, dusty Toyota with several dings in its beige body. She let out a little moan when he pulled up behind her car and she saw the parking ticket flapping under her windshield wipers.

He got out and raced around the hood to open her door, but before he could, she'd flung it open.

"You sure there isn't something wrong?" he asked.

She snatched the ticket, but before she could get in her car, he slid his arms around her waist from behind.

He felt so solid and strong and warm, she barely suppressed a sigh. She yearned to stay in his arms even though she knew she needed to get away from him as quickly as possible to regroup.

He turned her to face him and his fingertips traced the length of her cheek in a tender, burning caress, and for a long second he stared into her troubled eyes with a mixture of concern and barely suppressed impatience. He seemed to care.

Liar.

"It's not easy letting you go," he said.

"People are watching us," she said mildly, even as she seethed with outrage.

"So what? Last night was very special to me, Kira. I'm sorry if you're upset about it. I hope it's just that it all happened too fast. I wasn't too rough, was I?"

The concern in his voice shook her. "No." She looked away, too tempted to meet his gaze.

"It's never been like that for me. I…I couldn't control myself, especially this morning. I wanted you again… badly. This is all happening too fast for me, too. I prefer being able to plan."

That's not what he'd said on the phone. Quinn seemed to have damn sure had a plan. Marry a Murray daughter. And he was sticking to it.

"Yes, it is happening…too fast." She bit her lip. "But… I'm okay." She wanted to brush off his words, to pretend she didn't care that he'd apologized and seemed genuinely worried about her physical and emotional state. He seemed all too likable. She almost believed him.

"Do you have a business card?" he asked gently.

She shook her head. "Nope. At least, not on me."

He flipped a card out of his pocket. "Well, here is mine. You can call me anytime. I want to see you again…as soon as possible. There's something very important I want to discuss with you."

The intensity of his gaze made her heart speed up. "You are not going back on your word about marrying Jaycee, are you?"

"How can you even ask? I'll call it off as soon as I leave you. Unfortunately, after that, I have to be away on business for several days, first to New York, then London. Murray Oil is in the middle of negotiating a big deal with the European Union. My meeting tonight in New York ends at eight, so call me after that. On my cell."

Did he intend to propose over the phone? Her throat felt thick as she forced herself to nod. Whipping out a pen and a pad, she wrote down her cell phone number. "Will you text me as soon as you break up with my sister?"

"Can I take that to mean you care about me…a little?" he asked.

"Sure," she whispered, exhaling a pent-up breath. How did he lie so easily? "Take it any way you like."

She had to get away from him, to be alone to think. Everything he said, everything he did, made her want him—even though she knew, after what she'd heard this morning, that she'd never been anything but a pawn in the game he was playing to exact revenge against her father.

She wasn't special to him. And if she didn't stand up for herself now, she never would be.

She would not let her father sell Jaycee *or* her to this man!

Four

"You're her father. I still can't believe you don't have a clue where Kira could be. Hell, she's been gone for nearly three weeks."

Shaking his head, Earl stalked across Quinn's corner office at Murray Oil to look out the window. "I told you, she's probably off somewhere painting. She does that."

Quinn hated himself for having practically ordered the infuriating Murray to his office again today. But he was that desperate to know Kira was safe. Her safety aside, he had a wedding planned and a bride to locate.

"You're sure she's not in any trouble?"

"Are *you* sure she didn't realize you were about to demand that she marry you?"

Other than wanting Kira to take Jaycee's place, he wasn't sure about a damn thing! Well, except that maybe he'd pushed Kira too fast and too far. Hell, she could have overheard him talking to Habib. She'd damn sure gotten quiet and sulky before they parted ways.

"I don't think—"

"I'd bet money she got wise to you and decided to let you stew in your own juices. She may seem sweet and malleable, but she's always had a mind of her own. She's impossible to control. It's why she lost her job. It's why I suggested you choose Jaycee in the first place. Jaycee is biddable."

Quinn felt heat climb his neck. He didn't want Jaycee. He'd never wanted Jaycee. He wanted Kira…sweet, passionate Kira who went wild every time he touched her. Her passion thrilled him as nothing else had in years.

The trouble was, after he'd made love to her that morning, he'd felt completely besotted and then out of sorts as a result. He hadn't wanted to dwell on what feeling such an all-consuming attraction so quickly might mean. Now he knew that if anything had happened to her, he'd never forgive himself.

"I couldn't ask her to marry me after our dinner. It was too soon. Hell, maybe she did figure it all out and run off before I could explain."

"Well, I checked our hunting lodges at the ranch where she goes to paint wildlife, and I've left messages with my caretaker at the island where she paints birds. Nobody's seen her. Sooner or later she'll turn up. She always does. You'll just have to be patient."

"Not my forte."

"Quinn, she's okay. When she's in between museum jobs, she runs around like this. She's always been a free spirit."

"Right." Quinn almost growled. He disliked that the other man could see he was vulnerable and crazed by Kira's disappearance. The need to find her, to find out why she'd vanished, had been building inside him. He couldn't go on if he didn't solve this mystery—and not just because the wedding date loomed.

His one night with Kira had been the closest thing to perfection he'd known since before his dad had died. Never had he experienced with any other woman anything like what he'd shared with Kira. Hell, he hadn't known such closeness was possible. He'd lost himself completely in her, talked to her as he'd never talked to another person.

Even though she'd seemed distant the next morning, he'd thought she'd felt the same wealth of emotion he had and was running scared. But no—something else had made her vanish without a word, even before he'd told her she'd have to marry him if Jaycee didn't. Thinking back, all he could imagine was that she'd felt vulnerable and afraid after their shared night—or that she *had* overheard him talking to Habib.

Then the day after he'd dropped her at her car, Quinn had texted her, as he'd promised, to let her know he'd actually broken it off with Jacinda. She'd never called him back. Nor had she answered her phone since then. She'd never returned to her tiny apartment or her place of employment.

Kira had called her friend Betty to check in, and promised she'd call weekly to keep in touch, but she hadn't given an explanation for her departure or an estimation for when she'd return.

Quinn had to rethink his situation. He'd stopped romancing Jacinda, but he hadn't canceled the wedding because he planned to marry Kira instead. Come Saturday, a thousand people expected him to marry a Murray daughter.

Apparently, his future father-in-law's mind was running along the same worrisome track.

"Quinn, you've got to be reasonable. We've got to call off the wedding," Earl said.

"I'm going to marry Kira."

"You're talking nonsense. Kira's gone. Without a bride, you're going to piss off the very people we want to reassure. Stockholders, clients and employees of Murray Oil. Not to mention—this whole thing is stressing the hell out of Vera, and in her condition that isn't good."

Several months earlier, when Quinn had stalked into Earl's office with enough shares to demand control of Murray Oil, Earl, his eyes blurry and his shoulders slumped, had sat behind his desk already looking defeated.

The older man had wearily confided that his wife was seriously ill. Not only had Earl not cared that Quinn would soon be in charge of Murray Oil, he'd said the takeover was the answer to a prayer. It was time he retired. With Murray Oil in good hands, he could devote himself to his beloved wife, who was sick and maybe dying.

"She's everything to me," he'd whispered. "The way your father was to you and the way your mother was to him before she left him."

"Why tell me—your enemy?" Quinn had asked.

"I don't think of you as my enemy. I never was one to see the world in black or white, the way Kade, your dad, did—the way you've chosen to see it since his death. Whether you believe me or not, I loved your father, and I was sorry about our misunderstanding. You're just like him, you know, so now that I've got my own challenge to face, there's nobody I'd rather turn the company over to than you.

"Vera doesn't want me talking about her illness to friends and family. She can't stand the thought of people, even her daughters, thinking of her as weak and sick. I'm glad I finally have someone I can tell."

Quinn had been stunned. For years, he had hated Earl, had wanted revenge, had looked forward to bringing the man to his knees. But ever since that conversation his feelings had begun to change. The connection he'd found with Kira had hastened that process.

He'd begun to rethink his choices, reconsider his past. Not all his memories of Earl were negative. He could remember some wonderful times hunting and fishing with the blunt-spoken Earl and his dad. As a kid, he'd loved the stories Earl had told around the campfire.

Maybe the bastard had been partially responsible for his father's death. But maybe an equal share of the blame lay with his own father.

Not that Quinn trusted his new attitude. He'd gone too far toward his goal of vengeance not to seize Murray Oil. And he still believed taking a Murray bride would make the acquisition run more smoothly.

"I will get married on Saturday," Quinn said. "All we have to do is convince Kira to come back and marry me."

"Right. But how? We don't even know where she is."

"We don't have to know. All we have to do is motivate her to return," Quinn said softly.

Seabirds raced along the beach, pecking at seaweed. Her jeans rolled to her knees, Kira stood in the shallow surf of Murray Island and wiggled her toes in the cool, damp sand as the wind whipped her hair against her cheeks. Blowing sand stung her bare arms and calves.

Kira needed to make her weekly phone call to Betty after her morning walk—a phone call she dreaded. Each week, it put her back in touch with reality, which was what she wanted to escape from.

Still, she'd known she couldn't stay on the island forever. She'd just thought that solitude would have cleared her head of Quinn by now. But it hadn't. She missed him.

Three weeks of being here alone had changed nothing. None of her confusion or despair about her emotional entanglement with Quinn had lifted.

Maybe if she hadn't been calling Betty to check in, she would be calmer. Betty had told her about Quinn's relentless visits to the restaurant. Thinking about Quinn looking for her had stirred up her emotions and had blocked her artistically. All she could paint was his handsome face.

Well, at least she was painting. When she'd been frustrated while working at the museum, she hadn't even been able to hold a paintbrush.

Since it was past time to call Betty again, she headed for the family beach house. When she climbed the wooden stairs and entered, the wind caught the screen door and banged it behind her.

She turned on her cell phone and climbed to the second floor where the signal and the views of the high surf were better.

Betty answered on the first ring. "You still okay all alone out there?"

"I'm fine. How's Rudy?"

She'd packed her cat and his toys and had taken him to Betty's, much to his dismay.

"Rudy's taken over as usual. Sleeps in my bed. He's right here. He can hear your voice on speakerphone. He's very excited, twitchin' his tail and all." She paused, then, "I worry about you out there alone, Kira."

"Jim's around. He checks on me."

Jim was the island's caretaker. She'd taken him into her confidence and asked him not to tell anyone, not even her father, where she was.

"Well, there's something I need to tell you, something I've been dreadin' tellin' you," Betty began.

"What?"

"That fella of yours, Quinn..."

"He's not my fella."

"Well, he sure acts like he's your guy when he drops by. He's been drillin' the staff, makin' sure you weren't datin' anyone. Said he didn't want to lay claim to a woman who belonged to another."

Lay claim? Kira caught her breath. Just thinking about Quinn in the restaurant looking for her made her breasts swell and her heart throb.

Darn it—would she never forget him?

"Well, today he comes over just as I'm unlocking the door and launches into a tirade about how he's gonna have to break his promise to you and marry your sister, Jaycee! This Saturday!

"I thought it right funny at first, him sayin' that, when he comes by lookin' haunted, askin' after you all the time, so I said up front I didn't buy it. Called him a liar, I did.

"He said maybe he preferred you, but you'd forced his hand. He had to marry a Murray daughter for business reasons, so he would. Everything is set. He told me to read the newspapers, if I didn't believe him. And I did. They're really getting married. It's all over the internet, too."

"What?"

"Tomorrow! Saturday! I know he told you he broke off his wedding plans, but if he did, they're on again. He's every bit as bad as you said. You were right to go away. If I was you, I'd never come back."

So, since he'd never cared which Murray sister he married, he was going to marry Jaycee after all.

Well, she'd stop him. She'd go back—at once—and she'd stop him cold.

Five

A sign in front of the church displayed a calendar that said Murray-Sullivan Wedding: 7:30 p.m.

It was five-thirty as Kira swung into the mostly empty parking lot.

Good. No guests had arrived. She'd made it in time.

The sun was low; the shadows long; the light a rosy gold. Not that she took the time to notice the clarity of the light or the rich green of the grass or the tiny spring leaves budding on the trees. Her heart was pounding. She was perspiring as she hit the brakes and jumped out of her Toyota.

The drive from the coast hadn't taken much more than three hours, but the trip had tired her. Feeling betrayed and yet desperate to find her sister and stop this travesty before it was too late, Kira ran toward the back of the church where the dressing rooms were. Inside, dashing from room to room, she threw open doors, calling her sister's name. Then, suddenly, in the last room, she found Jaycee, wearing a blue cotton dress with a strand of pearls at her throat. With her blond hair cascading down her back, Jaycee sat quietly in front of a long, gilt mirror, applying lipstick. She looked as if she'd been carefully posed by a photographer.

"Jaycee!" Kira cried breathlessly. "At last… Why aren't you wearing…a wedding dress?"

Then she saw the most beautiful silk gown seeded with tiny pearls lying across a sofa and a pair of white satin shoes on the floor.

"Oh, but that's why you're here…to dress… Of course. Where's Mother? Why isn't Mother here to help you?"

"She's not feeling well. I think she's resting. Mother and Quinn told me to wait here."

Odd. Usually when it came to organizing any social affair, their mother had endless reserves of energy that lasted her until the very end of the event.

"Where are your bridesmaids?"

Turning like an actress compelled by her cue, Jaycee pressed her lips together and then put her lipstick inside her blue purse. "I was so worried you wouldn't come," she said. "I was truly afraid you wouldn't show. We all were. Quinn most especially. But me, too. He'll be so happy you're here. I don't know what he would have done if you hadn't gotten here in time. You don't know how important you are to him."

Right. That's why he's marrying you without a qualm.

As always, Jaycee worried about everyone she loved. Kira very much doubted that Quinn would be happy with her once she finished talking to Jaycee.

Guilt flooded Kira. How would she ever find the words to explain to her trusting sister why she couldn't marry Quinn? Jaycee, who'd always been loved by everybody, probably couldn't imagine there was a soul in the world who wouldn't love her if she tried hard enough to win him. After all, Daddy had given his blessing.

"You can't marry Quinn today," Kira stated flatly.

"I know that. He told me all about you two. When Daddy asked me to marry Quinn, I tried to tell myself it was the right thing to do. For the family and all. But…when I found out he wanted to marry you…it was such a relief."

"Why did you show up here today if you knew all this?"

"Quinn will…explain everything." Jaycee's eyes widened as the door opened. Kira whirled to tell their visitor that this was a private conversation, but her words died in a convulsive little growl. Quinn, dressed in a tux that set off his broad shoulders and stunning dark looks to heart-stopping perfection, strode masterfully into the room.

Feeling cornered, Kira sank closer to Jaycee. When he saw her, he stopped, his eyes flashing with hurt and anger before he caught her mood and stiffened.

"I was hoping you'd make it in time for the wedding," he said, his deep baritone cutting her to the quick.

"Damn you!" Her throat tightened as she arose. "Liar! How could you do this?"

"I'm thrilled to see you, too, darlin'," he murmured, his gaze devouring her. "You do look lovely."

Kira, who'd driven straight from the island without making a single stop, was wearing a pair of worn, tight jeans and a T-shirt that hugged her curves. She hadn't bothered with makeup or a comb for her tangled hair. She could do nothing but take in a mortified breath at his comment while she stared at his dark face, the face she'd painted so many times even when images of him had blurred through her tears.

"What is the meaning of this?" she screamed.

"There's no need for hysterics, darlin'," he said calmly.

"Don't *darlin'* me! You have no right to call me that!"

she shrieked. "I haven't even begun to show you hysterics! I'm going to tear you limb from limb. Pound you into this tile floor… Skin you alive—"

"Kira, Quinn's been so worried about you. Frantic that you wouldn't show up in time," Jaycee began. "Talk about wedding jitters. He's had a full-blown case…"

"I'll just bet he has!"

"I see we misunderstand each other, Kira. I was afraid of this. Jacinda," he said in a silky tone that maddened Kira further because it made her feel jealous of her innocent sister, "could you give us a minute? I need to talk to Kira alone."

With a quick, nervous glance in Kira's direction, Jaycee said, "Kira, are you sure you'll be okay? You don't look so good."

Kira nodded mutely, wanting to spare Jaycee any necessary embarrassment. So Jaycee slipped out of the room and closed the door quietly.

Her hand raised, Kira bounded toward him like a charging lioness ready to claw her prey, but he caught her wrist and used it to lever her closer.

"Let me go!" she cried.

"Not while you're in such a violent mood, darlin'. You'd only scratch me or do something worse that you'd regret."

"I don't think so."

"This storm will pass, as all storms do. You'll see. Because it's due to a misunderstanding."

"A misunderstanding? I don't think so! You promised you'd break up with my sister, and I, being a fool, believed you. Then you slept with me. How could you go back on a promise like that after what we—"

"I wouldn't. I didn't." His voice was calm, dangerously soft. "I've kept my promise."

"Liar. If I hadn't shown up, you would have married my sister."

"The hell I would have! It was a bluff. How else could I get you to come back to San Antonio? I was going mad not knowing where you were or if you were all right. If you hadn't shown up, I would have looked like a fool, but I wouldn't have married your sister."

"But the newspapers all say you're going to marry her. Here. Today."

"I know what they say because my people wrote the press releases. That was all part of the bluff—to get you here. We'll have to write a correction now, won't we? The only Murray sister I plan to marry today is you, darlin'. If it'll help to convince you, I'll repeat myself on bended knee."

When he began to kneel, she shrieked at him, "Don't you dare…or I'll kick you. This is not a proposal. This is a farce."

"I'm asking you to marry me, darlin'."

He didn't love her. He never would. His was a damaged soul. He'd told her that in plain, hurtful terms right after he'd made love to her.

The details of the conversation she'd overheard came back to her.

"Let me get this straight," she said. "You always intended to marry a Murray daughter."

"And your father suggested Jaycee because he thought she would agree more easily."

"Then I came to your office and asked you not to marry her, and after dinner and sex, you decided one sister was as good as the other. So, why not marry the *easy* sister? Is that about it?"

"Easy?" He snorted. "I wish to hell you were easy, but no, you disappeared for weeks."

"Back to the basics. Marrying one of the Murray daughters is about business and nothing more to you?"

"In the beginning…maybe that was true…"

"I repeat—I heard you talking to Habib, whoever the hell he is, the morning after we made love. And your conversation made it seem that your relationship with me, with any Murray daughter, was still about business. Your voice was cold, matter-of-fact and all too believable."

"Habib works for me. Why would I tell him how I felt when I'd only known you a day and was still reeling, trying to figure it out for myself?"

"Oh, so now you're Mr. Sensitive. Well, I don't believe you, and I won't marry you. I've always dreamed of marrying for love. I know that is an emotion you despise and are incapable of feeling. Maybe that's why you can be so high-handed about forcing me to take my sister's place and marry you. I think you…are despicable…and cold. This whole situation is too cynical for words."

"It's true that our marriage will make Murray Oil employees see this change of leadership in a less hostile way, as for the rest—"

"So, for you, it's business. I will not be bought and sold like so many shares of stock. I am a human being. An educated, Western woman with a woman's dreams and feelings."

"I know that. It's what makes you so enchanting."

"Bull. You've chosen to ride roughshod over me and my family. You don't care what any of us want or feel."

"I do care what you feel. I care too damn much. It's driven me mad these last few weeks, worrying about you. I wished you'd never walked into my office, never made me feel… Hell! You've made me crazy, woman."

Before she had any idea of what he was about to do, he

took a long step toward her. Seizing her, he crushed her against his tall, hard body.

His hands gripping her close, his mouth slanted across hers with enough force to leave her breathless and have her moaning…and then, dear God, as his masterful kiss went on and on and on, she wanted nothing except more of him. Melting, she opened her mouth and her heart. How could she need him so much? She'd missed him terribly—every day they'd been apart.

Needle-sharp thrills raced down her spine. His tongue plunged inside her lips, and soon she was so drunk on his taste and passion, her nails dug into his back. She wanted to be somewhere else, somewhere more private.

She'd missed him. She'd wanted this. She hadn't been able to admit it. His clean, male scent intoxicated her. The length of his all-too-familiar body pressing against hers felt necessary. Every second, asleep and awake, she had thought of him, craved him—craved this. Being held by him only made the need more bittersweet. How could she want such a cold man so desperately?

"We can't feel this, do this," she whispered in a tortured breath even as she clung to him.

"Says who?"

"We're in a church."

His arms tightened their hold. "Marry me, and we can do all we want to each other—tonight…and forever," he said huskily. "It will become a sacred marital right."

How could he say that when he didn't care which Murray sister walked down the aisle as long as it saved him a few million dollars?

The thought hissed through her like cold water splashed onto a fire.

Her parents' love had carried them through many difficulties. Her dad was a workaholic. Her mother was a perfectionist, a status-seeking socialite. But they had always been madly in love.

Kira had grown up believing in the sanctity of marriage. How could she even consider a marriage that would be nothing more than a business deal to her husband?

A potential husband who had lapped up women the way she might attack a box of chocolates. Maybe he temporarily lusted after her, but he didn't love her and never could, as he'd told her. No doubt some other woman would soon catch his fancy.

Even wanting him as she did, she wasn't ready to settle for a marriage based on poor judgment, a momentary sexual connection, shallow lust, revenge and business.

She sucked in a breath and pushed against his massive chest. His grip eased slightly, maybe because the handsome rat thought he'd bent her to his will with his heated words and kisses.

"Listen to me," she said softly. "Are *you* listening?"

"Yes, darlin'."

"I won't marry you. Or any man who could dream up such a cold, cynical scheme."

"How can you call this cold when we're both burning up with desire?" He traced a fingertip along her cheek that made her jump and shiver before she jerked her head away.

"Cheap tricks like that won't induce me to change my mind. There's nothing you can say or do that will convince me. No masterful seduction technique that you honed in other women's bedrooms will do the job, either."

"I wish I had the time to woo you properly and make you believe how special you are."

Special. Now, *there* was a word that hit a nerve. She'd always wanted to feel beloved to those she cared about. How did he know that? It infuriated her that he could guess her sensibilities and so easily use them to manipulate her.

"What you want is revenge and money. If you had all of eternity, it wouldn't be long enough. I won't have you or your loveless deal. That's final."

"We'll see."

His silky baritone was so blatantly confident it sent an icy chill shivering down her spine.

Six

"You told him—the enemy—that Mother might be dying, and you didn't tell me or Jaycee! And you did this behind my back—weeks and weeks ago!"

Kira fisted and unfisted her hands as she sat beside her father in the preacher's library. Rage and hurt shot through her.

"How could you be so disloyal? I've never felt so completely betrayed. Sometimes I feel like a stray you picked up on the side of the road. You didn't really want me—only you have to keep me because it's the right thing to do."

"Nonsense! You're our daughter."

He blanched at her harsh condemnation, and she hung her head in guilt. "I'm sorry," she muttered.

She wanted to weep and scream, but she wouldn't be able to think if she lost all control.

"You know your mother and how she always wants to protect you. I thought only of her when I confided in him."

"First, you sell Jaycee to him because, as always, she's your first choice."

"Kira…"

"Now, it's me."

"Don't blame me. He wants *you!*"

"As if that makes you blameless. Why didn't either of my parents think about protecting their daughters from Quinn?"

"It's complicated. Even if your mother weren't sick, we need someone younger at the top, someone with a clearer vision of the future. Quinn's not what you think. Not what the press thinks. I knew him as a boy. This can be a win-win situation for you both."

"He grew into a vengeful man who hates us."

"You're wrong. He doesn't hate you. You'll never make me believe that. You should have seen how he acted when you disappeared. I think he'll make you a good husband."

"You don't care about that. You don't care about me. You only care about Murray Oil's bottom line, about retiring and being with Mother."

"How can you say that? I care about you, and I care about this family as much as you do. Yes, I need to take care of your mother now, but like I said—I know Quinn. I've watched him. He's good, smart, solid. And he's a brilliant businessman who will be the best possible CEO for Murray Oil during these tumultuous economic times. He's done great things already. If I had time, I'd fill you in on how he helped organize a deal with the EU while you were gone. He's still in the middle of it at the moment."

"For years he's worked to destroy you."

"Hell, maybe he believed that's what he was doing, maybe others bought it, too, but I never did. I don't think *he* knew what was driving him. This company is his heritage, too. And I saw how he was when you were gone.

The man was beside himself. He was afraid you were in trouble. I don't know what happened between the two of you before you ran away, but I know caring when I see it. Quinn cares for you. He's just like his father. You should have seen how Kade loved his wife, Esther. Then you'd know the love Quinn is capable of."

"You think Quinn will come to love me? Are you crazy? Quinn doesn't believe he can love again. The man has lived his life fueled by hate. Hatred for all of us. How many times do I have to repeat it?"

"Maybe so, but the only reason his hatred was so strong was that the love that drove it was just as strong. You're equally passionate. You just haven't found your calling yet." Her father took her hands in his as he continued, "You should have seen him the day he came to tell me he had me by the balls and was set to take over Murray Oil. He could have broken me that day. Instead, he choked when I told him about Vera because he's more decent than he knows. He's ten times the man that his father ever was, that's for sure. Maybe you two didn't meet under ideal circumstances, but he'll make you a good husband."

"You believe that only because you want to believe it. You're as cold and calculating as he is."

"I want what's best for all of us."

"This is a deal to you—just like it is to him. Neither of you care which daughter marries Quinn today, as long as the deal is completed for Murray Oil."

"I suggested Jaycee primarily to avoid a scene like the one we're having, but Quinn wants you. He won't even consider Jaycee now, even though he was willing to marry her before you meddled."

"Oh, so this fiasco is my fault."

"Someday you'll thank me."

"I'm not marrying him. I won't be sacrificed."

"Before you make your decision, your mother wants to talk to you." He pressed a couple of buttons on his phone, and the door behind him opened as if by magic. Her mother's perfectly coiffed blonde head caught the light of the overhead lamp. She was gripping her cell phone with clawlike hands.

She looked so tiny. Why hadn't Kira noticed how thin and colorless her once-vital mother had become? How frail and tired she looked?

"Dear God," Kira whispered as she got up and folded her precious mother into her arms. She felt her mother's ribs and spine as she pressed her body closer. Her mother was fading away right before her eyes.

"Please," her mother whispered. "I'm not asking you to do this for me, but for your father. I need all my strength to fight this illness. He can't be worried about Murray Oil. Or you. Or Jaycee. I've always been the strong one, you know. I can't fight this if I have to worry about him. And I can't leave him alone. He'd be lost without me."

"I—I…"

"I'm sure your father's told you there's a very important international deal with the EU on the table right now. It can make or break our company."

"*His* company."

"Your father and I and the employees of Murray Oil need your help, Kira. Your marriage to Quinn would endorse his leadership both here and abroad. Have I ever asked you for anything before?"

Of course she had. She'd been an ambitious and very demanding mother. Kira had always hoped that when she married and had children, she'd finally be part of a family where she felt as if she belonged, where she was accepted, flaws and all. How ironic that when her parents finally needed her to play a role they saw as vital to their survival, their need trampled on her heartfelt dream to be at the core of her own happy family.

Would she ever matter to her husband the way her mother mattered to her father? Not if the man who was forcing her to marry him valued her only as a business prize. Once Quinn had Murray Oil under his control, how long would she be of any importance to him?

Still, what choice did she have? For the first time ever, her family really needed her. And she'd always wanted that above all things.

"I don't want to marry you! But yes!" she spat at Quinn after he had ushered her into one of the private dressing rooms. She'd spun around to face him in the deadly quiet. "*Yes!* I will marry you, since you insist on having your answer today."

"Since I insist we marry today!"

Never had she seemed lovelier than with her dark, heavily lashed eyes glittering with anger and her slender hands fisted defiantly on her hips. He was so glad to have found her. So glad she was all right. So glad she'd agreed without wasting any more precious time. Once she was his, they'd get past this.

"Then I'll probably hate you forever for forcing me to make such a terrible bargain."

Her words stabbed him with pain, but he steeled himself not to show it. She looked mad enough to spit fire and stood at least ten feet from him so he couldn't touch her.

Looking down, staring anywhere but at her, he fought to hide the hurt and relief he felt at her answer, as well as the regret he felt for having bullied her.

Bottom line—she would be his. Today. The thought of any man touching her as Quinn had touched her their one night together seemed a sacrilege worthy of vengeful murder.

"Good. I'm glad that's finally settled and we can move on," he said in a cool tone that masked his own seething passions. "I've hired people to help you get ready. Beauticians. Designers. I selected a wedding gown that I hope you'll like, and I have a fitter here in case I misjudged your size."

"You did all that?" Her narrow brows arched with icy contempt. "You were that sure I'd say yes? You thought I was some doll you could dress up in white satin..."

"Silk, actually, and no, I don't think you're some doll—" He stopped. He wasn't about to admit how desperate he'd felt during the dark days of her absence, or how out of control, even though his silence only seemed to make her angrier.

"Look, just because you bullied me into saying yes doesn't mean I like the way you manipulated my family into taking your side. And, since this is strictly a business deal to all of you, I want you to know it's nothing but a business deal to me, too. So, I'm here by agreeing to a marriage in name only. The only reasons I'm marrying you are to help my father and mother and Murray Oil and to save Jaycee from you."

His lips thinned. "There's too much heat in you. You won't be satisfied with that kind of marriage...any more than I will."

"Well, I won't marry you unless you agree to it."

He would have agreed to sell his soul to the devil to have her. "Fine," he said. "Suit yourself, but when you change your mind, I won't hold you to your promise."

"I won't change my mind."

He didn't argue the point or try to seduce her. He'd

make the necessary concessions to get her to the altar. He'd pushed her way too far already.

He was willing to wait, to give her the time she needed. He didn't expect it would be long before he'd have her in his bed once more. And perhaps it was for the best that they take a break from the unexpected passion they'd found.

Maybe he wanted her to believe his motive for marrying her was business related, but it was far from the truth. Need—pure, raw, unadulterated need—was what drove him. If they didn't make love for a while, perhaps he could get control over all his emotions.

After they'd made love the last time, he'd felt too much, had felt too bound to her. Her power over him scared the hell out of him. She'd left him just as carelessly as his own mother had left his father, hadn't she?

He needed her like the air he breathed. Kira had simply become essential.

But he wasn't about to tell her that. No way could he trust this overwhelming need for any woman. Hadn't his father's love for Quinn's own mother played the largest part in his father's downfall? And then his own love for his father had crushed him when his father died.

Grief was too big a price to pay for love. He never wanted to be weak and needy like that again.

Seven

"You look…absolutely amazing," her mother said, sounding almost as pleased as she usually did when she complimented Jaycee. "Don't frown! You know you do!"

In a trancelike daze, Kira stared at the vision in the gilt mirror. How had Quinn's beauty experts made her look like herself and yet so much better? They'd tugged and pulled, clipped and sprayed unmercifully, and now here she was, a sexy, glowing beauty in a diaphanous silk gown that clung much too revealingly. The dress flattered her slim figure perfectly. How had he known her exact size and what would most become her?

All those blondes, she told herself. He understood glamour and women, not her. The dress wasn't about her. He wanted her to be like them.

Still, until this moment, she'd never realized how thoroughly into the Cinderella fantasy she'd been. Not that she would ever admit that, on some deep level, he'd pleased her.

"How can I walk down the aisle in a dress you can see straight through?"

"You're stunning. The man has flawless taste."

"Another reason to hate him," Kira mumbled, brushing aside her mother's hard-won approval and pleasure for fear of having it soften her attitude toward Quinn.

"Haven't I always told you, you should have been playing up your assets all along," her mother said.

"Straight guys aren't supposed to know how to do stuff like this."

"Count yourself lucky your man has such a rare talent. You'll have to start letting him dress you. Maybe he knows how to bring out your best self in other areas, as well. If he does, you'll amaze yourself."

The way he had during their one night together. A shiver traced through her. "May I remind you that this is not a real marriage?"

"If you'd quit saying that in such a sulky, stubborn tone, maybe it would become one, and very soon. He's very handsome. I'll bet there isn't a single woman in this church who wouldn't trade places with you."

"He doesn't love me."

"Well, why don't you start talking to him in a sweet voice? More like the one that you always use with that impossible cat of yours?"

"Maybe because he's not my loyal, beloved pet. Maybe because being bullied into a relationship with him does not make me feel sweet and tender."

"Well, if you ask me, the men you've chosen freely weren't much to brag about. Quinn is so well educated and well respected."

A few minutes later, when the wedding march started, Kira glided down the aisle in white satin slippers holding on to her father's arm. When she heard awed gasps from the guests, she lifted her eyes from the carpet, but in the sea of faces it was Quinn's proud smile alone that made her heart leap and brought a quick, happy blush to her cheeks.

Then her tummy flipped as their souls connected in that uncanny way that made her feel stripped bare. Fortunately, her father angled himself between them, and she got a brief reprieve from Quinn's mesmerizing spell.

Not that it was long before her father had handed her over to her bridegroom where she became her awkward, uncertain self again. As she stood beside Quinn at the altar, she fidgeted while they exchanged rings and vows. With a smile, he clasped her hand in his. Threading her fingers through his, he held them still. Somehow, his warm touch reassured her, and she was able to pledge herself to him forever in a strong, clear voice.

This isn't a real marriage, she reminded herself, even as that bitter truth tore at her heart.

But the tall man beside her, the music, the church and the incredibly beautiful dress, combined with the memory of her own radiance in the mirror, made her doubt what she knew to be true. Was she a simple-minded romantic after all, or just a normal girl who wanted to marry a man she loved?

After the preacher told Quinn he could kiss his bride, Quinn's arms encased her slim body with infinite gentleness. His eyes went dark in that final moment before he lowered his beautifully sculpted mouth to hers. Despite her intention not to react to his lips, to feel nothing when he kissed her, her blood pulsed. Gripping his arms, she leaned into him.

"We'd better make this count because if you have your way, it will probably be a while before I convince you to let me kiss you again," he teased huskily.

She threw her arms around his warm, bronzed neck, her

fingers stroking his thick hair, and drew his head down. Fool that she was, it felt glorious to be in his arms as he claimed her before a thousand witnesses.

Such a ceremonial kiss shouldn't mean anything, she told herself. He was just going through the motions. As was she.

"Darlin'," he murmured. "Sweet darlin' Kira. You are incredibly beautiful, incredibly dear. I want you so much. No bridegroom has ever felt prouder of his bride."

The compliment brought her startled eyes up to his, and his tender expression fulfilled her long-felt secret desire to be special to someone. For one shining instant, she believed the dream. If a man as sophisticated as he was could really be proud of her and want her…

He didn't, of course… Oh, but if only he could…

Then his mouth was on hers. His tongue inside the moist recesses of her lips had her blood heating and her breath shuddering in her lungs. Her limbs went as limp as a rag doll's. When she felt his heart hammering against her shoulder blade, she let him pull her even closer.

The last thing she wanted was to feel this swift rush of warm pleasure, but she couldn't stop herself. How could a single, staged kiss affect her so powerfully?

He was the first to pull away. His smile was slow and sweet. "Don't forget—the last thing I want is for our marriage to be business-only," he whispered against her ravaged lips. "You can change your mind anytime, darlin'. Anytime. Nothing would please me more than to take you to my bed again."

"Well, I won't change my mind! Not ever!" she snapped much too vehemently.

He laughed and hugged her close. "You will. I should warn you that nothing appeals to me more than a challenge."

After a lengthy photography session—she was surprised that he wanted photos of a wedding that couldn't possibly mean anything to him—they were driven by limousine to the reception, held at his opulent club in an older section of San Antonio.

Once again he'd planned everything—decorations in the lavish ballroom, the menu, the band—with enough attention to detail that her critical mother was thoroughly impressed and radiantly aglow with pride. Vera sailed through the glittering throng like a bejeweled queen among awed subjects as she admired the banks of flowers, frozen sculptures and the sumptuous food and arrangements. Kira was secretly pleased Quinn had at least married her under circumstances that gave her mother, who loved to impress, so much pleasure.

With a few exceptions, the majority of the guests were employees and clients of Murray Oil. The few personal friends and family attending included Quinn's uncle Jerry, who'd been his best man, and her friend Betty. The guest list also included a few important people from the Texas art world, mostly museum directors, including Gary Whitehall, the former boss who'd let her go…for daring to have an opinion of her own.

Since the wedding was a business affair, Kira was surprised that Quinn had allowed his employees to bring their children, but he had. And no one was enjoying themselves more than the kids. They danced wildly and chased each other around the edges of the dance floor, and when a father spoke harshly to the little flower girl for doing cartwheels in her long velvet gown, Quinn soothed the child.

Watching the way the little girl brightened under his tender ministrations, Kira's heart softened.

"He's very good with children," Betty whispered into her ear. "He'll make a wonderful father."

"This is not a real marriage."

"You could have fooled me. I get all mushy inside every time he looks at you. He's *so* good-looking."

"He's taken over my life."

"Well, I'd be glad to take him off your hands. I think he's hunky. And so polite. Did I tell you how nice he was to Rudy after he found out the reason the beast wouldn't stop meowing was because he missed you? He sat down with that cat and commiserated. Made me give the beast some tuna."

"I'll bet he got you to feed him, too."

"Well, every time Quinn came to the restaurant he did sit down with me and whoever was waiting tables, like he was one of us. He bragged on my pies."

"Which got him free pies I bet."

"His favorite is the same as yours."

"Your gooey lemon meringue?"

"I thought he was sweet to remember to invite me to the wedding. He called this evening after you showed up."

Betty hushed when Quinn appeared at his bride's side and stayed, playing the attentive groom long after his duties in the receiving line ended. Even when several beauties—one a flashy blonde he'd once dated named Cristina, whom he'd apparently hired as a junior executive—came up and flirted boldly, he'd threaded his fingers through Kira's and tucked her closer.

For more than an hour, ignoring all others, he danced only with Kira. He was such a strong partner, she found herself enjoying the reception immensely as he whirled her around the room. She could see the admiring glances following them. He smiled down at her often, no doubt to give the appearance that she delighted him. The women who'd flirted with him watched him with intense interest, especially Cristina, whose lovely mouth began to pout.

"I've never been much of a dancer," Kira confessed during a slow number.

"You could've fooled me. Just goes to show that all you need is a little self-confidence."

Had his attentiveness given her that, at least briefly? When Gary Whitehall's gaze met hers over Quinn's broad shoulder, he smiled tightly. As Quinn's wife, she'd taken a huge step up in the art world. Was Gary wishing he'd let someone else go other than her when the budget had been tight? Why had Quinn included him on the guest list?

After a fast number, when Kira admitted she was thirsty, Quinn left her to get champagne. Seeing his chance, Gary rushed up to her.

"You look lovely," he said, smiling in the way he used to smile at major artists and important donors. How rare had been the smiles and compliments he'd bestowed on his lowly curator for her hard work. "I'm very happy for you," he said.

She nodded, embarrassed to be so pleased that her marriage had won his respect.

"If I can do anything for you, anything at all, just call me. I am rewriting your letter of recommendation. Not that you'll need to work now."

"I intend to work again. I loved my job."

"Your husband has been most generous to the museum. We value his friendship and expertise almost as much as we will value yours—as his wife," he gushed. "I have a feeling we may have a position for a curator opening up soon. If so, I'll give you a call."

She thought about what Gary had said about a position possibly being available and was surprised she was so pleased. Maybe...she would consider working for him again...if he made her the right offer. She would, however, demand to have more power.

Stunned, she stared at him. Then Quinn returned with her champagne. The two men shook hands and exchanged pleasantries. When Quinn made it clear he preferred his bride's conversation to art talk, Gary quickly eased himself back into the crowd. But every time after that conversation, when their eyes met, Gary smiled at her.

For a man who supposedly hated her family, Quinn was excessively attentive to her mother and father and Jaycee. He talked to them, ordered them wine and appetizers, acted as if he actually wished to please them. He was especially solicitous of her mother, who positively glowed.

Kira watched him during dinner, and his warm smiles and polite comments rang with sincerity. If she hadn't known better, she wouldn't have believed he was simply acting a part in order to reassure oil company clients and executives that Murray Oil was in good hands.

Never had a bridegroom appeared more enthusiastic, even when his uncle Jerry congratulated him on his marriage.

"Kira, he's had his nose to the grindstone so long, we were beginning to think that's all he'd ever do," Jerry said. "We'd given up on you, son. Now I see you just hadn't met the right girl. Sooner or later, if we're lucky, love comes our way. The trick is to know it and appreciate it. When you fall in love, wanting to spend the rest of your life with the same woman doesn't seem that hard to imagine."

Quinn stared at her as if he agreed. The two men shook hands again and laughed. But since Quinn's heart wasn't really in their marriage, she wondered how soon he'd give up trying to pretend to people like his uncle. After that, when she felt herself too charmed by one of Quinn's thoughtful smiles or gestures, she reminded herself that she'd be a fool if she fell for his act. Their marriage was a business deal. She didn't matter to him. She never would.

All too soon the dinner and dancing came to an end, and she and Quinn had changed into street clothes and were dashing out to his limo while cheering guests showered them with birdseed. When someone threw seeds straight at her eyes, and a tear streamed down her cheek, Quinn took out his monogrammed handkerchief and dabbed her face while everybody cheered.

She expected to be driven to his loft. Instead, the limo whisked them to his sleek private jet, which had been prepared for flight and was waiting outside a hangar at the San Antonio International Airport.

"Where are we going?" she asked as he helped her out into the blinding glare of dozens of flashes.

"Honeymoon," he whispered, his mouth so close to her ear she felt the heat of his breath. Her heart raced until she reminded herself he was only staging a romantic shot for the press.

Putting his arm around her, he faced the reporters, who asked him questions about his pending international oil deal as well as his marriage.

With abundant charm and smiles, he answered a few and then, grabbing her by the elbow, propelled her into his jet.

"Surely a honeymoon isn't necessary," she said when they were safely on board.

He smiled down at her. "A man only marries once."

"Like that reporter asked—how can you afford the time when you're working on that important EU deal?"

"You have to make time…for what's important."

"So, why did you notify the press about our honeymoon? Was it only so the EU people would know you married into the Murray family?"

"Why don't you relax? Step one, quit asking so many questions. Step two, just enjoy."

"You're thorough. I'll have to give you that. Even so,

how can I leave town when I haven't even packed for a trip," she said. "Besides, I have a cat—Rudy. I promised Betty I'd relieve her… He's been crying for me."

"I know. Rudy's all taken care of. Jacinda's going to look after him at your apartment. So, he'll be on his own turf. I bought him a case of tuna."

"You shopped for Rudy?"

"Okay—so I sent my assistant. And your mother helped me shop and pack for you."

"I'll bet she loved that."

"She did—although I did make certain key choices."

"Such as?"

"The lingerie and bikinis."

"Lingerie? I'm not much for lingerie! Or bikinis!"

"Good. Then you'll be exquisite in nothing. You slept in my arms like that all night, remember."

Hot color flooded her face. "Don't!"

"With your legs wrapped silkily around me," he added. "You were so warm and sweet, I can't believe you really intend to sleep alone tonight."

The images he aroused in her, coupled with his warm gaze and sexy grin, made her blood hum.

"I meant I feel bad about going away again so soon without telling Betty."

"Already done. Betty's fine with the idea."

"You *are* thorough."

When her temples began to throb, Kira squeezed her eyes shut. "Did everyone, absolutely everyone, know I was getting married to you today before I did?"

"Not me, darlin'. I was scared sick you wouldn't turn up or that you'd order me straight to hell after I proposed."

Had he really felt that way? Did he care a little?

No! She couldn't let herself ask such questions.

Or care at all what the answers might be.

Eight

An hour later, after a flight to the coast and a brief but exciting helicopter ride over Galveston Island, they dropped out of the night sky onto the sleek, upper deck of the white floating palace he kept moored at the Galveston marina. She took his arm when the rotors stopped and sucked in a breath as he helped her onto his yacht. Gusts of thick, humid air that smelled of the sea whipped her clothes and hair.

Promising to give her a tour of the megayacht the next day, the captain led them down a flight of steep, white stairs and through a wood-lined corridor to Quinn's master stateroom. Clearly the captain hadn't been told that they would not be sharing a room. Crewmen followed at a brisk pace to deliver their bags.

Once alone with Quinn in his palatial, brass-studded cabin, her brows knitted in concern as she stared at the mountain of bags.

"Don't worry. If you really insist on sleeping alone, I'll move mine."

Shooting a nervous glance toward his big bed, she felt her body heat.

Above the headboard hung a magnificent painting of a nude blonde by an artist she admired. The subject was lying on her tummy across a tumble of satin sheets, her slender back arched to reveal ample breasts. Long-lashed, come-hither eyes compelled the viewer not to look away. Surely such a wanton creature would never send her husband away on their wedding night.

"Last chance to change your mind," he said.

Feeling strangely shy, Kira crossed her arms over her own breasts and shook her head. "So, where will you sleep?"

"Next door." There was a mesmerizing intensity in his eyes. "Would you like to see my room?"

She twisted her hands. "I'll be just fine right here. So, if that's settled, I guess we'll see each other in the morning."

"Right." He hesitated. "If you need anything, all you have to do is punch this button on your bedside table and one of the staff will answer. If you want me, I'll leave my door unlocked. Or, if you prefer me to come to you, you could ring through on that phone over there."

"Thanks."

He turned, opened the door, shoved his bags into the passageway and stepped outside. When the door slammed behind him, and she was alone with his come-hither blonde, a heavy emotion that felt too much like disappointment gripped her.

To distract herself, she studied the painting for another moment, noting that the artist had used linseed oil most effectively to capture the effect of satin.

Feeling a vague disquiet as she considered the nude,

she decided the best thing to do was shower and get ready for bed. As she rummaged in her suitcase, she found all sorts of beautiful clothes that she never would have picked out. Still, as she touched the soft fabrics and imagined her mother shopping for such things without her there to discourage such absurd purchases, she couldn't help smiling. Her mother had always wanted to dress Kira in beautiful things, but being a tomboy, Kira had preferred jeans and T-shirts.

What was the point of fancy clothes for someone who lived as she had, spending time in art vaults, or painting, or waiting tables? But now, she supposed, for however long she was married to a billionaire with his own jet and megayacht, she would run in different circles and have fundraisers and parties to attend. Maybe she did need to upgrade her wardrobe.

Usually, she slept in an overlarge, faded T-shirt. In her suitcase all she found for pajamas were thin satin gowns and sheer robes, the kind that would cling so seductively she almost regretted she wouldn't be wearing them for Quinn.

Instead of the satin gown, which reminded her too much of the blonde above the bed, she chose black lace. Had he touched the gown, imagining her in it, when he'd picked it out? As the gossamer garment slipped through her fingers she shivered.

Go to bed. Don't dwell on what might have been. He's ruined enough of your day and night as it is.

But how not to think of him as she stripped and stepped into her shower? What was he doing next door? Was his tall, bronzed body naked, too? Her heart hammered much too fast.

Lathering her body underneath a flow of warm water, she imagined him doing the same in his own shower. Leaning against the wet tile wall, she grew hotter and hotter as the water streamed over her. She stood beneath the spray until her fingers grew too numb to hold the slippery bar of soap. When it fell, she snapped out of her spell.

Drying off and then slipping into the black gown, she slid into his big bed with a magazine. Unable to do more than flip pages and stare unseeingly at the pictures because she couldn't stop thinking about Quinn, she eventually drifted to sleep. But once asleep, she didn't dream of him.

Instead, she dreamed she was a small child in her pink bedroom with its wall-to-wall white carpet. All her books were lined up just perfectly, the way her mother liked them to be, in her small white bookcase beneath the window.

Somewhere in the house she heard laughter and hushed endearments, the sort of affection she'd never been able to get enough of. Then her door opened and her parents rushed inside her bedroom. Only they didn't take her into their arms as they usually did. Her mother was cooing over a bundle she held against her heart, and her father was staring down at what her mother held as if it were the most precious thing in the world.

She wanted them to look at her like that.

"Kira, we've brought your new baby sister, Jaycee, for a visit."

A baby sister? "Where did she come from?"

"The hospital."

"Is that where you got me?"

Her mother paled. Her father looked as uneasy as her mother, but he nodded.

What was going on?

"Do you love me, too?" Kira whispered.

"Yes, of course," her father said. "You're our big girl now, so your job will be to help us take care of Jaycee.

She's *our* special baby. We're all going to work hard to take very good care of Jaycee."

Suddenly, the bundle in her mother's arms began to shriek frantically.

"What can I do?" Kira had said, terrified as she ran toward them. "How can I help? Tell me what to do!"

But they'd turned away from her. "Why don't you just play," her father suggested absently.

Feeling lonely and left out as she eyed her dolls and books, she slowly backed away from them and walked out of her room, down the tall stairs to the front door, all the while hoping their concerned voices would call her back as they usually did. She wasn't supposed to be downstairs at night.

But this time, they didn't call her. Instead, her parents carried the new baby into a bedroom down the hall and stayed with her.

They had a new baby. They didn't need her anymore.

Kira opened the big front door. They didn't notice when she stepped outside. Why should they? They had Jaycee, who was special. They didn't care about Kira anymore. Maybe they'd never really cared.

Suddenly, everything grew black and cold, and a fierce wind began to blow, sweeping away everything familiar. The house vanished, and she was all alone in a strange, dark wood with nobody to hear her cries. Terrified, she ran deeper into the woods.

If her family didn't love her anymore, if nobody loved her, she didn't know what she would do.

Hysterical, she began sobbing their names. "Mother! Daddy! Somebody! Please…love me. I want to be special, too…"

Quinn opened her door and hurled himself into her stateroom.

"Kira!" He switched on a light. She blinked against the blinding glare of gold with heavy-lidded eyes.

"Are you okay?" he demanded. "Wake up!"

"Quinn?" Focusing on his broad shoulders, she blinked away the last remnants of that terrifying forest. He was huge and shirtless and so starkly handsome in the half shadows she hissed in a breath.

Her husband. What a fool she'd been to send him away when that was the last thing she really wanted.

When he sat down on the bed, she flung herself against his massive bare chest and clung. He felt so hard and strong and hot.

Snugging her close against his muscular body, he rocked her gently and spoke in soothing tones. "There…there…"

Wrapped in his warmth, she almost felt safe…and loved.

"I was a little girl again. Only I ran away and got lost. In a forest."

He petted her hair as his voice soothed her. "You were only dreaming."

She stared up at his shadowed face. In the aftermath of her dream, she was too open to her need of him. Her grip on him tightened. She felt his breath hitch and his heart thud faster. If only *he* loved her…maybe the importance of her childhood fears would recede.

"Darlin', it was just a dream. You're okay."

Slowly, because he held her, the horror of feeling lost and alone diminished and reality returned.

She was on his megayacht. In Galveston. He'd forced her to marry him and come on a honeymoon. She was in his bed where she'd been sleeping alone. This was supposed to be their wedding night, but she'd sent him away.

Yet somehow *she* was the one who felt lonely and rejected.

She liked being cradled in his strong arms, against his

virile body. Too much. She grew conscious of the danger of letting him linger in her bedroom.

"You want me to go?" he whispered roughly.

No. She wanted to cling to him…to be adored by him…. Another impossible dream.

When she hesitated, he said, "If you don't send me packing, I will take this as an invitation."

"It's no invitation," she finally murmured, but sulkily. Her heart wasn't in her statement.

"How come you don't sound sure?" He ran a rough palm across her cheek. Did she only imagine the intimate plea in his voice? Was he as lonely as she was?

Even as she felt herself softening under his affectionate touch and gentle tone, she forced herself to remember all the reasons she'd be a fool to trust him. Squeezing her eyes shut, she took a deep breath. "Thanks for coming, but go! Please—just go."

She felt his body tighten as he stared into her eyes. Time ticked for an endless moment before he released her.

Without a word he got up and left.

Alone again, she felt she might burst with sheer longing. When she didn't sleep until dawn, she blamed him for not going farther than the room next to hers. He was too close. Knowing that all she had to do was go to him increased her frustration. Because he'd made it clear he would not send her away.

Twisting and turning, she fought to settle into slumber, but could not. First, she was too hot for the covers. Then she was so cold she'd burrowed under them.

It was nearly dawn when she finally did sleep. Then, after less than an hour, loud voices in the passageway startled her into grouchy wakefulness. As she buried her head in her pillow, her first thought was of Quinn. He'd probably slept like a baby.

When the sun climbed high and his crewmen began shouting to one another on deck, she strained to hear Quinn's voice among theirs shouts, but didn't.

Sitting up, alone, she pulled the covers to her throat. Surely he couldn't still be sleeping. Where was he?

A dark thought hit her. Last night he'd left her so easily, when what she'd craved was for him to stay. Had she already served her purpose by marrying him? Was he finished with her?

Feeling the need for a strong cup of coffee, Kira slipped into a pair of tight, white shorts and a skimpy, beige knit top. Outside, the sky was blue, the sun brilliant. Normally, when she wasn't bleary from lack of sleep, Kira loved water, boats and beaches. Had Quinn been in love with her, a honeymoon on his luxurious yacht would have been exceedingly romantic. Instead, she felt strange and alone and much too needily self-conscious.

Was his crew spying on her? Did they know Quinn hadn't slept with her? Did they pity her?

Anxious to find Quinn, Kira grabbed a white sweater and left the stateroom. When he didn't answer her knock, she cracked open his door. A glance at the perfectly made spread and his unopened luggage told her he'd spent the night elsewhere. Pivoting, she stepped back into the corridor so fast she nearly slammed headlong into a crewman.

"May I help you, Mrs. Sullivan?"

"Just taking a private tour," she lied. On the off chance he'd think she knew where she was going, she strode purposefully past him down the wood-lined passageway.

Outside, the gulf stretched in endless sapphire sparkle toward a shimmering horizon. Not that she paid much attention to the dazzling view. Intent on finding Quinn, she was too busy opening every door on the sumptuously appointed decks. Too proud to ask the numerous crew members she passed for help, she averted her eyes when she chanced to meet one of them for fear they'd quiz her.

The yacht seemed even bigger on close inspection. So far she'd found six luxury staterooms, a cinema, multiple decks, a helipad and a grand salon.

Just when she was about to give up her search for Quinn, she opened a door on the uppermost deck and found him slumped over a desk in a cluttered office. Noting the numerous documents scattered on chairs, desks, tables and even the floor, she crossed the room to his side. Unfinished cups of coffee sat atop the jumbled stacks. Obviously, he'd worked through the night on a caffeine high.

At the sight of his exhausted face, her heart constricted. Even as she smoothed her hand lightly through his rumpled hair, she chastised herself for feeling sympathy for him. Hadn't he bullied her into their forced, loveless marriage?

Now that she knew where he was, she should go, order herself coffee and breakfast, read her magazine in some pristine chaise lounge, sunbathe—in short, ignore him. Thinking she would do just that, she stepped away from him. Then, driven by warring emotions she refused to analyze, she quickly scampered back to his side.

Foolishly, she felt tempted to neaten his office, but since she didn't know what went where, she sank into the chair opposite his. Bringing her knees against her chest, she hugged them tightly and was pleased when he slept another hour under her benevolent guardianship. Then, without warning, his beautiful eyes snapped open and seared her.

"What the hell are you doing here?" he demanded.

She nearly jumped out of her chair. "He awakens—like a grumpy old bear," she teased.

Managing a lopsided grin, he ran a hand through his

spiked, rumpled hair. "You were a bit grumpy…the morning after…you slept with me in San Antonio, as I recall."

"Don't remind me of that disastrous night, please."

"It's one of my fondest memories," he said softly.

"I said don't!"

"I love it when you blush like that. It makes you look so…cute. You should have awakened me the minute you came in."

"How could I be so heartlessly cruel when you came to my rescue in the middle of the night? If you couldn't sleep, it was my fault."

When his beautiful white teeth flashed in a teasing grin, she couldn't help smiling back at him.

"I could bring you some coffee. Frankly, I could use a cup myself," she said.

He sat up straighter and stretched. "Sorry this place is such a mess, but as I'm not through here, I don't want anybody straightening it up yet."

She nodded. "I sort of thought that might be the case."

"What about breakfast…on deck, then? I have a crew ready to wait on us hand and foot. They're well trained in all things—food service…emergencies at sea…"

"They didn't come when I screamed last night," she said softly. "You did."

"Only because you didn't call for their help on the proper phone."

"So, it's my fault, is it?" Where had the lilt in her light tone come from?

Remembering how safe she'd felt in his arms last night, a fierce tenderness toward him welled up in her heart. He must have sensed what she felt, because his eyes flared darkly before he looked away.

Again, she wished this were a real honeymoon, wished that he loved her rather than only lusted for her, wished that she was allowed to love him back. If only she hadn't demanded separate bedrooms, then she would be lying in his arms looking forward to making love with him again this morning.

At the thought, her neck grew warm. She'd been wishing for the wrong stuff her whole life. It was time she grew up and figured out what her life was to be about. The sooner she got started on that serious journey, one that could never include him, the better.

Nine

Breakfast on deck with his long-limbed bride in her sexy short shorts was proving to be an unbearable torture. She squirmed when his gaze strayed to her lips or her breasts or when it ran down those long, lovely legs.

If only he could forget how she'd clung to him last night or how her big eyes had adored him when he'd first woken up this morning.

"I wish you wouldn't stare so," she said as she licked chocolate off a fingertip. "It makes me feel self-conscious about eating this and making such a mess."

"Sorry," he muttered.

He tried to look away, but found he could not. What else was there to look at besides endless sapphire dazzle? Why shouldn't he enjoy watching her greedily devour her fresh-baked croissants and *pain du chocolat?* The way she licked chocolate off her fingers made him remember her mouth and tongue on him that night in his loft. *Torture.*

Even though he was sitting in the shade and the gulf breeze was cool, his skin heated. His bride was too sexy for words.

If he were to survive the morning without grabbing her like a besotted teenager and making a fool of himself, he needed to quickly get back to his office and the EU deal.

But he knew he wouldn't be able to concentrate on the deal while his forbidden bride was aboard. No. He'd go to the gym and follow his workout with a long, cold shower. Only then would he attempt another try at the office.

Dear God, why was it that ever since she'd said no sex, bedding her was all he could think about?

With the fortitude that was so much a part of his character, he steeled himself to endure her beauty and her provocative sensuality, at least until breakfast was over and they parted ways.

"So, are we heading somewhere in particular?" she asked playfully.

"Do you like to snorkel?"

"I do, but I've only snorkeled in lakes and shallow coves in the Caribbean."

"Once we get into really deep water, the gulf will be clear. I thought we'd snorkel off one of my oil rigs. It's always struck me as ironic the way marine life flourishes around a rig. You're in for a treat."

Her brief smile charmed him. "I read somewhere that rigs act like artificial reefs." She stopped eating her orange. "But you don't need to interrupt your precious work to entertain me."

"I'll set my own work schedule, if you don't mind."

"You're the boss, my lord and master. Sorry I keep forgetting that all-important fact." Again her playful tone teased him.

"Right." He smiled grimly. What could he say?

They lapsed into an uncomfortable silence. Focusing on his eggs and bacon, he fought to ignore her. Not that he didn't want to talk to her, because he did. Very much. But small talk with his bride was not proving to be an easy matter.

"I'd best get busy," he said when he'd finished his eggs and she her orange.

"Okay. Don't worry about me. Like I said, I can entertain myself. I love the water. As you know, I spent the past few weeks on Murray Island. I don't know where we are, but we probably aren't that far from it."

Scanning the horizon, he frowned. He didn't like remembering how much her stay at her family's isolated island had worried him.

How had he become so attached—or whatever the hell he was—to her so fast? They'd only had one night together!

Biting out a terse goodbye that made her pretty smile falter, he stood abruptly. Pivoting, he headed to his gym and that icy shower while she set off to her stateroom.

The gym and shower didn't do any good. No sooner did he return to his office on the upper deck than who should he find sunbathing right outside his door practically naked but his delectable bride.

She lay on a vivid splash of red terry cloth atop one of his chaise lounges, wearing the white thong bikini he'd picked out for her while under the influence of a lurid male fantasy.

He'd imagined her in it. Hell, yes, he had. But not like this—not with her body forbidden to him by her decree and his unwillingness to become any more attached to her. He would never have bought those three tiny triangles if he'd had any idea what torture watching her would give him.

Clenching his fists, he told himself to snap the blinds shut and forget her. Instead, mesmerized, he crossed his office with the long strides of a large, predatory cat and stood at a porthole, staring at her hungrily, ravenous for whatever scraps of tenderness the sexy witch might bestow. He willed her to look at him.

She flipped a magazine page carelessly and continued to read with the most maddening intensity. Not once did she so much as glance his way.

Damn her.

She was on her tummy in the exact position of the girl in the painting over his bed. He watched her long, dark hair glint with fiery highlights and blow about her slim, bare shoulders. He watched her long, graceful fingers flip more pages and occasionally smooth back flying strands of her hair. Every movement of her slim wrist had her dainty silver bracelet flashing.

Was she really as cool and collected as she appeared?

How could she be, when she'd given herself to him so quickly and completely that first night? Her eyes had shone with desire, and she'd trembled and quivered at his touch. She hadn't faked her response. He'd bet his life on it. He would never have forced her to marry him if he'd thought her cold and indifferent.

And last night he'd definitely felt her holding on to him as if she didn't want to let go.

So, she must be clinging to her position of abstinence out of principle. Wasn't she turning those pages much too fast? Was she even reading that magazine? Or was she as distracted as he was? Did she sense him watching her and take perverse delight in her power over him?

Damn the fates that had sent her to him!

Always, before Kira, he'd gone for voluptuous blondes with modern morals, curvy women who knew how to dress, women who thought their main purpose was to please a man. Women with whom he'd felt safe because they'd wanted his money and position more than they'd valued his heart.

This slim, coltishly long-limbed girl hadn't yet learned what she was about or even how to please herself, much less how to seduce a man. But her innocence in these matters appealed to him.

Why?

Again, he told himself to forget her, but when he went to his desk, he just sat there for a full half hour unable to concentrate. Her image had burned itself into his brain. She had his loins hard and aching. The woman lured him from his work like the Sirens had lured Ulysses after Troy.

He began to worry that she hadn't put on enough sunblock. Weren't there places on that long, slim body she couldn't reach?

Hardly knowing what he was about, he slammed out of his office and found himself outside, towering grimly over her. Not that she so much as bothered to glance away from her damn magazine, even though she must have heard his heavy footsteps, even though he cast a shadow over the pages.

He felt like a fool.

"You're going to burn," he growled with some annoyance.

"Do you think so? I've got lotion on, and my hat. But maybe you're right. I need to turn over for a while." She lowered her sunglasses to the tip of her nose and peered up at him saucily with bright, dark eyes.

Was she flirting with him? Damn her to hell and back if she was.

"Since you're out here, would you mind being a dear and rubbing some lotion on my back for me?"

He sank to his haunches, his excitement so profound at the thought of touching her that he didn't worry about her request for lotion on her back being illogical. Hadn't she forbidden his touch? And didn't she just say she intended to turn over onto her back?

He didn't care.

The lotion was warm from the sun, and her silky skin was even warmer as he rubbed the cream into it.

A moan of pure pleasure escaped her lips as his large palm made circular motions in the center of her back, and his heart raced at her response. He felt a visceral connection to her deep in his groin.

"You have strong hands. The lotion smells so deliciously sweet. Feels good, too," she whispered silkily, stretching like a cat as he stroked her.

"Thanks," he growled.

She rolled over and lay on her towel. Throwing him a dismissive glance, she lifted her magazine to shut him out.

"You can go now," she whispered.

Feeling stubborn and moody, he didn't budge. Only when he saw his oil rig looming off the starboard side did he arise and ask his crew to assemble their diving gear: fins, wet suits, marker floats and masks.

So much for working on the EU deal…

Later, when he and she stood on the teak diving platform at the stern of the yacht in their wet suits, she noticed nobody had thrown out an anchor.

"What if your yacht drifts while we're in the water?"

"She won't," he replied. "*Pegasus* is equipped with a sophisticated navigational system called dynamic positioning. On a day this calm she'll stay exactly where we position her. Believe me, it's much better than an anchor, which would allow her to swing back and forth."

"You plan so much that you think of everything. Does your planning and your fortune allow you to have everything you want?"

"Not quite everything," he murmured as he stared hungrily at her trim body.

Didn't she know she had changed everything?

For years, he'd been driven to avenge himself against her father, but no sooner had he been poised to seize his prize than he'd learned of Vera's illness. From that moment, his victory had begun to feel hollow.

Just when he'd wondered what new challenge could ever drive him as passionately as revenge once did, Kira had walked into his office to fight for her sister. He'd known he had to have her.

Trouble was, he was beginning to want more than he'd ever allowed himself to dream of wanting before. He wanted a life with her, a future, everything he'd told himself he could never risk having.

Kira stood on the platform watching Quinn in the water as he adjusted his mask.

"Come on in," he yelled.

She was removing her silver jewelry because he'd told her the flash of it might attract sharks.

"You know how I told you I've mainly confined my snorkeling to lakes or shallow lagoons," she began. "Well, the gulf's beginning to seem too big and too deep."

"I'll be right beside you, and Skip and Chuck are in the tender."

"I've seen all the *Jaws* movies."

"Not a good time to think about them."

She squinted, searching the vast expanse of the gulf for fins.

"Are you coming in or not?" he demanded.

Despite her doubts, she sucked in a deep breath and jumped in.

As she swam out to him, the water felt refreshingly cool.

After she got her mask on she and Quinn were soon surrounded by red snapper and amberjack. She was enjoying their cool, blue world so much that when he pointed out a giant grouper gliding by, she stared in awe instead of fear. Quinn's sure presence beside her in the water instilled in her a confidence she wouldn't have believed possible.

Snorkeling soon had her feeling weightless. It was as if she were flying in an alien world that dissolved into endless deep blue nothingness. As he'd promised, Quinn stayed beside her for nearly an hour. Enjoying herself, she forgot the vast blue darkness beneath them and what it concealed.

Just when she was starting to relax, a tiger shark zoomed out of the depths straight at Quinn. In her panic, she did exactly what she shouldn't have done. Kicking and thrashing wildly, she gulped in too much water. Choking, she yanked off her mask. As the fin vanished, Quinn ordered her to swim to the yacht.

In seconds, the fin was back, circling Quinn before diving again. Then the shark returned, dashing right at Quinn, who rammed it in the nose and made a motion with his arm for her to quit watching and start swimming. Staying behind her so he could keep his body between hers and the shark, he headed for the yacht, as well.

A tense knot of crewmen on the platform were shouting to them when she finally reached the yacht.

"Quinn," she yelled even as strong arms yanked her on board. "Quinn!" She barely heard his men shouting to him as she stood on the teak platform panting for breath. Then the dorsal fin slashed viciously right beside Quinn, and her fear mushroomed.

"Get him out! Somebody do something! Quinn! *Darling!*" she screamed.

Quinn swam in smooth, rapid strokes toward the stern. When he made it to the ladder, his crewmen sprang forward and hauled him roughly aboard, slamming him onto the teak platform.

Quinn tore off his mask. When he stood up, he turned to Kira, who took the desperate glint in his eyes as an invitation to hurl herself into his arms.

"You're as white as bleached bone," he said, gripping her tightly. "You're sure you're okay?"

The blaze of concern in his eyes and his tone mirrored her own wild fears for him.

"If you're okay, I'm okay," she whispered shakily, snuggling closer. She was so happy he was alive and unhurt.

"You're overreacting. It would take more than one little shark—"

"Don't joke! He could have torn off your arm!"

"He was probably just curious."

"Curious! I saw the movies, remember?"

He stared down at her in a way that made her skin heat. "In a funny way I feel indebted to the shark. Because of him, you called me darling."

"Did not!"

"Did, too," he drawled in that low tone that mesmerized her.

When she wrenched free of him, he laughed. "Okay. It must have been wishful thinking on a doomed man's part. Guess it was Chuck who let out the *d*-word."

She bit her lip to keep from smiling.

After they dressed, they met on the upper deck where they'd had breakfast earlier. Quinn wore jeans and a blue Hawaiian shirt that made his eyes seem as brilliant as the dazzling sky.

He ordered pineapple and mangoes and coffee. She was still so glad he was alive and had all his body parts she couldn't take her eyes off him.

"I have an idea," she said. "I mean…if we're looking for a less exciting adventure."

"What?"

"I could show you Murray Island."

"Where is it?"

"South of Galveston. Since I don't know where we are, I can't tell you how to get there. But it's on all the charts."

He picked up a phone and talked to his captain. When he hung up, he said, "Apparently, we're about forty nautical miles from your island. The captain says we could run into some weather, but if you want to go there, we will."

"What's a raindrop or two compared to being lunch for Jaws?"

"I love your vivid imagination."

In little over an hour, *Pegasus* was positioned off the shore of Murray Island, and Kira and Quinn were climbing down into the tender together. After Quinn revved the outboard, they sped toward the breaking surf, making for the pass between the barrier islands and the tiny harbor on the island's leeward side.

The bouncy ride beneath thickening gray storm clouds was wet and choppy. Heedless of the iffy weather, she stared ahead, laughing as the spray hit them. Quinn's eyes never strayed from his course—except when they veered to her face, which secretly thrilled her. She knew she shouldn't crave his attention so much, but ever since the shark incident, her emotions refused to behave sensibly.

He's alive. I have this moment with him. It's our honeymoon. Why not enjoy it? Why not share this island sanctuary I love with him?

Ten

Quinn watched his beachcombing bride much too avidly for his liking. He hated feeling so powerfully attracted to her. It was incomprehensible. She was Earl's daughter, a woman he barely knew, a wife who wouldn't even share his bed.

She'd slept with him once and then she'd left him, causing a pain too similar to what he'd felt after his father's death. The tenderness he continued to feel for her put him on dangerous ground, but still she possessed him in a way no other woman ever had.

It was the shark. Before they'd snorkeled, he'd been able to tell himself that he was under a temporary spell, that he could vanquish his burning need for her simply by staying out of her bed.

But he'd been afraid for her when she'd been swimming for the boat, more afraid than he'd ever been in his life.

Then he'd seen her bone-white face and the wild terror in her eyes when she'd imagined him in danger.

Once he'd been safely on board, her slim face had become luminous with joy. She'd hurled herself into his arms so violently she'd all but knocked them both back into the water again.

Nobody had ever looked at him like that.

Surely his father had loved him more, but she was here, and so beautiful, and so alive, and his—if only he could win her.

The prevailing southeasterly wind, cooler now because of the dark gray clouds, licked the crests of the waves into a foaming fury and sent her dark chestnut hair streaming back from her face as she scampered at the surf's edge. Every few steps, she knelt, not caring if a wave splashed her toes. Crouching, she examined the beach debris: tangles of seaweed, driftwood and shells.

Her long slim feet were bare, her toenails unpolished. Flip-flops dangled from her left hand.

For twenty years, his determination to succeed and get revenge had made time seem too valuable for him to waste on a beach with a woman. Most nights he'd worked, and most mornings, he'd left for his office before dawn. Driven by his dark goals, he'd often worked through entire weekends and holidays. His main sources of relaxation had been the gym or a willing woman and a glass of scotch before he hit his bed or desk again. He'd been more machine than human.

But that was before Kira.

Memories, long suppressed, stirred. As a child, he'd looked forward to the hour when his father's key would turn in the lock and he'd holler Quinn's name.

Quinn would race into his father's arms. After hugging him close, his father would lift him so high in the air

Quinn could touch the ceiling. So high, he'd felt as if he was flying. Then his dad would set him down and ruffle his hair and ask him about his day.

Never had his father been too tired to pass a football around the yard or take him to the park to chase geese. His father had helped with Quinn's homework, helped him build models, played endless games with him. His mother, on the other hand, had always been too busy to play. Then his father had died, and Quinn had known grief and loneliness.

For the first time, while indulging in this simple walk on the beach with Kira, Quinn felt a glimmer of the warmth that had lit his life before his father's death.

His father would want him to stop grieving, he realized. He'd want him to choose life, to choose the future.

Kira didn't realize she was beautiful, or that her lack of pretention and artifice made her even more attractive. Her every movement was graceful and natural. On the beach, she seemed a lovely wild thing running free.

This island was her refuge. For however long they were together, he would have to accept her world if he wanted her to accept his. No doubt, she would need to come here again from time to time.

He frowned, not liking the thought of her leaving him to stay out here all alone. Anyone could beach a small boat or tie up at her dock. Jim, the island's caretaker, had the faraway look of a man who'd checked out of life a long time ago. Quinn wasn't about to trust a dropout like him as her protector. No, he would have to get his security team to figure out how to make her safe here without intruding on her privacy. She was a free spirit, and Quinn wanted her to be happy, the way she was now, but safe, as well.

The sky was rapidly darkening from gray to black. Not that Kira seemed concerned about the gathering storm as she leaned down and picked up a shell. When she twisted, their gazes met. At her enchanting smile, his heart brimmed with way too much emotion. Then she ran over to show him her newfound treasure. When she held it up, her eyes shone, and the tiny window that had opened into his soul widened even further.

"Look, it's a lightning whelk," she cried.

"It's huge," he said, turning the cone-shaped shell over in his hand to properly admire it.

"At least a foot long. I've never seen one so big. And it's in perfect condition. Did you know it's the state shell of Texas?"

Shaking his head, he shot a glance at the darkening sky before he handed it back to her. "Do you collect shells?"

"Not really, but I'd like to give you this one. So you can remember Murray Island."

And *her,* he thought. "As if I could ever forget," he said. "I'll cherish it."

"I'm sure." She attempted a laugh and failed. "A new gem for your art collection."

"It's already my favorite thing."

Stronger now, the wind whipped her hair, and the sand bit into his legs.

"We should take cover," he said. "Storm's coming in. Fast. I think we'd better make a run for the house!"

"I'll race you!" Giggling as she danced on her toes, she sprinted toward the house, and because he liked watching her cute butt when she ran, he held back and let her win.

Darting from room to room as the wind howled and the frame structure shuddered, she gave him a quick tour of the house. A shady front porch looked out onto the raging gulf. Two bedrooms, a bath and a kitchen were connected by screened breezeways to each other and to the porch.

The southern bedroom had a wall of windows. "This is my favorite room," she said. "There's always a breeze, so I usually sleep here."

When she cracked a window, the room cooled instantly as storm gusts swept through it.

Deliberately, he stared outside at the rain instead of at her narrow bed. Since it was much too easy to imagine her long, lithe body on that mattress beneath him, he concentrated on the fat raindrops splatting on sand.

"With all the doors and windows open, the prevailing breezes cool the house on the hottest summer days," she said.

"If you open everything up, doesn't that make you vulnerable to a break-in?"

"No one usually comes here except me and Jim."

All anybody had to do was slit a screen to get inside. She would be defenseless. If Quinn had known how vulnerable she was while she'd been gone, he would have been even crazier with worry.

"Would you like some tea?" she said. "While we wait out the weather?"

"Sure."

When he nodded, she disappeared into the kitchen, leaving him to explore the room. A violent gust hit the house as the storm broke with full force. Somewhere, a breezeway door slammed so hard the entire house shook. Then papers fluttered under her bed. Curious, he knelt and pulled them out.

To his amazement, he discovered dozens of watercolors, all of himself, all ripped in two. He was trying to shove the entire collection back under the bed, when he heard her light footsteps at the doorway.

"Oh, my God," she said. "I forgot about those. Don't think… I mean… They don't mean anything!"

"Right."

You just painted picture after picture of me with violent, vivid brushstrokes. Then you shredded them all. For no reason.

"You obviously weren't too happy with me," he muttered.

"I really don't want to talk about it."

"Did you paint anything else…besides me?"

"A few birds."

"How many?"

"Not so many. One actually." She turned away as if uncomfortable with that admission.

Obviously, she was just as uneasy about her feelings for him as he was about his obsession with her.

"Why don't we drink our tea and go back to the yacht," he said brusquely.

"Fine with me."

"I shouldn't have pulled those pictures out," he said.

"We said we were going to forget about them."

"Right. We did." So, while he'd been obsessing about her absence, maybe she'd done a bit of obsessing herself. He took a long breath.

They sat on the porch drinking tea as the gray fury of the storm lashed the island. Now that he wanted to leave, the weather wasn't cooperating. To the contrary. Monstrous black waves thundered against the beach while rain drummed endlessly against the metal roof. No way could he trust his small tender in such high seas.

"Looks like we're stuck here for the duration," he said. So much for distracting himself from his bride anytime soon.

She nodded, her expression equally grim. "Sorry I suggested coming here."

The squalls continued into the night, so for supper she

heated a can of beans and opened cans of peaches and tomatoes. Happily, she produced a bottle of scotch that she said she kept hidden.

"We have to hide liquor from the pirates," she told him with a shy smile.

"Pirates?" he asked.

"We call anyone who lands on the island pirates. We leave the house open so they don't have to break in. Because they will if we don't."

"So, you're not entirely unaware of the dangers of being here all alone?"

"Jim's here."

"Right. Jim."

Quinn poured himself a drink and toasted good old Jim. Then he poured another. When he'd drained the second, she began to glow. Her smile and eyes looked so fresh and sparkly, he saw the danger of more liquor and suggested they go to bed.

"Separate bedrooms, of course," he said, "since that's what you want."

Nodding primly, she arose and led him to the guest bedroom. When she left him, he stripped off his shirt and lay down. She wouldn't leave his thoughts. He remembered her brilliant eyes lighting up when she saw him hauled safely onto *Pegasus*. He remembered how shyly she'd blushed every time she'd looked at him in his office, when she'd faced him down to ask him not to marry her sister. He remembered her breasts in the skimpy T-shirt she'd worn today and her cute butt and long legs in her white shorts as she'd raced him across the deep sand back to the house.

With the scotch still causing visions of her to warm his blood, he couldn't sleep for thinking of her on her narrow bed in the next room. Would she sleep curled in a ball like a child or stretched out like a woman? Was she naked? Or in her bra and panties? Did she desire him, too?

Remembering all the things she'd done to him in his loft in San Antonio, he began to fantasize that she was in the bed with him, her long legs tangled with his. That got him even hotter.

If only they were on board the yacht so he could hide out in his office on the upper deck and bury himself in paperwork. Here, there was nothing to think about but her lying in the bed next door.

At some point, he managed to fall asleep only to dream of her. In his dream, she slipped as lightly as a shadow into his bedroom. Slim, teasing fingers pulled back his sheet. Then, calling his name in husky, velvet tones, she slid into bed beside him. Her eyes blazed with the same fierce passion he'd seen when she'd realized he was safely back on board the yacht, away from the shark's teeth.

His heart constricted. Was this love? If it wasn't, it felt too dangerously close to the emotion for comfort. Even in his dream he recoiled from that dark emotion. Love had ruined his life and the life of his father. Hadn't it?

Then, in the dream, she kissed him, her sensual mouth and tongue running wildly over his lips and body while her hands moved between his legs and began to stroke. Soon he forgot about the danger of love and lost all power to resist her.

Lightning crashed, startling him. When his eyes flew open he heard the roar of the surf. He was alone in a strange, dark bedroom with sweat dripping from his long, lean body onto damp sheets, aching all over because he wanted to make love to his forbidden wife.

She was driving him crazy. On a low, frustrated groan, he hurled himself out of bed and stalked onto the breezeway in the hope that the chill, damp wind whipping through the screens would cool his feverish body and restore his sanity.

"Quinn!" came Kira's soft, startled cry, the sexy sound setting his testosterone-charged nerves on high alert.

He whirled to face her just as a bolt of lightning flashed. Her hair streaming in the wind, she leaned against a post some ten feet away, in the shadows. Momentarily blinded from the lightning, he couldn't make her out in the darkness. Imagining the rest of her, his blood notched a degree hotter.

"You'd better get back to your room," he rasped.

"What's the use when I couldn't sleep even if I did? Storms like this are exciting, aren't they?"

"Just do as I said and go."

"This is my house. Why should I do what you say, if I prefer watching the storm…and you?" she said in a low, breathless tone.

"Because if you plan to keep me in a separate bedroom, it's the smart thing to do."

"Used to giving orders, aren't you? Well, I'm not used to taking them. Since I'm your wife, maybe it's time I taught you that. I could teach you a lot…"

Thunder rolled, and rain slashed through the breezeway furiously, sending rivulets of water across the concrete floor.

"Go," he muttered.

"Maybe I will." But her husky laughter defied him. "Then, maybe not."

When she turned, instead of heading across the breezeway toward her bedroom, she unlatched a screen door behind her and ran onto the beach. As she did, a blaze of white fire screamed from the wet black sky to the beach.

Hell! She was going to get herself fried if he didn't bring her back.

"Kira!" he yelled after her.

When she kept running, he heaved himself after her, his bare feet sinking deeply into the soft, wet sand and crushed shells as he sprinted. Sheets of rain soaked him through within seconds.

She didn't get more than twenty feet before he caught her by the waist and pulled her roughly into his arms. She was wet and breathless, her long hair glued to her face, her T-shirt clinging to her erect nipples.

Quinn closed his eyes and willed himself to think of something besides her breasts and the light in her eyes. But as the cold rain pounded him, her soft warmth and beauty and the sweetness of her scent drew him. He opened his eyes and stared down at her. Slowly, she put her arms around him and looked at him as she had in his dreams, with her heart shining in her eyes.

Laughing, she said, "Have you ever seen anything so wild? Don't you love it?"

He hadn't deliberately stood in the rain or stomped in a puddle since he'd been a kid, when his dad had encouraged him to be a boy, as he'd put it. Hell, maybe that was his loss. Maybe it wasn't right for him to control himself so tightly.

As the torrents washed them, he picked her up and spun her crazily, high above his head. Then he lowered her, slowly, oh, so slowly. He let her breasts and tummy and thighs slide against his body, which became even harder in response to hers.

If only she'd stop looking at him with such fire in her eyes… She made him crave a different kind of life.… One of brightness, warmth and love.

"Kiss me," she whispered, pressing herself into his rock-hard thighs, smiling wantonly up at him when she felt his impressive erection.

So—she wanted him, too.

Kissing her so hard she gasped, he plunged his tongue into her mouth. The rain streamed over their fused bodies and the lightning flashed and the thunder rolled. He knew he should take her inside, but she tasted so good that, for the life of him, he couldn't let her go.

He would regret this, he was sure. But later. Not now, when she smelled of rain. Not when the wild surf roared on all sides of them. Not when his blood roared even louder.

Tonight, he had to have her.

Eleven

When he stripped her and laid her on the bed, she closed her eyes. With her face softly lit by an expectant smile and her damp hair fanning darkly across her pillow, she looked too lovely and precious for words.

"I wanted you to come to me… Even before…you appeared in the breezeway," she admitted, blushing shyly. "I know I shouldn't have…but I just lay on my bed craving you."

"Imagine that. We're on the same page for once."

"I don't want to want you…"

"I know exactly how you feel."

Thank God, he'd thought to stuff some condoms into his wallet before they'd left the yacht—just in case. Thinking about them now made him remember the first time—the one time he'd failed to protect her—and the little clock ticking in the back of his mind ticked a little louder.

She could be pregnant.

Part of him hoped she *was* pregnant…with a son. His son… No, *their* son. A little boy with dark hair who he could play ball with as his father had played with him. They would call him Kade. Quinn would come home, call his name, and the boy would come running.

Foolish dream.

Stripping off his wet jeans and Jockey shorts, he pulled the condoms out of his wallet and laid them on the bedside table. Still thinking she could very well be pregnant and that he wouldn't mind nearly as much as he should, he stroked the creaminess of her cheek with his thumb. When her eyes sparked with anticipation, he kissed each eyelid and then her smiling mouth.

"Such tiny wrists," he said as he lifted them to his lips. He let his warm breath whisper across her soft skin. "Your heart is beating faster than a rabbit's. So, you did want me…my darlin'. Feed my bruised ego—admit it."

She laughed helplessly. "Okay—I'm tingling in so many places, I feel weak enough to faint."

He touched her breasts, her slender waist, the thatch of silken curls where her thighs were joined. He pressed his lips to all those secret places so reverently that his kisses transcended the physical.

"Better." He smiled. "I told you that you'd change your mind about sex." Triumphantly, he skimmed his mouth along her jawline. With each kiss that he bestowed, she claimed another piece of his heart.

"That you did. Are you always right? Is that how you became so rich?"

He kissed her earlobe, chuckling when she shivered in response.

"Focus is the key in so many endeavors. It only took a day, and I didn't once try to seduce you, now, did I?"

"Stop crowing like a rooster who's conquered a henhouse! I see you brought plenty of protection…which means you intended this to happen."

"I was hopeful. I usually feel optimistic about achieving my goals." He trailed the tip of his tongue along her collarbone.

She moved restlessly beneath him. "You're rubbing it in, and I said don't gloat." When he licked her earlobe again, she shuddered, causing a blazing rush of fire to sizzle through him. "Just do it," she begged.

"Why are you always in such a hurry, sweet Kira?"

Because she was unable to take her eyes from his face, she blew out a breath. Except for clenching her fingers and pressing her lips together, she lay still, as if fighting for patience.

"After all," he continued, "for all practical purposes, this is our wedding night."

Her quick scowl made him wonder why the hell he'd reminded them both of the marriage he'd forced her into.

Before she could protest, he kissed her lips. Soon her breathing was deep and ragged, and it wasn't long until she was quivering beneath his lips and begging him for more.

Her hands moved over his chest and then lower, down his torso and dipping lower still. When her fingers finally curled firmly around the swollen length of his shaft, he shuddered. Soon she had him as hot and eager to hurry as she was. He was out of control, completely in her thrall.

"I bet we're on the same page now," she said huskily, a triumphant lilt in her husky tone.

"Sexy, wanton witch." Unwrapping a condom, he sheathed himself.

Compelled to claim her as his, he plunged into tight, satiny warmth. Stomach to stomach. Thigh to thigh. The moment he was inside her, she wrapped her legs around his waist and urged him even deeper.

"Yes," she whispered as a tortured moan was torn from her lips.

"Yes," he growled, holding her even closer.

Then, some force began to build as he stroked in and out of her, his rhythm growing as hard and steady as the surf dancing rhythmically against the shore. His blood heated; his heart drummed faster. When he fought to slow down, she clung tighter, writhing, begging, urging him not to stop—shattering what was left of his fragile control.

With a savage cry, he climaxed. She felt so good, so soft, so delectable. Grabbing her bottom, he ground himself into her, plunging deeper. As she arched against him, he spilled himself inside her.

She went wild, trembling, screaming his name, and her excitement sent him over the fatal edge he'd vowed never to cross. Walls inside him tumbled. He didn't want to feel like this—not toward her, not toward any woman.

But he did.

Long minutes after he rolled off her, he lay beside her, fighting for breath and control.

"Wow," she said.

Even though sex had never felt so intense before, he didn't trust his feelings. Why give her any more power than she already had by admitting them? But though he confessed nothing, her sweet warmth invaded him, soothing all the broken parts of his soul.

She sidled closer and touched his lips with feverish fingertips, her eyes alight with sensual invitation. As she stroked his mouth and cheek teasingly, desire sizzled through him. He was rock-hard in another instant.

No way in hell would one time suffice. For either of them. With one sure, swift movement, he slid nearer so that his sex touched hers. When she stared up at him hungrily, he kissed her brow, her eyelids and then the tip of her pert nose. Then he edged lower, kissing her breasts and navel. Spreading her legs, he went all the way down, laving those sweet forbidden lips that opened to him like the silken petals of a warm flower. The tip of his tongue flicked inside, causing her to moan.

"Darlin'," he said softly. "You're perfect."

"I want you inside me. So much."

He wanted that, too, so he eased into her, gently this time, and held her tight against him. How could she feel so wonderful in his arms? So right? Like she belonged there, always, till the end of time? How could this be? She was Earl's daughter, a woman he'd coerced into marriage.

"How can this be?" she asked, her words mirroring his dark thoughts.

He took his time, and when it ended in violent, bittersweet waves of mutual passion, he felt again the inexplicable peace that left no space for hate or thoughts of revenge. He simply wanted her, wanted to be with her. He didn't want to hurt anything or anybody she loved.

"You're dangerously addictive," he whispered against her earlobe.

Her sweet face was flushed; her lips bruised and swollen from his kisses.

"So are you," she said with a tremulous smile even as her wary eyes reminded him that she hadn't married him for this. "This wasn't supposed to happen, was it? You didn't want this connection any more than I did."

"No…" His mood darkened as he remembered she didn't believe this was a real marriage.

His old doubts hit him with sweeping force. Tomorrow… if it would make her happy, he'd swear to her he'd never touch her again. But not tonight. Tonight, he had to hold her close, breathe in her scent, lose himself in her…dream of a different kind of life with her.

Just for tonight she was completely his.

Hugging him close, she sighed and fell asleep. Beside her, he lay awake for hours watching her beautiful face in the dark, longing and…wishing for the impossible.

When Kira awoke, her arms and legs were tangled around Quinn's. She'd slept so well. For a fleeting instant she felt happy just to be with him.

Last night he'd made her feel precious and adored. Until…the end. With a frown, she remembered how tense and uncertain he'd seemed right before he'd crushed her close and she'd fallen asleep in his arms.

How could she have thrown herself at him? Begged him? He was determined never to love again. Sex, even great sex, would not change his mind.

Despite regrets and misgivings, the gray morning was beautiful. Rain was falling softly, scenting the island with its freshness. A gentle breeze whirred in the eaves while dazzling sunlight splashed the far wall with vivid white.

Had she been sure of Quinn's love, it would have felt romantic to be nestled so warmly in his strong arms. She would have reveled in the sensual heat created by his breath stirring her hair.

But wrapped in cocoonlike warmth with him when she knew he couldn't ever care for her only aroused longings for forbidden things like friendship and affection.

He was going to break her heart. She knew it.

Slowly, she shifted to her side of the bed. Careful not to wake him, she eased herself to her feet. When he smiled in his sleep, she couldn't help thinking him the most stunningly handsome man she'd ever seen.

He looked so relaxed. So peaceful. Last night, he'd taken great care to make her happy in bed. Longing to brush his thick hair away from his brow filled her. Because of what they'd shared, she simply wanted to touch him.

No... She had to remember his experience. He was probably just a great lover and had taken no special pains with her.

Fearing she'd accidentally awaken him if she didn't stop gaping at his virile, male beauty, she tiptoed onto the breezeway where salty air assaulted her. When her tummy flipped violently, causing a brief dizzy spell, she sank against the doorjamb.

After a deep breath, the dizziness loosened its hold. She wasn't sick exactly, but her face felt clammy and she was queasy in a way she'd never been before.

Alarmed, she swallowed. Shakily, she smoothed her damp hair back from her face.

Again, she remembered that Quinn hadn't used a condom their first time in bed. In her head, she began to count the days since her last period, which she already knew was a little late. It was time...past time...for her period to start...and under the circumstances, her odd lightheadedness made her anxious.

What if she were pregnant? How would Quinn react? He had not married her because he loved her or wanted a family. Quite the opposite. He'd used protection every single time since that first lapse. She'd never want to force him to stay married to her because of a baby. She wanted love, acceptance. Making their marriage of convenience a permanent situation was the best way to guarantee she'd never find it.

Quickly, she said a little prayer and decided not to borrow trouble just yet. Why upset him until she knew for sure? Still, no matter how she denied it, a seed of worry had taken root.

By the time Quinn had awakened, yanked on his jeans

and called for her, Kira had had her first cup of coffee and felt almost calm enough to face him. As she sat on the front porch, she watched the last gusts of the storm whip the high waves into a frenzy and hurl them against the shore.

At the sound of his approaching footsteps her belly tightened. Then she reminded herself there had only been one lapse…so there really wasn't much danger of pregnancy, was there?

"Kira?"

Concentrating on the angry seas, she wondered how soon the waves would calm down enough for them to leave. When she heard Quinn turning away from the porch, maybe because she hadn't answered, and stomping around somewhere inside the kitchen calling her name, she sensed he was out of sorts, too.

The door behind her creaked.

"Why didn't you answer when I called you?" His low voice was harsh, uncertain. "Avoiding me, are you?"

She didn't turn around to look at him. "Maybe I didn't hear you."

"Maybe you did."

"The seas are still so high, it may be a while before we can leave," she said.

"I see. After last night, you're too embarrassed to talk about anything but the weather. Are you blaming me because I didn't stick to our no-sex deal?"

Hot color climbed her cheeks. "No. I know that what happened was as much my fault as yours."

"But you don't like it."

"Look, what I don't like is being bullied into this marriage in the first place."

"Right."

"If you hadn't forced me to marry you, we wouldn't be

trapped on this island together. Then last night wouldn't have happened."

"Okay, then. So, am I to assume from your mutinous expression that you want to go back to our no-sex deal?"

Why were men always so maddeningly literal? All she wanted was a little reassurance. Instead, he'd launched into the blame game.

Well, she wasn't about to admit she'd craved him last night or that she'd enjoyed everything they'd done together. Nor would she admit that despite everything, she still wanted him. That the last thing she wanted was their no-sex deal. To admit any of that would prove her irrational and give him too much power over her.

When she sat staring at the stormy gulf in silence, he squared his shoulders. "It's too bad the waters are so rough and you're stuck with me, but if we've waited it out this long, I don't intend to push our luck by trying to take the tender out when we could capsize. I'm hungry. Do you want to share that last can of pork and beans with me for breakfast or not?"

The mere thought of canned pork and beans made her mouth go dry and her tummy flip. Within seconds, she began to perspire.

"Or not," she whispered, shaking her head fiercely as she inhaled a deep breath to settle her stomach.

"Are you all right? You look a little pale," he said, stepping closer. "Sick almost."

"I'm fine," she snapped, turning away so he couldn't read her face.

"I wasn't too rough last night, was I?" he asked, the genuine concern in his low tone touching her.

"The less said about what happened the better!"

With a weary look, he nodded. "I talked to my captain via satellite phone. *Pegasus* held up well under the rough seas and squalls. The crew had a bit of a bad night, but other than a case or two of seasickness, all is well."

"I'm glad."

"Look, for what it's worth, I'm sorry I reneged on our bargain and made love to you."

She knotted her hands and unknotted them.

"I took advantage."

"No, you didn't! I was the one who ran out in the storm and lured you after me!" She jumped up. Hugging herself, she walked over to the window. "I'm sure any man would have done the same."

"Look, I'm not just some guy you picked up off the street who is out to get what he can get."

She whirled on him. "Whatever you may think because of that night we shared in San Antonio, I don't do one-night stands, either!"

"I know that. I believe that. I wouldn't have married you otherwise."

"I wonder. Did anything besides my last name really matter to you?"

His face went cold. "I'm your husband. Last night I knew what you wanted and what you didn't want. But in the end, it didn't matter."

"You told me you'd have me in your bed in no time, and you did. So why don't you chalk up another win for your side in your little plan to get revenge against my father."

"Damn it. Because that's not how I feel about it! Or about you!"

"Don't romanticize what happened! We were bored and trapped. Big deal. It's over."

"The hell it is."

"Ours is only a marriage of convenience."

"Do you have to constantly remind me of that?"

"Why not, if it's the truth?"

"Is it? Does it have to be?"

"Yes! Yes!"

He was silent for a long moment. "If that's really how you feel, I won't sleep with you again. You can have your marriage of convenience—permanently. I hope it makes you happy!"

His cold announcement chilled her. Not that she was about to let him see how hurt she felt.

"Great! Now that that's settled, go! Eat your beans and leave me alone!"

"All right. And after I eat them, I'm going out. For a walk. To check on the tender. And I won't be back till the storm's over."

"Great! Perfect!"

When he slammed out of the porch and stalked toward the kitchen, her stomach twisted sharply. She felt ill, really ill. Clutching her stomach, she ran out the back door so he wouldn't see, knelt on the damp sand in the lightly falling rain, and was sick.

She *was* pregnant. She just knew she was.

His strides long and quick because he was anxious to get as far from the house—and from her—as fast as he could, Quinn stalked down the beach toward the dock. As his heels thudded into the deep sand, his head pounded viciously. Their quarrel had given him the headache from hell.

How different he felt now than he had when he'd first woken up. The air had smelled so fresh. He'd lain in bed, his eyes closed, drinking in a contentment he hadn't known in years. Then, he'd reached for her and discovered cool sheets instead of her warm, silky body, and some part of him had gone cold.

He didn't regret his harsh words because she'd smashed

his heart. He didn't regret the sex, either. She'd been sweet, and she'd felt too good—so good that just thinking of her naked and writhing in his arms, her shining eyes big as she'd begged for more had him brick-hard all over again.

When he saw the dock up ahead and the tender riding the waves, he felt intense relief.

He wasn't used to second-guessing himself or feeling the slightest guilt or confusion after sex. In his whole life he'd never awakened beside a woman who hadn't wanted him. Quite the opposite. They always clung, wanting more than he could give. Then he'd be the one to pull away. With her, he felt different. That's probably why he'd been fool enough to marry her.

From the moment Kira had shown up in his office to beg him not to marry her sister, he'd changed all the rules he'd lived by for so long. She'd tangled his emotions into a painful knot.

For some insane, ridiculous reason, he wanted to please her. He'd actually hoped she'd be happier with him after last night, so her obvious misery this morning ate at him all the more.

In his frustration, he broke into a jog. His marriage be damned. The sooner he ended this farce of a honeymoon and got back to business the better.

From now on, their marriage would be as she wished—all for show. He'd ignore the hell out of her except when there were in public.

When he reached the dock, he grabbed the stern line. After snugging the tender closer, he sprang on board.

Crafted of teak for the turbulent waters of the North Sea, she was an efficient, self-bailing craft. Maybe that was why she hadn't sunk. Also, the dock was on the leeward side of the island and in a well-protected cove.

He started the engine and smiled grimly when it purred

to life. Once he made sure the tender was sound, he shut it off, sat down and let the wind buffet him.

In no mood to return to the house or to his wife, he kept an eye on the distant horizon. As soon as the seas calmed, he'd take his bride home and get back to work. He'd lose himself in negotiations with the European Union and forget all about Kira.

His marriage was turning out to be the last thing from convenient, whatever Kira might say to the contrary.

Twelve

Quinn spoke to her as little as possible now.

If Kira had wondered how long Quinn would pretend to be interested in her, she had her answer and was miserable as a result.

No sooner had they returned to San Antonio than he'd made it clear he intended to live as he had before his marriage—working nearly every waking hour.

"The EU deal is going to command my full attention, so I won't be around much for a while," he'd said.

"Fine. I understand."

"Jason will come promptly at ten every morning to take care of you and the house."

"Jason?"

"My houseman. He's at your command. You'll find him highly competent."

Quinn had ensconced her in his fabulous loft apartment, and yes, he'd given her the master bedroom. Now she slept alone in the vast bed they'd shared that first night. As for himself, their first evening home, he'd packed a suitcase and moved his things into a second bedroom. Then he'd politely bid her a terse good-night, gone to bed early and left for work the next morning hours before she'd woken up.

That first morning Jason, a much older man, who was thin-lipped and skeletal, had greeted her so haughtily in the kitchen, she'd felt she was invading his territory.

"I'm Jason," he'd said with a vague sneer in his upper-class tone. "I'm here for whatever you need, cleaning, shopping, cooking—anything. It is my duty and privilege to please you, madam."

Madam?

"Wow! I'm really not used to being waited on. I can't think of a thing for you to do. I mean, I can pour my own cereal out of a box, can't I?"

"Cereal?" He scowled briefly. "Would you prefer an omelet?" he'd suggested with a contemptuous lift of his brows.

"Well, why not," she'd whispered, sensing they were getting off to a bad start. She wanted to be agreeable, yet she despised herself for giving in to him when he was supposed to be serving her. The man made her feel more out of place in Quinn's home than she'd felt before.

Jason had cooked a very good ham-and-vegetable omelet, and she'd dutifully eaten it. Then she'd rushed off to Betty's restaurant to help out while one of the waitresses was away, and the kitchen smells had bothered her way more than usual.

The rest of the week followed the same pattern with Quinn leaving early and returning late. Jason cooked her breakfast and made her dinner, and she began to feel grateful for his presence since it meant she wasn't totally alone.

Since Quinn was gone all the time, she might hardly have noticed she was married if she hadn't missed him so much. She was on her own, as she had been before her marriage, but because her husband was a man she found exceedingly attractive, she felt rejected and constantly unsettled. If he was home behind his shut door, she thought of him every minute.

When he was gone, she felt lost. With every passing day she grew more acutely sensitive to odors, which made her increasingly worried that he'd made her pregnant. She wanted to talk to Quinn about the situation, but she dreaded the conversation, especially now that he was so intent on avoiding her.

On the eighth day of their return, when her period still hadn't started and she was queasier than ever, she called her doctor and made an appointment for the next morning. She'd agreed to take her mother to a routine chemo treatment the same afternoon.

Jaycee had called her earlier in the week, begging her to pick up their mother for her appointment as a favor because escorting her mother for treatment made Jaycee so sad.

"So, how's it going with Quinn?" Jaycee had asked after Kira agreed.

"Fine."

"Fine? Hmm? Well, they do say the first few months are an adjustment."

"I said we're fine."

"I know you don't believe this, but he cares about you. He wanted to marry you."

"Right."

"He bought you that beautiful wedding dress, and you should have seen him when you were gone and nobody knew where you were."

"Well, he's ignoring me now," Kira confided.

"Did you two have a fight?"

She didn't answer.

"If you did, and I think you did, you need to find a way to kiss and make up."

"Why bother to make up, if we have no future?"

Kira changed the subject to her cat, Rudy, and asked if Jaycee minded keeping him a while longer. "I don't want him attaching himself to Quinn…if we're just going to break up."

"He's only a cat."

"Rudy's sensitive."

"And Quinn's not? If I were you, I'd worry more about your husband."

She was; she just wasn't going to admit it.

When Jaycee hung up, Kira had marked her mother's appointment on her calendar. She was glad to have something other than Quinn and her possible pregnancy to concentrate on.

Hours later, she was in bed that night with her light out when she heard Quinn at the door. Throwing off her covers, she started to go out and greet him. Then, pride made her stay where she was.

Wishing he'd knock on her door, she counted his approaching footsteps as he walked across the great room before he made his way down the hall.

When he paused at her door her heart beat very fast. But after a minute, he resumed walking to his own bedroom.

When his door slammed, a strangled sob rose in her throat. With a little cry, she got out of bed and ran to her window. Staring out at the brilliant city, she imagined other married couples, happier couples, slipping into bed together, snuggling close, talking about their day or their children, taking such blissful marital pleasures for granted.

Suddenly, Kira felt as lonely as a butterfly trapped in a child's glass jar.

Pulling on her robe, she wandered out into the great room. Baby or not, she could not live like this, with a husband who didn't want her.

Behind her, she heard a floorboard creak. Whirling, she caught her breath at the sight of Quinn standing bare-chested in the dark. His shadowed eyes looked haunted.

"You okay?" His low, harsh voice made her shiver. She wanted to be held, loved and crushed against him.

"I'm fine. And you?"

"A little tired, but the deal with the EU seems to be coming together. I'll be going to London for a few days."

"Oh."

"A car's coming for me at 5:00 a.m. Don't worry. I'll be careful so as not to wake you."

How could he be so obtuse? Was he just indifferent? Or was he still angry with her for their harsh exchange on the island?

She wanted to scream at him that he should kiss her goodbye properly. She wanted to drive him to the airport herself. But she kept such foolish thoughts to herself, and he only stared at her from the dark with his intense, burning gaze. She thought he was watching her, waiting—but for what?

Jaycee had advised her to kiss and make up. But how? To what purpose, when he so clearly had his mind on more important things?

After a few minutes of staring at each other in stony silence, he said good-night.

The next morning, when she heard the front door close behind him, she got up. Throwing away all pride, she rushed from her room into the foyer that was filled with crimson light, managing to catch up to him as he waited for the elevator.

"Sorry to wake you," he murmured, concern in his eyes.

"Don't be. I had to say goodbye and wish you a safe journey, didn't I," she whispered, surprised that she could sound so calm, so normal when she felt so incredibly depressed. "I'll miss you."

His dark brows arched warily. "Will you now?"

"I will," she said.

After another long moment spent considering her, he sighed and drew her close against his long, hard body. "I'll miss you, too." He paused. "Sorry about the last week or so."

"I'm sorry, too."

"Habib will call you later and give you all the numbers where I can be reached. I'll think of you in London. I really will miss you. You know that, don't you?" he murmured.

Would he really?

Wrapping her closer, he kissed her hard. She clung to him, probably revealing more of her real feelings than was wise. Then the elevator pinged, and he was forced to let her go or be late. Holding her gaze, he picked up his suitcase and strode through the doors.

She couldn't turn away or stop looking at him or take even one step toward the loft until the door shut.

Pregnant! Needing a moment to take in that news, Kira clenched the steering wheel of her Toyota as she sat in the parking lot of the medical complex and kneaded her forehead with her knuckles.

After a brief exam, the doctor had ripped off his latex gloves and confirmed she was pregnant.

"How do you know? You haven't even tested me."

"When you've been doing this as long as I have, young lady, you just know."

Within minutes, a pregnancy test administered in his office confirmed his opinion.

After the office visit, she felt both numb and tingly as she sat in her car. Biting her lip, she pulled out the slip of paper where she'd written all the numbers Habib had given her earlier. After calculating the time difference between the U.K. and Texas, she grabbed her cell phone and started dialing. Then she stopped. Quinn was probably extremely busy or in an important meeting. Her news would distract him from what was all-important to him—the deal. Better to share the news with him in person when she was sure she had his full attention and could gauge his reaction.

Still, her heart felt as if it was brimming over. She was bursting to tell someone…who would be every bit as excited as she was.

Mother. Suddenly, she was very glad she would be taking her mother to treatment today. Who better to confide in than her precious baby's grandmother? Nobody adored babies, anybody's babies, more than her mother did. Her mother would be happier about this news than anyone, and goodness knew, with all she was going through, she needed a cheerful future to contemplate.

"Oh, my dear," her mother gushed, setting her flowered china teacup aside and seizing Kira's hand in both of her thin ones. Kira had waited until after her mother's treatment, when they could sit down together at Betty's, to share the news.

How weak her mother's grasp felt, even if her eyes were alight with joy.

"Such wonderful news! The best ever! Unbelievable! And it was so easy for you two! And so soon!"

A fierce rush of pride swamped Kira. Never had her mother been so pleased with her. Such rapture had always been reserved for Jaycee's accomplishments.

"Have you told Quinn yet?" her mother asked.

"I started to call him. Then I thought I'd wait…until he comes home, until he's not so distracted."

"So, I'm the first!" Her mother beamed so brightly she almost looked as she had before the illness. Her grip strengthened. "I'm going to beat this thing and live for a very long time. I have to…if I'm to see my darling grand-baby grow up."

Kira's gaze blurred, and she had to turn away to hide her emotion. She felt exhilarated and proud, and a big part of her pleasure had to do with the fact that for once she'd trumped Jaycee.

Oh, why hadn't she ever felt sure of her parents' love?

The river sparkled beside their table outside Betty's. Kira was thrilled her mother's fighting spirit was intact and that she felt reasonably strong. But most of all, she couldn't help being glad that she'd been the one to make her mother so happy.

"Your father will be just as excited as I am. He's very up on Quinn's successes in London, too. So this will be a doubly great day for him."

"Oh, so he's already heard from Quinn?" Kira whispered, feeling more than a little hurt that Quinn had called her father and not her.

"Yes, and it sounds like things are going very well," her mother replied. "Am I to assume by the way you're biting your lip that *you* haven't spoken to him?"

"He texted me, saying he'd arrived in London safely. I'm not hurt. Not in the least."

After studying her for a long moment, her mother looked

dubious. "Well, I'm sure he'll be so happy to hear your exciting news."

Would he be? Oh, how she hoped so, but her doubts soon had her biting her lower lip again.

"Don't do that, dear. How many times have I told you that biting your lip like that chaps your beautiful mouth?"

"When I was a child, Mother!"

"Well, just the same, I know you want to be beautiful for Quinn when he comes home, now, don't you?"

"Right. I do." She glanced at the muddy green river and tried to focus on a white duck. "Frankly, I'm a little worried about telling him. You know…we didn't marry under the best of circumstances."

"I wish you wouldn't make so much of that. I really think it means something when a couple gets pregnant so easily," her mother said almost enviously.

"What are you saying?"

"Sometimes it doesn't work that way… Earl and I had a terrible time getting pregnant with…with you. But let's not go there."

Did she only imagine the shadow that passed over her mother's thin face?

"Is anything wrong, Mother?"

"No, dear."

But her mother looked away and something in her manner and stiff posture rang alarm bells inside Kira. When the silence between them lengthened and grew more strained, she was sure her mother was worrying about something.

"What's wrong? Have I upset you?"

Her mother stared at her, hesitating. "I guess…it's only natural that your news would stir up the past."

"When you were pregnant with me?"

A single tear traced down her mother's cheek. "No..." She clenched her napkin.

"Did the doctor tell you something when you were alone with her that has you upset? Bad news of some kind?"

"Dear God, no!" Her mother took her hand. "No. It's not that. It's nothing like that. It's about you..." Her mother's eyes filled with some unfathomable emotion. "I was never pregnant with you."

"What?"

"I...*we* tried so hard, your father and I, to have a baby. So dreadfully hard. You know how I am. I took my temperature all the time. Ten times a day. But I didn't...I couldn't get pregnant...no matter what I did. We went to so many specialists, and they told us that it was my fault, not your father's. Some hormone imbalance. And then...we never told anyone, not even you, the truth."

"What truth?" Under the table Kira's hands fisted so tightly her nails dug bloody crescents into her palms.

"I couldn't conceive, so, in the end, we adopted."

"What?"

"You're adopted. Please don't look so upset! I could never have had a daughter of my own as wonderful as you. You've always been so sweet. Like now. Coming with me for my treatment when poor Jaycee couldn't bear it. She hates thinking of me being sick. She's too much like me, you see. I'm strong in some ways, but weak in others. Until now, I could never admit, not to anyone, that you weren't my biological child. It represented my biggest imperfection as a woman."

"Oh, my God." Kira felt overwhelmed, hollow. Suddenly she remembered all the little things that had never added up in her life. The rest of her family members were blond and blue-eyed, while she had dark eyes and hair. She was tall and slim, while her mother and Jaycee were more petite and curvy.

She'd never been as interested in style or fashion as they were. She'd been wired more emotionally and hadn't thought as logically as they did. Maybe this was why she'd always felt as if she hadn't belonged in her family. Maybe she'd always sensed this huge falsehood in her life.

"I felt like such a failure," her mother continued. "As a woman. For not being able to conceive a child. And then suddenly, inexplicably, when you were two years old, I became pregnant with Jaycee...without even trying. When she was so perfect, so gorgeous, I felt I'd achieved something grand by giving birth. But really, having you was always just as big an achievement. Only I never appreciated it until now. Illness like this can change you, make you wiser somehow.

"I was silly and so unsure when I was young. I know I haven't always understood you, but you are very precious to me."

Kira could say nothing. She was as overwhelmed as a stage actress in a drama who'd forgotten all her lines. Her mind had gone blank.

"I'm so glad you have Quinn. We all suffered so much when Kade died right after selling the company to us. Your father loved Kade like a brother. And then, all these years later, to have Quinn take over the company at the best possible moment for us was a fortunate irony. And now this baby. This wonderful baby will make everything right again. I just know it will.

"I'll get well, and you'll be happy with Quinn. You'll quit...doubting you belong together because you'll have this baby to love together. Nothing can bring a couple closer than a child."

"If only life were that simple."

"Sometimes it is."

Kira couldn't think about her adoption and what it meant right now. So she focused on finding out more about Quinn's past.

Squeezing her eyes shut, she reopened them. "Mother, why did Quinn blame Daddy for his father's death?"

"Your father and Kade Sullivan created Murray Oil. Well, back then it was Sullivan and Murray Oil. Esther Sullivan was extravagant, but Kade adored her. Of course, he was always borrowing from Earl, always needing more... because of her, you see. Esther's needs were insatiable. In time, Kade began to gamble on the side and play the market. For years he was lucky, but then one day his luck ran out.

"When money went missing at the company, from accounts he was responsible for, your father asked him some pointed questions. Kade got angry. The money was found eventually, but the misunderstanding had caused a rift between them.

"Kade said he wanted out, so Earl bought him out. But when times got better and the stock price took off, Kade got hard feelings and started drinking and bad-mouthing your father, especially to Quinn, I think. Around that time, Esther divorced Kade and took whatever he had left.

"Not too long afterward, Earl made a deal that tripled the worth of Murray Oil. Kade claimed the deal had been his idea and wanted compensation, so he sued. He lost the suit, and Quinn discovered his father's body in his shop off the garage. Supposedly Kade had been cleaning his shotgun and it went off. Accidentally. But who knows? Not that Kade ever seemed like the kind of man who'd kill himself. In fact, your father definitely believes it was an accident.

"Oh, my darling, let's not talk of such depressing things.

I much prefer to think about my future grandbaby. Do you want a boy or a girl?"

"A little boy," she whispered. "A little boy with blue eyes who looks just like Quinn and Kade."

"So, you're beginning to love him a little."

With all her heart. Yet she wasn't ready to admit that, not even to her mother.

But her mother saw the truth. "I told you so," she said triumphantly. "And no wonder. He's everything any woman with half a brain would want in a husband."

Not quite everything. He could never return her love, Kira thought.

Thirteen

Quinn remained in London for a week, during which time Kira ached for him. She didn't know how she could miss a man who'd worked so hard to ignore her before he'd left, but she did.

Then, suddenly he sent her a brief text informing her of his flight information for the next day. He said he'd hired a driver to pick him up. Then, right before he boarded his plane, he called her cell while she was still asleep. When she didn't answer, he left a message saying he'd called to remind her of a company party they were attending that evening an hour after his flight was scheduled to land.

So, there would be no private time together his first night home.

"You can call my secretary to find out what to wear," he'd said over the phone. Then his voice had lowered. "Missed you…worse than I thought I would," he'd whispered before ending the call.

Damn. Damn. Damn. What rotten luck that she'd missed his call. What else might he have said if they'd actually talked? She replayed his message several times just to hear his mesmerizing voice say he'd missed her.

A lump formed in her throat. Why had she muted her phone before laying it on her bedside table?

Dialing his secretary, she asked what she should wear to the party.

"It's formal, but Mr. Sullivan did tell me to suggest you wear something red."

"Why red?"

"He didn't say. The deal he pulled off with the EU will have far-reaching consequences for Murray Oil, hopefully positive. Since he's returning in triumph, the party's important to him. I'd suggest you go with his color choice, in case it fits with a bigger plan."

Her heart thumping wildly, Kira took off early from Betty's to indulge in a shopping spree with her mother in search of the perfect sexy red dress. Then she rushed home, with her low-cut scarlet gown and a pair of new heels, so she could take special pains getting dressed.

After the party, if Quinn was in a good mood, she would tell him she was pregnant.

At six, while she was combing her hair, his driver called to tell her Quinn's plane had just landed. "I'll have him home soon."

"Can I please talk to him?"

"He's on the phone. Business. But I'll tell him to call you as soon as he finishes."

When Quinn's key turned in the lock, Kira hurried to the door to greet him. His luggage thumped heavily on the floor. Then he strode through the foyer with his phone still pressed to his ear.

His voice rang with authority as he stepped into the living room. When she met his hard, dark eyes, she saw the shadows of weariness under them. Even if he hadn't bothered to call her from the car, she was so thrilled he was home, her heart leaped with pure joy.

"Gotta go," he said abruptly. "We'll wrap this up in the morning." He flipped his phone shut and stared at her. "Sorry about the phone call. Business."

"Of course. I understand." She smiled tremulously.

His mouth curved, but his smile played out before it reached his eyes.

She wanted to rush into his arms, and it was only with great effort that she remained where she was. No matter how eager she felt, she would not throw herself at him.

"You look pale," he said. "Thinner. Are you okay?"

She hadn't been eating as regularly due to her morning sickness, but she couldn't tell him that. At least, not now.

"I'm fine," she whispered.

"Right. Why is that answer always your first line of defense?"

She didn't know what to say to him. If only he would take her in his arms and kiss her, maybe that would break down the barriers between them.

His eyes burned her, and his hands were clenched. Was being married to her so difficult for him?

"I like the dress. It becomes you," he murmured.

She blushed, pleased.

"I bought you something." He tossed a box onto the sofa carelessly. "Open it and see if you like it." He spoke casually, as if the gift was a token and nothing more.

When he turned sharply and walked down the hall to his bedroom, she felt a sickening sensation of loss. How foolish she'd been to dream they might have a new beginning.

Sinking onto the sofa, she opened the black box and let

out a pleased cry when a necklace and earrings of rubies and diamonds exploded in fiery brilliance. He'd tucked his business card inside the box. On the back of it, scrawled in bold black ink, she read, "For my beautiful wife."

Tears filled her eyes as she hesitantly touched the necklace. She quickly brushed the dampness away. The necklace was exquisite. Nobody had ever given her anything half so lovely.

In the next breath, she told herself the gift meant nothing. He was wealthy. It was for show. He'd bought the jewels to impress Murray Oil's clients, stockholders and employees. He'd probably had someone pick them up for her. The gift wasn't personal.

"Do you like it?" Tall and dark, he stood in the doorway looking gravely handsome in his elegant black suit.

"It's too beautiful," she whispered. "You shouldn't have, but thank you."

"Then stand up, and I'll help you put it on. You have no idea how many necklaces I looked at. Nothing seemed right until I found this one."

"You shopped for it yourself?"

"Indeed. Who could I possibly trust to select the right gift for my bride? The wrong necklace could overpower you."

He let her secure the earrings to her ears before he lifted the necklace from the black velvet box and fastened it around her neck.

At the warmth of his fingertips against her nape, her skin tingled and her heart beat wildly. Was it possible to have an orgasm from sheer longing?

"With your dark hair, I thought rubies would become you, and they do," he said, staring so long at the sparkle on her slim neck his gaze made her skin burn. "I imagined you wearing them and nothing else."

In spite of herself, she giggled. *This was more like the homecoming she'd fantasized about.* In another moment, he would kiss her.

He stepped back to admire her and shot her an answering grin. Why, oh, why hadn't he kissed her?

She pursed her lips, touched her hand to her throat.

His face grew guarded again; his lips set in that firm line she'd come to dread. Instead of taking her in his arms, he backed away almost violently. "Shall we go?" he said, his tone rough and deliberately impersonal.

Cut to the quick, she didn't dare look at him as she nodded. During the short drive, he didn't speak to her again.

As soon as they arrived at the party, he put his arm around her as executives and clients rushed up and surrounded him, all clamoring to congratulate Quinn on his successes in London.

Black silk rustling, Cristina was among the first who hurried to his side. Barely managing a cool smile for Kira, she placed a bejeweled, exquisitely manicured hand on Quinn's cheek with practiced ease and kissed him lightly.

"I'm *so* proud of you," she gushed in a low, intimate tone. "I knew you'd pull it off. See—everybody loves you now. Worries over."

Clearly, he'd taken the time to inform *her* personally of his successes.

"So the deal went well?" Kira whispered into his ear when the lovely Cristina glided away.

He nodded absently as he continued shaking everybody's hand.

"Why didn't you tell me?"

"You know now, don't you?"

"But I'm your wife…"

"Unwillingly, as you keep reminding me. Which is why

I've been working hard not to burden you with too much attention."

Stung, her eyes burning and her heart heavy, she turned away. Why did it hurt that he saw no need to share the things that mattered to him when she'd known all along their marriage was for show?

She was sure he had a duty to mingle, so she was surprised when Quinn stayed by her side. When she noticed a dark-skinned man talking animatedly to her family, she asked Quinn who he was.

"Habib."

"The man you were talking to after we made love that first time?"

He nodded. "I thought you two had met…at the wedding."

"No, but we've talked on the phone this past week. Why did he think you should marry Jaycee instead of me?"

"Whatever he thought, he was wrong. What difference does it make now?"

"My mother told me today that I was adopted."

When Quinn's blue eyes darkened, she sensed that he knew more than he wanted to let on.

"Something you said that morning made me wonder if you and he somehow knew that," she persisted.

He stiffened warily.

"I thought that if you had known, maybe you assumed my family cared more about her…and maybe that was why Habib concurred with my father that she was the better choice…?"

"Habib's research did indicate a partiality on your father's part for Jacinda."

Her chest constricted. That truth was one of the reasons being loved in her own right by her husband was something that was beginning to matter to Kira more than anything.

"I preferred you from the first," he countered.

He kept saying that. Could she dare to believe him?

"Doesn't that count for something?" he asked.

"Our marriage was a business deal."

"So you keep reminding me."

"You only married me to make taking over Murray Oil go more smoothly, and now that you've made a place for yourself, your need for me is at an end."

"I'll decide when my need for you is at end. What do you say we end this depressing conversation and dance?" He took her hand. "Shall we?"

"You don't really want to dance with me— I'm just—"

"Don't put yourself down," he growled as he pulled her into his hard arms. "You're my wife."

"So, dancing with me at the company party is expected?" she said.

"I suppose." His grip strengthening, he smiled grimly down at her. "Did it ever occur to you that I might want to dance with you even if it wasn't expected?"

She was aware of people watching them and reminded herself that he was only dancing with her to make the guests believe their marriage was real.

From a corner, her laughing parents and a smiling Jaycee watched them, too. Looking at them, so happy together, Kira felt left out, as usual. Even being in Quinn's arms, knowing she was pregnant with his child, gave her no joy. How could it? Had he touched her other than for public viewing, or shown her any affection since he'd returned? Their marriage was a business deal to him, and one that wasn't nearly as important as the one he'd just concluded in London.

"Quit thinking dark, mutinous thoughts, and just dance," he whispered against her ear. "Relax. Enjoy. You're very beautiful, you know, and I'd seize any excuse to hold you in my arms."

Despite her determination to resist his appeal, his words, his nearness and his warm breath against her earlobe had her blood beating wildly.

She knew it was illogical, but being held in his arms reassured her. Soon she almost forgot dancing with him was just for show. Everyone in the gilded room blurred except her handsome husband.

They didn't speak again, but his eyes lingered on her lips as the music washed through her. Did he want to kiss her? She wanted it so much, she felt sick with longing. Surely he knew it. If so, he gave no indication, and, after a while, all the spinning about began to make her feel dizzy and much too hot.

She didn't want to be sick. Not now…not when he was finally holding her, when he seemed almost happy to be with her. Still, she couldn't take another step or she'd faint.

"I need some air," she whispered.

"All right." He led her round along the shadowy edges of the room until they came to a pair of tall French doors that opened onto a balcony overlooking the sparkling city. Gallantly, he pulled her outside. The night was mild, pleasant even. Once they were alone, his grip around her tightened in concern and he pressed her close.

"You look so strained and pale. Are you sure you're okay?"

She gulped in a breath of air. And then another. "I'm perfectly fine," she lied, believing that surely in a minute or two she would be.

"Obviously, even being in my arms is an ordeal."

"No!"

"You don't have to lie. I know well enough that I've given you ample reason to dislike me."

"I don't dislike you."

"But you don't like me. How could you? I was your father's enemy."

"Quinn—"

"No, hear me out. Since the island, I've kept my distance in order to make our marriage less onerous to you. I know I pushed you into this situation too hard and too fast, and I took advantage of you the night of the storm. I'm not proud of that. But do you have any idea how difficult it's been to stay away from you ever since?

"I wanted to give you your precious space and time to get used to our arrangement. I prayed that a week's separation would give me the strength to resist you when I returned," he muttered. "So, I didn't call you from London, and when I came home, I tried to be the cold husband you desire. But after our days apart, when you looked so ethereal and beautiful in your flashy red dress, my vow not to touch you drove me crazy. God help me, ever since the first day I saw you at your parents' ranch, you've obsessed me."

"But I don't desire a cold husband. I've wanted you, too," she whispered, wishing her feet felt a little steadier beneath her. Despite the fresh air, she was beginning to feel light-headed again.

"You have?"

Whatever encouragement he sought in her eyes, he found. Instantly, his lips were on hers, but when he crushed her closer, holding her tightly and kissing her, her dizziness returned in a sickening rush.

"I've wanted you so much," he murmured. "Missed you so much. You have no idea. Darlin', tell me you missed me, at least a little?"

Her heart beat violently even as she gulped in another breath. "Of course I did," she managed to say even as his dear face blurred and the walls of the building and the twinkling lights beneath them whirled dizzyingly like bright colors dancing in a kaleidoscope.

She willed herself to be strong, to fight the dizziness. "I did... But there's something I have to tell you, Quinn. Something...wonderful."

Little blue stars whirred. *Not good.* On the next beat the bottom dropped out of her tummy, and try as she might to save herself by gulping in mouthfuls of air, she couldn't get her breath.

"Quinn—"

Her hands, which had been pushing frantically against his hard chest, lost their strength. She was falling into a heavy darkness that was hot and swirling and all-enveloping.

The last thing she saw was Quinn's anxious face as his arms closed around her.

Fourteen

When Kira regained consciousness, Quinn was leaning over her in a small room, pressing a cool rag to her brow. To his right, a tall blond man with an air of grave authority had a finger pressed to her wrist while he studied his watch.

"Dennis is a doctor, and he wants me to ask you if…if you could possibly be pregnant," Quinn said.

"I wanted to tell…you. First thing… I really did."

"What?"

"Yes!" She blushed guiltily as Quinn stared down at her. "Yes. I'm pregnant. "I…I think that's why I got too hot while we were dancing. I've been having morning sickness while you were gone."

"That's why you were so pale. Why didn't you call me? Or tell me when I got home?" Quinn's hand tightened on her arm, and his expression grew grim. "Because you were unhappy about the baby? Were you planning to end the pregnancy without telling me?"

"No!" she exclaimed, horrified.

Quinn turned to the doctor and grilled him about her condition. The man quickly reassured him that her pulse and blood pressure were just fine. Still, he advised that she see her own doctor the next day, just to make sure.

"We're going home," Quinn said. "You're going to bed. No wonder I thought you looked thin. You should have told me."

"I was going to…"

"When?" he demanded so coldly she couldn't answer him.

That was the last word either of them said until they reached his loft. In the car, he gripped the steering wheel with clenched fists, while his profile seemed fashioned of unyielding granite. Never once did he look her way. Deliberately, he shut her out. The walls between them thickened and grew taller. Would she ever be able to reach him again?

Once inside the loft, he lingered in the crimson shower of light by the door while she fled to the master bedroom.

Alone in the vast room, she stared at the bed they'd shared. Silently, she kicked off her heels and pulled off the red dress and then slipped into a frothy white nightgown.

This wasn't the way she'd imagined telling him about the baby.

The rubies on her neck felt heavy, unbearable, but when she went to undo the clasp, her fingers shook too badly for her to manage it. The weight on her heart was even heavier. How could he have thought, even for one second, she might want to end her pregnancy? How could she go to bed when heartbreak was suffocating her?

She had to talk to him, to at least try to make things

right. Without remembering to grab a robe, she raced to the huge living room. It was empty, so she tiptoed back down the hall to his bedroom door, which he'd shut against her. She called his name, softly at first. When he didn't answer, she knocked.

His door swung open and he stood before her, his powerful, bare-chested body backlit by the lamp on his nightstand. He looked so glorious, she caught her breath. For a long moment, she could only stare at his bronzed muscles with bemused fascination. He was so fit and hard. If only she could throw herself into his arms and tell him she loved him and his baby.

But she knew he didn't want her love.

"I want this baby, and I was going to tell you," she whispered.

She watched his magnificent muscles cord as he pushed the door wider. "When?" he muttered roughly, disbelieving her.

"Just before I passed out at the party. I wanted to tell you in person, and… It was just that I was scared," she continued breathlessly. "I—I…couldn't believe you'd want my baby, too."

"Our baby," he corrected in a tight tone. "Couldn't the baby give us something more positive to build on?"

"How? If you regret marrying me. And blame our child for trapping you into a permanent involvement with a woman you don't want.

"Quinn, if you'd planned to dissolve our marriage after your takeover of Murray Oil, you don't have to stay with me because of this. I hope you know that. This doesn't have to change the businesslike nature of our arrangement."

He sucked in a breath. "Damn it. Are you ever going to quit telling me what I feel?"

"But isn't that…how you feel?"

For a long moment he was silent. "Would you listen to me for once, instead of being so sure you've got me pegged?"

"Yes. All right."

After another lengthy interval, his expression softened. "I guess I'm a little scared by your news," he said simply.

"Because you know our marriage isn't real?"

His mouth tensed. "No! Because babies are a lifetime commitment. Because they are so little…and so helpless. Because they know how to turn their parents into doting sots—and they do it with charm, in no time flat. Anything could happen to a baby." He caught her hand, and when she didn't struggle, he pulled her into his arms. "Or to you… while you're pregnant. I couldn't bear it." He kissed her brow.

It was bliss to be in his arms.

So he didn't love her, couldn't love anybody. But he cared. She was sure he cared, at least a little. He was holding her as if he did.

"But nothing will happen because we'll take good care of the baby…and me," she said reassuringly.

"My father was strong, and he died. We're all only a heartbeat away from death." There was so much grief and passion in his voice she felt hot tears sting the back of her eyelids.

"Which is why we have to live each moment to the fullest," she whispered. In a burst of tenderness, she raised her fingertips to stroke his temples in consolation. "We don't have a second to waste. We might as well be dead if we're afraid to live." To love, she wanted to add.

Quinn's arms tightened around her. He lowered his face and this time it was her mouth he sought. When he found it, he kissed her long and deeply. She opened her lips and sighed. She'd wanted him to kiss her like this for hours, days. Maybe that was why she couldn't help shivering in delight and giving him everything—all her love, even her soul—when she kissed him back.

"Oh, Kira…" For an endless time, he couldn't seem to stop kissing her. Then, suddenly, he let her go and jerked free of her embrace.

"Forgive me. I forgot—you don't want me pawing you. That's what made you sick, earlier." His dark face was flushed and his breathing ragged.

"No… I told you… I've had morning sickness. Only sometimes it's not just in the morning."

"Go to your own room. We can talk tomorrow." Even as his harsh rejection wounded, his eyes continued to hungrily devour her.

He wanted her. He was pushing her away *because* he desired her so much. And because she'd made him promise not to sleep with her.

She'd been wrong, impossible from the first. She'd missed him while he was away. She was carrying his child.

Everything had changed for them.

If she had to beg, she would.

"Don't make me sleep alone tonight," she pleaded. "Because I won't sleep. I'll just lie there…wanting you."

"I won't sleep, either. Still, in the morning you'll regret it if you don't go." His expression darkened. "Like you did before…on the island."

But she hadn't regretted it. He had.

"I don't think so," she said. "You did say we should focus on the positive…for the baby's sake. Am I right?"

His sensual mouth quirked ever so charmingly, and the heat in his gaze soon had her bones melting.

"How do you make me break every rule that allowed me to survive during my long, dark years of grief?"

"I get that you don't want to love anybody ever again.

Especially not me," she whispered. "But I'm not asking for your love tonight."

When he would have protested, she sealed his lips with a fingertip. "I'm not asking for anything you can't give. I just want to be with you."

"My father loved my mother too much, and…she destroyed him…when she left. I can't help thinking you're just waiting for the right moment to walk out."

Don't you know how much I love you? Don't you know that if only you loved me, I would never leave you?

Her knees were so weak with desire, she could barely stand. No way did she possess the courage to voice her true thoughts. She was afraid they would only drive him further away.

Her hold on him was tenuous, and only sexual. She had to accept that, use it and hope that someday she could build on that foundation.

Reaching toward him, she splayed her fingertips against his massive chest. Flesh and bone and sinew felt solid and warm beneath her open palm. When she ran her fingers over his nipples and through the dark hair that matted his torso, he groaned, which pleased her.

"Kira. Darlin'." On a shuddering sigh, he pulled her close and teased her lips and jawline with his mouth and tongue.

Lifting her, he carried her to the bed. There, he slid off his belt and slacks and pushed her nightgown down her shoulders. As it pooled onto the floor, he pulled her against him and pushed inside her slick satin warmth. Riding their mutual passion, they let it carry them like a charging black steed, faster and faster, until they soared together in torrid surrender. Afterward, as she held on to him, her sated body melted into his.

"You've ruined me," he whispered.

"Whiner," she teased.

"Seriously. I'll never be able to move again," he said.

She laughed. "Sure you will. And it better be sooner than you think. Because I'm going to be wanting more... very soon. You've neglected me...you know."

"Have I now? And whose fault was that, darlin' Kira?"

For an entire hour, he held her against his body as if she was precious to him. When she kissed his rough cheek, his throat, his nipples, he muttered huskily, "You weren't kidding, were you?"

"I've missed you."

"Slave driver."

But he smiled and ran his hands through her hair as he pulled her close.

This time his love was sweeter, and slower, and afterward, when he kissed her belly gently, he showed her that his intense passion included their precious child.

"So, you want my baby, do you?" he whispered.

"So much, too much," she admitted in a breathless whisper as she pressed his dark head against her flat stomach. "More than anything. In fact, I hope the baby's a boy and that he looks just like you."

He laughed in husky delight and nuzzled her tummy with his feverish lips. "Be careful what you wish for. He'll be a handful, I assure you."

"I can't wait."

When he held her close like this and was so teasingly affectionate, she could almost forget he didn't love her, that he never could. She could almost forget how inadequate and uncertain she'd always felt.

Almost...

He was a handsome billionaire, who could have any woman he wanted. What could she do to hold him?

Nestled in his arms, she fell into a restless sleep and

dreamed. She was a child again, standing beside her parents as they cheered Jaycee and her basketball team to victory. Then she was sitting in her room alone. The house was empty because her mother and father had driven Jaycee to a slumber party.

Older now, Kira was walking across the stage at Princeton where she'd graduated with honors. As she posed for photographs, she smiled brightly through her disappointment. None of her family was in the audience because Jaycee had a conflicting high school event. The picture was all they'd have to remember this huge milestone in Kira's life.

"Remember to smile," her mother had commanded over the phone. "You never smile." A pause. "Oh, how I wish I could be there to see you graduate!"

"Couldn't Daddy stay with Jaycee?"

"You know your father. He's no good at those high school functions without me."

The dream darkened into a nightmare. Quinn was standing in a shower of crimson light, holding Cristina against his long, lean body. "I have to marry *her,* don't you understand? I don't want to. You're the one who's special to me. Don't ever forget that my marriage to her is strictly business. You're the woman who really matters. Who will always matter. Nothing will change between us. You'll see."

Then he kissed Cristina as those awful words repeated themselves in her mind. "Strictly business..."

Kira woke up crying that phrase even as Quinn wrapped his arms around her and held her close.

"Hush. It's okay, baby. You were only dreaming."

Was she? Or were her dreams where she faced the harsh truths she denied when awake?

"I'm fine," she murmured, pushing him away. "You

don't have to comfort me. I can take care of myself—just like I always have. I didn't ask you to love me—did I?"

"No, you damn sure didn't."

Strictly business.

God, if only Quinn could feel that way, too, maybe then he'd survive this nightmare.

As soon as Kira's breathing had become regular again and Quinn was sure she was asleep, he'd tossed his own covers aside and shot out of bed.

Groping clumsily for his slacks on the dark floor, he yanked them on and stalked out of the bedroom in bare feet. When he got to the bar, he splashed a shot of vodka into a glass.

Strictly business.

Damn her! Not that he didn't feel sorry for her, because he did. Even now, her stricken cries echoed in his mind. She was no happier than he was.

He'd been right to think she'd regret the sex. So, why the hell had she slept with him when he'd given her an out?

He'd never figure her out. She might regret what had happened, but he couldn't. She'd been too sweet, and he'd craved her too desperately. Hell, it embarrassed him to think of how needy he'd felt all week without her in London.

Frowning as he stared into his glass, he remembered how he'd grabbed his cell phone at least a dozen times in his eagerness to call her, only to shove it back in his pocket. All he'd wanted was to hear her soft voice. Without her, he'd felt cut off, alone, alienated in a city he usually enjoyed.

Once in San Antonio, he'd rushed home. And when he'd seen her, he'd wanted nothing except to sweep her into his arms and kiss her endlessly. But she'd been pale and withdrawn.

Every day his obsession for her increased. If she could not reciprocate, they were shackled together on the same fatal course his own parents had traveled. He would not endure that kind of marriage.

His father had given his mother everything, and it hadn't been enough.

He would not make the same mistake.

Fifteen

Quinn's side of the bed was ice-cold.

Nothing had changed.

He was gone.

It wasn't the first time Kira had woken up alone in Quinn's bed, but this morning, she felt needier than usual. Maybe because of what they'd shared the night before, or maybe because of her bad dreams, she wanted a good-morning kiss. And maybe breakfast together punctuated with a lot more kisses.

But he'd left her for work, which was all-important to him. Hadn't business been the sole reason he'd married her?

To him, last night must have been about sex and nothing more. She'd known that, hadn't she? Still, as she lay in bed, her body sore from making love, she felt lonely. Would it always be like this?

Stretching, she rolled onto his side of the bed where his

scent lingered and hugged his pillow. Then, realizing what an idiot she was, she hurled his pillow at the wall. It struck an etching, which crashed to the floor.

Footsteps in the corridor brought a quick blush to her face.

"Mrs. Sullivan? Is that you? Do you need my assistance?" Jason sounded so stiff and formal, she cringed. She wanted her husband, not some uptight houseman with high-class British airs.

"I'm fine," she cried.

How was she going to get from Quinn's room to hers in her sheer nightie without Jason seeing her wrapped in a blanket? Such an encounter would be embarrassing for both of them.

When five minutes passed without another sound, she cracked the door. There was no sign of him, so she ripped a blanket off the bed, covered herself and shot down the hall on flying tiptoes. Once inside her bedroom, she bolted the door.

As she dressed, taking her time because it was hours before she needed to be at Betty's, she turned on the television. Murray Oil and the EU deal were all over the news.

Both the local news channels and the national ones were full of stories about Quinn's heady successes. In too many shots, a beaming Cristina stood so close to Quinn the pair seemed joined at the hip. Why hadn't Quinn told her that Cristina had gone to London with him?

Cristina worked for him. Surely he'd taken other executives. It was no big deal.

But in her fragile mood, and after her dream last night, it felt like a big deal to her.

You can't blame a man for something you dreamed!

Maybe not, but she still had to ask him about Cristina and his reasons for taking the woman to London. So, when the phone rang, she rushed to pick it up, hoping it was Quinn.

"Hello!" she said a little too brightly.

"Kira? You don't sound like yourself."

The critical male tone was very familiar. Still, because she was focused on Quinn, it took her a second to place the voice. Then it came to her: Gary Whitehall, her former boss.

"Hi, Gary."

"Are you still looking for a job?"

"I am," she said.

"Even though you're Quinn Sullivan's wife?"

"Yes, even though. He's a very busy man, and I love doing what I'm trained to do."

"Well, Maria is retiring because she needs more time to help her daughter. The minute she told me she wanted to play grandmother, well, naturally, we all thought of you."

She lifted a brow. *And Quinn.*

"You could have your old job back… Although, like I said, I wasn't at all sure you'd be interested now that you're *the* Mrs. Sullivan."

"Well, I am, so…this is wonderful news."

"Then you'll make yourself available for a meeting? No hurry, though. Don't want to pressure you."

"I'm available. In fact, I'm free for an hour or two this afternoon."

They agreed upon a time and hung up.

The call boosted her mood until she remembered how Quinn had rushed off to work this morning without even a goodbye. Until she remembered what a gorgeous couple he and Cristina had made on television. They were both so stylish and good-looking. They had business concerns in common, too.

With an effort, she quit thinking about Cristina and refocused on Gary's offer. She was glad Gary had called, even if it was her marriage to Quinn that had made her more attractive as a job applicant.

On a whim, she decided to call Quinn and run the job idea by him just to see what he'd say.

Oh, be honest, Kira, you just want to hear his sexy voice and distract him from Cristina.

Kira made the call, only to be deflated when his secretary told her, "I'll have him return your call. He's in a meeting."

"With whom?"

"Cristina Gold. They're taking a last look at the contracts for the EU deal before everything is finalized."

Don't ask a question if you don't want the answer.

"Would you please tell him…that I'll be on my cell."

"Are you all right, Mrs. Sullivan?"

"I'm fine," she whispered as she hung up.

Perfectly fine.

Clutching the phone to her breast, she sank onto her bed. She didn't feel fine. She felt more uncertain than ever.

Leave it alone. Cristina works for him. That's all there is to it. Go to Betty's. Do the interview with Gary. Forget your stupid nightmare.

But being pregnant had her feeling highly emotional. She couldn't leave it alone. She had to see him. After last night, she had to know how he felt.

Dressing hurriedly, she was in his office in less than an hour. The same beautiful blonde secretary who'd greeted her on her first visit greeted her again, more warmly this time.

"Mr. Sullivan told me you two are expecting a baby. He sounded so happy about it. Congratulations."

"Thank you."

"Would you like coffee? Or a soda?"

"I just want to talk to my husband. He didn't call me back, and since I was in the neighborhood…"

"I'm afraid he's still going over those contracts."

"With Miss Gold?"

The young woman nodded. "I'm afraid the documents are long and very complicated. A mistake could cost millions. Miss Gold is one of our attorneys, you see. She had several concerns."

"Please tell him I'm here."

After the young woman buzzed him, she looked up almost immediately. "He says he'll see you. Now."

Intending to lead her down the hall, she arose, but Kira held up a hand. "I remember the way."

When Kira reached his office, Cristina was just exiting with a thick sheaf of documents. She tossed Kira a tight smile. Behind Cristina, Quinn leaned negligently against the doorjamb.

When he opened the door, Kira said, "I hope I'm not interrupting."

"Glad that meeting's over. And doubly glad to see you." He shut the door. "I needed a break."

Despite the welcoming words, when their eyes met, she felt a sudden unbearable tension coming from him.

"Sorry I left so early this morning, but I had a couple of urgent texts."

"From Cristina?"

"One was. Unfortunately, I still have a lot of balls in the air related to the EU deal," he said.

"No problem."

"You look upset." His voice was flat.

"I didn't realize Cristina went to London with you… until I saw some of the news coverage on television."

A cynical black brow lifted. "I took a team of ten. She

was part of the team. She's very talented at what she does, or I never would have hired her."

"Not only is she talented, but she's beautiful, too."

He stood very still. "I imagine her looks are part of why she made it into so many of the TV shots. Look, there's no need for you to be jealous of her…if that's what this is."

"I'm not."

"I'm married to you, and whether you believe it or not, that means something to me."

What did it really mean if he could never love her?

"Since you obviously want to know more about Cristina and me," he began in the maddening, matter-of-fact tone of a lawyer presenting his case, "I'll clarify our relationship. We dated briefly. The press gave our romance more attention than it deserved.

"Then she broke up with me—for another man with whom she's still seriously involved. At the time, she complained I never had time for her. He did. Naturally, I was angry, but since then I've realized she was right."

"A vengeful man might have held what she did against her," she said coolly. "Why did you hire her?"

"We worked together on several projects before we dated. She will do a lot for Murray Oil."

"So, as always, business is all-important to you? Does nothing else ever matter? Not even your own injured feelings?"

He shrugged. "They weren't that injured. I got over her pretty quickly."

Would he get over Kira and be this matter-of-fact about it? At the thought, Kira cringed.

"Business will always be an important part of my life. I don't deny that. It's part of who I am. I hired her…before I met you." He paused. "What is it you want from me this morning, Kira?"

"Right. I'm interrupting you. You're a busy man. You probably have many more important meetings to get through today. All those balls in the air. And here I am, your pregnant, overly emotional wife needing reassurance."

He studied her warily. "What do you want, Kira?"

Why couldn't she be as cool and logical as he was? Because everything in her life was out of balance. She was pregnant and feeling needy. There were too many unanswered questions in their relationship, and she was still reeling from the discovery that she'd been adopted.

She wanted to belong somewhere, to someone. She wanted to matter to *Quinn*. If she'd been more important to him, wouldn't he have kept her in the loop while he was gone? Wouldn't he have shared more details concerning his oil deal?

"I guess I want the impossible," she blurted out. "I want a real marriage."

"Now you want a real marriage, when all along you've said that's the last thing you want? Last night you woke up crying from some dream, apparently about me, demanding 'strictly business.' You pushed me away as if you wanted nothing to do with me. If I give you space it's wrong. If I push myself on you it's wrong."

"I know I'm not making sense," she said. "Our marriage was never based on love, mutual understanding or anything that makes up a true partnership. I guess I'm upset because…because I don't know… I just know I can't go on like this!"

"As soon as I complete this deal, I'll have more time…"

"How will that matter if you don't want the same kind of marriage I do? Now, maybe because of the baby and finding out I was adopted, I have this huge need for things to be right between us. I want more. I've wanted more my whole life. I don't want to feel left out anymore. Most of all, I want to count to my husband."

"If you wanted to belong in this marriage, then why did you tell me from the first that you didn't want to sleep with me?"

"I guess to protect myself…from ever feeling like I feel now—needy…confused. I knew this marriage was only a business deal for you. I didn't want to get my heart broken," she whispered.

"What are you saying?"

"What we have isn't enough. Not for me…or for you."

"You're pregnant. We can't just walk away from each other. It's not about you and me anymore, or even Murray Oil. We have a child to think about now."

"That's all the more reason I don't want us trapped in a loveless marriage. I want a husband who can love me. I want my child to grow up in a loving home. After the deal you just made, the executives at Murray Oil trust you. You don't need to be married to me anymore. You can divorce me and date somebody who understands you, someone who can make you happy…someone like Cristina."

"Damn it. I don't want a divorce. Or Cristina. Like I said—if you'd ever once listen to me—she's practically engaged."

"But you don't love me…"

"Well, I damn sure don't love anyone else. And I'm not lusting after anybody else. I'm focused solely on you! You're very important to me, Kira. Vital. Still, it's true that I'm not sure I'll ever be capable of loving anyone—even you. Maybe I've been hard and dark and driven for too long."

"Well, I want a man who will commit his heart to me, or I want out."

"Okay," he said in a tone that was cold, infuriatingly

logical and final. "Now that our marriage has served its purpose, you want out. Well, I don't want out, and I'm not ready to let you go. But if that's what you want, I won't hold you against your will any longer."

"What?"

"I'll give you what you say you want. You're free to leave. But understand this—I intend to take an active role in raising our child."

"Of course," she whispered, feeling shattered.

"Then so be it," he said.

He stared at her, waiting for her to walk out the door, and, for a brief moment, his guard fell. She saw longing and pain flash in his eyes.

Suddenly, she realized just how much she'd wanted him to fight for her, for them.

After stumbling blindly out of his office, she sat behind the wheel of her car, clenching her keys in her hand. All her life she'd wanted someone to fight for her, someone to put her first. She'd had a right to push for more from her marriage.

He wasn't willing to fight for her as he'd fought for his oil deal in London, so she would do the fighting.

She would fight for her self-respect, and she would teach their child to fight for his, too.

Kira had been in no condition to be interviewed by Gary the afternoon she'd parted from Quinn, so she'd rescheduled.

Two miserable days later, she still didn't feel strong enough, but here she sat, facing Gary across his wide, cluttered desk in his flashy corner office that overlooked the museum grounds and the busy street that fronted the modern building.

If only she could stop thinking about Quinn and how

bereft she'd felt ever since he'd agreed to end their marriage.

Concentrating on Gary, who wasn't the most fascinating man, was difficult. Lately, everything had been difficult. Returning to Quinn's gorgeous loft, packing the beautiful clothes that she would no longer need and then moving back into her cramped apartment with her dead plants and resentful cat had been full of emotional hurdles.

Rudy wouldn't sit on her lap or use his scratching post. Only this morning he'd peed on her pillow just to show her how much he resented being abandoned.

"Quit feeling sorry for yourself! I'm the one who got married and pregnant…and separated," she'd yelled at him.

Swishing his tail, he'd flattened his ears and stalked indifferently to his bowl where he'd howled for more tuna.

She tried to pay attention to Gary, she really did, but her mind constantly wandered to her miserable new separated state and to Quinn and how cold he'd been right before he'd watched her walk away.

Suddenly, she found Gary's droning insufferable and longed to be anywhere else, even home alone with her sullen cat. If she didn't interrupt Gary, he might easily rant on for another half an hour.

"Gary, this is all very fascinating, but I need to ask a question."

He frowned.

"Is this job offer contingent on me remaining married to Quinn?"

"What?"

"Let me be blunt."

His mouth tightened. "You do that so well."

"Quinn and I have separated. Do you still want me for this job? "

His face fell. "Separated?" Flushing, he pushed himself

back from his desk. "Well, that does change things." Recovering quickly, he ran a nervous hand through his hair. "Still, I want you to work here, of course."

Her voice was equally silky as she leaned toward him. "*Of course.* I'm so glad we understand each other."

A few minutes later he hastily concluded the interview. "I'll call you," he said.

She left, wondering if he would.

As she stood on the curb outside the museum, about to cross the street, Jaycee called her on her cell.

"How are things going?"

"I've been better," Kira replied. "The interview with Gary went okay, I guess."

"And Rudy?"

"He peed on my pillow this morning."

"Well, you abandoned him. He's still mad at you."

"I guess. Hold on—"

Pressing the phone against her ear, she looked both ways to cross the street. But just as she jumped into the crosswalk a motorcycle made a left turn, going too fast.

She felt a surge of panic, but it was too late. In the next moment, she was hurled into the air.

It was true what they said about your life flashing before your eyes.

She saw Quinn's darkly handsome face and knew suddenly, without a doubt, that she loved him.

It didn't matter that he could never love her. Or maybe she knew, on some deep level, that he must love her, too—at least a little.

She remembered all the times he'd looked at her and she'd felt her soul join to his.

She'd been an idiot to walk out on the man she loved, to

abandon a man so afraid of love that he denied what was in his own heart. He needed her.

She wanted to get up and run back to his office. She wanted to beg him for another chance. But when she tried to sit up, her body felt as if it were made of concrete.

Someone knelt over her, but she couldn't see his face.

"Quinn," she cried. "I want Quinn."

The man spoke, but she couldn't hear what he said.

Then everything went black.

"A Jerry Sullivan is here to see you," Quinn's secretary informed him crisply. "Says he's family."

"Show him in," Quinn ordered in a dull voice as he set the lightning whelk Kira had given him back on the shelf. "He's my uncle. He'll want coffee with cream and sugar."

Uncle Jerry didn't wait for Quinn's secretary to return with his coffee before he pounced.

"Sorry to interrupt you, but I just heard you separated from your beautiful wife. I'd ask you to tell me it isn't true, but since you look like something my dog dragged in from the gutter, I won't bother."

"Good to see you, too, Uncle J."

"What the hell did you do to drive her away?"

"I never should have married her in the first place."

"If you let her go, you'll be making the biggest mistake of your life. You've already wasted too many years of your life alone."

"Let me be, why don't you?"

"You're still in love with her. I can see it!"

"The hell I am. Did anybody ever tell you to mind your own business?"

"Sure. You. Plenty of times. Good thing I've got better sense than to listen to the likes of an upstart nephew who doesn't have a clue about what's good for him."

"I think some men are better off single. And I'm probably one of them."

"Bull. I saw the way you were with her. You're like your father. He was the most loving man I ever knew."

"And what did it get him—other than a broken heart and an early grave?"

"You're not your father. Kira's not Esther. Kira's the real thing. Esther was a beautiful woman who knew how to play your dad. And, yes, your dad foolishly loved her with all his heart—just like he loved you. But when you get down to it, even when you're wrong about the people you love, loving is still the best way to live. That's why we still miss Kade. He loved us all so much!"

"My father killed himself because my mother left him."

"You'll never make me believe that! Kade wouldn't ever deliberately walk out on you. You were everything to him. His death was an accident."

"Uncle Jerry, thanks for coming by."

"Great. Now you're giving me the brush-off."

"I know you mean well...but I'm a grown man—"

"Who has the right to screw up his life royally and who's doing a damn good job of it."

"If you've said your piece, I've got work to do."

"You've always got work to do! Maybe it's time you got a life." Uncle Jerry smiled grimly. "Okay, I'll leave you to it, not that it's any fun watching my favorite nephew walk out on the best thing that ever happened to him."

"I didn't walk out on her! Damn it! She left me!"

"So, quit sulking, and go after her!"

"If only it were that easy!"

"Trust me—it is. The only thing stopping you is your damn arrogance."

"Get the hell out of here!"

Holding a silver tray with a coffee cup, Quinn's secretary pushed the door open and would have entered except Quinn held up a hand. "Uncle Jerry won't be having coffee after all. He's leaving."

For some time after his uncle had gone, Quinn sat in his office and seethed. Slowly, as he cooled down, everything the older man had said began replaying in his mind. Since his father's death, Uncle Jerry was the one person Quinn had been able to count on.

Quinn walked over to the shelf where he'd placed the lightning whelk. How full of hope he'd felt when she'd given it to him. He remembered her shining eyes, her glowing beauty.

Turning away, he grabbed his cell phone. For a long moment he just held it.

Quinn didn't just want to call Kira for his own selfish reasons. He was genuinely worried about her and the baby. The longer he went without talking to her, the more worried he grew. Would it be so wrong to call just to make sure she and the baby were all right? Would it? Even if they never got back together, she was the mother of his future child.

Swallowing his pride, he lifted his phone and punched in her number. As he waited for her to answer, his gut clenched.

Then, on the third ring, a man answered.

"I want Kira," Quinn thundered. "I need to speak to my wife."

"Sir, I'm so sorry. I'm terribly afraid there's been an accident..."

The man introduced himself as someone working at the local hospital. He said something about a motorcycle hitting Kira and that Kira had been taken to his emergency room by ambulance. After getting the specifics, Quinn hung up and was grabbing his jacket and on his way to the door, when Earl Murray rang his cell phone.

Quinn picked up on the first ring. "I just heard Kira's been hurt."

"Apparently, Jaycee was talking to her when the motorcycle hit her… I don't know anything else."

"Then I'll meet you at the hospital," Quinn said. His heart was in his throat as he bolted out of his office in a dead run, praying he wouldn't be too late.

Sixteen

Quinn had never been as scared in his life as he was when he stood over Kira watching the IV drip clear liquid into her veins. Her narrow face had the awful grayish tint Quinn had seen only one time before—on his father's face as he'd lain in a pool of his own blood.

"Tell me she's going to be all right. Tell me the baby's all right."

"I've told you," the doctor repeated patiently. "Apparently, she was thrown onto the pavement, but seems to have suffered only a concussion and a few bruises. After a night or two of rest, she and the baby will be fine. She's one lucky young lady."

"You're sure?" For some reason, the facts weren't sticking in Quinn's head as they usually did.

"As sure as I can be under the circumstances."

"When will she wake up?"

"Like I told you before—soon. You just have to be patient."

An hour later, the longest hour of Quinn's life, her long lashes fluttered. Sensing that she was struggling to focus on him, Quinn gripped her hand and leaned forward.

"Kira… Darlin'…"

"Quinn… I wanted you to come. I wanted it so much."

"Kira, you're in a hospital. You're going to be okay. The baby, too."

"I love you," she said softly. "I was such a fool."

Rather than terrifying him, those three words brought a rush of joy.

"I love you, too. More than anything." He squeezed her hand tightly. "So much it scares the hell out of me."

It had only taken her admission to make him brave enough to admit his own feelings for her.

With glistening eyes, she laughed softly. "You really love me?"

"Yes. Maybe even from the first moment I saw you. I just didn't know what had hit me." He paused. "Jaycee's here, along with your parents. We've all been so scared for you and the baby. Half out of our minds."

"They're all here, too?"

"Of course we're here," her father roared.

Kira smiled radiantly up at them. "It's almost worth getting hit by a motorcycle to have all of you all here… together, knowing…knowing that you love me."

They moved closer, circling her bed. Holding hands, they smiled down at her. "Of course we love you," her father said. "You're our girl."

"You gave us a terrible scare," her mother said. "You're very important to all of us."

"I'm so happy," Kira whispered. "I've never been happier."

"By the way," her father said, "your old boss called and said you'd better get well soon because you've got a big job at the museum waiting for you. So, no more waitressing…"

Kira smiled weakly. "I guess that's good news…but not nearly as good as all of you being here." Her grip on Quinn's hand tightened as she looked up at him. "I never, ever want to let go of you again."

"You won't have to."

Quinn needed no further encouragement to lean forward and kiss her. Very carefully, so as not to hurt her, he pressed his mouth to her lips.

As always, she gave her entire being to him, causing warmth and happiness to flow from her soul into his.

She was everything to him. He would love her and cherish her always, or at least until the last breath left his body.

"Darlin'," he whispered. "Promise me you'll never leave me again."

She nodded. "Never. I swear it. Like I said, I was a fool."

Circling his neck with her hands, she brought his face down to hers and kissed him again.

Epilogue

One Year Later
July the Fourth
Wimberley, Texas

Kira looked across the green lawns that sloped down to cypress trees shading the sparkling river. The air stirring through the leaves was warm, while the water was clear and icy.

Kira couldn't believe her happiness. Ever since that afternoon in the hospital, when she'd awakened to Quinn and her family gathered around her bed, her happiness had grown a little every day.

Despite the pain in her shoulder and back, she'd seen the love shining in all their eyes.

Love for her.

Had it always been there? Whether it had or not, all her doubts about herself, about Quinn, about her adoption, had vanished. She'd simply known that she mattered—to all of them.

She belonged.

Knowing she was truly loved, her confidence had grown in every aspect of her life, including in her career as a curator. Naturally, Gary had been thrilled that she was to remain Mrs. Sullivan. Quinn had thrilled him even more by being most generous to the museum, stipulating with every donation that his wife be in charge of the funds.

This lazy summer afternoon on the grounds of the Sullivans' new weekend home on the Blanco was perfect for a July Fourth celebration that included friends, family and business associates. The star of the show was only a few months old.

Thomas Kade Sullivan fulfilled his mother's most fervent hopes as he sat on his red-and-blue quilt by the water, holding court. He shook his rattle while Aunt Jaycee laughed and held up a stuffed bunny rabbit. With his brilliant blue eyes, Tommy Kade was every bit as handsome as his father.

Off to one side, a band played as their guests took turns swimming in the cool waters or serving themselves barbecue.

Quinn left the men he'd been talking to and walked up to her. Grinning down at her, he circled her with his arms. Contentment made her feel soft and warm as he held her close. Never had she dreamed she'd feel this complete with anyone.

She smiled at the sight of her mother ordering the caterers about. With her illness in remission, her mother was her old formidable self. When Vera had been well enough for Kira's dad to leave her at home, Quinn had made a place for him at Murray Oil.

"Murray Oil's too big for one man to run," Quinn had said when Kira had tried to thank him.

Life was good, she thought as her husband brushed his lips against her cheek. Very good.

"Happy July Fourth," Quinn said.

"The happiest ever."

"For me, too. Because you're in my life," he murmured huskily. "You're the best thing that ever happened to me… besides Tommy Kade. And you're responsible for him, too."

"Stop. We're at a party. We have to behave."

"Maybe I don't want to behave."

He drew her away from the crowd into the shade of the towering cypress trees. Once they were hidden from their guests, he wrapped her in his arms and kissed her long and deeply.

"I love you," he whispered. "I love you, and I always will. We have a real marriage, now—wouldn't you agree?"

The most wonderful thing of all was that she knew it and accepted it—down to her bones—because she felt exactly the same way. "I would! And I love you, too," she murmured. "Oh, how I love you."

* * * * *

AN OUTRAGEOUS PROPOSAL

BY
MAUREEN CHILD

Maureen Child is a California native who loves to travel. Every chance they get, she and her husband are taking off on another research trip. An author of more than sixty books, Maureen loves a happy ending and still swears that she has the best job in the world. She lives in Southern California with her husband, two children and a golden retriever with delusions of grandeur. Visit Maureen's website, www.maureenchild.com.

For two wonderful writers who are fabulous
friends, Kate Carlisle and Jennifer Lyon.
Thank you both for always being there.

One

"For the love of all that's holy, *don't push!*" Sean Connolly kept one wary eye on the rearview mirror and the other on the curving road stretching out in front of him. Why the hell was *he* the designated driver to the hospital?

"Just mind the road and drive, Sean," his cousin Ronan complained from the backseat. He had one arm around his hugely pregnant wife, drawing her toward him despite the seat belts.

"He's right," Georgia Page said from the passenger seat. "Just drive, Sean." She half turned to look into the back. "Hang on, Laura," she told her sister. "We'll be there soon."

"You can all relax, you know," Laura countered. "I'm not giving birth in the car."

"Please, God," Sean muttered and gave the car more gas.

Never before in his life had he had reason to curse the

narrow, winding roads of his native Ireland. But tonight, all he wanted was about thirty kilometers of smooth highway to get them all to the hospital in Westport.

"You're not helping," Georgia muttered with a quick look at him.

"I'm driving," he told her and chanced another look into the rearview mirror just in time to see Laura's features twist in pain.

She moaned, and Sean gritted his teeth. The normal sense of panic a man felt around a woman in labor was heightened by the fact that his cousin was half excited and half mad with worry for the wife he doted on. A part of Sean envied Ronan even while the larger part of him was standing back and muttering, *Aye, Ronan, better you than me.*

Funny how complicated a man's life could get when he wasn't even paying attention to it. A year or so ago, he and his cousin Ronan were happily single, each of them with an eye toward remaining that way. Now, Ronan was married, about to be a father, and Sean was as involved in the coming birth of the next generation of Connollys as he could be. He and Ronan lived only minutes apart, and the two of them had grown up more brothers than cousins.

"Can't you go any faster?" Georgia whispered, leaning in toward him.

Then there was Laura's sister. Georgia was a smart, slightly cynical, beautiful woman who engaged Sean's brain even while she attracted him on a much more basic level. So far, he'd kept his distance, though. Getting involved with Georgia Page would only complicate things. What with her sister married to his cousin, and Ronan suddenly becoming insanely protective about the women he claimed were in "his charge."

Damned old-fashioned for a man who had spent most

of his adult years mowing through legions of adoring females.

Still, Sean was glad to have Georgia along. For the sanity she provided, if nothing else. Georgia and Sean would at least have each other to turn to during all of this, and he was grateful for it.

Sean gave her a quick glance and kept his voice low. "I go much faster on these roads at night, we'll *all* need a room in hospital."

"Right." Georgia's gaze fixed on the road ahead, and she leaned forward as if trying to make the car speed up through sheer force of will.

Well, Sean told himself, if anyone could pull that off, it would be Georgia Page. In the light from the dashboard, her dark blue eyes looked fathomless and her honey-colored hair looked more red than blond.

He'd first met her at Ronan and Laura's wedding a year or so ago, but with her many trips to Ireland to visit her sister, he'd come to know Georgia and he liked her. He liked her quick wit, her sarcasm and her sense of family loyalty—which he shared.

All around them, the darkness was complete, the headlights of his car illuminating the narrow track winding out in front of them. This far from the city, it was mainly farmland stretching out behind the high, thick hedges that lined the road. The occasional lighted window in a farmhouse stood out like beacons, urging them on.

At last, a distant glow appeared and Sean knew it was the lights of Westport, staining the night sky. They were close, and he took his first easy breath in what felt like hours.

"Nearly there," he announced, and glanced at Georgia. She gave him a quick grin, and he felt the solid punch of it.

From the backseat, Laura cried out and just like that, Sean's relief was cut short. They weren't safe yet. Focusing on the task at hand, he pushed his car as fast as he dared.

What felt like days—and was in reality only hours and hours later—Sean and Georgia walked out of the hospital like survivors of a grueling battle.

"God," Sean said, as they stepped into the soft rain of an Irish afternoon in winter. The wind blew like ice, and the rain fell from clouds that looked close enough to touch. He tipped his face back and stared up into the gray. It was good to be outside, away from the sounds and smells of the hospital. Even better to know that the latest Connolly had arrived safely.

"That was the longest night and day of my life, I think," he said with feeling.

"Mine, too," Georgia agreed, shrugging deeper into the navy blue coat she wore. "But it was worth it."

He looked over at her. "Oh, aye, it was indeed. She's a beauty."

"She is, isn't she?" Georgia grinned. "Fiona Connolly. It's a good name. Beautiful, but strong, too."

"It is, and by the look of her, she's already got her da wrapped around her tiny fingers." He shook his head as he remembered the expression on his cousin's face as Ronan held his new daughter for the first time. Almost enough to make a jaded man believe in—never mind.

"I'm exhausted and energized all at the same time."

"Me, as well," Sean agreed, happy to steer his mind away from dangerous territory. "Feel as though I've been running a marathon."

"And all we did was wait."

"I think the waiting is the hardest thing of all."

Georgia laughed. "And I think Laura would disagree."

Ruefully, he nodded. "You've a point there."

Georgia sighed, stepped up to Sean and threaded her arm through his. "Ronan will be a great father. And Laura…she wanted this so much." She sniffed and swiped her fingers under her eyes.

"No more crying," Sean said, giving her arm a squeeze. "Already I feel as though I've been riding a tide of tears all day. Between the new mother and father and you, it's been weepy eyes and sniffles for hours."

"I saw your eyes get a little misty, too, tough guy."

"Aye, well, we Irish are a sentimental lot," he admitted, then started for the car park, Georgia's arm still tucked through his.

"It's one of the things I like best about you—"

He gave her a look.

"—the Irish in general, I mean," she qualified.

"Ah, well then." He smiled to himself at her backtracking. It was a lovely afternoon. Soft rain, cold wind and new life wailing in the hospital behind them. "You've been to Ireland so often in the last year, you're very nearly an honorary Irishman yourself, aren't you?"

"I've been thinking about that," she admitted. They walked up to his car, and Sean hit the unlock button on his keypad.

"What's that then?" he asked, as he opened the passenger door for her and held it, waiting. Fatigue clawed at him, but just beneath that was a buoyant feeling that had him smile at the woman looking up at him.

"About being an honorary Irishman. Or at least," she said, looking around her at the car park, the hospital and the city beyond, "moving here. Permanently."

"Really?" Intrigued, he leaned his forearms on the top

of the door. "And what's brought this on then? Is it your brand-new niece?"

She shrugged. "Partly, sure. But mostly, it's this country. It's gorgeous and friendly, and I've really come to love being here."

"Does Laura know about this?"

"Not yet," she admitted, and shifted her gaze back to him. "So don't say anything. She's got enough on her mind at the moment."

"True enough," he said. "But I'm thinking she'd be pleased to have her sister so close."

She flashed him a brilliant smile then slid into her seat. As Sean closed the door after her and walked around the car, he was forced to admit that *he* wouldn't mind having Georgia close, either.

A half hour later, Georgia opened the door to Laura and Ronan's expansive stone manor house and looked back over her shoulder at Sean. "Want to come in for a drink?"

"I think we've earned one," he said, stepping inside and closing the door behind him. "Or even a dozen."

She laughed and it felt good. Heck, *she* felt good. Her sister was a mother, and Georgia was so glad she had made the decision to come to Ireland to be present for the baby's birth. She hated to think about what it would have been like, being a half a world away right now.

"Ronan's housekeeper, Patsy, is off in Dublin visiting her daughter Sinead," Georgia reminded him. "So we're on our own for food."

"It's not food I want at the moment anyway," Sean told her.

Was he flirting with her? Georgia wondered, then

dismissed the notion. She shook her head and reminded herself that they were here for a drink. Or several.

As he spoke, a long, ululating howl erupted from deep within the house. Georgia actually jumped at the sound and then laughed. “With the rain, the dogs have probably let themselves into the kitchen.”

“Probably hungry now, too,” Sean said, and walked beside her toward the back of the house.

Georgia knew her sister’s house as if it were her own. Whenever she was in Ireland, she stayed here at the manor, since it was so huge they could comfortably hold a family reunion for a hundred. She opened the door into a sprawling kitchen with top-of-the-line appliances and what looked like miles of granite countertops. Everything was tidy—but for the two dogs scrambling toward her for some attention.

Deidre was a big, clumsy English sheepdog with so much hair over her eyes, it was a wonder she didn’t walk into walls. And Beast—huge, homely—the best that could be said about him was what he lacked in beauty he made up for in heart. Since Beast reached her first, Georgia scratched behind his ears and sent the big dog into quivers of delight. Deidre was right behind him, nudging her mate out of her way.

“Okay then, food for the dogs, then drinks for us,” Georgia announced.

“Already on it,” Sean assured her, making his way to the wide pantry, stepping over and around Beast as the dog wound his way in and out of Sean’s feet.

Within a few minutes, they had the dogs fed and watered and then left them there, sleeping on their beds in front of the now cold kitchen hearth. Cuddled up together, the dogs looked snug and happy.

Then Georgia led the way back down the hall, the

short heels of her shoes clicking against the wood floor. At the door to the parlor, Sean asked, "So, Patsy's in Dublin with her daughter. Sinead's doing well then, with her new family?"

"According to Patsy, everything's great," Georgia said.

Laura had told her the whole story of the pregnant Sinead marrying in a hurry. Sinead was now the mother of an infant son and her new husband was, at the moment, making a demo CD. He and his friends played traditional Irish music and, thanks to Ronan's influence with a recording company, had a real chance to do something with it. "She misses Sinead living close by, but once they get the demo done, they'll all be coming back to Dunley."

"Home does draw a body back no matter how far you intend to roam," Sean mused, as he followed her into the front parlor. "And yet, you're thinking of leaving your home to make a new one."

"I guess I am."

Hearing him say it aloud made the whole idea seem more real than it had in the past week or so that it had been floating around in her mind. But it also felt…right. Okay, scary, but good. After all, it wasn't as if she was giving up a lot. And the plus side was, she could leave behind all of the tension and bad memories of a marriage that had dissolved so abruptly.

Moving to Ireland was a big change, she knew. But wasn't change a good thing? Shake up your life from time to time just to keep it interesting?

At that thought, she smiled to herself. Interesting. Moving to a different country. Leaving the familiar to go to the…okay, also familiar. Since Laura had married Ronan and moved to Ireland, Georgia had made the long trek to visit four times. And each time she came, it was harder to leave. To go back to her empty condo in Huntington Beach, California. To sit at her desk, alone in the real estate office she and Laura had opened together.

Not that she was feeling sorry for herself—she wasn't. But she had started thinking that maybe there was more to life than sitting behind a desk hoping to sell a house.

In the parlor, Georgia paused, as she always did, just to enjoy the beauty of the room. A white-tiled hearth, cold now, but stacked with kindling that Sean was already working to light against the chill gloom of the day. Pale green walls dotted with seascapes and oversize couches facing each other across a low table that held a Waterford crystal bowl filled with late chrysanthemums in tones of russet and gold. The wide front windows looked out over a sweep of lawn that was drenched with the rain still falling softly against the glass.

When he had the fire going to his satisfaction, Sean stood up and brushed his palms together, then moved to the spindle table in the corner that held a collection of crystal decanters. Ignoring them, he bent to the small refrigerator tucked into the corner behind the table.

"Now, about that celebratory drink," he muttered.

Georgia smiled and joined him at the table, leaning her palms on the glossy top as she watched him open the fridge. "We earned it all right, but I wouldn't have missed it. The worry, the panic—" She was still smiling as he glanced up at her. "And I was seriously panicked. It was hard knowing Laura was in pain and not being able to do anything about it."

"Would it make me seem less manly to you if I admitted to sheer terror?" he asked, as he reached into the refrigerator.

"Your manhood is safe," Georgia assured him.

In fact, she had never known a man who needed to worry less about his manhood than Sean Connolly. He was gorgeous, charming and oozed sex appeal. Good thing, she thought, that she was immune. Well, nearly.

Even she, a woman who knew better, had been tempted by Sean's charms. Of course, it would be much better—safer—to keep him in the "friend" zone. Starting up anything with him would not only be dangerous but awkward, as well. Since her sister was married to his cousin, any kind of turmoil between them could start a family war.

And there was *always* turmoil when a man was involved, she thought with an inner sigh. But she'd learned her lesson there. She could enjoy Sean's company without letting herself get…involved. Her gaze skimmed over his tall, nicely packed yet lanky body, and something inside her sizzled like a trapped flame struggling to grow into a bonfire. She so didn't need that.

Nope, she told herself, just enjoy looking at him and keep your hormones on a tight leash. When he sent her a quick wink and a wild grin, Georgia amended that last thought to a tight, *short,* leash.

To divert herself from her own thoughts, Georgia sighed and asked, "Isn't she beautiful? The baby?"

"She is indeed," Sean agreed, pulling a bottle of champagne from the fridge and holding it aloft like a hard-won trophy. "And she has a clever father, as well. Our Ronan's stocked the fridge with not one but three bottles of champagne, bless him."

"Very thoughtful," she agreed.

He grabbed two crystal flutes from the shelf behind the bar, then set them down on the table and worked at the champagne wire and cork. "Did you get hold of your parents with the news?"

"I did," Georgia said, remembering how her mother had cried over the phone hearing the news about her first grandchild. "I called from Laura's room when you took Ronan down to buy flowers. Laura got to talk to them and they heard the baby cry." She smiled. "Mom cried along with her. Ronan's already promised to fly them in whenever they're ready."

"That's lovely then." The cork popped with a cheerful sound, and Sean poured out two glasses. Bubbling froth filled the flutes, looking like liquid sunshine. "So, champagne?"

"Absolutely."

She took a glass and paused when Sean said, "To Fiona Connolly. May her life be long and happy. May she be a stranger to sorrow and a friend to joy."

The sting of tears burned Georgia's eyes. Shaking her head, she took a sip of champagne and said, "That was beautiful, Sean."

He gave her a grin, then took her free hand in his and led her over to one of the sofas. There, he sat her down and then went back to the bar for the bottle of champagne. He set it on the table in front of them, then took a seat beside Georgia on the couch.

"A hell of a day all in all, wouldn't you say?"

"It was," she agreed, then amended, *"is."* Another sip of champagne and she added, "I'm tired, but I don't think I could close my eyes, you know? Too much leftover adrenaline pumping away inside."

"I feel the same," he told her, "so it's lucky we can keep each other company."

"Yeah, I guess it is," Georgia agreed. Kicking her shoes off, she drew her feet up onto the sofa and idly rubbed her arches.

The snap and hiss of the fire along with the patter of rain on the window made for a cozy scene. Taking a sip of her champagne, she let her head fall back against the couch.

"So," Sean said a moment or two later, "tell me about this plan of yours to move to Ireland."

She lifted her head to look at him. His brown hair was tousled, his brown eyes tired but interested and the half smile on his face could have tempted a saint. Georgia took another sip of champagne, hoping the icy liquor would dampen the heat beginning to build inside.

"I've been thinking about it for a while," she admitted, her voice soft. "Actually since my last visit. When I left for home, I remember sitting on the airplane as it was taxiing and wondering why I was leaving."

He nodded as if he understood completely, and that settled her enough to continue.

"I mean, you should be happy to go home after a trip, right?" She asked the question more of herself than of Sean and answered it the same way. "Looking forward to going back to your routine. Your everyday life. But I wasn't. There was just this niggling sense of disappointment that seemed to get bigger the closer I got to home."

"Maybe some of that was just because you were leaving your sister," he said quietly.

"Probably," she admitted with a nod and another sip of champagne. "I mean, Laura's more than my sister, she's my best friend." Looking at him, she gave him a small smile. "I really miss having her around, you know?"

"I do," he said, reaching for the champagne, then topping off their glasses. "When Ronan was in California, I found I missed going to the pub with him. I missed the laughter. And the arguments." He grinned. "Though if you repeat any of this, I'll deny it to my last breath."

"Oh, understood," she replied with a laugh. "Anyway, I got home, went to our—*my*—real estate office and stared out the front window. Waiting for clients to call or come in is a long, boring process." She stared down into her champagne. "And while I was staring out that window, watching the world go by, I realized that everyone outside the glass was doing what they wanted to do. Everyone but me."

"I thought you enjoyed selling real estate," Sean said. "The way Laura tells it, the two of you were just beginning to build the business."

"We were," she agreed. "But it wasn't what either of us wanted. Isn't that ridiculous?" Georgia shifted on the couch, half turning to face Sean more fully.

Wow, she thought, *he really is gorgeous.*

She blinked, then looked at the champagne suspiciously. Maybe the bubbles were infiltrating her mind, making her more susceptible to the Connolly charm and good looks. But no, she decided a moment later, she'd always been susceptible. Just able to resist. But now…

Georgia cleared her throat and banished her wayward thoughts. What had she been saying? Oh, yeah.

"I mean, think about it. Laura's an artist, and I was an interior designer once upon a time. And yet there we were, building a business neither of us was really interested in."

"Why is that?" He watched her out of those beautiful brown eyes and seemed genuinely curious. "Why would you put so much of yourselves into a thing you'd no interest in?"

"Well, that's the question, isn't it?" she asked, gesturing with her glass and cringing a little when the champagne slopped over the brim. To help fix that situation, she sipped the contents down a bit lower. "It started simply enough," she continued. "Laura couldn't make a living painting, so she took classes and became a real estate agent because she'd rather be her own boss, you know?"

"I do," he said with a knowing nod.

Of course he understood that part, Georgia thought. As the owner of Irish Air, a huge and growing airline, Sean made his own rules. Sure, their situations were wildly different, but he would still get the feeling of being answerable only to oneself.

"Then my marriage dissolved," she said, the words still tasting a little bitter. Georgia was mostly over it all, since it had been a few years now, but if she allowed herself to remember… "I moved out to live with Laura, and rather than try to build up a brand-new business of my own—and let's face it, in California, you practically stumble across an interior designer every few steps, so they didn't really need another one—I took classes and the two of us opened our own company."

Shaking her head, she drank more of the champagne and sighed. "So basically, we both backed into a business we didn't really want, but couldn't think of a way to get out of. Does that make sense?"

"Completely," Sean told her. "What it comes down to is, you weren't happy."

"*Exactly*." She took a deep breath and let it go again. What was it about him? she wondered. So easy to talk to. So nice to look at, a tiny voice added from the back of her mind. Those eyes of his seemed to look deep inside her, while the lilt of Ireland sang in his voice. A heady combination, she warned herself. "I wasn't happy. And, since I'm free and on my own, why shouldn't I move to Ireland? Be closer to my sister? Live in a place I've come to love?"

"No reason a'tall," he assured her companionably. Picking up the champagne bottle he refilled both of their glasses again, and Georgia nodded her thanks. “So, I’m guessing you won’t be after selling real estate here then?”

“No, thank you,” she said on a sigh. God, it felt wonderful to know that soon she wouldn’t have to deal with recalcitrant sellers and pushy buyers. When people came to her for design work, they would be buying her talent, not whatever house happened to be on the market.

“I’m going to open my own design shop. Of course, I’ll have to check everything out first, see what I have to do to get a business license in Ireland and to have my interior design credentials checked. And I’ll have to have a house…”

“You could always stay here,” he said with a shrug. “I’m sure Ronan and Laura would love to have you here with them, and God knows the place is big enough…”

“It is that,” she mused, shifting her gaze around the parlor of the luxurious manor house. In fact, the lovely old house was probably big enough for two or three families. “But I’d rather have a home of my own. My own place, not too far. I’m thinking of opening my shop in Dunley…”

Sean choked on a sip of champagne, then laughed a second later. “*Dunley?* You want to open a design shop in the *village?*”

Irritated, she scowled at him. And he’d been doing so nicely on the understanding thing, too. “What’s wrong with that?”

“Well, let’s just say I can’t see Danny Muldoon hiring you to give the Pennywhistle pub a makeover anytime soon.”

“Funny,” she muttered.

“Ah now,” Sean said, smile still firmly in place, “don’t get yourself in a twist. I’m only saying that perhaps the city might be a better spot for a design shop.”

Still frowning, she gave him a regal half nod. "Maybe. But Dunley is about halfway between Galway and Westport—two big cities, you'll agree—"

"I do."

"So, the village is centrally located, and I'd rather be in a small town than a big one anyway. And I can buy a cottage close by and walk to work. Living in the village, I'll be a part of things as I wouldn't if I lived in Galway and only visited on weekends. *And,*" she added, on a roll, "I'd be close to Laura to visit or help with the baby. Not to mention—"

"You're right, absolutely." He held up both hands, then noticed his champagne glass was nearly empty. He refilled his, and hers, and then lifted his glass in a toast. "I'm sorry I doubted you for a moment. You've thought this through."

"I really have," she said, a little mellower now, thanks not only to the wine, but to the gleam of admiration in Sean's gaze. "I want to do this. I'm *going* to do this," she added, a promise to herself and the universe at large.

"And so you will, I've no doubt," Sean told her, leaning forward. "To the start of more than *one* new life this day. I wish you happiness, Georgia, with your decision and your shop."

"Thanks," she said, clinking her glass against his, making the heavy crystal sing. "I appreciate it."

When they'd both had a sip to seal the toast, Sean mused, "So we'll be neighbors."

"We will."

"And friends."

"That, too," she agreed, feeling just a little unsettled by his steady stare and the twisting sensation in the pit of her stomach.

"And as your friend," Sean said softly, "I think I should tell you that when you're excited about something, your eyes go as dark as a twilight sky."

Two

"What?"

Sean watched the expression on her face shift from confusion to a quick flash of desire that was born and then gone again in a blink. But he'd seen it, and his response to it was immediate.

"Am I making you nervous, Georgia?"

"No," she said and he read the lie in the way she let her gaze slide from his. After taking another sip of champagne, she licked a stray drop from her lip, and Sean's insides fisted into knots.

Odd, he'd known Georgia for about a year now and though he'd been attracted, he'd never before been tempted. Now he was. Most definitely. Being here with her in the fire-lit shadows while rain pattered at the windows was, he thought, more than tempting. There was an intimacy here, two people who had shared a hellishly long day together. Now, in the quiet shadows, there was something new and…compelling rising up between them.

He knew she felt it, too, despite the wary gleam in her eyes as she watched him. Still, he wanted her breathless, not guarded, so he eased back and gave her a half smile. "I'm only saying you're a beautiful woman, Georgia."

"Hmm…" She tipped her head to one side, studying him.

"Surely it's not the first time you've heard that from a man."

"Oh, no," she answered. "Men actually chase me down the street to tell me I have twilight eyes."

He grinned. He did appreciate a quick wit. "Maybe I'm just more observant than most men."

"And maybe you're up to something," she said thoughtfully. "What is it, Sean?"

"Not a thing," he said, all innocence.

"Well, that's good." She nodded and reached down absently to rub at the arch of her foot. "I mean, we both know anything else would just be…complicated."

"Aye, it would at that," he agreed, and admitted silently that complicated might be worth it. "Your feet hurt?"

"What?" She glanced down to where her hand rubbed the arch of her right foot and smiled ruefully. "Yeah, they do."

"A long day of standing, wasn't it?"

"It was."

She sipped at her champagne and a log shifted in the fire. As the flames hissed and spat, she closed her eyes—a little dreamily, he thought, and he felt that fist inside him tighten even further. The woman was unknowingly seducing him.

Logic and a stern warning sounded out in his mind, and he firmly shut them down. There was a time for a cool head, and there was a time for finding out just where the road you found yourself on would end up. So far, he liked this particular road very much.

He set his glass on the table in front of them, then sat back and dragged her feet onto his lap. Georgia looked at him and he gave her a quick grin. “I’m offering a one-night-only special. A foot rub.”

“Sean…”

He knew what she was thinking because his own mind was running along the same paths. Back up—or, stay the course and see what happened. As she tried to draw her feet away, he held them still in his lap and pushed his thumbs into her arch.

She groaned and let her head fall back and he knew he had her.

“Oh, that feels too good,” she whispered, as he continued to rub and stroke her skin.

“Just enjoy it for a bit then,” he murmured.

That had her lifting her head to look at him with the wariness back, glinting in those twilight depths. “What’re you up to?”

“Your ankles,” he said, sliding his hands higher to match his words. “Give me a minute, though, and ask again.”

She laughed as he’d meant her to, and the wariness edged off a bit.

“So,” she asked a moment later, “why do I rate a foot rub tonight?”

“I’m feeling generous, just becoming an uncle and all.” He paused, and let that settle. Of course, he and Ronan weren’t actually brothers, but they might as well have been. “Not really an uncle, but that’s how it feels.”

“You’re an uncle,” she told him. “You and Ronan are every bit as tight as Laura and I are.”

"True," he murmured, and rubbed his thumb into the arches of her small, narrow feet. Her toes were painted a dark pink, and he smiled at the silver toe ring she wore on her left foot.

She sighed heavily and whispered, "Oh, my…you've got great hands."

"So I've been told," he said on a laugh. He slid his great hands a bit higher, stroking her ankles and then up along the line of her calves. Her skin was soft, smooth and warm, now that the fire had chased away the chill of the afternoon.

"Maybe it's the champagne talking," she said softly, "but what you're doing feels way too good."

"'Tisn't the champagne," he told her, meeting her eyes when she looked at him. "We've not had enough yet to blur the lines between us."

"Then it's the fire," she whispered, "and the rain outside sealing us into this pretty room together."

"Could be," he allowed, sliding his hands even higher now, stroking the backs of her knees and watching her eyes close as she sighed. "And it could just be that you're a lovely thing, here in the firelight, and I'm overcome."

She snorted and he grinned in response.

"Oh, yes, overcome," she said, staring into his eyes again, as if trying to see the plans he had, the plans he might come up with. "Sean Connolly, you're a man who always knows what he's doing. So answer me this. Are you trying to seduce me?"

"Ah, the shoe is on the other foot entirely, Georgia," he murmured, his fingertips moving higher still, up her thighs, inch by inch. He hadn't thought of it earlier, but now he was grateful she'd been wearing a skirt for their mad ride to the hospital. Made things so much simpler.

"Right," she said. "I'm seducing you? You're the one

giving out foot rubs that have now escalated—" her breath caught briefly before she released it on a sigh "—to *thigh* rubs."

"And do you like it?"

"I'd be a fool not to," she admitted, and he liked her even more for her straightforwardness.

"Well then…"

"But the question remains," she said, reaching down to capture one of his hands in hers, stilling his caresses. "If you're seducing me, I have to ask, why now? We've known each other for so long, Sean, and we've never—"

"True enough," he murmured, "but this is the first time we've been alone, isn't it?" He set her hand aside and continued to stroke the outsides of her thighs before slowly edging around to the inside.

She squirmed, and he went hard as stone.

"Think of it, Georgia," he continued, though his voice was strained and it felt as though there were a rock lodged in his throat. "'Tis just us here for the night. No Ronan, no Laura, no Patsy, running in and out with her tea trays. Even the dogs are in the kitchen sleeping."

Georgia laughed a little. "You're right. I don't think I've ever been in this house alone before. But…"

"No buts," he interrupted, then leaned out and picked up the champagne bottle. Refilling her glass and then his own, he set the bottle down again and lifted his glass with one hand while keeping her feet trapped in his lap with the other. "I think we need more of this, then we'll…*talk* about this some more."

"After enough champagne, we won't want to talk at all," she said, though she sipped at the wine anyway.

"And isn't that a lovely thought?" he asked, giving her a wink as he drained his glass.

She was watching him, and her eyes were filled with

the same heat that burned inside him. For the life of him, Sean couldn't figure out how he'd managed to keep his hands off of her for the past year or more. Right now, the desire leaping inside him had him hard and eager for the taste of her. The feel of her beneath his hands. He wanted to hear her sigh, hear her call his name as she erupted beneath him. Wanted to bury himself inside her heat and feel her surrounding him.

"That look in your eyes tells me exactly what you're thinking," Georgia said, and this time she took a long drink of champagne.

"And are you thinking the same?" he asked.

"I shouldn't be."

"That wasn't the question."

Never breaking her gaze from his, Georgia blew out a breath and admitted, "Okay, yes, I'm thinking the same."

"Thank the gods for that," he said, a smile curving his mouth.

She chuckled, and the sound was rich and full. "I think you've got more in common with the devils than you do with the gods."

"Isn't that a lovely thing to say then?" he quipped. Reaching out, he plucked the champagne flute from her hand and set it onto the table.

"I wasn't finished," she told him.

"We'll have more later. *After,*" he promised.

She took a deep breath and said, "This is probably a mistake, you know."

"Aye, probably is. Would you have us stop then, before we get started?" He hoped to hell she said no, because if she said yes, he'd have to leave. And right now, leaving was the very last thing he wanted to do.

"I really should say yes, because we absolutely should stop. Probably," she said quietly.

He liked the hesitation in that statement. "But?"

"But," she added, "I'm tired of being sensible. I want you to touch me, Sean. I think I've wanted that right from the beginning, but we were being too sensible for me to admit to it."

He pulled her up and over to him, settling her on his lap where she'd be sure to feel the hard length of him pressing into her bottom. "You can readily see that I feel the same."

"Yeah," she said, turning her face up to his. "I'm getting that."

"Not yet," he teased, "but you're about to."

"Promises, promises…"

"Well then, enough talking, yes?"

"Oh, yes."

He kissed her, softly at first, a brush of the lips, a connection that was as swift and sweet as innocence. It was a tease. Something short to ease them both into this new wrinkle in their relationship.

But with that first kiss, something incredible happened. Sean felt a jolt of white-hot electricity zip through him in an instant. His eyes widened as he looked at her, and he knew the surprise he read on her face was also etched on his own.

"That was… Let's just see if we can make that happen again, shall we?"

She nodded and arched into him, parting her lips for him when he kissed her, and this time Sean fed that electrical jolt that sizzled between them. He deepened the kiss, tangling his tongue with hers, pulling her closer, tighter, to him. Her arms came up around his neck and held on. She kissed him back, feverishly, as if every ounce of passion within her had been unleashed at once.

She stabbed her fingers through his hair, nails dragging along his scalp. She twisted on his lap, rubbing her behind against his erection until a groan slid from his throat. The glorious friction of her body against his would only get better, he thought, if he could just get her out of these bloody clothes.

He broke the kiss and dragged in a breath of air, hoping to steady the racing beat of his heart. It didn't help. Nothing would. Not until he'd had her, all of her. Only then would he be able to douse the fire inside. To cool the need and regain his control.

But for now, all he needed was her. Georgia Page, temptress with eyes of twilight and a mouth designed to drive a man wild.

"You've too many clothes on," he muttered, dropping his hands to the buttons on her dark blue shirt.

"You, too," she said, tugging the tail of his white, long-sleeved shirt free of the black jeans he wore. She fumbled at the buttons and then laughed at herself. "Can't get them undone, damn it."

"No need," he snapped and, gripping both sides of his shirt, ripped it open, sending small white buttons flying around the room like tiny missiles.

She laughed again and slapped both palms to his chest. At the first touch of her skin to his, Sean hissed in a breath and held it. He savored every stroke, every caress, while she explored his skin as if determined to map every inch of him.

He was willing to lie still for that exploration, too, as long as he could do the same for her. He got the last of her buttons undone and slid her shirt off her shoulders and down her arms. She helped him with it, and then her skin was bared to him, all but her lovely breasts, hidden behind the pale, sky-blue lace of her bra. His mouth went dry.

Tossing her honey-blond hair back from her face, Georgia met his gaze as she unhooked the front clasp of that bra and then slipped out of it completely. Sean's hands cupped her, his thumbs and forefingers brushing across the rigid peaks of her dark pink nipples until she sighed and cupped his hands with her own.

"You're lovely, Georgia. More lovely than I'd imagined," he whispered, then winked. "And my imagination was pretty damned good."

She grinned, then whispered, "My turn." She pushed his shirt off and skimmed her small, elegant hands slowly over his shoulders and arms, and every touch was a kiss of fire. Every caress a temptation.

He leaned over, laying her back on the sofa until she was staring up at him. Firelight played over her skin, light and shadow dancing in tandem, making her seem almost ethereal. But she was a real woman with a real need, and Sean was the man to meet it.

Deftly, he undid the waist button and the zipper of the skirt she wore, then slowly tugged the fabric down and off before tossing it to the floor. She wore a scrap of blue lace panties that were somehow even more erotic than seeing her naked would have been. Made him want to take that elastic band between his teeth and—

"Sean!" She half sat up and for a dark second or two, Sean was worried she'd changed her mind at the last. The thought of that nearly brought him to his knees.

"What is it?"

"Protection," she said. "I'm not on the pill, and I don't really travel with condoms." Worrying her bottom lip with her teeth, she blurted, "Maybe Ronan's got some old ones upstairs…"

"No need," he said and stood. "I've some in the glove box of the car."

She just looked at him. "You keep condoms in the glove compartment?"

Truthfully, he hadn't used any of the stash he kept there for emergencies in longer than he cared to admit. There hadn't been a woman for him in months. Maybe, he thought now, it was because he'd been too tangled up in thoughts of twilight eyes and kissable lips. Well, he didn't much care for the sound of that, so he told himself that maybe he'd just been too bloody busy getting his airline off the ground, so to speak.

"Pays to be prepared," was all he said.

Georgia's lips twitched. "I didn't realize Ireland *had* Boy Scouts."

"What?"

"Never mind," she whispered, lifting her hips and pulling her panties off. "Just...hurry."

"I bloody well will." He scraped one hand across his face, then turned and bolted for the front door. It cost him to leave her, even for the few moments this necessary trip would take.

He was through the front door and out to his car in a blink. He hardly felt the misting rain as it covered him in an icy, wet blanket. The night was quiet; the only light came from that of the fire within the parlor, a mere echo of light out here, battling and losing against the darkness and the rain.

He tore through the glove box, grabbed the box of condoms and slammed the door closed again. Back inside the house, he staggered to a stop on the threshold of the parlor. She'd moved from the couch, and now she lay stretched out, naked, on the rug before the fire, her head on one of the countless pillows she'd brought down there with her.

Sean's gaze moved over her in a flash and then again,

more slowly, so he could savor everything she was. Mouth dry, heartbeat hammering in his chest, he thought he'd never seen a more beautiful picture than the one she made in the firelight.

"You're wet," she whispered.

Sean shoved one hand through his rain-soaked hair, then shrugged off his shirt. "Hadn't noticed."

"Cold?" she asked, and levered herself up on one elbow to watch him.

The curve of her hip, the swell of her breasts and the heat in her eyes all came together to flash into an inferno inside him. "Cold? Not likely."

Never taking his gaze from hers, he pulled off the rest of his clothes and simply dropped them onto the colorful rug beneath his feet. He went to her, laser-focused on the woman stretched out beside him on the carpet in the firelight.

She reached up and cupped his cheek before smiling. "I thought we'd have more room down here than on the couch."

"Very sensible," he muttered, kissing her palm then dipping to claim her lips in a brief, hard kiss. "Nothing more sexy than a smart woman."

"Always nice to hear." She grinned and moved into him, pressing her mouth to his. Opening for him, welcoming the taste of him as he devoured her. Bells clanged in his mind, warning or jubilation he didn't care which.

All that mattered now was the next touch. The next taste. She filled him as he'd never been filled before and all Sean could think was *Why had it taken them so bloody long to do this?*

Then his thoughts dissolved under an onslaught of sensations that flooded his system. He tore his mouth from hers to nibble at the underside of her jaw. To drag lips and tongue along the line of her throat while she sighed with pleasure and slid her hands up and down his back.

She was soft, smooth and smelled of flowers, and every breath he took drew her deeper inside him. He lost himself in the discovery of her, sliding his palms over her curves. He took first one nipple, then the other, into his mouth, tasting, suckling, driving her sighs into desperate gasps for air. She touched him, too, sliding her hands across his back and around to his chest and then down, to his abdomen. Then further still, until she curled her fingers around his length and Sean lifted his head, looked down into her eyes and let her see what she was doing to him.

Firelight flickered, rain spattered against the windows and the wind rattled the glass.

Her breath came fast and heavy. His heart galloped in his chest. Reaching for the condoms he'd tossed to the hearth, he tore one packet open, sheathed himself, then moved to kneel between her legs.

She planted her feet and lifted her hips in invitation and Sean couldn't wait another damn minute. He needed this. Needed *her* as he'd never needed anything before.

Scooping his hands beneath her butt, he lifted her and, in one swift push, buried himself inside her.

Her head fell back, and a soft moan slid from her lips. His jaw tight, he swallowed the groan trying to escape his throat. Then she wrapped her legs around his middle, lifted her arms and drew him in deeper, closer. He bent over her and kissed her as the rhythm of this ancient, powerful dance swept them both away.

They moved together as if they'd been partners for years. Each seemed to know instinctively what would most touch, most inflame, the other. Their shadows moved on the walls and the night crowded closer as Sean pushed Georgia higher and higher.

His gaze locked with hers, he watched her eyes flash, felt her body tremble as her release exploded inside her. Lost himself in the pleasure glittering in her twilight eyes and then, finally, his control snapped completely. Taking her mouth with his, he kissed her deeply as his body shattered.

Georgia felt…fabulous.

Heat from the fire warmed her on one side, while Sean's amazing body warmed her from the other. And of the two, she preferred the heat pumping from the tall, gorgeous man laying beside her.

Turning to face him, she smiled. "That was—"

"Aye, it was," he agreed.

"Worth waiting for," she confessed.

He skimmed a palm along the curve of her hip and she shivered. "And I was just wondering why in the hell we waited as long as we did."

"Worried about complications, remember?" she asked, and only now felt the first niggling doubt about whether or not they'd done the right thing. Probably not, she mused, but it was hard to regret any of it.

"There's always complications to good sex," he said softly, "and that wasn't just good, it was—"

"Yeah," she said, "it was."

"So the question arises," he continued, smoothing his hand now across her bottom, "what do we do about this?"

She really hadn't had time to consider all the options, and Georgia was a woman who spent most of her life looking at any given situation from every angle possible. Well, until tonight anyway. Now, her brain was scrambling to come up with coherent thoughts in spite of the fact that her body was still buzzing and even now hoping for more.

Still, one thing did come to mind, though she didn't much care for it. "We could just stop whatever this is. Pretend tonight never happened and go back to the way things were."

"And is that what you really want to do?" he asked, leaning forward to plant a kiss on her mouth.

She licked her lips as if to savor the taste of him, then sighed and shook her head. "No, I really don't. But those complications will only get worse if we keep doing this."

"Life is complicated, Georgia," he said, smoothing his hand around her body to tug playfully at one nipple.

She sucked in a gulp of air and blew it out again. "True."

"And, pretending it didn't happen won't work, as every time I see you, I'll want to do this again…"

"There is that," she said, reaching out to smooth his hair back from his forehead. Heck, she *already* wanted to do it all again. Feel that moment when his body slid into hers. Experience the sensation of his body filling hers completely. That indescribable friction that only happened when sex was done really well. And this *so* had been.

His eyes in the firelight glittered as if there were sparks dancing in their depths, and Georgia knew she was a goner. At least for now, anyway. She might regret it all later, but if she did, she would still walk away with some amazing memories.

"So," he said softly, "we'll take the complications as they come and do as we choose?"

"Yes," she said after giving the thought of never being with him again no more than a moment's consideration.

"We'll take the complications. We're adults. We know what we're doing."

"We certainly seemed to a few minutes ago," he said with a teasing grin.

"Okay, then. No strings. No expectations. Just…*us*. For however long it lasts."

"Sounds good." He pushed himself to his feet and walked naked to the table where they'd abandoned their wineglasses and the now nearly empty bottle of champagne.

"What're you doing?"

He passed her the glasses as she sat up, then held the empty bottle aloft. "I'm going to open another of Ronan's fine bottles of champagne. The first we drank to our new and lovely Fiona. The second we'll drink to *us*. And the bargain we've just made."

She looked up at him, her gaze moving over every square inch of that deliciously toned and rangy body. He looked like some pagan god, doused in firelight, and her breath stuttered in her chest. She could only nod to his suggestion because her throat was so suddenly tight with need, with passion, with…other things she didn't even want to contemplate.

Sean Connolly wasn't a forever kind of man—but, Georgia reminded herself as she watched him move to the tiny refrigerator and open it, she wasn't looking for forever. She'd already tried that and had survived the crash-and-burn. Sure, he wasn't the man her ex had been. But why even go there? Why try to make more out of this than it was? Great sex didn't have to be forever.

And as a right-now kind of man, Sean was perfect.

Three

The next couple of weeks were busy.

Laura was just settling into life as a mother, and both she and Ronan looked asleep on their feet half the time. But there was happiness in the house, and Georgia was determined to find some of that happy for herself.

Sean had been a big help in navigating village society. Most of the people who lived and worked in Dunley had been there for generations. And though they might like the idea of a new shop in town, the reality of it slammed up against the whole aversion-to-change thing. Still, since Georgia was no longer a complete stranger, most of the people in town were more interested than resentful.

"A design shop, you say?"

"That's right," Georgia answered, turning to look at Maeve Carrol. At five feet two inches tall, the seventy-year-old woman had been Ronan's nanny once upon a long-ago time. Since then, she was the self-appointed chieftain of the village and kept up with everything that was happening.

Her white hair was piled at the top of her head in a lopsided bun. Her cheeks were red from the wind, and her blue eyes were sharp enough that Georgia was willing to bet Maeve didn't miss much. Buttoned up in a Kelly green cardigan and black slacks, she looked snug, right down to the soles of her bright pink sneakers.

"And you'll draw up pictures of things to be done to peoples' homes."

"Yes, and businesses, as well," Georgia said, "just about anything. It's all about the flow of a space. Not exactly feng shui but along the same lines."

Maeve's nose twitched and a smile hovered at the corners of her mouth. "Fing Shooey—not a lot of that in the village."

Georgia smiled at Maeve's pronunciation of the design philosophy, then said, "Doesn't matter. Some will want help redecorating, and there will be customers for me in Westport and Galway…"

"True enough," Maeve allowed.

Georgia paused to take a look up and down the main street she'd come to love over the past year. There really wasn't much to the village, all in all. The main street held a few shops, the Pennywhistle pub, a grocer's, the post office and a row of two-story cottages brightly painted.

The sidewalks were swept every morning by the shop owners, and flowers spilled from pots beside every doorway. The doors were painted in brilliant colors, scarlet, blue, yellow and green, as if the bright shades could offset the ever-present gray clouds.

There were more homes, of course, some above the shops and some just outside the village proper on the narrow track that wound through the local farmers' fields.

Dunley had probably looked much the same for centuries, she thought, and liked the idea very much.

It would be good to have roots. To belong. After her divorce, Georgia had felt so…untethered. She'd lived in Laura's house, joined Laura's business. Hadn't really had something to call *hers*. This was a new beginning. A chapter in her life that she would write in her own way in her own time. It was a heady feeling.

Outside of town was a cemetery with graves dating back five hundred years or more, each of them still lovingly tended by the descendants of those who lay there. The ruins of once-grand castles stubbled the countryside and often stood side by side with the modern buildings that would never be able to match the staying power of those ancient structures.

And soon, she would be a part of it.

"It's a pretty village," Georgia said with a little sigh.

"It is at that," Maeve agreed. "We won the Tidy Town award back in '74, you know. The Mayor's ever after us to win it again."

"Tidy Town." She smiled as she repeated the words and loved the fact that soon she would be a part of the village life. She might always be called "the Yank," but it would be said with affection, she thought, and one day, everyone might even forget that Georgia Page hadn't always been there.

She hoped so, anyway. This was important to her. This life makeover. And she wanted—needed—it to work.

"You've your heart set on this place, have you?" Maeve asked.

Georgia grinned at the older woman then shifted her gaze to the empty building in front of them. It was at the end of the village itself and had been standing empty for a couple of years. The last renter had given up on making a go of it and had left for America.

"I have," Georgia said with a sharp nod for emphasis. "It's a great space, Maeve—"

"Surely a lot of it," the older woman agreed, peering through dirty windows to the interior. "Colin Ferris now, he never did have a head for business. Imagine trying to make a living selling interwebbing things in a village the size of Dunley."

Apparently Colin hadn't been able to convince the villagers that an internet café was a good idea. And there hadn't been enough of the tourist trade to tide him over.

"'Twas no surprise to me he headed off to America." She looked over at Georgia. "Seems only right that one goes and one comes, doesn't it?"

"It does." She hadn't looked at it that way before, but there was a sort of synchronicity to the whole thing. Colin left for America, and Georgia left America for Dunley.

"So you've your path laid out then?"

"What? Oh. Yes, I guess I have," Georgia said, smiling around the words. She had found the building she would rent for her business, and maybe in a couple of years, she'd be doing so well she would buy it. It was all happening, she thought with an inner grin. Her whole life was changing right before her eyes. Georgia would never again be the same woman she had been when Mike had walked out of her life, taking her self-confidence with him.

"Our Sean's been busy as well, hasn't he?" Maeve mused aloud. "Been a help to you right along?"

Cautious, Georgia slid a glance at the canny woman beside her. So far she and Sean had kept their…relationship under the radar. And in a village the size of Dunley, that had been a minor miracle. But if Maeve Carrol was paying attention, their little secret could be out.

And Maeve wasn't the only one paying attention. Laura was starting to give Georgia contemplative looks that had to mean she was wondering about all the time Georgia and Sean were spending together.

Keeping her voice cool and her manner even cooler, Georgia said only, "Sean's been great. He's helped me get the paperwork going on getting my business license—" Which was turning out to be more complicated than she'd anticipated.

"He's a sharp one, is Sean," Maeve said. "No one better at wangling his way around to what he wants in the end."

"Uh-huh."

"Maggie Culhane told me yesterday that she and Colleen Leary were having tea at the pub and heard Sean talking to Brian Connor about his mum's cottage, it standing empty this last year or more."

Georgia sighed inwardly. The grapevine in Dunley was really incredible.

"Yes, Sean was asking about the cottage for me. I'd really like to live in the village if I can."

"I see," Maeve murmured, her gaze on Georgia as sharp as any cop's, waiting for a confession.

"Oh, look," Georgia blurted, "here comes Mary Donohue with the keys to the store."

Thank God, she thought, grateful for the reprieve in the conversation. Maeve was a sweetie, but she had a laserlike focus that Georgia would just as soon avoid. And she and Sean were keeping whatever it was between them quiet. There was no need for anyone else to know, anyway. Neither one of them was interested in feeding the local gossips—and Georgia really didn't want to hear advice from her sister.

"Sorry I'm late," Mary called out when she got closer. "I was showing a farm to a client, and wouldn't you know he'd be late and then insist on walking over every bloody blade of grass in the fields?"

She shook her mass of thick red hair back from her face, produced a key from her suitcase-sized purse and opened the door to the shop. "Now then," she announced, standing back to allow Georgia to pass in front of her. "If this isn't perfect for what you're wanting, I'll be shocked."

It *was* perfect, Georgia thought, wandering into the empty space. The floor was wood, scarred from generations of feet tracking across its surface. But with some polish, it would look great. The walls were in need of a coat of paint, but all in all, the place really worked for Georgia. In her mind, she set up a desk and chairs and shelves with samples stacked neatly. She walked through, the heels of her boots clacking against the floor. She gave a quick look to the small kitchen in the back, the closet-sized bath and the storeroom. She'd already been through the place once and knew it was the one for her. But today was to settle the last of her nerves before she signed the rental papers.

The main room was long and narrow, and the window let in a wide swath of daylight even in the gray afternoon. She had a great view of the main street, looking out directly across the road at a small bakery where she could go for her lunch every day and get tea and a sandwich. She'd be a part of Dunley, and she could grow the kind of business she'd always wanted to have.

Georgia breathed deep and realized that Mary was giving her spiel, and she grinned when she realized she would never have to do that herself, again. Maeve wandered the room, inspecting the space as if she'd never seen it before. Outside, two or three curious villagers began to gather, peering into the windows, hands cupped around their eyes.

Another quick smile from Georgia as she turned to Mary and said, "Yes. It's perfect."

Sean came rushing through the front door just in time to hear her announcement. He gave her a wide smile and walked across the room to her. Dropping both hands onto her shoulders, he gave her a fast, hard kiss, and said, "That's for congratulations."

Georgia's lips buzzed in reaction to that spontaneous kiss even while she worried about Maeve and Mary being witnesses to it. Sean didn't seem to mind, though. But then, he was such an outgoing guy, maybe no one would think anything of it.

"We used handshakes for that in my day," Maeve murmured.

"Ah, Maeve my darlin', did you want a kiss, too?" Sean swept the older woman up, planted a quick kiss on her mouth and had her back on her feet, swatting the air at him a second later.

"Go on, Sean Connolly, you always were free with your kisses."

"He was indeed," Mary said with a wink for Georgia. "Talk of the village he was. Why when my Kitty was young, I used to warn her about our Sean here."

Sean slapped one hand to his chest in mock offense. "You're a hard woman, Mary Donohue, when you know Kitty was the first to break my heart."

Mary snorted. "Hard to break a thing that's never been used."

No one else seemed to notice, but Georgia saw a flash of something in Sean's eyes that made her wonder if

Mary's words hadn't cut a little deeper than she'd meant. But a moment later, Sean was speaking again in that teasing tone she knew so well.

"Pretty women were meant to be kissed. You can't blame me for doing what's expected, can you?"

"You always did have as much brass as a marching band," Maeve told him, but she was smiling.

"So then, it's settled." Sean looked from Georgia to Mary. "You'll be taking the shop."

"I am," she said, "if Mary's brought the papers with her."

"I have indeed," that woman said and again dipped into her massive handbag.

Georgia followed her off a few steps to take care of business while Sean stood beside Maeve and watched her go.

"And just what kind of deviltry are you up to this time, Sean Connolly?" Maeve whispered.

Sean didn't look at the older woman. Couldn't seem to tear his gaze off of Georgia. Nothing new there. She had been uppermost in his mind for the past two weeks. Since the first time he'd touched her, Sean had thought about little else but touching her again. He hadn't meant to kiss her like that in front of witnesses—especially Maeve—but damned if he'd been able to help himself.

"I don't know what you mean, Maeve."

"Oh, yes," the older woman said with a knowing look, "it's clear I've confused you..."

"Leave off, Maeve," he murmured. "I'm here only to help if I can."

"Being the generous sort," she muttered right back.

He shot her a quick look and sighed. There was no putting anything over on Maeve Carrol. When they were boys, he and Ronan had tried too many times to count to get away with some trouble or other only to be stopped short by the tiny woman now beside him.

Frowning a bit, he turned to watch Georgia as she read over the real estate agent's papers. She was small but, as he knew too well, curvy in all the right places. In her faded blue jeans and dark scarlet, thickly knit sweater, she looked too good. Standing here in this worn, empty store, she looked vivid. Alive. In a way that made everything else around her look as gray as the skies covering Dunley.

"Ronan says you haven't been by the house much," Maeve mentioned.

"Ah, well, I'm giving them time to settle in with Fiona. Don't need people dropping in right and left."

"You've been *dropping* in since you were a boy, Sean." She clucked her tongue and mused, "Makes a body wonder what you've found that's kept you so busy."

"I've got a business to run, don't I?" he argued in a lame defense, for Maeve knew as well as he did that his presence wasn't required daily at the offices of Irish Air. There was plenty of time for him to stop in at Ronan's house as he always had. But before, he hadn't been trying to cover up an affair with his…what was Georgia to him? A cousin-in-law? He shook his head. Didn't matter. "I'll go to the house, Maeve."

"See that you do. Ronan's wanting to show off his baby girl to you, so mind you go to there soon."

"I will and all," he assured her, then snatched at his ringing cell phone as he would a lifeline tossed into a churning sea. Lifting one finger to Maeve as if to tell her one moment, he turned and answered, "Sean Connolly."

A cool, dispassionate voice started speaking and he actually *felt* a ball of ice drop into the pit of his stomach.

"Repeat that if you please," he ordered, though he didn't want to hear the news again. He had to have the information.

His gaze moved to Georgia, who had turned to look at him, a question in her eyes. His tone of voice must have alerted her to a problem.

"I understand," he said into the phone. "I'm on my way."

He snapped the phone closed.

Georgia walked up to him. "What is it?"

Sean could hardly say the words, but he forced them out. "It's my mother. She's in hospital." It didn't sound real. Didn't feel real. But according to the nurse who'd just hung up on him, it was. "She's had a heart attack."

"Ah, Sean," Maeve said, sympathy rich in her voice.

He didn't want pity. More than that though, he didn't want to be in a position to need it. "She's in Westport. I have to go."

He headed for the door, mind already racing two or three steps ahead. He'd get to the hospital, talk to the doctors, then figure out what to do next. His mother was hale and hearty—usually—so he wouldn't worry until he knew more. An instant later, he told himself *Bollocks to that,* as he realized the worry and fear had already started.

Georgia was right behind him. "Let me come with you."

"No." He stopped, looked down into her eyes and saw her concern for him and knew that if she were with him, her fears would only multiply his own. Sounded foolish even to him, but he had to do this alone. "I have to go—"

Then he hit the door at a dead run and kept running until he'd reached his car.

* * *

Ailish Connolly was not the kind of woman to be still.

So seeing his mother lying in a hospital bed, hooked up to machinery that beeped and whistled an ungodly tune was nearly enough to bring Sean to his knees. Disjointed but heartfelt prayers raced through his mind as he reached for the faith of his childhood in this time of panic.

It had been too long since he'd been to Mass. Hadn't graced a church with his presence in too many years to count. But now, at this moment, he wanted to fling himself at the foot of an altar and beg God for help.

Sean shoved one hand through his hair and bit back the impatience clawing inside him. He felt so bloody helpless, and that, he thought, was the worst of it. Nothing he could do but sit and wait, and as he wasn't a patient man by nature…the waiting came hard.

The private room he had arranged for his mother smelled like her garden, since he'd bought every single flower in the gift shop. That was what he'd been reduced to. Shopping for flowers while his mother lay still and quiet. He wasn't accustomed to being unable to affect change around him.

Sean Connolly was a man who got things done. Always. Yet here, in the Westport hospital, he could do not a bloody thing to get action. To even get a damned doctor to answer his questions. So far, all he'd managed to do was irritate the nurses and that, he knew, was no way to gain cooperation. Irish nurses were a tough bunch and took no trouble from anyone.

Sitting beside his mother's bed in a torture chair designed to make visiting an ordeal, Sean braced his elbows on his knees and cupped his face in his palms. It had been only his mother and he for so long, he couldn't remember his life any other way. His father had died when Sean was just a boy, and Ailish had done the heroic task of two parents.

Then when Ronan's parents had died in that accident, Ailish had stepped in for him, as well. She was strong, remarkably self-possessed and until today, Sean would have thought, invulnerable. He lifted his gaze to the small woman with short, dark red hair. There was gray mixed with the red, he noticed for the first time. Not a lot, but enough to shake him.

When had his mother gotten old? Why was she here? She'd been to lunch with her friends and had felt a pain that had worried her enough she had come to the hospital to have it checked. And once the bloody doctors got their hands on you, you were good and fixed, Sean thought grimly, firing a glare at the closed door and the busy corridor beyond.

They'd slapped Ailish in to be examined and now, several hours later, he was still waiting to hear what the dozens of tests they'd done would tell them. The waiting, as he had told Georgia not so very long ago, was the hardest.

Georgia.

He wished he had brought her with him. She was a calm, cool head, and at the moment he needed that. Because what he was tempted to do was have his mother transferred to a bigger hospital in Dublin. To fly in specialists. "To *buy* the damned hospital so *someone* would come in and talk to me."

"Sean," his mother whispered, opening her eyes and turning her face toward him, "don't swear."

"Mother." He stood up, curled one hand around the bar of her bed and reached down with the other to take hers in his. "How are you?"

"I'm fine," she insisted. "Or I was, having a lovely nap until my son's cursing woke me."

"Sorry." She still had the ability to make him feel like a guilty boy. He supposed all mothers had that power, though at the moment, only *his* mother concerned him. "But no one will talk to me. No one will tell me a bloody—" He cut himself off. "I can't get answers from anyone in this place."

"Perhaps they don't have any to give yet," she pointed out.

That didn't ease his mind any.

Her face was pale, her sharp green eyes were a little watery, and the pale wash of freckles on her cheeks stood out like gold paint flicked atop a saucer of milk.

His heart actually ached to see her here. Like this. Fear wasn't something he normally even considered, but the thought of his mother perhaps being at death's bleeding door with not a doctor in sight cut him right down to the bone.

"Do you know what I was thinking," she said softly, giving her son's hand a gentle squeeze, "when they were sticking their wires and such to me?"

He could imagine. She must have been terrified. "No," he said. "Tell me."

"All I could think was, I was going to die and leave you alone," she murmured, and a single tear fell from the corner of her eye to roll down her temple and into her hair.

"There'll be no talk of dying," he told her, instinctively fighting against the fear that crouched inside him. "And I'm not alone. I've friends, and Ronan and Laura, and now the baby..."

"And no family of your own," she pointed out.

"And what're you then?" Sean teased.

She shook her head and fixed her gaze with his. "You

should have a wife. A family, Sean. A man shouldn't live his life alone."

It was an old argument. Ailish was forever trying to marry off her only child. But now, for the first time, Sean felt guilty. She should have been concerned for herself; instead she was worried for him. Worried *about* him. He hated that she was lying there so still and pale, and that there was nothing he could do for her. Bloody hell, he couldn't even get the damn doctor to step into the room.

"Ronan's settled and happy now," Ailish said softly. "And so should you be."

Her fingers felt small and fragile in his grip, and the fear and worry bottled up inside Sean seemed to spill over. "I am," he blurted before he was even aware of speaking.

Her gaze sharpened. "You are what?"

"Settled," he lied valiantly. He hadn't planned to. But seeing her worry needlessly had torn something inside Sean and had him telling himself that this at least, he could do for her. A small lie couldn't be that bad, could it, if it brought peace? And what if she *was* dying, God forbid, but how was he to know since no one would tell him anything. Wouldn't it be better for her to go believing that Sean was happy?

"I'm engaged," he continued, and gave his mother a smile. "I was going to tell you next week," he added, as the lie built up steam and began to travel on its own.

Her eyes shone and a smile curved her mouth even as twin spots of color flushed her pale cheeks. "That's wonderful," she said. "Who is she?"

Who indeed?

Brain racing, Sean could think of only one woman who would fit this particular bill, but even he couldn't drag Georgia into this lie without some warning. "I'll tell you as soon as you're fit and out of here."

Now those sharp green eyes narrowed on him. "If this is a trick…"

He slapped one hand to his chest and hoped not to be struck down as he said, "Would I lie about something this important?"

"No," she said after a long moment, "no, you wouldn't."

Guilt took another nibble of his soul.

"There you are then," he pronounced. "Now try to get some sleep."

She nodded, closed her eyes and still with a smile on her face, was asleep in minutes. Which left Sean alone with his thoughts—

A few hours later the doctor finally deigned to make an appearance, and though Sean was furious, he bit his tongue and was glad he had. A minor heart attack. No damage to her heart, really, just a warning of sorts for Ailish to slow down a bit and take better care of herself.

The doctor also wanted a few more tests to be sure of his results, which left Sean both relieved and worried. A minor heart attack was still serious enough. Was she well enough to find out he'd…*exaggerated* his engagement?

She would be in hospital for a week, resting under doctor's orders, so Sean wouldn't have to decide about telling her the truth right away. But he *did* have to have a chat with Georgia. Just in case.

Four

He left his mother sleeping and made his way out of the hospital, grateful to leave behind its smell of antiseptic and fear. Stepping into a soft, evening mist, Sean stopped dead when a familiar voice spoke up.

"Sean?"

He turned and felt a well of pleasure open up inside as Georgia walked toward him. "What're you doing here?" he asked, wrapping both arms around her and holding on.

She hugged him, then pulled her head back to look up at him. "When we didn't hear anything, I got worried. So I came here to wait for you. How's your mom?"

Pleasure tangled with gratitude as he realized just how much he'd needed to see her. He'd been a man alone for most of his adult life, never asking for anything, never expecting anyone to go an extra meter for him. Yet here she was, stepping out of the mist and cold, and Sean had never been happier to see anyone.

"She's well, though the doctor's holding on to her for a week or so. More tests, he says, and he wants her to rest. Never could get my mother to slow down long enough to *rest,* so God help the nurses trying to hold her down in that bed," he said, dropping a quick kiss on her forehead. "Scared me, Georgia. I don't even remember the last time anything has."

"Family does that to you," she told him. "But she's okay?"

"Will be," he said firmly. "It was a 'minor' heart attack, they say. No permanent damage, though, so that's good. She's to take it easy for a few weeks, no upsets. But yes, she'll be fine."

"Good news." Georgia's gaze narrowed on him. "So why do you look more worried than relieved?"

"I'll tell you all. But first, I've a need to get away from this place. Feels like I've been here for years instead of hours." Frowning, he looked out at the car park. "How did you get here?"

"Called a cab." She shrugged. "Laura was going to drive me, but I told her and Ronan that I'd be fine and you'd bring me home."

"As I will," he said, taking her arm and steering her toward his car. "But first, we'll go to my house. We need to talk."

"You'll tell me on the way?"

"I think not," he hedged. "I'm a man in desperate need of a beer, and I'm thinking you'll be needing wine to hear this."

There wasn't enough wine in the world.

"Are you insane?" Georgia jumped off the comfortable sofa in Sean's front room and stared down at him in stunned shock. "I mean, seriously. Maybe we should have had *you* examined at the hospital while we were there."

Sean huffed out a breath and took a long drink of the beer he'd poured for himself as soon as they reached his home. Watching him, Georgia took a sip of her Chardonnay, to ease the tightness in her own throat.

Then he leaned forward and set the glass of beer onto the table in front of him. "I'm not insane, no. Crazy perhaps, but not insane."

"Fine line, if you ask me."

He pushed one hand through his hair and muttered, "I'm not explaining this well a'tall."

"Oh, I don't know." Georgia sipped at her wine, then set her own glass down beside his. Still standing, she crossed both arms over her chest and said, "You were pretty clear. You want me to *pretend* to be engaged to you so you can lie to your mother. That about cover it?"

He scowled and stood up, Georgia thought, just so he could loom over her from his much greater height.

"Well, when you put it like that," he muttered, "it sounds—"

"Terrible? Is that the word you're looking for?"

He winced as he scrubbed one hand across his face. Georgia felt a pang of sympathy for him even though a part of her wanted to kick him.

"I thought she was dying."

"So you lied to her to give her a good send-off?"

He glared at her, and for the first time since she'd known him, she wasn't seeing the teasing, laughing, charming Sean…but instead the hard-lined owner of Irish Air. This was the man who'd bought out a struggling airline and built it into the premier luxury line in the world. The man who had become a billionaire through sheer strength of will. His eyes flashed with heat, with temper, and his mouth, the one she knew so well, was now flattened into a grim line.

Georgia, who had a temper of her own and just as hard a head, was unimpressed.

"If you think I enjoy lying to her, you're wrong."

"Well, good, because I *like* your mother."

"As do I," he argued.

"Then tell her the truth."

"I will," he countered, "as soon as the doctor says she's well again. Until then, would it really be so bad to let her believe a small lie?"

"Small." She shook her head and walked toward the wide stone hearth, where a fire burned against the cold night. On the mantel above the fire were framed family photos. Sean and Ronan. Sean and his mother. Laura and Georgia captured forever the day Ronan and Sean had taken them to the Burren—a lonely, desolate spot just a few miles outside Galway. Family was important to him, she knew that. Seeing these photos only brought that truth back to her.

She turned her back to the flames and looked at him, across the room from her. Sean's and Ronan's houses were both huge, sprawling manors, but Sean's was more…casual, she supposed was the right word. He'd lived alone here, but for his housekeeper and any number of people who worked on the estate, so he'd done as he pleased with the furniture.

Oversize sofas covered in soft fabric in muted shades of gray and blue crowded the room. Heavy, carved wooden tables dotted the interior, brass-based reading lamps tossed golden circles of light across gleaming wood floors and midnight-blue rugs. The walls were stone as well, interspersed with heavy wooden beams, and the wide front windows provided a view of a lawn that looked as if the gardener had gone over it on his knees with a pair of scissors, it was so elegantly tended.

"Is it really such a chore to pretend to be mad about me?" he asked, a half smile curving his mouth.

She looked at him and thought, no, pretending to be crazy about him wasn't a problem. Which should probably *be* a problem, she told herself, but that was a worry for another day.

"You want me to lie to Ailish."

"For only a while," he said smoothly. "To give me time to see her settled." He frowned a bit and added quietly, "She's…important to me, Georgia. I don't want her hurt."

God, was there anything sexier than a man unafraid to show his love for someone? Knowing how much Ailish meant to Sean touched Georgia deeply, but she was still unconvinced that his plan was a good one. Still, she remembered clearly how devastated she had been when she'd discovered all of her ex-husband's lies to her. Wouldn't Ailish feel the same sort of betrayal?

She shook her head slowly. "And you don't think she'll be hurt when she discovers she's been tricked?"

"Ah, but she won't find that out, will she?" Sean said, and he was smiling again, his temper having blown away as fast as it had come. "When the time is right, you'll throw me over, as well you should, and I'll bravely go on with my heart shattered to jagged pieces."

She snorted a laugh before she could stop it.

"So I get to be the bad guy, too?" She walked back, picked up her wine and took another sip. "Wow, I'm a lucky woman, all right. You remember I'm moving to Dunley, don't you? I'll see Ailish all the time, Sean, and she's going to think I'm a hideous person for dumping her son."

"She won't blame you," he assured her, "I'll see to it."

"Uh-huh."

"Georgia love," he said with a sigh, "you're my only chance at pulling this off."

"I don't like it."

"Of course you don't, being an honest woman." He plucked the wineglass from her fingers and set it aside. Then, stroking his hands up and down her arms, he added, "But being a warm-hearted, generous one as well, you can see this is the best way, can't you?"

"You think you can smooth me into this with a caress and a kiss?"

He bent down until his eyes were fixed on hers. "Aye, I do." Before she could respond to that arrogant admission, he added, "But I don't think I'll have to, will I? You've a kind heart, Georgia, and I know you can see why I've to do this."

Okay, yes, she could. Irritating to admit that even to herself. She understood the fear that must have choked him when he thought his mother was going to die. But damn it. Memories fluttered in her mind like a swarm of butterflies. "Lies never go well, Sean."

"But we're not lying to each other now, are we? So between the two of us, everything is on the up and up, and my mother will get over the disappointment—when she's well."

"It's not *just* your mother, though," she said. "The whole village will know. They'll all think I'm a jerk for dumping you."

"Hah!" Sean grinned widely. "Most of those in Dunley will think you a fool for agreeing to marry me in the first place and will swear you've come to your senses when we end it. And if that doesn't do the job, I'll take the blame entirely."

She laughed, because he looked so pleased with that statement. "You're completely shameless, aren't you?"

"Absolutely," he agreed, with that grin that always managed to make her stomach take a slow bump and roll. "So will you do it then, Georgia? Will you pretend to be engaged to me?"

She was tempted, she could admit that much to herself. It was a small thing, after all. Just to help her lover out of a tight spot. And oh, he was a wonderful lover, she thought, her heart beginning to trip wildly in her chest. The time spent with him in the past couple of weeks had been…fabulous. But this was something else again.

"I can help you get your business license," he offered. "You're bogged down in the mire of bureaucratic speak, and I don't know as you'd noticed or not, but things in Ireland move at their own pace. You could be a woman with a walker by the time you got that license pushed through on your own."

She gave him a hard look. "But you're a magician?"

"I've a way about me, that's true. But also, I know some of those that are in charge of these things and frankly, as the owner of Irish Air, I carry a bit more weight to my words than you would."

He could. Darn it. She'd already seen for herself that working her way through the reams of paperwork was going to be mind-boggling.

"I could see you settled and ready for business much faster than you could do it on your own."

"Are you trying to bribe me?"

He grinned, unashamed. "I am and doing a damn fine job of it if you ask me."

Staring up into his brown eyes, shining now with the excitement for his plan, Georgia knew she was pretty much done. And let's face it, she told herself, he'd had her from the jump. Not only was it a great excuse to keep their affair going—but she knew how worried he was about Ailish and she felt for him. He had probably never doubted for a moment that he'd be able to talk her into joining him in his insanity. Even *before* the really superior bribe.

He was unlike anyone she'd ever known, Georgia thought. Everything about him was outrageous. Why wouldn't a proposal from Sean Connolly be the same?

"And, did you know there's a cottage for sale at the edge of the village?"

"Is that the one I hear you were talking to someone named Brian about?"

"Ah, the Dunley express," he said with a grin. "Talk about it in the pub and it's as good as published in the paper. No, this isn't Brian's mum's place. He's rented it just last week to Sinead and Michael when they come home."

"Oh." Well, there went a perfectly good cottage. "I spoke to Mary this afternoon, and she didn't say a thing about a cottage for sale."

"She doesn't know all," Sean said, bending to plant one quick, hard kiss on her lips. "For example, I own two of the cottages near the close at the end of main. Not far from your new shop…"

That last bit he let hang there long enough for Georgia to consider it. Then he continued.

"They're small, but well kept. Close to the village center and with a faery wood in the back."

She shook her head and laughed. "A what?"

He smiled, that delicious, slow curve of his mouth that promised wickedness done to perfection. "A faery wood, where if you stand and make a wish on the full of the moon, you might get just what your heart yearns for." He paused. "Or, the faeries might snatch you away to live forever in their raft beneath the trees."

With the song of Ireland in his voice, even the crazy sounded perfectly reasonable. "Faeries."

"You'd live in Ireland and dismiss them?" he challenged, his eyes practically twinkling now with good humor and banked laughter.

"Sean..."

"I could be convinced to make you a very good deal on either of the cottages, if..."

"You're evil," she said softly. "My mother used to warn me about men like you."

"An intelligent woman to be sure. I liked her very much when we met at Ronan's wedding."

Her mother had liked him, too. But then, her mom liked everybody. Georgia could remember being like that once upon a time. Before her ex-husband had left her for her cheerleader cousin and cleaned out their joint accounts on his way out of town. Just remembering the betrayal, the hurt, stiffened her spine even while her mind raced. Too many thoughts piling together were jumbled up in possibilities and possible disasters.

She was torn, seriously. She really did like Sean's mother and she hated the thought of lying to her. But Sean would be the *real* liar, right? Oh, man, even she couldn't buy that one. She would be in this right up to her neck if she said yes. But how could she not? Sean was offering to help her get her new life started, and all she had to do was pretend to be in love with him.

And that wasn't going to be too difficult, she warned herself. Just standing here beside him was dangerous. She knew all too well what it was like to have his hands and his mouth on her. Having a lover like Sean—much less a fiancé, pretend or not—was really a slippery slope toward something she had to guard against.

She wasn't interested in trusting another man. Giving her heart over to him. Giving him the chance to crush her again. Sure, Sean was nothing like her ex, but he was still *male.*

"What do you say, Georgia?" he asked, reaching down to take her hands in his and give them a squeeze. "Will you pretend-marry me?"

She couldn't think. Not with him holding on to her. Not with his eyes staring into hers. Not with the heat of him reaching for her, promising even *more* heat if she let him get any closer. And if she did that, she would agree to anything, because she well knew the man could have her half out of her mind in seconds.

Georgia pulled her hands free of his and took one long step back. "This isn't the kind of thing I can decide on in a minute, Sean. There's a lot to consider. So I'll think about it and let you know tomorrow, okay?"

He opened his mouth as if to argue, then, a moment later, changed his mind. Nodding, he closed the distance between them again and pulled her into the circle of his arms. Georgia leaned into him, giving herself this moment to feel the rush of something spectacular that happened every time he touched her.

Kissing the top of her head, he whispered, "Fine then. That'll do. For now."

With him holding on to her, the beat of his heart beneath her ear, Georgia was tempted to do all sorts of things, so she looked away from him, out the window to the rain-drenched evening. Lamps lining the drive shone like diamonds in the gray. But the darkness and the incessant rain couldn't disguise the beauty that was Ireland.

Just like, she thought, looking up at Sean, a lie couldn't

hide what was already between the two of them. She didn't know where it was going, but she had a feeling the ride was going to be much bumpier than she had planned.

"I feel like I haven't slept in years," Laura groaned over her coffee the following morning.

"At least you can have caffeine again," Georgia said.

"Yes." Her sister paused. "Is it wrong to be nearly grateful that Fiona had no interest in nursing just so I can have coffee again?"

"If it is, I won't tell."

"You're the best." Laura slouched in a chair near the end of the couch where Georgia sat, checking email on her computer tablet.

Though she'd never been much of a morning person, it was hard to remain crabby when you got to sit in this beautiful parlor sipping coffee every morning. Of course, the baby had jumbled life in the manor, but she had to admit she loved being around her niece. Georgia glanced out the window at a sun-washed vista of sloping yard and trees beginning to lose their leaves for winter. For the first time in days, the sky was clear, but the cold Irish wind was tossing leaves into the air and making the trees dance and sway.

"I'm so excited that you're moving to Ireland," Laura said. "I really miss you when you're not around."

Georgia smiled at her sister. "I know, me, too. And it is exciting to move," she said, as she reached out for the silver pot on the rolling tea table in front of them. Hefting it, she refilled both her own and Laura's cups. Tea might be the big thing over here, but thankfully Patsy Brennan was willing to brew a pot of coffee for the Page sisters every morning. "Also, moving is terrifying. Not only going to a new place and starting over, but it's all the logistics of the thing. Canceling mail and utilities, starting them up somewhere else, and the packing."

Georgia shuddered and took a sip of coffee to bolster her.

"I get that. I was worried when I first moved here with Ronan, but everything went great."

"You had Ronan."

"And you have *me*."

"Ever the optimist," Georgia noted.

"No point in being a pessimist," Laura countered. "If you go around all grim, expecting the worst, when it happens, you've been suffering longer than you had to."

Georgia just blinked at her. "I'll work on that one and let you know when I figure it out."

Laura grinned, then sobered up again. "I wish you'd reconsider living here with us. There's plenty of room."

She knew her sister meant it, and having her offer was really wonderful. Even though having a secret affair was hard to manage when you were living with your sister. "I know, and I appreciate the offer. Just like I appreciate you letting me stay here when I visit. But I want my own place, Laura."

"Yeah, I know."

Morning light filtered into the room, and the winter sunshine was pale and soft. The baby monitor receiver that Laura carried with her at all times sat on the coffee table in front of them, and from it came the soft sounds of Fiona's breathing and the tiny sniffling sounds she made as she slept.

"Yesterday, Sean told me he owns a couple of cottages at the edge of the village," Georgia said. "He's going to sell me one of them."

"And that," Laura said thoughtfully, "brings us to the

main question for the day. What's going on with you and Sean?"

She went still and dropped her gaze to the black coffee in her cup. "Nothing."

"Right. What am I, blind? I gave birth in the hospital, Georgia," her sister pointed out, "I didn't have a lobotomy."

"Laura..." Georgia had known this was coming. Actually, it was probably only because Laura was so wrapped up in Fiona that she hadn't noticed earlier. Laura wasn't stupid and as she just mentioned, not blind, either.

"I can see how you guys are around each other," Laura was saying, tapping her fingernails lightly against the arm of the chair. "He watches you."

"Oooh, that's suspicious."

"I said he *watches* you. Like a man dying of thirst and you're a fountain of ice-cold water."

Something inside her stirred and heat began to crawl through Georgia's veins, in spite of her effort to put a stop to it. After that proposal Sean had made last night, he'd kissed her senseless, then dropped her off here at the manor, leaving Georgia so stirred up she'd hardly slept. Now, just the thought of Sean was enough to light up the ever-present kindling inside her.

Shaking her head, she said only, "Leave it alone, Laura."

"Sure. I'll do that. I'm sorry. Have we met?" Laura leaned toward her. "Honey, don't get me wrong. I'm glad you're having fun finally. God knows it took you long enough to put what's-his-name in the past—"

At the mention of Georgia's ex, she frowned. Okay, fine. It had taken her some time to get past the fury of being used, betrayed and then finally, publicly *dumped.*

But she figured most women would have come out of that situation filled with righteous fury.

"Gee, thanks."

"—I just don't want you to get crushed again."

"What happened to that optimism?"

Laura frowned at her. "This is different. What if you guys crash and burn? Then you'll be living here, with Sean right around the corner practically and seeing him all the time and you'll be miserable. I don't want that for you."

Georgia sighed and gave her sister's hand a pat. "I know. But you don't get to decide that, Laura. And we're not going to crash and burn. We're just…"

"…yeah?"

"I was going to say we're just lovers."

"There's no 'just' about it for you, Georgia," Laura sputtered. "Not for either one of us. We're not built that way. We don't do 'easy.'"

"I know that, too," Georgia argued, "but I did the cautious thing for years, and what did it get me? I thought Mike was the one, remember? Did everything right. Dated for two years, was engaged for one of those two. Big wedding, nice house, working together to build something, and what happened?"

Laura winced.

Georgia saw it and nodded. "Exactly. Mike runs off with Misty, who, if she had two thoughts running around in that tiny brain of hers, would rattle like BBs in a jar."

Laura smiled, but sadly. "That's no reason to jump into something with a man like Sean."

Suddenly forced to defend the man she was currently sleeping with, Georgia said, "What does that mean, 'a man like Sean'? He's charming and treats me great. We have fun together, and that's all either one of us is looking for."

"For now."

Georgia shook her head and smiled. "All I'm interested in at the moment is 'for now,' Laura. I did the whole cautious thing for way too long. Maybe it's time to cut loose a little. Stop thinking nonstop about the future and just enjoy today."

A long moment passed before Laura sighed and said, "Maybe you're right. Sean is a sweetie, but Georgia—"

"Don't worry," she said, holding up one hand to stave off any more advice. "I'm not looking for marriage and family. I don't know that I ever will."

"Of course you will," Laura told her, sympathy and understanding shining in her eyes. "That's who you are. But if this is what you need right now, I'm on your side."

"Thanks. And," Georgia added, "as long as we're talking about this, you should know that last night Sean asked me to help him out."

In a few short sentences, she explained Sean's plan and watched Laura's mouth drop open. "You can't be serious."

"I think I am."

"Let me count the ways this could go bad."

"Do me a favor and don't, okay?" Georgia glanced down at her email and idly deleted a couple of the latest letters from people offering to send her the winnings to contests she'd never entered. "I've thought about it, and I understand why he's doing it."

"So do I. That doesn't make it a good idea."

"What's not a good idea?" Ronan asked, as he walked into the room and paused long enough to kiss his wife good morning before reaching out to grab a cup and pour himself some coffee.

"Your idiot cousin," Laura started, firing a glare at her

husband as if this were all his fault, "wants my sister to pretend they're engaged."

While Laura filled Ronan in, Georgia sat back and concentrated on her coffee. She had a feeling she was going to need all the caffeine she could get.

Five

When Laura finally wound down and sat in her chair, alternately glowering at Ronan and then her sister, Georgia finally spoke up.

"Sean can sell me a cottage," she said calmly. "He can help push through my business license and speed things up along the bureaucratic conga line."

"Ronan can do that, too, you know."

"I know he can," Georgia said with a smile for her brother-in-law. "Sean's already volunteered."

"And…" Laura said.

"And what?"

"And you're already lovers, so this is going to complicate things."

"Oh," Ronan muttered, "when did that happen? No. Never mind. I don't need to know this."

"It's not going to get complicated," Georgia insisted.

"Everything gets complicated," Laura argued. "Heck,

look at me! I broke up with Ronan last year, remember? Now here I sit, in Ireland, married, with a baby daughter."

Ronan asked wryly, "Are you complaining?"

Laura shot a look at the man studying her through warm brown eyes. "No way. Wouldn't change a thing. I'm just saying," she continued, shifting her gaze back to Georgia, "that even when you think you know what's going to happen, things suddenly turn upside down on you."

A warbling cry erupted from the baby monitor on the table in front of Laura. Picking it up, she turned off the volume and stood.

"I have to go get the baby, but we're not done here," she warned, as she left the dining room.

"Laura's just worried for you." Ronan poured himself more coffee, then sat back and crossed his legs, propping one foot on the opposite knee.

"I know." She looked at him and asked, "But you've known Sean forever. What do you think?"

"I think I warned Sean to keep his distance from you already, for all the good that's done." Then he thought about it for a moment or two, and said, "It's a good idea."

Georgia smiled and eased back in her chair. "Glad to hear you say that."

"But," he added.

"There's always a *but,* isn't there?"

"Right enough," he said. "I can see why Sean wants to do this. Keep his mother happy until she's well. And you helping him is a grand thing as long as you remember that Sean's not the man to *actually* fall for."

"I'm not an idiot," Georgia reminded him.

"And who knows that better than I?" Ronan countered with a smile. "You helped me out last year when Laura was making my life a misery—"

"You're welcome."

"—and I'll do the same now. Sean is a brother to me, and so if he hurts you and I'm forced to kill him, it would pain me."

Georgia grinned. "Thanks. I never had a big brother threaten to beat up a boy who was mean to me."

He toasted her with his coffee cup. "Well, you do now."

She laughed a little. "Good to know."

"You'd already made up your mind to go along with Sean's plan, even before you told Laura, hadn't you?"

"Just about," she admitted. But until Ronan had thrown in on her side, she had still had a few doubts. Being close with Sean was no hardship, but getting much closer could be dangerous to her own peace of mind. Laura was right. Georgia wasn't the "take a lover, use him and lose him" kind of woman. So her heart would be at risk unless she guarded it vigilantly.

"So you've signed your rental agreement on the shop?"

"I did, and I'm going into Galway this morning to look at furnishings." She glanced down at her computer tablet as a sound signaled an incoming email. "I'm really excited about the store, too. Of course it needs some fresh paint and—" She broke off as her gaze skimmed the e-vite she had just received. "You have *got* to be kidding me."

"What is it?" All serious now, Ronan demanded, "What's wrong?"

Georgia hardly heard him over the roaring in her ears. She read the email again and then once more, just to be sure she was seeing it right. She was.

"That miserable, rotten, cheating, lying…"

"Who's that then?"

"My *ex*-husband and my *ex*-cousin," Georgia grumbled. "Of all the— I can't believe this. I mean seriously, could this be any more tacky? Even for *them?*"

"Ah," Ronan muttered. "This may be more in Laura's line…"

Georgia tossed her computer tablet to the couch cushion beside her, set her coffee cup down with a clatter and stood up, riding the wings of pure rage. "I'll see you later, Ronan."

"What?" He stood too and watched as she headed for the back door that led to the stone patio, the garden and the fields beyond. "Where are you going? What am I to tell Laura?"

"Tell her I just got engaged."

Then she was through the door and across the patio.

She could have taken a car and driven along the narrow, curving road to Sean's place. But as angry as she was, Georgia couldn't have sat still for that long. Instead, she took the shortcut. Straight across a sunlit pasture so green it hurt her eyes to look at it. Stone fences rambled across the fields, and she was forced to scramble over them to go on her way.

Normally, she loved this walk. On the right was the round tower that stood near an ancient cemetery on Ronan's land. To her left was Lough Mask, a wide lake fringed by more trees swaying in the wind. In the distance, she heard the whisper of the ocean and the low grumbling of a farmer's tractor. The sky above was a brilliant blue, and the wind that flew at her carried the chill of the sea.

Georgia was too furious to feel the cold.

Her steps were quick, and she kept her gaze focused on her target. The roof of Sean's manor house was just visible above the tips of the trees, and she headed there with a steely determination.

She crossed the field, walked into the wood and only then remembered Sean saying something about the faeries and how they might snatch her away.

"Well, I'd like to see them try it today," she murmured.

Georgia came out of the thick stand of trees at the edge of Sean's driveway. A wide gravel drive swung in a graceful arch in front of the stone-and-timber manor. Leaded windows glinted in the sunlight. As she neared the house, Sean stepped out and walked to meet her. He was wearing black slacks, a cream-colored sweater and a black jacket. His dark hair ruffled in the wind, and his hands were tucked into his pockets.

"Georgia!" He grinned at her. "I was going to stop to see you on my way to hospital to check in on my mother."

She pushed her tangled hair back from her face and stomped the dew and grass from her knee-high black boots. She wore her favorite, dark green sweater dress, and the wind flipped the hem around her knees. She had one short flash that for something this big, she should have worn something better than a dress she'd had for five years. But then, she wasn't really getting engaged, was she? It was a joke. A pretense.

Just like her first marriage had been.

"Are you all right?" he asked, his smile fading as he really looked at her. Walking closer, he pulled his hands from his pockets and reached out to take hold of her shoulders.

"Really not." Georgia took a deep breath of the cold Irish air and *willed* it to settle some of the roaring heat she still felt inside. It didn't work.

"What's wrong then?"

There was real concern on his face and for that, she

was grateful. Sean was exactly who he claimed to be. There was no hidden agenda with him. There were no secrets. He wouldn't cheat on a woman and sneak out of town with every cent she owned. It wouldn't even occur to him. She could admire that about him since she had already survived the man who was the exact opposite of Sean Connolly.

That thought brought her right back to the reason for her mad rush across the open field.

"You offered me a deal yesterday," she said.

"I did."

"Now I've got one for you."

Sean released her, but didn't step back. His gaze was still fixed on her and concern was still etched on his face. "All right then, let's hear it."

"I don't even know where to start," she said suddenly, then blurted out, "I just got an email from my cousin Misty. The woman my ex-husband ran off with."

"Ah." He nodded as if he could understand now why she was so upset.

"Actually, the email was an e-vite to their *wedding*."

His jaw dropped, and she could have kissed him for that alone. That he would *get* it, right away, no explanation necessary, meant more to Georgia than she could have said.

"She sent you an e-vite?" He snorted a laugh, then noted her scowl and sobered up fast. "Bloody rude."

"You think?" Shaking her head, Georgia started pacing back and forth on the gravel drive, hearing the grinding noise of the pebbles beneath her boots. "First, that she's tacky enough to use e-vites as wedding invitations!" She shot him a look and threw both hands in the air. "Who does that?"

"I wouldn't know."

"Of course you wouldn't, because *no one* does that!" Back to pacing, the *crunch, crunch* of the gravel sounding out in a rapid rhythm. "And really? You send one of your stupid, tacky e-vites to the woman your fiancé cheated on? The one he left for *you?*"

"The pronouns are starting to get confusing, in case you were wondering," Sean told her.

She ignored that. "And Mike. What the hell was *he* thinking?" Georgia demanded. "He thinks it's okay to invite me to his wedding? What're we now? Old *friends?* I'm supposed to be civilized?"

"What fun is civilized?" Sean asked.

"Exactly!" She stabbed a finger at him. "Not that I care who the creep marries and if you ask me, the two of them deserve each other, but why does either one of them think I want to be there to watch the beginning of a marriage that is absolutely doomed from the start?"

"Couldn't say," Sean said.

"No one could, because it doesn't make sense," Georgia continued, letting the words rush from her on a torrent of indignation. Then something occurred to her. "They probably don't expect me to actually *go* to the wedding."

"No?"

"No." She stopped dead, faced Sean and said, "Misty just wants me to *know* that she finally got Mike to marry her. Thinks it'll hurt me somehow."

"And of course she's wrong about that," Sean mused.

She narrowed her eyes on him. "Do I look hurt to you?"

"Not a bit," he said quickly. "You look furious and well you should be."

"Damn right." She set both hands on her hips and tapped the toe of one boot against the gravel, only absently noting the rapid *tappity, tappity, tap* sound. "But you know what? I'm *going* to that wedding. I'm going to be the chill kiss of death for those two at the happy festivities."

Sean laughed. "I do admire a woman with fire in her eyes."

"Then stick around," she snapped. "I'm going to show them just how little they mean to me."

"Good on you," Sean said.

"And the kicker is, I'm going to be arriving at their wedding in Brookhollow, Ohio, with my gorgeous, fabulously wealthy Irish fiancé."

One corner of his mouth tipped up. "Are you now?"

"That's the deal," Georgia said calmly, now that the last of her outrage had been allowed to spill free. "I'll help you keep your mom happy until she's well if you go to this wedding with me and convince everyone there that you're nuts about me."

"That's a deal," he said quickly and walked toward her.

She skipped back a step and held up one hand to keep him at bay. "And you'll help me get my license and sell me that cottage, too, right?"

"Absolutely."

"Okay, then." She huffed out a breath as if she'd been running a marathon.

"We've a deal, Georgia Page, and I think we'll both come out of this for the better."

"I hope you're right," she said and held out her right hand to take his in a handshake.

He smirked and shook his head. "That's no way to seal a deal between lovers."

Then he swooped in, grabbed her tightly and swung her into a dip that had her head spinning even *before* he kissed her blind.

* * *

The next few days flew past.

Georgia could even forget, occasionally, that what was between she and Sean wasn't actually *real*. He played his part so well. The doting fiancé. The man in love. Seriously, if she hadn't known it was an act, she would have tumbled headfirst into love with him.

And wouldn't that be awkward?

True to his word, Sean had pushed through the paperwork for her business license, and in just a week or two she would have it in hand. He sold her one of the cottages he owned and made her such a good deal on it she almost felt guilty, then she reminded herself that it was all part of the agreement they had struck. And with that reminder came the annoying tug of memory about her ex and the wedding Sean would be attending with her.

Georgia squared her shoulders and steeled her spine. She'd made her decision and wouldn't back away now. Besides, her new life was coming together. She had her lover. A shop. A new home.

And all of it built on a tower of lies, her mind whispered.

"The question is," she asked herself aloud, "what part of it will survive when the tower collapses?" Frowning at the pessimistic thoughts that she was determined to avoid, she added, "Not helping."

She had chosen her road and wouldn't change directions now. Whatever happened, she and Sean would deal with it. They were two adults after all. They could have sex. Have…whatever it was they had, without destroying each other. And then, there was the fact that even if she had been willing to consider ending their deal, she was in too deep to find a way out anyway. So instead, she would suck it up, follow the plan Sean had laid out and hope for the best.

Meanwhile, she had a shop to get ready and a new cottage to decorate and furnish.

She stepped back to take a look at her handiwork and smiled at the wash of palest yellow paint on one of the walls of her new office. It was cheerful and just bright enough to ease back the gray days that seemed to be a perpetual part of the Irish life. The smell of paint was strong, so she had propped open the front door. That cold wind she was so accustomed to now whipped through the opening and tugged at her hair as she worked.

All morning, people in the village had been stopping in, to offer help—which Georgia didn't need, since she wanted to do this part herself—or to offer congratulations on her upcoming marriage. So she hardly jumped when a voice spoke up from the doorway.

"It's lovely."

Georgia turned to smile at Ailish as Sean's mother walked into the shop just a step or two ahead of her son.

"Thanks." Georgia smiled at both of them. "I didn't know you were stopping by. Ailish, it's so good to see you out of the hospital."

"It's even better from my perspective," she answered quickly, a soft smile curving her mouth. "I can't tell you how badly I wanted to be home again. Of course, I was planning on going back to my own home in Dublin, but my son insists I stay at the family manor until I'm recovered—which I am even now, thanks very much."

"You're not recovered yet and you'll take it easy as the doctor advised," Sean told her.

"Take it easy," Ailish sniffed. "How'm I to do that with you and everyone else hovering?"

Georgia grinned at the expression of helpless frustration on Sean's face. She understood how he was feeling, but she really identified with Ailish. Georgia didn't appreciate hovering, either. "How're you feeling?"

The smaller woman hurried across the tarp-draped floor and took Georgia in a hard, brief hug. "I'm wonderful is what I am," she said. "Sean's told me your news and I couldn't be happier."

Guilt flew like an arrow and stabbed straight into Georgia's heart. She looked into Ailish's sharp green eyes and felt *terrible* for her part in this lie. But at the same time, she could see that Sean's mother's face was pale and there were shadows beneath those lovely eyes of hers. So she wasn't as well as she claimed and maybe, Georgia thought wildly, that was enough of a reason to carry on with the lie.

"Isn't it lovely that you and your sister both will be here, married and building families?" Ailish sighed at the romance of it. "I couldn't ask for a more perfect daughter-in-law."

"Thank you, Ailish," Georgia said and simply embraced the guilt, accepting that it would now be a part of her life. At least for a while.

"Now," Ailish said, grabbing Georgia's left hand. "Let me see the ring..."

There was no ring.

Georgia curled her fingers into her palm and threw a fast look at Sean who mimed slapping his hand to his forehead.

"We've not picked one out yet," he said quickly. "It has to be just right, doesn't it?"

"Hmm..." Ailish patted Georgia's hand even as she slid a curious look at her son. "Well, I'll look forward to seeing it."

"So," Georgia said into the quiet, "you're not heading home to Dublin?"

"Not for a bit yet," she said, "though I do long for my own things about me."

"The manor was your home until four years ago, mother," Sean reminded her. "There's plenty of your things there, as well. And someone to look after you."

"I don't need a keeper," Ailish told him. "Though there were plenty of times I was convinced you did. Until you had the sense to become engaged to Georgia."

"Thanks very much," Sean muttered, stuffing his hands into the pockets of his slacks.

"Now, if you don't mind, I think I'll go sit in the car again until you're ready to leave, Sean. Georgia," she added, leaning in to kiss her cheek, "I couldn't be happier for the both of you. It'll be a lovely wedding, and you know I think this one should be held in Dunley, as Ronan and Laura were married in California."

"Um, sure," Georgia said, as the pile of lies she was standing on grew higher and higher. "Only fair."

"Exactly." Ailish took a breath and let it slide from her lungs as she smiled. "Have you thought about when the wedding will be?"

"We really haven't gotten that far yet," Sean told her. "What with Georgia opening a new business and moving here and all, we've been too busy to set a date."

"Sometime soon then," Ailish went on in a rush. "Perhaps a Christmas wedding? Wouldn't that be lovely? Sean will send a plane for your parents of course, and perhaps they'd like to come out early, so we could all work on the wedding preparations together."

"I'll, um, ask them."

"Wonderful." Ailish smiled even wider, then turned

for a look at her son. "I'll speak to Father Leary tomorrow and see about having the banns read at Mass."

"All right then," Sean said stiffly, "I'll leave it in your hands."

"Good. That's settled. Now," Ailish added, "you two don't mind me. I'll be in the car, Sean, whenever you're ready."

They watched her through the window to make sure she was all right, and once she was safely in the car again, Georgia grabbed his arm. "The priest? She's going to have the banns read in church?"

This was suddenly way more complicated. For three weeks running, the priest would read the names of the couples wanting to be married, giving anyone with a legal or civil objection a chance to speak up. But that just meant the news would fly around Dunley even faster than they'd expected.

He pushed one hand through his hair. "Aye, well, that's the way it's done, isn't it?"

"Can't you ask her to wait?"

"And use what for a reason?" He shook his head. "No, the banns will be read but it changes nothing. We'll still call it off when you break up with me. It'll all be fine, Georgia. You'll see." He grabbed her left hand and ran his thumb over her ring finger. "I'm sorry though, that I forgot about a ring."

"It isn't important."

His gaze locked with hers. "It is, and it'll be taken care of today. I'll see to it."

"Sean," she whispered, moving in close, then sliding a quick look at Ailish to make absolutely certain the woman couldn't overhear them, "are you really *sure* we're doing the right thing?"

"I am," he insisted, dipping his head to hers. "She's

tired, Georgia. I've never seen my mother so pale, and I've no wish to give her a setback right now. Let's see her up and moving around and back to herself before we end this. We have a deal, right?"

She sighed miserably. "We do."

"Good then." He kissed her hard and fast. "I'll just take mother to the manor house, then I'll come back and help you paint."

Surrendering, she smiled and asked, "Are you a good painter?"

"I'm a man of many talents," he reminded her.

And as he walked out of the shop, Georgia thought, he really hadn't needed to remind her of that at all.

Six

"I've an itch between my shoulder blades," Sean confessed the following day, as he followed Ronan into the front parlor of his cousin's house.

He felt as if he were surrounded by women lately. Ordinarily, not a bad thing at all. But just now, between Georgia and his mother and his housekeeper and even Laura, who was giving him a glare every time they met up, he was ready for some strictly male company. And his cousin was the one to understand how he was feeling. Or so he thought.

"Not surprising." Ronan walked to the corner, where an elegant table stood in for a bar, and headed for the small refrigerator that held the beer he and Sean both needed. "It's probably much what a rabbit feels when the hunter's got his gun trained on it."

Sean winced and glared at his cousin's back. "Thanks for that. I've come to you looking for solidarity and you turn on me like a snake. Are you going to be no comfort to me in this?"

"I won't." Ronan bent to the fridge, opened it and pulled out two beers. As he closed the door again, he spotted something small and white beside it on the floor and picked it up. "A shirt button?"

"What?"

"A shirt button," Ronan repeated, standing up and glancing down at his own shirt front as if expecting to see that one of the buttons had leaped free of the fabric. "Where did that come from?"

Sean knew exactly where. It was one of his, after all, torn from his shirt the first night he and Georgia had made love, right here in this room, before a roaring fire. At the thought of that, he went hard as stone and covered his discomfort by snapping, "How'm I to know why your shirt button is on the bloody floor? Did you not hear me, Ronan? I said I'm in trouble."

Frowning still at the button, Ronan tossed it onto the table, then crossed the room and handed one of the beers to Sean. "'Tis no more than you deserve," he said, tearing off the bottle cap and taking a long drink. "I warned you, didn't I, at my own bleeding wedding, to keep your hands off our Georgia?"

Sean uncapped his beer as well and took a long, thirsty drink. Ronan had indeed warned him off, but even now, when things had gotten so completely confused, he couldn't bring himself to regret ignoring that warning.

"When a man's tempted by a woman like her," Sean mused, "he's hard put to remember unwanted advice."

"And yet, when the shite hits the fan, you come to me for more of that advice."

Sean scowled at his cousin. He'd thought to find a little male solidarity here in this house that had been as much his home as Ronan's since he was a child. Seems he'd been wrong. "When you've done gloating, let me know."

"I'll be a while yet," Ronan mused and dropped onto the sofa. Propping his booted feet up on the table in front of him, he glanced up at Sean and said, "What's got you so itchy, then?"

"What hasn't?" Shaking his head, Sean wandered the room, unable to settle. Unable to clear his mind enough to examine exactly why he felt as though he were doing a fast step-toe dance on a hot skillet—barefoot.

"Then pick one out of the bunch to start with."

"Fine." Sean whirled around, back to the fire, to face his cousin. Heat seared him from head to toe, and still there was a tiny chill inside it couldn't reach. "Father Leary dropped in on me this morning, wanting to have a 'pre-marriage' chat."

Ronan snorted. "Aye, I had one with the old man, as well. Always amazed me, bachelor priests thinking they know enough about marriage to be handing out counsel on how to treat a wife."

"Worse than that, he wanted to tell me all about how sex with a wife is different from sex with a mistress."

Ronan choked on a sip of beer, then burst out laughing. "That's what you get for having a reputation as quite the ladies' man. Father didn't feel it necessary to warn me of such things." As Ronan considered that, he frowned, clearly wondering whether or not he should be insulted.

"Fine for you," Sean grumbled. "I don't know which of us was more uncomfortable with that conversation—me, or the good father himself."

"I'd bet on you."

"You'd win that one, all right," Sean said, then took another drink of his beer. Shaking his head, he pushed that confrontation with the village priest out of his head. "Then there's Katie—"

"Your housekeeper?"

"No, the other Katie in my life, of *course* my bloody housekeeper," Sean snapped. "She's buying up bridal magazines and bringing them to Mother, who's chortling over them as if she's planning a grand invasion. She's already talked to me about flowers, as if I know a rose from a daisy, and do we want to rent a canvas to stretch over the gardens for the reception in case of rain—"

"Shouldn't be news to you," Ronan said mildly. "Not the first time you've been engaged, after all."

"'Tisn't the same," Sean muttered.

"Aye, no, because that time it wasn't a game, was it? And when Noreen dumped your ass and moved on, you couldn't have cared less."

All true, Sean thought. He'd asked Noreen Callahan to marry him more than three years ago now. It had seemed, he considered now, the thing to do at the time. After all, Noreen was witty and beautiful, and she liked nothing better than going to all the fancy dos he was forced to attend as Irish Air made a name for itself.

But he hadn't put in the time. He'd spent every minute on his business, and finally Noreen had had enough. She'd come to understand that not even getting her mitts on Sean's millions was enough motivation to live with a man who barely noticed her existence.

Sean had hardly noticed when she left. So what did that say about him? He'd decided then that he wasn't the marrying sort and nothing yet had happened to change his mind.

"This was all your idea," Ronan reminded him.

"Do you think I don't know that?" He scrubbed one hand across his face, then pushed that hand through his hair, fingers stabbing viciously. The longer this lie went on, the more it evolved. "There's a pool at the Pennywhistle, you know. Picking out dates for the wedding *and* the birth of our first child."

"I've five euros on December twenty-third myself." Ronan studied the label on his bottle of Harp.

"Why the bloody hell would you do that? You *know* there's not to be a wedding!"

"And if I don't enter a pool about your wedding, don't you think those in the village would wonder why?"

"Aye, I suppose." Sean shook his head and looked out the window at the sunny afternoon. Shadows slid across the lawn like specters as the trees that made them swayed in the wind. "No one in the village was this interested in my life when it was Noreen who was the expected bride."

"Because no one in the village could stand the woman," Ronan told him flatly. "A more nose-in-the-air, pretentious female I've never come across."

Hard to argue with that assessment, Sean thought, so he kept his mouth shut.

"But everyone around here *likes* Georgia. She's a fine woman."

"As if I didn't know that already."

"Just as you knew this would happen, Sean. It can't be a surprise to you."

"No, it's not," he admitted, still staring out the glass, as if searching for an answer to his troubles. "But it all feels as though it's slipping out of my control, and I've no idea how to pull it all back in again."

"You can't," Ronan said easily, and Sean wanted to kick him.

"Thanks for that, too." He sipped at his beer again and got no pleasure from the cold, familiar taste. "I'm seeing this whole marriage thing get bigger and bigger, and I've no idea what's going to happen when we finally call it off."

"Should've thought of that before this half-brained scheme of yours landed you in such a fix."

"Again, you're a comfort to me," he said, sarcasm dripping in his tone. "I've told Georgia I'll see to it that everyone blames me. But now I'm seeing that it's more complicated than that. Did you know, my assistant's already fielding requests for wedding invitations from some of my business associates?"

"Lies take on a life of their own," Ronan said quietly.

"True enough." Sean's back teeth clenched, as he remembered exactly how he'd gotten into this whole thing, and for the life of him, he couldn't say for sure now that he would have done it differently if given a chance. "You didn't see my mother lying in that hospital bed, Ronan. Wondering if she'd recover—or if, God forbid, I was going to lose her. Seeing her face so pale and then the tears on her cheeks as she worried for me." He paused and shook his head. "Scared me."

"Scared me, too," Ronan admitted. "Your mother's important to me, you know."

"I do know that." Sean took a deep breath, shook off the tattered remnants of that fear and demanded, "So out of your fondness for my mother, why not help save her son?"

"Ah no, lad. You're on your own in this."

"Thanks for that, as well."

"I will say that if Georgia ends up shedding one tear over what you've dragged her into," Ronan told him, "I will beat you bloody."

"I know that, too." Sean walked back and sat down beside Ronan. He kicked his feet up onto the table and rested his bottle of beer on his abdomen. "I'd expect nothing less."

"Well then, we're agreed." Ronan reached over and clinked the neck of his beer against Sean's. "You're in a hole that's getting deeper with every step you take, Sean. Mind you don't go in over your head."

As he drank to that discomforting toast, Sean could only think that Ronan was too late with this particular warning. He knew damn well he was already so deep, he couldn't see sky.

From Georgia's cottage kitchen downstairs came the incredible scent of potato-leek soup and fresh bread.

Georgia inhaled sharply, then sighed as she looked at her sister. "I think I'm going to keep Patsy here with me. You go on home to Ronan and have him cook for you."

"Never gonna happen," Laura told her on a laugh. "Besides, Patsy wouldn't leave now even if I wanted her to—which I don't—she's too crazy about Fiona."

Georgia looked down at the tiny baby cuddled in her arms and smiled wistfully. Milk-white skin, jet-black eyelashes lying in a curve on tiny, round cheeks. Wisps of reddish-brown hair and a tiny mouth pursed in sleep. A well of love opened in Georgia's heart, and she wondered how anything so young, so helpless, could completely change the look of the entire world in less than a month.

"Can't blame Patsy for that. I know I'm Fiona's aunt, but really, isn't she just beautiful?"

"I think so," Laura answered, and plopped down onto Georgia's new bed. "It's so huge, Georgia. The love I have for her is so immense. I just never knew anything could feel like this."

A trickle of envy wound its way around Georgia's heart before she recognized it, then banished it. She didn't begrudge her sister one moment of her happiness. But Georgia could admit, at least to herself, that she wished for some of the same for herself.

But maybe that just wasn't going to happen for her. The whole "husband and family" thing. A pang of regret sliced through her at that thought, but she had to accept that not everyone found love. Not everyone got to have their dreams come true. And sometimes, she told herself, reality just sucked.

"It's terrific," Georgia said, and jiggled the baby gently when she stirred and made a soft mewing sound. "You've got Ronan, Fiona, you're painting again..." As Georgia had given up on her design dreams to sell real estate, Laura had set aside her paints and easel in favor of practicality. Knowing that she'd rediscovered her art, had found the inspiration to begin painting again, made Georgia's heart swell. "I'm really happy for you, Laura."

"I know you are," her sister said. "I want *you* to be happy, too, you know."

"Sure I know. But I am happy," Georgia said, adding a smile to the words to really sell it. "Honest. I'm starting a new business. I'm moving to a new country. I've got a brand-new niece and a new home—what's not to be happy about?"

"I notice you didn't mention your new faux fiancé."

Georgia frowned a bit. "I don't *have* Sean."

"As far as the whole village of Dunley is concerned you do."

"Laura..." Georgia sighed a little, then crossed the bedroom and handed the baby back to her mother. She understood why her sister was concerned, but hearing about it all the time didn't help and it didn't change anything.

"All I'm saying is," Laura said, as she snuggled her

daughter close, "well, I don't really know what I'm saying. But the point is, I'm worried about you."

"Don't be."

"Oh, okay. All better." Laura blew out an exasperated breath. "I love Sean and all, but *you're* my sister, and I'm worried that this is going to blow up in your face. The whole village is counting on this wedding now. What happens when you call it off?"

Niggling doubts had Georgia chewing at her bottom lip. Hadn't she been concerned about the same thing from the very beginning? Everyone in Dunley was excited about the "wedding." Ailish had ordered a cake from the baker and then gleefully told Georgia that it was all taken care of.

"I don't know, but it's too late to worry about that now," she said firmly, and crossed the room to tug at the hem of the new curtains over one of the three narrow windows overlooking Sean's faery wood. A smile curved her mouth as she thought of him.

"I see that."

"What?"

"That smile. You're thinking about him."

"Stop being insightful. It's disturbing."

Laura laughed and shook her head. "Fine. I'll back off. For now."

"It's appreciated." Georgia didn't need her sister's worries crowding into her head. She barely had room for her own.

"So, do you need help packing?"

Now it was Georgia's turn to laugh. "For a trip I'm not taking until next week?"

"Fine, fine." Laura sighed a little. "I'm just trying to help out. I want you settled in and happy here, Georgia."

"I *am*." She looked around the bedroom of her new cottage.

It really helped knowing the owner, since Sean had given her the keys so she could move in *before* escrow closed on the place. It was good to have her own home, even though it wouldn't really feel like hers until she had some of her own furniture and things around her. Thank God, though, as a rental it had come furnished, so she at least had a place to sit and sleep, and pots and pans for the kitchen.

She'd taken the smaller of the two cottages Sean had shown her. The other one had been a row cottage, differentiated from the homes on either side of it only by the shade of emerald green painted on the front door. It was bigger and more modern, but the moment Georgia had seen *this* one, she'd been lost.

Mainly because this cottage appealed to her sense of whimsy.

It was a freestanding home, with a thatched roof and white-washed walls. Empty flower boxes were attached to the front windows like hope for spring. The door was fire-engine red, and the back door opened onto a tiny yard with a flower bed and a path that led into the faery wood.

The living room was small, with colorful rugs strewn across a cement floor that was painted a deep blue. A child-sized fireplace was tucked into one wall with two chairs pulled up in front of it. The kitchen was like something out of the forties, but everything worked beautifully. The staircase to the second floor was as steep as a ladder, and her bedroom was small with her bed snuggled under a sloping ceiling. But the windows looked out over the woods, and the bathroom had been updated recently to include a tub big enough to stretch out in.

It was a fairy-tale cottage, and Georgia already loved it.

This would be her first night in her new place, and she was anxious to nudge Laura on her way so that she could relax in that beautiful tub and pour herself a glass of wine to celebrate the brand-new chapter in her life.

"It is a great cottage." Laura looked at her for a long minute then frowned and asked, "You sure you don't want Fiona and me along for the trip back to California?"

"Absolutely not." On this, Georgia was firm. "I'm not going to be there for long, and all I have to do is sign the papers to put the condo up for sale. After that, when they find a buyer for the place, they can fax me the paperwork and I'll handle it from here. Then I'll arrange for my stuff to be shipped to Ireland and I'll be done. Besides," she added with a grim nod, "when I leave California, I'll be stopping in Ohio for the wedding."

Laura shook her head. "Why you're insisting on going to that is beyond me. I mean come on. You're over Mike, so what do you care?"

"I don't." And she realized as she said it that she really didn't care about her ex-husband and his soon-to-be wife, the husband-stealing former cheerleader. After all, if Mike hadn't been willing to cheat on his wife, Misty never would have gotten him in the first place.

So Georgia figured she was much better off without him anyway. "It's the principle of the thing, really. You know damn well Misty only sent me that tacky invitation to rub in my face that she and Mike are getting married. They never for a minute expect me to show up. So why shouldn't I? At the very least I should be allowed the pleasure of ruining their big day for them."

Laura chuckled. "I guess you're right. And seriously? Misty deserves to be miserable."

"She will be," Georgia promised with a laugh. "She's

marrying Mike, after all. May they be blessed with a dozen sons, every one of them just like their father."

"Wow," Laura said, obviously impressed, "you're really getting the hang of being Irish. A blessing and a curse all at the same time."

"It's a gift."

Georgia glanced down at her ring finger. She still wasn't entirely accustomed to the weight of the emerald and diamond ring Sean had given her for the length of their "engagement."

The dark green of the stone swam with color, and the diamonds winked in the light. It occurred to her then that while her new life was beginning with a lie—Mike was apparently *happy* with his. It didn't matter so much to her anymore, though Georgia could admit, if only to herself, that she'd spent far too much time wrapped up in anger and bitterness and wishing a meteor to crash down on her ex-husband's head.

It was irritating to have to acknowledge just how much time she had wasted and how much useless energy had been spent thinking about how her marriage had ended while the man who had made her so miserable wasn't suffering at all.

She had locked her heart away to avoid being hurt again, which was just stupid. She could see that now. Being hurt only meant that you were alive enough to feel it. And if her soul wasn't alive, then why bother going through the motions trying to pretend different? At least, she told herself, using her thumb against the gleaming gold band of the ring on her finger, she'd gotten past it, had moved on.

Then a voice inside her laughed. Sure, she'd moved on. To a ring that meant nothing and planning a fake future with a fake fiancé.

Wow. How had all of this happened anyway?

Still befuddled by her train of thought, she didn't notice Laura scooting off the bed until her sister was standing beside her.

"I should gather up Patsy and go," she said. "It's nearly time to feed Fiona, and Ronan's probably starving, as well."

Pleased at the idea of having some time to herself, Georgia lovingly nudged her sister to the door. "Go home. Feed the baby. Kiss your husband. I've got a lot to do around here before I leave for my trip next week. Don't worry, you'll have plenty of time to nag me before I leave. And then I'll be back before you even miss me."

"Okay." Laura gave her a one-armed hug and kissed her cheek. "Be careful. And for heaven's sake, take a picture of Misty's wedding gown. That's bound to be entertaining."

Laughing, Georgia vowed, "I will."

"And about Sean—"

"You said you were backing off."

"Right." Laura snapped her mouth shut firmly, took a breath and said, "Okay, then. Enjoy your new house and the supper Patsy left for you. Then have a great trip with your pretend fiancé and hurry home."

When her sister had gone down the stairs and she and Patsy had both shouted a goodbye, Georgia dropped onto the edge of her bed, relishing the sudden silence.

Home, she thought with a sigh. This cottage, in Dunley, Ireland, was now *home*.

It felt good.

She took a long bath, savored a glass of wine in the stillness, then dressed in what she thought of as her Ireland winter wear—jeans, sneakers and a shirt with one of her thick, cable-knit sweaters, this one a dark red, over it—and went downstairs.

Restless, she wandered through her new home, passing through the kitchen to break off a piece of the fresh bread Patsy had left for her. Walking back to the small living room, she paused in the center and did a slow turn.

There were still changes to be made, of course. She wouldn't bring all of her things from America, but the few items she loved would fit in here and make it all seem more *hers* somehow. Though already she felt more at home here than she ever had in the plush condo in Huntington Beach.

The fire in the hearth glowed with banked heat, its red embers shining into the room. Outside her windows, the world was dark as it could be only in the country. The streetlights of the village were a faint smudge in the blackness.

Georgia turned on the television. Then, the instant the sound erupted, turned it off again. She hugged herself and wished for company. Not the tinny, artificially cheerful voice of some unknown news anchor.

"Maybe I should get a dog," she mused aloud, listening to the sound of her own voice whisper into the stillness around her. She smiled at the thought of a clumsy puppy running through the cottage, and she promised herself that when she left America to come home to Dunley for good, she would find a puppy. She missed Beast. And Deidre. And the sound of Ronan's and Laura's voices. And the baby's cries. And Patsy's quiet singing when she was working in the kitchen.

She wanted another heartbeat in the house.

Georgia frowned as she realized the hard truth. What she wanted was Sean.

She could call him, of course, and actually started

for her phone before stopping again. Not a good idea to turn to him when she was lonely. He wouldn't always be there, right? Better she stand on her own, right from the beginning.

Plus, if she was making Dunley her home now, then she might as well get used to going about the village on her own. With that thought in mind, she snagged her jacket off the coat tree by the door and headed for the Pennywhistle.

It was a short walk from her door to the main street of the village, and from there only a bit more to the pub, but she fought for every step. The wind roared along the narrow track, pushing at Georgia and the few other hardy souls wandering the sidewalks with icy hands, as if trying to steer them all back to their homes.

Finally, though, she reached the pub, yanked open the heavy door and stepped into what felt like a *wall* of sound. The silence of the night was shattered by the rise and fall of conversations and laughter, the quick, energetic pulse of the traditional music flowing from the corner and the heavy stomp of booted feet dancing madly to the tune.

Just what I need, Georgia thought, and threw herself into the crush.

Seven

Georgia edged her way to the bar, slipping out of her jacket as she went. The heat inside was nearly stifling, what with the crowd of people and the fire burning merrily in the corner. Waitresses moved through the mob of people with the sort of deft grace ballet dancers would envy, carrying trays loaded with beer, whiskey, soft drinks and cups of tea.

A few people called hello to her as she made her way to the bar and Georgia grinned. This was just what she needed, she thought, to remind herself that she *did* have a real life; it merely also included a fake fiancé. She had friends here. She belonged, and that felt wonderful.

Jack Murphy, the postmaster, a man of about fifty with graying hair and a spreading girth, leaped nimbly off his stool at the bar and offered it to her. She knew better than to wave off his chivalry, though she felt a bit guilty for chasing him out of his seat.

"Thanks, Jack," she said, loud enough to be heard. "Looks like a busy night."

"Ah, well, on a cold night, what's better than a room full of friends and a pint?"

"Good point," she said, and, still smiling, turned to Danny Muldoon, the proprietor of the Pennywhistle.

A big man with a barrel chest, thinning hair and a mischievous smile, he had a bar towel slung over one shoulder and a clean white apron strung around his waist. He was manning the beer taps like a concert pianist as he built a Guinness with one hand and poured a Harp with another. He glanced up at her and asked, "Will it be your usual then, love?"

Her usual.

She loved that. "Yes, Danny, thanks. The Chardonnay when you get a minute."

He laughed, loud and long. "That'll be tomorrow morning by the looks of this crowd, but I'll see you put right as soon as I've finished with this."

Georgia nodded and turned on her stool to look over the crowd. With her jacket draped across her knees, she studied the scene spread out in front of her. Every table was jammed with glassware, every chair filled, and the tiny cleared area closest to the musicians was busy with people dancing to the wild and energetic tunes being pumped out furiously by a fiddle, a flute and a bodhran drum. Georgia spotted Sinead's husband, Michael, and watched as he closed his eyes and tapped his foot to the reel spinning from his fiddle. Sinead sat close by, her head bent to the baby in her arms as she smiled to the music her husband and his friends made.

Here was Dunley, Georgia thought. Everyone was welcome in Irish pubs. From the elderly couple sitting together and holding hands to the tiny girl trying to step-dance like her mother, they were all here. The village. The sense of community was staggering. They were part of each other's lives. They had a connection, one to the other, and the glorious part of it all, in Georgia's mind, was that they had included *her* in their family.

When the incredibly fast-paced song ended, the music slid into a ballad, the notes of which tugged at Georgia's heart. Then one voice in the crowd began to sing and was soon joined by another until half the pub was singing along.

She turned and saw her wine waiting for her and Georgia lifted it for a sip as she listened to the song and lost herself in the beauty of the moment.

She was so caught up, she didn't even notice when Sean appeared at her side until he bent his head and kissed her cheek.

"You've a look of haunted beauty about you," he whispered, and Georgia's head spun briefly.

She turned and looked up at him. "It's the song."

"Aye, 'The Rising of the Moon' is lovely."

"What's it about?"

He winked and grinned. "Rebellion. What we Irish do best."

That song ended on a flourish, and the musicians basked in applause before taking a beer break.

"What'll it be for you then, Sean?" Danny asked.

"A Jameson's if you please, Danny. *Tá sé an diabhal an oíche fuar féin.*"

"It is indeed," the barman answered with a laugh.

"What was that?" Georgia asked. "What did you say?"

Sean shrugged, picked up his glass and laid money down for both his and Georgia's drinks. "Just a bit of the Gaelic. I said it's the devil's own cold night."

"You speak *Gaelic?*"

"Some," he said.

Amazing. Every time she thought she knew him, she found something new. And this was touching, she thought. "It sounds…musical."

"We've music in us, that's for sure," Sean acknowledged. "A large part of County Mayo is Gaeltacht, you know. That means 'Irish-speaking.' Most of those who live here have at least a small understanding of the language. And some speak it at home as their first language."

She'd heard snippets of Gaelic since she first came to Ireland, but it had never occurred to her that it was still a living language. And, to be honest, some of the older people here spoke so quickly and had such thick accents, at first she'd thought they were speaking Gaelic—though it was English.

"Of course," she said after a sip of wine. "The aisle signs in the grocery store are in both English and Gaelic. And the street signs. I just thought maybe it was for the tourists, you know…"

He tapped one finger to her nose. "It's for us. The Irish language was near lost not so very long ago. After the division and the Republic was born, the government decided to reclaim all we'd nearly lost. Now our schools teach it and our children will never have to worry about losing a part of who they are."

Georgia just looked at him. There was a shine of pride in his eyes as he spoke, and she felt a rush of something warm and delicious spread through her in response.

"We're a small country but a proud one," he went on, staring down into his glass of whiskey. "We hang on to what we have and fight when another tries to take it." He shot a quick look at the man on the stool beside Georgia. "Isn't that so, Kevin Dooley?"

The man laughed. "I've fought you often enough for a beer or a woman or just for the hell of it."

"And never won," Sean countered, still grinning.

"There's time yet," Kevin warned companionably, then smiled and turned back to his conversation.

Georgia laughed, too, then leaned into Sean as the musicians picked up their instruments again and the ancient pub came alive with music that filled the heart and soul. With Sean's arm around her, Georgia allowed herself to be swept into the magic of the moment.

And she refused to remember, at least for tonight, that Sean was only hers temporarily.

Two hours later, Sean walked her to the cottage and waited on the step while she opened the door. Georgia went inside, then paused and looked at him.

For the first time in days, they were alone together. With his mother recuperating at his house and her at Ronan and Laura's, they'd been able to do little more than smile at each other in passing.

Until tonight.

Earlier that night, she'd been wishing for him and now, here he was.

He stood in the doorway, darkness behind him, lamplight shining across his face, defining the desire quickening in his eyes. The cold night air slipped inside, twisted with the heat from the banked fire and caused Georgia to shiver in response.

"Will you invite me in, Georgia?"

Her heartbeat sped up, and her mouth went dry. There was something about this man that reached her on levels she hadn't even been aware of before knowing him. He'd made a huge difference in her life, and she was only now realizing how all-encompassing that difference was.

Just now, just this very minute, she stared up at Sean and felt everything within her slide into place, like jagged puzzle pieces finally creating the picture they were meant to be.

There was more here, she thought, than a casual affair. There was affection and danger and excitement and a bone-deep knowledge that when her time with Sean was done, she'd never be the same again.

It was far too late to pull back, she thought wildly. And though she knew she'd be hurt when it was all over, she wouldn't have even if she could.

Because what she'd found with Sean was what she'd been looking for her whole life.

She'd found out who she was.

And more importantly, she *liked* the woman she'd discovered.

"Is it so hard then, to welcome me into your home?" Sean asked softly, when her silence became too much for him.

"No," she said, reaching out to grab hold of his shirtfront. She dragged him inside, closed the door then went up on her toes. "It's not hard at all," she said, and then she kissed him.

At the first long taste of him, that wildness inside her softened. Her bones seemed to melt until she was leaning into him, the only thing holding her up was the strength of Sean's arms wrapped around her.

Her body went up like a torch. Heat suffused her, swamping Georgia with a need so deep, so all-consuming, she could hardly draw breath. When he tore his mouth from hers, she groaned.

"You've a way about you, Georgia," he whispered, dipping his head to nibble at her ear.

She shivered and tipped her head to one side, giving

him easier access. “I was just thinking the same thing about you…” She sighed a little. “Oh, that feels so good.”

“You taste of lemons and smell like heaven.”

Georgia smiled as her eyes closed and she gave herself up to the sensations rattling through her. “I had a long soak in that wonderful tub upstairs.”

“Sorry to have missed that,” he murmured, dragging his lips and tongue and teeth along the line of her neck until she quivered in his arms and trembled, incredibly on the brink of a climax. Just his touch. Just the promise of what was to come was enough to send her body hurtling toward completion.

The man had some serious sexual power.

“I thought about you today,” he whispered, turning her to back her up against the front door. He lifted his head, looked her dead in the eye and fingered her hair as he spoke. “Thought I'd lose my mind at the office today, trying to work out the figures on the new planes we've ordered… Galway city never seemed so far from Dunley before.” He dropped his hands to her waist, pulled up the hem of her sweater and tugged at the snap of her jeans. “And all I could think about was you. Here. And finally having you all to myself again.”

The brush of his knuckles against the bare skin of her abdomen sent a zip of electricity shooting through her veins. Releasing him long enough to shrug out of her jacket, she let it fall to the floor, unheeded.

“You're here now,” she told him, reaching up to push his jacket off, as well. He helped her with that, then went back to the waistband of her jeans and worked the zipper down so slowly she wanted to scream.

“I am,” he said, dipping his head for a kiss. “And so're you.”

He had the fly of her jeans open, and he slid one hand

down across her abdomen, past the slip of elastic on her panties and down low enough to touch the aching core of her.

The moment his hand cupped her, she shattered. She couldn't stop it. Didn't want to. She had been primed and ready for his touch for days. Georgia cried out and rocked her hips into his hand. While her body trembled and shook, he kissed her, whispering bits and pieces of Gaelic that seemed to slide into her heart. He stroked her, his fingers dipping into her heat while she rode his hand feverishly, letting the ecstasy she'd found only with him take her up and then under.

When it was done and she could breathe again, she looked up into his eyes and found him watching her with a hunger she'd never seen before. His passion went deeper and gleamed more darkly in his eyes. He held her tenderly, as if she were fragile and about to splinter apart.

"Shatter tú liom," he said softly, gaze moving over her face like a touch.

Still trying to steady her breathing, she reached up to cup his cheek in her palm. The flash of her ring caught her eye but she ignored it. This wasn't fake, she thought. This, what she and Sean shared when they were together, was *very* real. She had no idea what it meant—and maybe it didn't have to *mean* anything. Maybe it was enough to just shut off her mind and enjoy what she had while she had it.

"What does that mean?"

He turned his face into her palm and kissed her. "'You shatter me,' that's what I said."

Her heartbeat jolted, and a sheen of unexpected tears welled up in her eyes, forcing her to blink them back before she could make a fool of herself and cry.

"I watch you tremble in my arms and you take my

knees out from under me, Georgia. That's God's truth." He kissed her, hard, fast, and made her brain spin. "What you do to me is nothing I've ever known before."

She knew exactly what he meant because she felt the same. What she had with Sean was unlike any previous relationship. Sometimes, she felt as though she were stumbling blindly down an unfamiliar road and the slightest misstep could have her falling off a cliff. How could anything feel so huge? How could it not be real? And still, this journey was one she wouldn't have missed for anything.

"Say something else," she urged. "In Gaelic, say something else."

He gave her a smile and whispered, *"Leat mo anáil uaidh."*

She returned his smile. "Now translate."

"'You take my breath away.'"

To disguise the quick flash of feelings too deep to explore at the moment, Georgia quipped, "Back atcha. That means 'same to you.'"

He chuckled, rested his forehead against hers, pulled his hand from her jeans and wrapped both arms around her. "I've got to have you, Georgia. It feels like years since I've felt your skin against mine. You're a hunger in me, and I'm a starving man."

Her stomach did a fast roll and her heartbeat leaped into a gallop. And still she teased him because she'd discovered she liked the teasing, flirtatious way they had together. "Starving? Patsy Brennan left some bread and soup in the kitchen."

"You're a hard woman," he said, but the curve of his mouth belied the words.

"Or," she invited, taking his hand in hers and heading

for the stairs, "you can come up with me and we'll find something else to ease your appetite."

"Lá nó oíche, Tá mé do fear."

She stopped and looked at him. "Now you're just doing that because you know what it does to me."

"I am indeed."

"What did you say that time?"

"I am indeed."

Her lips quirked at the humor in his eyes. "Funny. Before that, what did you say?"

"I said," he told her, swooping in to grab her close and hold on tight like a drowning man clinging to the only rope in a stormy sea, "'Day or night, I'm your man.'"

Then his mouth came down on hers and every thought but one dissolved.

Her man. Those two words repeated over and over again in her mind while Sean was busy kissing her into oblivion. He was hers. For now. For tonight. For however long they had together.

And that was going to have to be enough.

When he let her up for air, she held his hand and shakily led the way up the steep flight of stairs. The ancient treads groaned and squeaked beneath them, but it was a cozy sound. Intimate. At the head of the stairs, Georgia pulled Sean into her room and then turned to look up at him.

He glanced around the bedroom and smiled as he noted everything she'd done to it. "You've made it nice in here. In just a day."

She followed his gaze, noting the fresh curtains at the windows, the quilt on the bed and the colorful pillows tossed against the scrolled iron headboard.

"Laura and Patsy brought a few things over from the manor."

"You've made it a home already."

"I love it already, too," she confessed. "And when I get some of my own things in here, it'll be perfect."

"'Tis perfect right now," he said, moving in on her with a stealthy grace that made her insides tremble. "There's a bed after all."

"So there is."

"I've a need to have you stretched across that bed," he told her, undoing the buttons of his shirt so he could tear it off and throw it onto a nearby chair. "I've a need to touch every square inch of that luscious body of yours and then, when I've finished, to begin again."

Georgia drew a long, unsteady breath and yanked her sweater up and off, before throwing it aside with Sean's shirt. Her fingers were shaky as she tugged at the buttons on her blouse, but Sean's hands were suddenly there, making fast work of them. Then he pushed the fabric off her shoulders and let it slide down her arms to puddle on the floor.

Outside, the night was clear for a change. No rain pinged against the windows, but moonlight did a slow dance through the glass. Inside, the house was still, only the sounds of their ragged breathing to disturb the quiet.

Georgia couldn't hear anything over the pounding of her own heart, anyway. Sean undid the front clasp of her bra, and she slipped out of it eagerly. His hands at her waist, her hands at his, and he pushed her jeans down her hips as she undid the hook and zipper of his slacks, then pushed them down, as well.

In seconds they were naked, the rest of their clothes discarded as quickly as possible. Georgia threw herself into his arms, and when he lifted her off her feet she felt a thrill in her bones. He tucked her legs around his waist, and she hooked her ankles together at the small of his back.

He took two long steps to the nearest wall and braced her back against it. With her arms around his neck, she looked down into his eyes and said breathlessly, “I thought we needed the bed.”

“And so we will,” he promised. “When we’re too tired to stand.”

Then he entered her. His hard, thick length pushing into her welcoming body. Georgia could have sworn he went deep enough to touch the bottom of her heart. She felt him all through her, as if he’d laid claim to her body and soul and was only now letting her in on it.

The wall was cold against her back, but she didn’t feel it. All she was aware of was the tingling spread of something miraculous inside her. Her body was spiraling into that coil of need that would tighten until it burst from the pressure and sent jagged shards of sensation rippling through her.

Bracing one hand on the dresser beside her, Georgia clapped the other to his shoulder and moved with him as he set a frenetic pace. She watched his eyes glaze over, saw the mix of pleasure and tension etch themselves onto his features. Again and again he took her, pushing her higher and higher, faster and faster.

Her heels dug into his back, urging him on, and when the first hard jolt of release slammed into her, she shouted his name and clung desperately to him. She was still riding the ripples of her climax when he buried his face in the curve of her neck and joined her there.

A few miles away at Laura’s house, the phone rang and Laura picked it up on the run. She had just gotten the baby down for the night and she had a gorgeous husband waiting for her in the front parlor with a bottle of wine.

"Hello?"

"Laura, love," Ailish said. "And how's our darling Fiona this night?"

Sean's mother. Why was she calling? Did she suspect something? *This* was why Laura didn't like lies. They tangled everything up. Made her unsure what she could say and what she couldn't. Sean and Georgia were trying to protect Ailish, and what if Laura said something that blew the whole secret out of the water? What if she caused Ailish a heart attack? What if—

Laura stepped into the parlor, gave her husband a silent *Oh Dear God* look and answered, "The baby's wonderful, Ailish. I've just put her down."

"Lovely, then you have a moment?"

"Um, sure," she said desperately, "but wouldn't you like to say hello to Ronan?"

At that, her devoted husband shot out of his chair, shaking his head and waving both hands.

Laura scowled at him and mouthed the word *coward.*

He bowed at the waist, accepting the insult as if it were a trophy.

"No, dear, this is better between us, I think," Ailish told her through the phone.

Uh-oh. She didn't want to talk to Ronan? *Better between us?* That couldn't be good.

Deserted by the man she loved, Laura took a breath and waited for the metaphorical ax to fall.

"I just want to ask you one question."

No, no, no. That wasn't a good idea at all.

"Oh!" Laura interrupted her frantically, with one last try for escape. "Wait! I think I hear Fiona—"

"No, you don't. And there's no point trying to lie to me, Laura Connolly. You've no talent for it, dear."

It was the Irish way. A compliment and a slap all in the same sentence.

"Yes, ma'am," she said, throwing a trapped look at her husband. Ronan only shrugged and poured each of them a drink. When he was finished, he handed her the wine and Laura took a long gulp.

"Now then," Ailish said and Laura could picture the tiny, elegant woman perfectly. "I know my son, and I've a feeling there's more going on between him and Georgia than anyone is telling me."

"I don't—"

"No point in lying, Laura dear, remember?"

She sighed.

"That's better." Then to Sean's housekeeper, Ailish said, "Thank you, Katie. A cup of tea would be wonderful. And perhaps one or two of your scones? Laura and I are just settling down for a long chat."

Oh, God, Laura thought. A long chat? That wasn't good. Wasn't good at all. Quickly, she drained her glass and handed it to her husband for a refill.

Eight

For the entire next week, Sean felt that itch between his shoulder blades. And every day, it got a little sharper. A little harder to ignore. Everywhere he went, people in the village were talking about the upcoming wedding. It shouldn't have bothered him, as he'd known full well what would happen the moment he began this scheme. But knowing it and living it were two different things.

The pool in the pub was more popular than ever—with odds changing almost daily as people from outlying farms came in to make their bets on the date of the wedding. Even the Galway paper had carried an engagement announcement, he thought grimly, courtesy of Ailish.

From her sickbed, his mother had leaped into the planning of this not-to-be wedding with such enthusiasm, he shuddered to think what she might do once she was cleared by her doctor.

When the article in the paper had come out, it had

taken Sean more than an hour of fast talking with Georgia to smooth that particular bump in the road. She was less and less inclined to keep up the pretense as time went by, and even Sean was beginning to doubt the wisdom of the whole thing.

But then, he would see his mother moving slowly through the house and tell himself that he'd done the right thing. The only thing. Until Ailish was well and fit again, he was going to do whatever he had to.

Though to accomplish it, the annoying itch would become his constant companion.

Even Ronan and Laura had been acting strangely the past few days, Laura especially. She had practically sequestered herself in the manor, telling Georgia she was simply too exhausted with caring for the baby to be good company.

Frowning, Sean told himself there was definitely something going on there, but he hadn't a clue what it was. Which made this trip with Georgia to the States seem all the more attractive.

At the moment, getting away from everyone in Ireland for a week or so sounded like a bloody vacation. Going to California to close out Georgia's house and then on to Ohio, of all places, for the wedding, would give both of them a chance to relax away from the stress of the lies swarming around them like angry bees.

Or maybe it was the muted roar of the plane's engines making him think of swarming bees. He and Georgia had the jet to themselves for this trip, but for the pilots and Kelly, the flight attendant who had already brought them coffee right after takeoff and then disappeared into the front of the jet, giving them privacy.

He looked at Georgia, sitting across from him, and Sean felt that quick sizzle of heat and need that he'd become accustomed to feeling whenever he was close to her. Oh, since the moment he first met her at Ronan's wedding, he had felt the zing of attraction and interest any man would feel for a woman like Georgia.

But in the past few weeks, that zing had become something else entirely. He spent far too much time thinking about her. And when he was with her, he kept expecting to feel the edge of his need slackening off as it always had before with the women he was involved with. It hadn't happened, of course. Instead, that need only became sharper every time he was with her. As if feeding his hunger for her only defined his appetite, not quenched it.

It wasn't just the sex, either, he mused, studying her profile in the clear morning light. He liked the way her short, honey-blond hair swung at her chin. He liked the deep twilight of her eyes and how they darkened when he was inside her. He liked her sense of style—the black skirt, scooped-neck red blouse and the high heels that made her legs look bloody amazing. And he liked her mind. She had a quick wit, a sharp temper and a low tolerance for bullshit—all of which appealed to him.

She was on his mind all the bloody time and he couldn't say he minded it overmuch. The only thing that *did* bother him was the nagging sensation that he was coming to care for her more than he'd intended. Sean knew all too well that a man in love lost all control over a situation with his woman, and he wasn't a man who enjoyed that. He'd seen enough of his friends become fools over women. Even Ronan had lost a part of himself when he first tumbled for Laura.

No, Sean preferred knowing exactly what was happening and when, rather than being tossed about on a tide of emotion you couldn't really count on anyway.

And still…

There was a voice inside him whispering that perhaps *real* love was worth the risk. He argued that point silently as he'd no wish to find out.

A knot of something worrisome settled into the pit of his stomach and he determinedly chose to ignore it. No point in examining feelings at the moment anyway, was there? Right now, he was just going to enjoy watching her settle into the plush interior of one of his jets.

Her gaze didn't settle, but moved over the inside of the plane, checking out everything, missing nothing. Another thing to admire about her. She wasn't a woman to simply accept her surroundings. Georgia had enough curiosity to explore them. And Sean could admit that he wanted her opinion of his jets.

He was proud of what he'd built with Irish Air and had a million ideas for how to grow and expand the company. By the time he was finished, when someone thought luxury travel, he wanted Irish Air to be the name that came to mind.

"What do you think?" Sean had noticed how she had tensed up during takeoff, but now that they were at a cruising altitude, she was relaxed enough to ease her white-knuckled grip on the arms of the seat.

"Of the jet? It's great," she said. "Really beats flying coach."

"Should be our new slogan," Sean said, with a chuckle. "I'm glad you like it. Irish Air is a luxury airline. There are no coach seats. Everyone is a first-class passenger."

"A great idea, but I'm sure most of us couldn't afford to travel like this."

"It's not so dear as you'd think," Sean said. In fact, he'd made a point of doing as much as he could to keep the price down.

He was proud of what he'd built, but curious what

Georgia thought of his flagship. This plane was the one he used most often himself. But all of the others in his fleet were much like it.

Sean's idea had been to outfit a smaller plane with luxury accommodations. To give people who wouldn't ordinarily fly first class a chance to treat themselves. And yes, the price was a bit higher than coach, but still substantially less than that of a first-class ticket on an ordinary airline.

"It's cheaper than chartering a jet."

"Yeah," she said, flicking a curtain aside to take a look out the window at the clouds beneath them. "But coach is still way cheaper."

"You get what you pay for, don't you?" he asked, leaning back in his own seat to sip at his coffee. "When you fly Irish Air, your vacation begins the moment you board. You're treated like royalty. You arrive at your destination rested instead of wild-eyed and desperate for sleep."

"Oh, I get it," she said. "Believe me. And it's a great idea…"

He frowned as she left that thought hanging. *"But?"*

Georgia shot him a half grin. "But, okay." She set her coffee on the table. "You say your airline's different. Set apart."

"I do."

"But, inside, it's set up just like every other plane. A center aisle, seats on either side."

There was a shine in her eyes and Sean was paying more attention to that, than he was to her words. When what she'd said at last computed, he asked, "And how else should we have it arranged?"

"Well, that's the beauty of it, isn't it?" she countered. "It's your plane, Sean. You want to make Irish Air different from the crowd, so why even have them furnished like everyone else?"

She ran the flat of her hand across the leather arm rest and for a second, he allowed himself to picture that hand stroking him, instead. As his body tightened, he reminded himself they had a six-hour flight to New York and then another five to L.A. Plenty of time to show Georgia the owner's bedroom suite at the back of the jet. That brought a smile to his face, until he realized that Georgia was frowning thoughtfully.

"What is it you're thinking? Besides the fact that the seats are arranged wrong?"

"Hmm? Oh, nothing."

"It's something," he said, following her gaze as she studied the furnishings of the plane with a clearly critical eye. "Let's have it."

"I was just thinking…you say you started Irish Air as a way of giving people a real choice in flying."

"That's right," he said, leaning forward, bracing his elbows on his knees. "As I said, most can't afford first-class tickets on commercial airlines, and chartering a jet is well beyond them, as well. Irish Air," he said with a proud smile, "is in the buffer zone. I offer luxury travel for just a bit more than coach."

"How much is a bit?"

"More than a little," he hedged, "less than a lot. The theory being, if people save for an important vacation, then they might be willing to save a bit more to start their vacation the moment they board the plane." Warming to his theme, he continued. "You see, you fly coach, say from L.A. to Ireland. By the time you've arrived, you feel as though you've been dragged across a choppy sea. You're tired, you're angry, you're hungry. Then you've to rent a car and drive on a different side of the road when you're already on the ragged edge..."

"All true. I've done it," she said.

He nodded. "But, on Irish Air, you step aboard and you relax. There are fewer seats. The seats are wider, fold out into beds and there's a TV at every one of them. We offer WiFi on board and we serve *real* meals with actual knives and forks. When you arrive at your destination, you're rested, refreshed and feel as though your worries are behind you."

"You should do commercials," Georgia said with a smile. "With the way you look, that accent of yours and the way your eyes shine when you talk about Irish Air, you'd have women by the thousands lined up for tickets."

"That's the idea." He sat back, rested one foot on his opposite knee and glanced around. "By this time next year, Irish Air will be the most talked-about airline in the world. We'll be ordering a dozen new planes soon and—" He broke off when he saw her shift her gaze to one side and chew at her bottom lip. A sure sign that she had something to say and wasn't sure how to do it. "What is it?"

"You want the truth?"

"Absolutely," he told her.

"Okay, you want Irish Air to stand out from the crowd, right?"

"I do."

"So why are you creating such boring interiors?"

"What? Boring, did you say?" He glanced around the main cabin, saw nothing out of line and looked back at her for an explanation.

She half turned in her seat to face him, then slapped one hand against the armrest. "First, I already told you, the arrangement of the seats. There are only ten of them on this plane, but you've got them lined up in standard formation, with the aisle up the middle."

One eyebrow winged up. "There's a better way?"

"There's a *different* way, and that is what you said you wanted."

"True. All right then, tell me what you mean."

A light burned in her eyes as she gave him a quick grin. Unbuckling her seat belt, she stood up, looked down the length of the plane, then back to him.

"Okay. It's not just the seats," she said, "the colors are all wrong."

A bit insulted, as he'd paid a designer a huge sum to come up with a color palette that was both soothing and neutral, he asked, "What the bloody hell is wrong with beige?"

She shook her head sadly. "It's *beige,* Sean. Could any color be more ordinary?"

"I've had it on good authority that beige is calming and instills a sense of trust in the passenger."

"Who told you that?" she asked, tipping her head to one side as she studied him. "A man?"

He scowled. "I'm a man, if you've forgotten."

She gave him a wicked smile. "That's one thing I'm certain of."

He stood up, too, but she skipped back a pace to keep some distance between them. "*But* you're not a designer."

"I'm not, no." Considering, thinking, he watched her and said, "All right, then. Tell me what it is you're thinking, Georgia."

"Okay…" She took a breath and said, "First, the carpeting. It looks like the kind you see in a dentist's office. Trust me when I say *that* is not soothing."

He frowned thoughtfully at the serviceable, easy-to-clean carpet.

"It should be plush. Let a passenger's feet sink into it when they step on board." She wagged a finger at him. "Instant luxurious feel and people *will* notice."

"Thick carpet."

"Not beige," she added quickly. "I think blue. Like the color of a summer sky."

"Uh-huh."

She ran one hand across the back of the leather seat again. "These are comfortable, but again. Beige. Really?"

"You recommend blue again?" he asked, enjoying the animation on her face.

"No, for the seats, gray leather." She looked up at him. "The color of the fog that creeps in from the ocean at night. It'll go great with the blue carpet and it'll be different. Make Irish Air stand out from the crowd. And—" She paused as if she were wondering if she'd already gone too far.

He crossed his arms over his chest. "Go on, no reason to stop now."

"Okay, don't line the seats up like bored little soldiers. Clump them."

"Clump?"

"Yeah," she said. "In conversational groups. Like seats on a train. You said this is the midsize jet, right? So your others are even wider. Make use of that space. Make the interior welcoming. Two seats facing back, two forward. And stagger them slightly too, so the people sitting on the right side of the plane aren't directly opposite those on the left. Not everyone wants strangers listening in to conversations."

She walked down the aisle and pointed. "Have the last two back here, separate from the others. A romantic spot that seems cozy and set apart."

He looked at the configuration of his jet and in his

mind's eye, pictured what she was describing. He liked it. More, he could see that she was right. He'd seen the same sort of design on private corporate jets, of course, but not on a passenger line. Offering that kind of difference would help set Irish Air apart. The congenial airline. The jets that made travel a treat. And gray seats on pale blue carpet would look more attractive than the beige. Why hadn't he thought of that?

Better yet, why hadn't the "expert" he'd hired to design the interiors thought of it?

"Oh, and I hate those nasty little overhead light beams on airplanes. It's always so hard to arrow them down on what you want to read." Georgia looked at the slope of the walls, then back to him. "You could have small lamps attached to the hull. Like sconces. Brass—no, pewter. To go with the gray seats and offset the blue."

She reached down and lifted a table that was folded down into itself. Opening it, she pointed to the space on the wall just above. "And here, a bud vase, also affixed to the hull, with fresh flowers."

Sean liked it. Liked all of it. And the excitement in her eyes fired his own.

"Oh, and instead of the standard, plastic, pull-down shades on the windows, have individual drapes." She leaned over and put her hands to either side of one of the portholes. "Tiny, decorative curtain rods—also pewter—and a square of heavy, midnight-blue fabric..."

Before he could comment on that, she'd straightened up and walked past him to the small galley area. The flight attendant was sitting in the cockpit with the pilot and copilot, so there was no one in her way as she explored the functional kitchen setup.

She stepped out again and studied the wall with a

flat-screen television attached to it. "The bathroom is right here, yes?"

"One of them," he said. "There's another in the back."

"So, if you get rid of the big TV—and you should have individual screens at the seating clumps—and expand the bathroom wall another foot or so into the cabin," she took another quick look around the corner at the galley. "That gives you a matching extra space in the kitchen. And that means you could expand your menu. Offer a variety of foods that people won't get anywhere else."

He could bloody well see it, Sean thought. Frowning, he studied the interior of the jet and saw it not as it was now, but as it could be. As it *would* be, he told himself, the moment they got back to Ireland and he could fire the designer who'd suggested ordinary for his *extraordinary* airline.

Following Georgia's train of thought was dizzying, but the woman knew what she was talking about. She painted a picture a blind man could see and appreciate. Why she'd wasted her talent on selling houses, he couldn't imagine.

"You could even offer cribs for families traveling with babies." She was still talking. "If you bolt it down in the back there and have, I don't know, a harness or something for the baby to wear while it sleeps, that gives the mom a little time to relax, too."

He was nodding, making mental notes, astonished at the flow of brilliant ideas Georgia had. "You've a clever mind," he said softly. "And an artist's eye."

She grinned at him and the pleasure in her eyes was something else a blind man could see.

"What's in the back of the plane, through that door?" she asked, already headed toward it.

"Something I'd planned to show you later," he told her with a wink. Then he took her hand and led her down the narrow, ordinary aisle between boring beige seats. Opening the door, he ushered her inside, then followed her and closed the door behind them.

"You have a bedroom on your jets?" she asked, clearly shocked at the sight of the double bed, bedecked with a dark blue duvet and a half-dozen pillows. The shades were drawn over the windows, filling the room with shadow. Georgia looked up at him, shaking her head.

"This plane is mine," Sean told her. "I use it to fly all over the damn place for meetings and such, and so I want a place to sleep while I travel."

"And the seats that fold into beds aren't enough for you?"

"Call it owner's privilege," he said, walking closer, steadily urging her backward until the backs of her knees hit the edge of the mattress and she plopped down. Swinging her hair back from her face, she looked up at him.

"And do you need help designing this room, too?" she asked, tongue firmly in cheek.

"If I did, I now know who to call," he assured her.

"Does that door have a lock on it?" she asked, sliding her gaze to the closed door and then back to him.

"It does."

"Why don't you give it a turn, then?"

"Another excellent idea," Sean said, and moved to do just that.

Then he looked down at her and was caught by her eyes. The twilight shine of them. The clever mind behind them. Staring into her eyes was enough to mesmerize a man, Sean thought. He took a breath and dragged the scent of her into his lungs, knowing that air seemed empty without her scent flavoring it.

Slowly, she slipped her shoes off, then lay back on the mattress, spreading her arms wide, so that she looked like a sacrifice to one of the old gods. But the welcoming smile on her face told him that she wanted him as much as he did her.

In seconds, then, he was out of his clothes and helping her off with hers. The light was dim in the room, but he saw all he needed to see in her eyes. When he touched her, she arched into him and a sigh teased a smile onto her lips.

"Scáthanna bheith agat," he whispered. Amazing how often he felt the old language well up inside him when he was with her. It seemed only Irish could help him say what he was feeling.

She swept her fingers through his hair and said, "I love when you speak Gaelic. What did you say that time?"

"I said, 'Shadows become you,'" he told her, then dipped his head for a kiss.

"You make my heart melt sometimes, Sean," she admitted, her voice little more than a hush of sound.

That knot in his guts tightened further as words he might have said, but wouldn't, caught in his throat. Right now, more words were unnecessary anyway, he told himself.

Instead, he kissed her again, taking his time, tasting her, tangling his tongue with hers until neither of them were thinking. Until all either of them felt was the need for each other. He would take his time and savor every luscious inch of her. Indulge them both with a slow loving that would ease away the ragged edges they had been living with and remind them both how good they were together.

Well, Georgia told herself later that night, Sean was right about one thing. Flying Irish Air did deliver you to your destination feeling bright-eyed and alert. Of course, great sex followed by a nap on a real bed probably hadn't hurt, either.

Now Sean was out picking up some dinner, and she was left staring into her closet trying to decide what to pack, what to give away and what to toss.

"Who'm I trying to kid?" she asked aloud. "I'm taking my clothes with me. All of 'em."

She glanced at the stack of packing boxes on the floor beside her and sighed. Then her gaze moved around her bedroom in the condo she and Laura used to share.

She'd had good times in this house. Sort of surprising, too, since when she'd arrived here to move in with her sister, she hadn't really been in a good place mentally. Marriage dissolved, bank account stripped and ego crushed, she'd slowly, day by day, rebuilt a life for herself.

"And now," she whispered, "I'm building another."

"Talking to yourself? Not a good sign."

She whirled around to find Sean standing in the open doorway, holding a pizza box that smelled like heaven while he watched her with amusement glittering in his eyes.

In self-defense, she said, "I have to talk to myself, since I'm the only one who really understands me."

"*I* understand you, Georgia."

"Is that right?" She turned her back on the closet, the boxes and everything she had to do. Snatching the pizza box from him, she headed out of the bedroom and walked toward the stairs. He was right behind her. "Well then, why don't you tell me what I'm thinking?"

"Easily enough done," he said, his steps heavy on the stairs behind her. "You're excited, but worried. A bit embarrassed for having me catch you doing a monologue in your bedroom and you're hoping you've some wine in the kitchen to go with that pizza."

She looked over her shoulder at him and hoped the surprise she felt was carefully hidden. "You're right about two of them, but I happen to know I don't have a bottle of wine in the kitchen."

"You do now," he told her, and dropped an arm around her shoulders when they hit the bottom of the stairs. "I picked some up while I was out."

"I do like a man who plans ahead."

"Then you'll love me for the plans I have for later." He took the box from her, walked into the kitchen and set it down on the counter.

She stood in the doorway, her gaze following him as he searched through cupboards for plates and napkins and wineglasses. His hair was shaggy and needed a trim. The jeans he wore now were faded and clung to his butt and legs, displaying what she knew was a well-toned body. He whistled as he opened the bottle of wine and poured each of them a glass of what was probably an outrageously expensive red.

You'll love me for the plans I have for later.

His words echoed in her head, and Georgia tried to shrug them off. Not easy to do, though, when a new and startling discovery was still rattling through her system. Warning bells rang in her mind and a flutter of nerves woke up in the pit of her stomach.

Mouth dry, heart pounding, she looked at Sean and realized what her heart had been telling her for days. Maybe weeks.

She'd done the unthinkable.

She'd fallen in love with Sean Connolly.

Nine

Oh, absolutely not.

She refused to think about it. Simply slammed a wall up against that ridiculous thought and told herself it was jet lag. Or hunger. Probably hunger. Once she got some of that pizza into her, her mind would clear up and she'd be fine again.

"You know, you don't have to do the packing yourself," Sean was saying, and she told herself to pay attention.

"What?"

He snorted a laugh. "Off daydreaming while I'm slaving over a hot pizza box were you?"

"No." God, now she was nervous around him. How stupid was that? He'd seen her naked. She'd made love to the man in every way possible. How could she be nervous over what was, in essence, a blip on the radar?

This wasn't love. This was lust. Attraction. Hell, even *affection*.

But not love.

There, she told herself. Problem solved. *Love* was not a word she was going to be thinking ever again. "What did you say? About the packing?"

"While you take care of putting your house up for sale tomorrow, why don't I make some calls and see about getting movers in here?" He looked around the well-stocked condo kitchen. "You can go through, tell them what you want moved to Ireland and what you're getting rid of, and then stand back and watch burly men do the heavy lifting for you."

Tempting. And expensive. She argued with herself over it for a minute or two, but the truth was, if she did it Sean's way, the whole business could be finished much faster. And wasn't that worth a little extra expense?

Especially if it got her back to Ireland faster? And then hopefully in another week or two, they could end this pretend engagement? She glanced down at the emerald-and-diamond ring on her hand and idly rubbed at the band with her thumb. Soon, it wouldn't be hers anymore. Soon, *Sean* wouldn't be hers anymore.

She lifted her gaze to his and his soft brown eyes were locked on her. Another flutter of something nerve-racking moved in the pit of her stomach, but she pushed it aside. Not love, she reminded herself.

And still, she felt a little off balance. Georgia had to have some time to come to grips with this. To figure out a way to handle it while at the same time protecting herself.

She wasn't an idiot, after all. This hadn't been a part of their deal. It was supposed to be a red-hot affair with no strings attached. A pretend engagement that they would both walk away from when it was over.

And that was just what she would do.

Oh, it was going to hurt, she thought now, as Sean handed her a glass of wine, letting his fingers trail across her skin. When he was out of her life, out of her bed and still in her heart—not that she was admitting he was—it was going to be a pain like she'd never known before.

But she comforted herself with the knowledge that she would be in Ireland, near her sister. She'd have Laura and baby Fiona to help her get over Sean. Shouldn't take more than five or ten years, she told herself with an inner groan.

"So, what do you think?" Sean carried the wine to the table beside the window that overlooked the backyard. "We can have you packed up in a day or two. A lot of your things we can carry back on the jet, what we can't, we'll arrange to ship."

"That's a good idea, Sean." She took a seat, because her knees were still a little weak and it was better to sit down than to fall down. Taking a quick sip of the really great wine, she let it ease the knot in her throat.

Then she picked up the conversation and ran with it. Better to talk about the move. About packers and all of the things she had to do rather than entertain even for a minute that the affection she felt for him could be something else. Losing Sean now was going to hurt. But God help her, if she was really in *love,* the pain would be tremendous.

"There are really only a few things I want to take with me to Ireland," she said. "The rest I'll donate."

That thought appealed to her anyway. She was starting over in Ireland, and the cottage was already furnished, so there was no hurry to buy new things. She could take her time and decide later what she wanted. As for kitchen stuff, it didn't really make sense to ship pots and pans when she could replace them easily enough in Ireland.

All she really wanted from the condo aside from her clothes were family photos, Laura's paintings and a few other odds and ends. What did that say about her, that she'd been living in this condo, surrounded by *stuff* and none of it meant enough to take with her?

She had more of a connection with the cottage than she did with anything here.

"You know," she said, "it's kind of a sad statement that there's so little here I want to take with me. I mean, I was willing to stay here when it clearly didn't mean much to me."

"Why would that be sad?" He sat down opposite her, opened the pizza box and served each of them a slice. "You knew when it was time to move on, is all. Seems to me it's more brave than that. You're moving to a different country, Georgia. Why wouldn't you want to leave the past behind?"

She huffed out a breath and let go of the 'poor me' thoughts that had just begun to form. "How do you do that?"

"What?"

"Manage to say exactly the right thing," she said.

He laughed a little and took a bite of pizza. "Luck, I'd say. And knowing you as I've come to, I thought you might be getting twisted up over all there is to be done and then giving yourself a hard time over it."

Scowling, she told him, "It's a little creepy, knowing you can see into my head so easily."

He picked up his wineglass and toasted her with it. "Didn't say it was easy."

She hoped not, because she *really* didn't want him looking too closely into her mind right now. Twists of emotion tangled inside her and this time she didn't fight them.

Okay, yes. She had feelings for him. Why wouldn't she? He was charming and fun and smart and gorgeous. He was easy to talk to and great in bed, of course she cared about him.

That didn't mean she loved him. Didn't mean anything more than what they had together was important to her.

Even she wasn't buying that one.

Oh, God. No sense in lying to herself, Georgia thought. She'd sew her lips shut and lock herself in a deep dark hole for the rest of her life before she ever admitted the truth to Sean.

This wasn't affection. It wasn't lust. Or hunger.

It was love.

Nothing like the love she had thought she'd found once before.

Now, she couldn't imagine how she had ever convinced herself that she was in love with Mike. Because what she felt for Sean was so much bigger, so much… *brighter,* that it was like comparing an explosion to a sparkler. There simply wasn't a comparison.

This was the kind of love she used to dream of.

And wouldn't you know she'd find it with a man who wouldn't want it? Feelings hadn't been part of their agreement. Love had no place in a secret. A pretense.

So she'd keep her mouth shut and tuck what she felt for him aside until it withered in the dark. It would. Eventually. She hoped.

Oh, God.

She was such an idiot.

"Well," Sean said after a sip of his wine, "I'll admit to you now I've no notion of what you're thinking at this minute. But judging by your expression, it's not making you happy."

Understatement of the century.

"Nothing in particular," she lied smoothly. "Just how much I have to do and how little time I have to do it."

He looked at her for a long minute as if trying to decide to let it lay or not, and finally, thank God, he did.

"So no second thoughts? Being here," he said, glancing around the bright, modern kitchen, "doesn't make you want to rethink your decision?"

She followed his gaze, looking around the room where she'd spent so much alone time in the past year. It was a nice place, she thought, but it had never felt like *hers*. Not like the cottage in Ireland did.

"No," she said, shaking her head slowly. "I came here to live with Laura when my marriage ended and it was what I needed then. But it's not for me now, you know?"

"I do," he said, resting one elbow on the tabletop. "When you find your place, you know it."

"Exactly. What about you? Did you ever want to live somewhere else?"

He grinned. "Leave Dunley?" He shook his head. "I went to college in Dublin and thought it a fine place. I've been all over Europe and to New York several times as well, but none of those bright and busy places tug at me as Dunley does.

"The village is my place, as you said," he told her. "I've no need to leave it to prove anything to myself or anyone else."

"Have you always been so sure of yourself?" She was really curious. He seemed so together. Never doubting himself for a minute. She envied it. At the same time she simply couldn't understand it.

He laughed. "A man who doesn't question himself from time to time's a fool who will soon be slapped down by the fates or whatever gods are paying attention to the jackass of the moment. So of course I question," he said. "I just trust myself to come up with the right answers."

"I used to," she told him and pulled a slice of pepperoni free of the melted cheese and popped it into her mouth. "Then I married Mike and he left me for someone else and I didn't have a clue about it until he was walking out the door." Georgia took a breath and then let it go. "After that, I had plenty of questions, but no faith in my own answers."

"That's changed now, though," he said, his gaze fixed on hers. "You've rebuilt your life, haven't you? And you've done it the way *you* want to. So, I'm thinking your answers were always right, you just weren't ready to hear them."

"Maybe," she admitted. Then, since marriages, both real and pretend, were on her mind, asked, "So, why is it you've never been married?"

He choked on a sip of wine, then caught his breath and said, "There's a question out of the blue."

"Not really. We were talking about my ex—now it's my turn to hear your sad tales. I am your 'fiancée,' after all. Shouldn't I know these things?"

"I suppose you should," he said with a shrug. "Truth is, I was engaged once."

"Really?" A ping of something an awful lot like jealousy sounded inside her. Just went to show her mom was right. She used to tell Georgia, *Never ask a question you don't really want the answer to.*

"Didn't last long." He shrugged again and took a sip of his wine. "Noreen was more interested in my bank account than in me, and she finally decided that she deserved better than a husband who spent most of his time at work."

"Noreen." Harder somehow, knowing the woman's name.

"I let her maneuver me into the thought of marriage," Sean was saying, apparently not clueing in to Georgia's thoughts. "I remember thinking that maybe it was time to be married, and Noreen was there—"

"She was *there?"* Just as *she* had been there, Georgia thought now, when he'd needed a temporary fiancée. Hmm.

He gave her a wry smile. "Aye. I know how it sounds now, but at the time, it seemed easier to let her do what she would than to fight her over it. I was consumed at the time with taking Irish Air to the next level, and I suppose the truth is I didn't care enough to put a stop to Noreen's plans."

Dumbfounded, she just stared at him. "So you would have married her? Not really loving her, you would have married her anyway because it was easier than saying 'no thanks'?"

He shifted uneasily on his chair and frowned a bit at the way she'd put things. "No," he said finally. "I wouldn't have taken that trip down the aisle with her in the end. It wouldn't have worked and I knew it at the time. I was just…"

"Busy?" she asked.

"If you like. Point is," Sean said, "it worked out for the best all around. Noreen left me and married a bank president or some such. And I found you."

Yes, he'd found her. Another temporary fiancée. One he had no intention of escorting down an aisle of any kind. Best to remember that, she told herself.

He lifted his glass and held it out to her, a smile on

his face and warmth in his eyes. Love swam in the pit of her stomach, but Georgia put a lid on it fast. She hadn't planned to love him, and now that she did, she planned to get over it as fast as humanly possible.

So, she'd keep things as they had been between them. Light. Fun. Sexy and affectionate. And when it was over, she'd walk away with her head high, and Sean would never know how she really felt. Georgia tapped her wine-glass to his, and when she drank, she thought that the long-gone Noreen had gotten off easy.

Noreen hadn't really loved Sean when she left him, or she'd never have moved on so quickly to someone else.

Georgia on the other hand…it wasn't going to be simple walking away from Sean Connolly.

Georgia was glad they'd come to the wedding. Just seeing the look on Misty's face when she spotted Georgia and Sean had made the trip worthwhile. But it was more than that, too, she told herself. Maybe she'd *had* to attend this wedding. Maybe it was the last step in leaving behind her past so that she could walk straight ahead and never look back.

And dancing with her ex-husband, the groom, was all a part of that. What was interesting was, she felt nothing in Mike's arms. No tingle. No soft sigh of regret for old time's sake. Nothing.

She looked up at him and noticed for the first time that his blue eyes were a little beady. His hair was thinning on top, and she had the feeling that Mike would one day be a comb-over guy. His broad chest had slipped a little, making him a bit thick about the waist, and the whiskey on his breath didn't make the picture any prettier.

Once she had loved him. Or at least thought she had. She'd married him assuming they would be together forever, and yet here she was now, a few years after a divorce she hadn't seen coming and she felt…nothing.

Was that how it would be with Sean one day? Would her feelings for him simply dry up and blow away like autumn leaves in a cold wind?

"You look amazing," Mike said, tightening his arm around her waist.

She did and she knew it. Georgia had gone shopping for the occasion. Her dark red dress had long sleeves, a deep V neckline, and it flared out from the waist into a knee-length skirt that swirled when she moved.

"Thanks," she said, and glanced toward Sean, sitting alone at a table on the far side of the room. Then, willing to be generous, she added, "Misty makes a pretty bride."

"Yeah." But Mike wasn't looking at his new wife. Instead, he was staring at Georgia as if he'd never seen her before.

He executed a fast turn and Georgia had to grab hold of his shoulder to keep from stumbling. He pulled her in even closer in response. When she tried to put a little space between them, she couldn't quite manage it.

"You're engaged, huh?"

"Yes," she said, thumbing the band on her engagement ring. Sean had made quite the impression. Just as she'd hoped, he'd been charming, attentive and, in short, the perfect fiancé. "When we leave here, we're flying home to Ireland."

"Can't believe you're gonna be living in a foreign country," Mike said with a shake of his head. "I don't remember you being the adventurous type at all."

"Adventurous?"

"You know what I mean," he continued, apparently not noticing that Georgia's eyes were narrowed on him thoughtfully. "You were all about fixing up the house.

Making dinner. Working in the yard. Just so—" he shrugged "—boring."

"Excuse me?"

"Come on, Georgia, admit it. You never wanted to try anything new or exciting. All you ever wanted to do was talk about having kids and—" He broke off and sighed. "You're way more interesting now."

Was steam actually erupting from the top of her head? she wondered. Because it really felt like it. Georgia's blood pressure was mounting with every passing second. She had been *boring?* Talking about having kids with your husband was *boring?*

"So, because I was so uninteresting, that's why you slipped out with Misty?" she asked, her voice spiking a little higher than she'd planned. "Are you actually trying to tell me it's *my* fault you cheated on me?"

"Jeez, you always were too defensive," Mike said, and slid his hand down to her behind where he gave her a good squeeze.

Georgia's eyes went wild.

They made a good team.

Sean had been thinking about little else for the past several days. All through the mess of closing up her home and arranging for its sale. Through the packing and the donations to charity and ending the life she'd once lived, they'd worked together.

He was struck by how easy it was, being with her.

Her clever mind kept him on his toes and her luscious body kept him on his knees. A perfect situation, Sean told himself as he sat at the wedding, drinking a beer, considering ways to keep Georgia in his life.

Ever since she'd laid out her ideas to improve the look of his company jets, Sean had been intrigued by possibilities. They got along well. They were a good match. A team, as he'd thought only moments before.

"And damned if I want to lose what we've found," he muttered.

The simplest way, he knew, was to make their engagement reality. To convince her to marry him—not for love, of course, because that was a nebulous thing after all. But because they fit so well. And the more he thought about it, the better it sounded.

Hadn't his cousin Ronan offered very nearly the same deal to his Laura? A marriage based on mutual need and respect. That had worked out, hadn't it? Nodding to himself, he thought it a good plan. The challenge would be in convincing Georgia to agree with him.

But he had time for that, didn't he?

Watching her here, at the wedding of her ex-husband, he was struck again by her courage. Her boldness in facing down those who had hurt her with style and enough attitude to let everyone in the room know that she'd moved on. Happily.

The bride hadn't expected Georgia to show up for the wedding. That had been clear enough when he and Georgia arrived. The stunned shock on the bride's face mingled with the interest from the groom had been proof of that.

Sean frowned to himself and had a sip of the beer sitting in front of him. He didn't much care for the way Georgia's ex-husband took every chance he had to leer at her. But he couldn't blame the man for regretting letting Georgia go in favor of the empty-headed woman he'd now saddled himself with.

Georgia was as a bottle of fine wine while the bride seemed more of a can of flat soda in comparison.

The reception was being held at the clubhouse of a

golf course. Late fall in Ohio was cold, and so the hall was closed up against the night, making the room damn near stifling.

Crepe paper streamers sagged from the corners of the wall where the tape holding them in place was beginning to give. Balloons, as their helium drained away, began to dip and bob aimlessly, as if looking for a way out, and even the flowers in glass vases on every table were beginning to droop.

People who weren't dancing huddled together at tables or crowded what was left of the buffet. Sean was seated near the dance floor, watching Georgia slow dance in the arms of her ex, fighting the urge to go out there and snatch her away from the buffoon. He didn't like the man's hands on her. Didn't like the way Mike bent his head to Georgia and whispered in her ear.

Sean frowned as the music spilled from the speakers overhead and the groom pulled Georgia a bit too tightly against him. Something spiked inside Sean's head and he tightened his grip on the beer bottle so that it wouldn't have surprised him in the least to feel it shatter. Deliberately, he released his hold on the bottle, setting it down carefully on the table.

Then Sean breathed slow and deep, and rubbed the heel of his hand against the center of his chest, unconsciously trying to rub away the hard, cold knot that seemed to have settled there. He gritted his teeth and narrowed his eyes when the groom's hand slipped down to cup Georgia's behind.

Fury swamped his vision and dropped a red haze of anger over his mind. When Georgia struggled to pull free without success, something inside Sean simply snapped. The instinct to protect her roared into life and he went with it. *His* woman, mauled on a dance floor? He bloody well didn't think so.

Sean was halfway out of his chair when Georgia brought the sharp point of one of her high heels down onto the toe of the groom's shoe. While Mike hopped about, whinging about being in pain, Misty ran to her beloved's rescue, and Sean met Georgia halfway between the dance floor and the table.

Her eyes were glinting with outrage, color was high in her cheeks and she'd never been more vividly beautiful to him. She'd saved herself, leaving him nothing to do with the barely repressed anger churning inside him.

His woman, he thought again, and felt the truth of it right down to his bones. And even knowing that, he pulled away mentally from what that might mean. He wouldn't look at it. Not now. Instead, he focused a hard look at the groom and his new bride, then shifted his gaze back to Georgia.

"So then," Sean asked, "ready to leave?"

"Way past ready," Georgia admitted and stalked by him to their table to pick up her wrap and her purse.

He let her go, but was damned if he'd leave this place without making a few things clear to the man he'd like nothing better than to punch into the next week. Misty was clinging to Mike when Sean approached them, but he didn't even glance at the new bride. Instead, his gaze was for the groom, still hobbling unsteadily on one injured foot.

Voice low, eyes hard, Sean said, "I'll not beat a man on his wedding day, so you're safe from me."

Insulted, Mike sputtered, "What the—"

"But," Sean continued, letting the protective instincts rising inside him take over, "you even so much as *think* of Georgia again, I'll know of it. And you and I will have a word."

Misty's mouth flapped open and shut like a baby bird's. Mike flushed dark red, but his eyes showed him for the true coward he was, even before he nodded. Sean left them both standing there, thinking the two of them deserved each other.

When he draped Georgia's wrap about her shoulders, then slid one arm around her waist to escort her from the building, she looked up at him.

"What did you say to him?"

He glanced at her and gave her a quick smile to disguise the fury still pulsing within. "I thanked him for a lovely party and wished him a broken foot."

"I do like your style, Sean," she said, leaning her head against his shoulder.

He kissed the top of her head and took the opportunity to take a long breath of her scent. Then he quipped, "I believe the American thing to say would be, 'back atcha.'"

With the sound of her laughter in his ears, Sean steered her outside to the waiting limousine, and ushered her inside.

With a word to the driver, they were off for the airport so Sean could take his woman home to Ireland.

Ten

A few days later, Sean was standing in Ronan's office in Galway, looking for a little encouragement. Apparently, though, he'd come to the wrong place.

"You're out of your mind," Ronan said.

"Well, don't hold back, cousin," Sean countered, pacing the confines of the office. It was big and plush but at the moment, it felt as if it were the size of a box. There was too much frustrated energy pumping through Sean's brain to let him stand still, and walking in circles was getting him nowhere.

He stopped at the wide window that offered a view of Galway city and the bay beyond. Out over the ocean, layers of dark clouds huddled at the horizon, no doubt bunched up over England but planning their immediate assault on Ireland. Winter was coming in like a mean bitch.

Sean had come into Galway to see Ronan because

his cousin's office was the one place Sean could think of where they could have a conversation without interruptions from the seeming *multitude* of women in their lives. Ronan was, naturally, wrapped up in Laura and baby Fiona. For Sean, there was his mother, nearly recovered now, and there was Georgia. Beautiful Georgia who haunted his sleep and infiltrated his every waking thought.

His woman, he'd thought that night in Ohio, and that notion had stayed with him. There was something there between them. He knew it. Felt it. And he'd finally found a plan to solve his troubles, so he'd needed this time with Ronan to talk it all out. But for all the help he was finding, he might have stayed home.

"How is it crazy to go after what I want?" he argued now. "You did it."

Ronan sat back in the chair behind his uncluttered desk. Tapping the fingers of one hand against that glossy surface, he stared at Sean with a disbelieving gleam in his eyes.

"Aye, I did it, just as you're thinking to, so I'm the man to tell you that you're wrong. You can't ask Georgia to marry you as a sort of business arrangement."

"Why not?" Sean countered, glancing over his shoulder at his cousin before turning his gaze back to the window and the outside world beyond. "For all your calm reason now, you did the same with Laura and look how well that turned out for you."

Ronan scraped one hand across his face. "You idiot. I almost lost Laura through my own foolishness. She wouldn't have me, do you not remember that? How I was forced to chase her down to the airport as she was leaving me?"

Sean waved that off. The point was, it *had* worked out.

A bump or two in the road, he was expecting. Nothing worthwhile came easy, after all, but in the end, Georgia would agree with him. He'd done a lot of thinking about this, and he knew he was right. Georgia was much more sensible, more reasonable than her sister and he was sure she'd see the common sense in their getting married.

He'd worked it out in his mind so neatly, she had to see it. A businesslike offer of marriage was eminently sensible. With his mother on the mend, the time for ending their faux engagement was fast approaching. And Sean had discovered he didn't want his time with Georgia to be over. He wanted her even more now than he had when this had all begun.

He turned around, leaned one hip against the window jamb and looked at his cousin.

"Georgia's buying a house here," Sean pointed out. "She's opening her business. She won't be running off to California to escape me."

"Doesn't mean she'll greet you with open arms, either," Ronan snapped, then huffed out a breath filled with frustration. "She's already been married to a man who didn't treasure her. Why would she choose another who offers her the same?"

Sean came away from the window in a fast lunge and stood glaring down at Ronan. Damned if he'd be put in the same boat as the miserable bastard who'd caused Georgia nothing but pain. "Don't be comparing me to that appalling excuse of a man who hurt her. I'd not cheat on my wife."

"No, but you won't love her, either," Ronan said, jumping up from his chair to match his cousin glare for glare. "And as she's my sister now, I'll stand for her and tell you myself she *deserves* to be loved, and if you're not the man to do it then bloody well step aside and let her find the one who will."

Those words slapped at Sean's mind and heart, and he didn't much care for it. *Love* wasn't a word Sean was entirely comfortable with. He'd tried to be in love with Noreen and he'd failed. What if he tried with Georgia and failed there, as well? No, he wouldn't risk it. What they had now was good. Strong. Warmth beneath the heat. Caring to go with the passion. Affection that wasn't muddled by trying to label it. Wasn't that enough? Wasn't that more than a lot of people built a life around?

And he'd be damned before he stepped aside for some other man to snatch Georgia in front of his eyes. Which was one of the reasons he'd come up with this plan in the first place. If they ended their engagement—and since Ailish was recovering nicely, that time was coming fast—then he'd be forced to let Georgia go. Watch her find a new man. He'd have to imagine that lucky bastard touching her, kissing her, claiming her in the dark of night—and damned if he'd do *that,* either.

He alone would be the man touching Georgia Page, Sean assured himself, because he could accept no other option. If he did, he'd be over the edge and into insanity in no time at all.

"She had a man who promised her love, as you've just said yourself," Sean argued, jamming both hands into his pockets to hide the fists they'd curled into. Thinking about that man, Georgia's ex, made him want to punch something. That a man such as he had had Georgia and let her go was something Sean would never understand.

"What good did the promise of love do her then?" he asked, more quietly now. "I'm not talking of love but of building a life together."

"Without the first, the second's not much good," Ronan told him with a slow shake of his head.

"Without the first, the second is far less complicated,"

Sean argued. He knew Ronan loved his Laura, and good for him. But love wasn't the only answer. Love was too damn ephemeral. Hard to pin down. If he offered her love, why would she believe him? Why would she trust it when that bastard who had offered the same had crushed her spirit with the word?

No. He could offer Georgia what she wanted. A home. Family. A man to stand at her side and never hurt her as she'd been hurt before. Wasn't that worth something?

"You're a jackass if you really believe that bilge you're shoveling."

"Thanks very much," Sean muttered, then said, "You're missing the point of this, Ronan. If there's no love between us, there's no way for her to be hurt. She'll be safe. I'll see to it."

Ronan skewered him with a look. "You're set on this, aren't you?"

"I am. I've thought this through." In fact, he'd thought of little else since going on that trip to the States with Georgia. He wanted this and so, Sean knew, he could make it happen. He'd never before lost when something mattered as this did. Now wouldn't be the first time. "I know I'm right about this, Ronan."

"Ah, well then." Clapping one hand to Sean's shoulder, Ronan said, "I wish you luck with it, because you're going to need it. And when Georgia coshes you over the head with something heavy, don't be coming to me looking for sympathy."

A tiny speck of doubt floated through the river of Sean's surety, but he paid it no attention at all. Instead, he focused only on his plan, and how to present it to Georgia.

It stormed for a week.

Heavy, black clouds rolled in from the sea, riding an

icy wind that battered the village like a bad-tempered child. The weather kept everyone closed up in their own houses, and Georgia was no different. She'd spent her time hanging pictures and paintings, and putting out the other small things she'd brought with her from California until the cottage was cozy and felt more hers every day.

She missed Sean, though. She hadn't seen him in days. Had spoken to him only briefly on the phone. Laura had told her that Sean and Ronan had spent days and nights all over the countryside, helping the villagers and farmers who were having a hard time through the storm. They'd done everything from mending leaking roofs to ferrying a sick child to the hospital just in time for an emergency appendectomy.

Georgia admired their connection to the village and their determination to see everyone safely through the first big storm of the season. But, God, she'd missed him. And though it pained her, she had finally convinced herself that not seeing him, not having him with her, was probably for the best. Soon, she'd have to get accustomed to his absence, so she might as well start getting used to it.

But it was so much harder than she'd thought it would be. She hadn't planned on that, damn it. She'd wanted the affair with the gorgeous Irishman, and who wouldn't have?

But she hadn't wanted the risk of loving him, and the fact that she did was entirely *his* fault. If he hadn't been so blasted charming and sweet and sexy. If he hadn't been such an amazing lover and so much fun to be around, she never would have fallen. So really, Georgia told herself, none of this was her fault at all.

She'd been hit over the head by the Irish fates and the only way out was pain and suffering. He'd become such a part of her life that cutting him out of it was going to be like losing a limb. Which just irritated her immensely. That she could fall in love when she knew she shouldn't, because of the misery that was now headed her way, was both frustrating and infuriating.

The worst of it now was there was nothing she could do about it. The love was there and she was just going to have to hope that, eventually, it would fade away. In hindsight, she probably shouldn't have accepted Sean's bargain in the first place. But if she hadn't…she would have missed so much.

So she couldn't bring herself to wish away what she'd found with him, even though ending it was going to kill her.

When the sun finally came out, people streamed from their homes and businesses as if they were prisoners suddenly set loose from jail. And Georgia was one of them. She was so eager to get out of her own thoughts, and away from her own company, she raced into town to open her shop and start living the life she was ready to build.

The sidewalks were crowded with mothers who had spent a week trapped with bored children. The tea shop did a booming business as friends and neighbors gathered to tell war stories of storm survival. Shop owners were manning brooms, cleaning up the wreckage left behind and talking to friends as they worked.

Georgia was one of them now. Outside her new design shop, she wielded a broom with the rest of them, and once her place was set to rights, she walked back inside to brew some coffee. She might be in Ireland, but she hadn't yet switched her allegiance from coffee to tea.

The bell over the front door rang in a cheery rattle, and she hurried into the main room only to stop dead when she saw Sean. Everything in her kindled into life. Heat, excitement, want and tenderness tangled together making her nearly breathless. It felt like years since she'd seen him though it had only been a few days. Yes. Irritating.

He looked ragged, tired, and a curl of worry opened up in the center of her chest. The shadow of whiskers on his jaws and the way his hair jutted up, no doubt from him stabbing his fingers through it repeatedly, told her just what a hard few days he'd had. He wore faded jeans, a dark, thickly knit sweater and heavy work boots. And, she thought, he'd never looked more gorgeous.

"How are you?" she asked.

He rubbed one hand across his face, blinked a couple of times, then a half smile curved one corner of his mouth. "Tired. But otherwise, I'll do."

"Laura told me what you and Ronan have been up to. Was it bad?"

"The first big storm of the year is always bad," he said. "But we've got most of the problems in the area taken care of."

"I'm glad. It was scary around here for a day or two," she said, remembering how the wind had howled like the shrieks of the dying. At one point the rain had come down so fiercely, it had spattered into the fire in her hearth.

"I'm sorry I wasn't able to be with you during your first real storm in Dunley," he said, as sunlight outlined him in gold against the window.

"I was fine, Sean. Though I am thinking about getting a dog," she added with a smile. "For the company. Besides, it sounds like you and Ronan had your hands full."

"We did at that." He blew out a breath and tucked his hands into the back pockets of his jeans.

How could a man look *that* sexy in old jeans and beat-up work boots?

"Maeve Carrol's roof finally gave up the ghost and caved in on her."

Georgia started. "Oh, my God. Is she okay?"

"She's well," Sean said, walking farther into the shop, letting his gaze move over the room and all the changes she'd made to it. "Madder than the devil with a drop of holy water in his whiskey, but fine."

She smiled at the image and imagined just how furious Maeve was. The older woman was spectacularly self-sufficient. "So, I'm guessing you and Ronan finally talked her into letting you replace her roof."

"The woman finally had no choice as she's a hole in her roof and lots of water damage." He shook his head. "She nearly floated away on a tide of her own stubbornness. She'll be staying with Ronan and Laura until her cottage is livable again."

Georgia folded her arms across her chest to help her fight the urge to go and wrap her arms around him. "I'm guessing she's not happy about leaving her home."

"You'd think we'd threatened to drag her through the village tied to a rampaging horse." He snorted. "The old woman scared us both half to death. Ronan's been after her for years to let us replace that roof."

"I know. It's nice of you to look out for her."

He glanced at her. "Maeve is family."

"I know that, too," she said and felt that flutter of love inside her again. Honestly, who wouldn't be swooning at the feet of a man like this? Even as that thought circled her brain, Georgia steeled herself. If she wasn't careful, she was going to do something stupid that would alert him to just how much she cared about him.

And that couldn't happen. No way would she live in Dunley knowing that Sean was off at the manor feeling sorry for poor Georgia, who'd been foolish enough to fall in love with him.

"Anyway," she said with forced cheer, "my cottage is sound, thanks to the previous owner. So I was fine."

"Aye," he said softly, brown eyes locked on her face. "You are."

A ripple of sensation slid along her spine at the music in his voice, the heat in his eyes. He was temptation itself, she told herself, and she wondered how she was going to manage living in this town over the years, seeing him and not having him. Hearing the gossip in the village about the women he would be squiring around. And again, she wanted to kick herself for ever agreeing to his crazy proposal.

"You've been working here. Your shop looks good," he said, shifting a quick look around the space. "As do you."

Heat flared inside her, but she refused to acknowledge it. Instead, Georgia looked around her shop, letting her gaze slide over the soft gold walls, the paintings of Laura's that Georgia had hung only that morning.

"Thanks," she said. "The furniture I ordered from the shop in Galway should arrive by end of the week."

She could almost see it, a sleek, feminine desk with matching chair. More chairs for clients, and shelves for what would be her collection of design books. She'd have brightly colored rugs strewn across the polished wood floor and a sense of style that customers would feel the moment they stepped inside.

Georgia was excited about the future even as she felt a pang of regret that Sean wouldn't be a part of it. She took a steadying breath before looking into his soft brown eyes again. And still it wasn't enough. Probably never would be, she thought. He would always hold a piece of her heart, whether he wanted it or not.

Still, she forced a smile. "I think it's really coming along. I'm looking forward to opening the shop for business."

"You'll be brilliant," he said, his gaze level on hers.

"Thanks for that, too." She knew his words weren't empty flattery, and his confidence in her was a blossom of warmth inside her. "And as long as I'm thanking you…we'll add on that I appreciate all your help with the business license."

"We had a deal, didn't we?"

"Yeah," she said, biting at her bottom lip. "We did."

"I spoke to Tim Shannon this morning. He told me that your business license should be arriving by end of the week."

A swirl of nerves fluttered in the pit of her stomach, and she slapped both hands to her abdomen as if to still them.

"Never say you're nervous," he said, smiling.

"Okay, I won't tell you. But I am. A little." She turned her gaze on the front window and stared out at the sunlit street beyond. "This is important to me. I just want to do it right."

"And so you will," Sean said, "and to prove it, I want to hire you."

"What?" That she hadn't expected.

"Do you remember how you reeled off dozens of brilliant ideas on how to improve the interior of my planes?"

"Yes…"

He walked closer, tugged his hands from his pockets and laid them on her shoulders. "I want you to redesign the interiors of all the Irish Air jets."

"You…" She blinked at him.

"Not just the fleet we've got at the moment, either," he told her, giving her shoulders a squeeze. "I want you in on my talks with the plane builders. We can get your input from the beginning that way."

"Redesign your..." It was a wild, exciting idea. And Georgia's mind kicked into high gear despite the shock still numbing parts of her brain.

This was huge. Irish Air as her client would give her an instant name and credibility. It would be an enormous job, she warned herself, expecting nerves or fear to trickle in under the excitement, but they didn't come. All she felt was a rush of expectancy and a thrill that he trusted her enough to turn her loose on the business that meant so much to him.

"I can see the wheels in your mind turning," he said, his mouth curving slightly. "So add this to the mix. You'll have a free hand to make whatever changes you think best. We'll work together, Georgia, and together we'll make Irish Air legendary."

Together. Her heart stirred. Oh, she liked the sound of that, even though more time with Sean would only make the eventual parting that much more painful. How could she *not* love him? He was offering her carte blanche to remake Irish Air because he trusted her.

Shaking her head, she admitted, "I don't even know what to say."

He grinned and she felt a jolt.

"Say yes, of course. I'll be your first client, Georgia, but not your last." He pulled her closer and she looked up into deep brown eyes that shone with pleasure and... something else.

"With Irish Air on your résumé, I guarantee other companies will be beating down your door soon."

"It's great, Sean, really. You won't be sorry for this."

"I've no doubts about that, Georgia," he said, then lifted one hand to smooth her hair back from her face.

At his touch, everything in her trembled, but Georgia fought it. She *had* to fight it, for her own sake.

"There's something else I want to talk to you about." His voice was quiet, thoughtful.

And she knew instinctively what he was going to say. She should have known there would be another reason for his incredible offer. He had come here to tell her their engagement was done. Deal finished. Obviously, he'd offered her that job to take the sting out of the whole thing.

"Let me help," she said, pulling back and away from him. How could she think when his hands were on her? When she was looking into those eyes of his? "Laura told me that Ailish is mostly recovered now and I'm really glad."

"Thank you," he said, "and yes, she is. She'll see her doctor this week, then all will be back to normal."

Normal. Back to life without Sean.

"So she'll be headed back to Dublin?"

"No," Sean said. "Mother's decided she wants to come home to Dunley. I offered her the left wing of the manor, but she says she's no interest in living with her son." He shrugged and laughed a little. "So she's opted for moving into the gatehouse on the estate."

"The gatehouse?" Georgia didn't remember ever noticing a gatehouse at Sean's place.

"It's what we call it, anyway," he said with a smile. "It was originally built for my grandmother to live in when she moved out of the manor in favor of my parents. Mother's always loved it, and there's plenty of room there for her friends to visit."

"Oh, okay. Well, it's nice that she'll be closer. I really like your mother."

"I know you do," Sean said. "But the thing is, with mother recovering, it's time we talked about our bargain."

"It's okay." Georgia cut him off. She didn't want him to say the words. "You don't have to say it. Ailish is well, so we're finished with this charade."

She tugged at the ring on her finger, but he reached out and stilled her hand. Georgia looked up at him.

"I don't want to be done with it," he blurted, and hope shot through her like sunlight after the storm they'd just lived through.

She swallowed hard and asked, "What?"

"I want us to marry," he said, curling her fingers into her palm to prevent her from taking off the ring.

"You do?" Love dazzled her. She looked into his eyes and saw them shine. She felt everything in her world setting itself straight again. In one split instant, she saw their lives spiraling out into a wonderful future. The home they'd make. The children. The family. She saw love and happiness and everything she'd ever wished for.

The sad cynic inside her died, and Georgia was glad to see her go.

And then he continued talking.

"It makes sense," he told her, a gorgeous smile on his face. "The village is counting on it. My mother's got the thing half-planned already. We work well together. You must admit we make a hell of a good team. We're great in bed together. I think we should simply carry on with the engagement and go through with the marriage. No one ever has to know we didn't marry for love."

Eleven

There, Sean told himself. He'd done it. Laid out his plan for her, and now she'd see exactly what they could have together. Looking into her eyes, he saw them alight, then watched worriedly as that light dimmed. He spoke up fast, hoping to see her eyes shine again.

"There's no sense in us breaking up when any fool could see we've done well together," he said, words rushing from him as her eyes went cool and a distance seemed to leap up between them.

He moved in closer and told himself she hadn't actually moved *away,* just to one side. "You're a sensible woman, Georgia. Clear-thinking. I admire that about you, along with so many other facets of you."

"Well, how nice for you that I'm such a calm person."

"I thought so." He frowned. "But somehow, I've insulted you."

"Oh, why would I be insulted by *that?*"

"I've no idea," he said, but watched her warily. "I realize I've caught you off guard with this, but you'll see, Georgia. If you'll but take a moment to think it through, you'll agree that this is the best way for both of us."

"You've decided that, have you?" She snapped a look at him that had the hackles at the back of his neck standing straight up.

This wasn't going as he'd thought it would, yet he had no choice but to march on, to lay everything out for her.

"I did. I've done considerable thinking about the two of us since we took that trip to California."

"Have you?"

Her tone was sweet, calm, and he began to relax again. This was the Georgia he knew so well. A temper, aye. What's life without a little seasoning after all, but a reasonable woman at the heart of it.

"I'm saying we work well together and there's no reason for us to separate." When her gaze narrowed, he hurried on. "The entire village is expecting a wedding. If we end things now, there'll be questions and whispers and gossip that will last for years."

"That's not what you said when we started this," she countered. *"Oh, they'll all think you've come to your senses,"* she added in such a true mimic of his own voice and words she had him flinching.

"It's different now," he insisted.

"How? How is it different?"

He rubbed one hand over his face, fatigue clawing at him even as his muddled mind fought for survival. "You're a part of things in Dunley, as am I. They'll wonder. They'll talk."

"Let them," she snapped. "Isn't that what a *sensible* woman would say?"

"Clearly that word upsets you, though I've no idea

why. You're a lovely woman, Georgia, with a sound mind and a clear vision." He pushed on, determined to make her see things his way, though the ground beneath his feet felt suddenly unstable. "You're rational, able to look at a situation and see it for what it is. Which is why I know you'll agree with me on this. Ronan insisted you wouldn't, of course, but he doesn't know you as I do..."

"Ronan?" she asked, turning her head and glancing at him from the corner of her eye. "You discussed this with Ronan?"

"Why wouldn't I?" He stiffened. "He's as close as a brother to me, and I wanted to get it all set in my mind before I came to you with it."

"And now you have?"

"I do," Sean told her, and felt worry begin to slither through him. She wasn't reacting as he'd expected. He'd thought that his sensible Georgia would smile up at him and say, *Good idea, Sean. Let's do it.* Instead, the distance between them seemed to be growing despite the fact she was standing right in front of him.

She looked down at the emerald-and-diamond ring on her finger, and when he caught her hand in his, he felt better. She was considering his proposal, then, though he'd have expected a bit more excitement and a little less biting his damned head off.

"If you'll just take a moment to consider it, I know you'll agree. You're not a woman to muddy your thinking by looking through the wavery glass of emotion."

"Oh, no," she whispered, rubbing her thumb against the gold band of her ring. "I'm cool and calm. That's me. No emotions. Little robot Georgia."

"Robot?" He frowned at her. "What're you talking about?"

"Logical," she repeated. "Rational. If I come when you whistle I could be your dog."

He scrubbed the back of his neck. Maybe he shouldn't have come here first thing this morning. Maybe he should have waited. Gotten some damn sleep before talking to her. For now, he felt as though even his own thoughts were churning. He couldn't lay a finger on how he'd gone wrong here, but he knew he had.

The only way out was to keep talking, hoping he'd stumble on the words he needed so desperately. And why was it, he thought wildly, that when he most needed the words, they'd dried up on him?

"Not a robot now, but a dog?" Sean shook his head. "You've got this all wrong, Georgia. 'Tis my fault you're not understanding me," he said benevolently. "I've not made myself clear enough."

"Oh," she told him with a choked-off laugh, "you're coming through loud and clear."

"I can't be, no, or you wouldn't be standing there spitting fire at me with your eyes."

"Really?" She cocked her head to one side and studied him. "How should I react to this oh-so-generous proposal?"

Temper slapped him. He was offering marriage here, not a year in a dungeon. For all the way she was acting, you wouldn't believe he was trying to make her his wife but instead ordering her to swim her way back to America.

"A kiss wouldn't be out of hand, if you're asking me. It's not every day I ask a woman to marry me, you know."

"And so graciously, too." She fiddled with her ring again, thumb sliding across the big green stone. "I should probably apologize."

"No need for that," he said, worry easing back an inch or so now. "I've caught you by surprise, is all."

"Oh, you could say that." She pulled her hand free of his. "And your proposal to Noreen, was it every bit this romantic?"

"Romantic? What's romance to do with this?"

"Nothing, obviously," she muttered.

"And I never proposed to Noreen," he told her hotly. "That just…happened."

"Poor you," Georgia told him with sarcasm dripping off each word. "How you must have been taken advantage of."

"I didn't say that—" He shook his head and blew out a breath. "I've no idea what I'm saying now, you've got me running in circles so."

"Not sensible enough for you?"

"Not by half, no," he said flatly. "You're behaving oddly, Georgia, if you don't mind my saying." Reaching for her, he blinked when she batted his hands away. "What was that for?"

"Oh, let me count the reasons," she muttered, stalking away from him to pace back and forth across the narrow width of the shop.

The short heels of her boots clacked loudly against the wood floor and sounded to Sean like a thundering heartbeat.

"You want me to marry you because your mother's making plans and the *village* will be disappointed."

"That's only part of it," he argued, feeling control slipping away from him somehow.

"Yes, of course." She snapped him a furious glance. "There's how well we work together, too."

"There is."

"And we're such a good team, right?" Her eyes flashed. "And let's not forget how good we are in bed together."

"It's a consideration, I think you'll agree, when wanting to marry." His tone was as stiff as his spine as he faced the rising fury in her eyes.

"Sure, wouldn't want to waste your time on a sensible, rational, logical woman who sucked in bed."

"A harsh way of putting it—"

She held up one hand to keep him from saying anything else, and he was shocked enough to obey the silent command.

"So basically, you don't want anything as pesky as *love* involved in this at all."

"Who said anything about love?" he demanded, as something cold and hard settled in the center of his chest.

"Exactly my point."

Swallowing his rising anger, he kept his voice calm as he pointed out, "You're not talking sense, Georgia."

"Wow, I'm not?" She flashed him a look out of eyes that had gone as dark as the ocean at night. "How disappointing for you."

Watery winter sunlight slanted into the room through the front windows and seemed to lay across Georgia like a blessing. Her hair shone, her features were golden and the flash in her eyes was unmistakable.

Still, Sean had come here to claim her and he wasn't willing to give up on that. "You're taking this the wrong way entirely, Georgia. You care for me, and I for you—"

"Care for?" she repeated, her voice hitching higher. "Care for? I *love* you, you boob."

Sean was staggered, and for the first time in his life, speechless.

"Hah!" She stabbed one finger in the air, pointing it at him like a blade. "I see you hadn't considered *that* in all of your planning. Why would rational, logical, *sensible* Georgia be in love?"

She loved him? Heat blistered his insides even as words tangled on his tongue.

"Well, I can't explain that. It's really not sensible at all," Georgia muttered, pushing both hands through her hair before dropping her hands to her sides and glaring at him. "At the moment, it feels downright stupid."

"It's not stupid," Sean blurted out, crossing to her and taking hold of her shoulders before she could dodge his touch again. Love? She loved him? This was perfect. "It's more reason than ever for you to marry me. You love me, Georgia. Who the bloody hell else would you marry?"

"Nobody." She yanked free of his grip.

"That makes no sense at all."

"Then you're not paying attention," she snapped. "You think I want to marry a man who doesn't love me? *Again?* No, thanks. I've already had that and am in no way interested in doing it all over."

"I'm nothing like that inexcusable shite you married and you bloody well know it," he argued, feeling the need to defend himself.

"Maybe not, but what you're offering me is a fake marriage."

"It would be real."

"It would be legal," she argued. "Not real."

"What the bloody hell's the difference?"

"If you don't *know* what the difference is," she countered, "then there's no way to explain it to you." She took a long breath and said, "I've come to Ireland to build myself a life. *Myself.* And just because I made the mistake of falling in love with you doesn't mean I'm willing to throw those plans away."

"Who's asking you to?" he demanded, wondering if

she loved him as she claimed, how she could be so stubbornly blind to what they shared. What they *could* share.

"I'm done with you, Sean. It's over. No engagement. No marriage. No nothing." She grabbed his arm and tugged him toward the door.

Sunlight washed the street and, for the first time, Sean noted that a few of the villagers had gathered outside the door. Drawn, no doubt by the rising voices. Nothing an Irishman liked better than a good fight—either participating or witnessing.

"Now get out and go away."

"You're throwing me out of your shop?" He dug in his heels and she couldn't budge him another inch.

"Seems the 'sensible' thing to do," she countered, her gaze simply boiling with temper.

"There's nothing sensible about you at the moment, I'm sorry to say."

"Thank you! I don't feel sensible. In fact, I may never be sensible again." She tapped the tip of her index finger against the center of his chest. "In fact, I feel *great.* It's liberating to say exactly what you're thinking and feeling.

"I've always done the right thing—okay, the sensible thing. But no more. And if you don't want me to redesign Irish Air, that's fine with me." She shook her hair back from her face. "I hear Jefferson King lives somewhere around here—I'll go see *him* about a job if I have to."

"Jefferson King?" The American billionaire who now lived on a sheep farm near Craic? Just the thought of Georgia working in close quarters with another man gave Sean a hard knot in the pit of his belly. Even if that man was married and a father.

Georgia belonged here. With him. Nowhere else.

"There's no need for that," he said sharply. "I don't

break my word. I've hired you to do the job and I'll expect you to do it well."

Surprise flickered briefly in her eyes. At least he had that satisfaction. It didn't last long.

"Good." Georgia gave him a sharp nod. "Then we're agreed. Business. *No* pleasure."

Outside the shop, muttering and conversations rose along with the size of the crowd. All of Dunley would be out there soon, Sean thought, gritting his teeth. Damned if he'd give the village more grist to chew on. If she wouldn't see reason, then he'd leave her now and try again another day to batter his way through that hard head of hers.

He lowered his voice and said, "You've a head like stone, Georgia Page."

"And so is your heart, Sean Connolly," she told him furiously.

Someone outside gasped and someone else laughed.

"This is the way you talk to a man who offers you marriage?" he ground out.

"A man who offered me *nothing*. Nothing of himself. Nothing that matters."

"Nothing? I offer you my name and that's nothing?" His fury spiked as he stared down into those blue eyes flashing fire at him.

She didn't back down an inch and even while furious he could admire that, as well.

"Your name, yes," Georgia said. "But that's all. You don't offer your heart, do you, Sean? I don't think you'd know how."

"Is that right?" Her words slapped at him and a part of him agreed with her. He'd never once in his life risked love. Risked being out of control in that way. "Well, I don't remember hearts being a part of our bargain, do you?"

"No, but with *people,* sometimes hearts get in the way."

"Oooh," someone said from outside, "that was a good one."

"Hush," another voice urged, "we'll miss something."

Sean dragged in a breath and blew it out again, firing a furious glare at their audience then looking back again to Georgia. "I'll be on my way, then, since we've nothing more to talk about."

"Good idea." She folded her arms over her chest and tapped the toe of her shoe against the floor in a rapid staccato that sounded like machine gun fire.

"Fine, then." He turned, stepped outside and pushed his way through the small crowd until he was out on the street. All he wanted now was to walk off this mad and think things through. He stopped when Georgia called his name and turned to her, hoping—foolishly—that she'd changed her mind.

She whipped her right arm back and threw her engagement ring at him. It hit Sean dead in the forehead and pain erupted as she shouted, "No engagement. No marriage!"

She slammed the door to punctuate her less than sensible shout.

Sean heard someone say, "She's a good arm on her for all she's small."

Muttering beneath his breath, Sean bent down to pick up the ring and when he straightened, Tim Casey asked, "So, the wedding'll be delayed, then? If you can keep her angry at you until January, I'll win the pool."

Sean glanced at the closed door of the shop and imagined the furious woman inside. "Shouldn't be a problem, Tim."

* * *

An hour later, Ailish was sitting in Laura's front parlor, a twist of disgust on her lips. "Well, it's happened."

"What?" Laura served the older woman a cup of tea, then took one for herself before sitting down on the couch beside her. "What happened?"

"Just what we've been waiting for," Ailish told her. "I heard from Katie, Sean's housekeeper, that Mary Donohue told her that not an hour ago, your sister threw her engagement ring at Sean. I'd say that ends the 'bargain' you told me about."

Laura groaned. Since the phone call with Ailish, when the sly woman had gotten Laura to confess all about Sean's and Georgia's ridiculous "deal," the two of them had been co-conspirators. Sean's mother was determined to see him married to a "nice" woman and to start giving her grandchildren. Laura was just as determined to see her sister happy and in love. And from what Laura had noted lately, Georgia *was* in love. With Sean. So, if she could…help, she would.

But, this new wrinkle in the situation did not bode well.

Ailish had been convinced that if they simply treated the wedding as a fait accompli, then Sean and Georgia would fall into line. Laura, knowing her sister way better, hadn't bought it for a minute, but she hadn't been able to think of anything else, either. So Ailish had ordered a cake, Laura had reserved canvas tenting for the reception and had already made a few calls to caterers in Galway and Westport.

Not that they would need any of that, now.

"Then it's over," Laura said. "I was really hoping they might actually realize that they belonged together and that it would all work out."

"They *do* belong together," Ailish said firmly, pausing to take a sip of her tea. "We're not wrong about that."

"It doesn't really matter what we think though, does it?" Laura shook her head. "Damn it, I knew Georgia was going to end up hurt."

Ailish gave a delicate, ladylike snort. "From what I heard, I'd say Sean was the one hurt. That was a very big emerald, and apparently she hit him square in the middle of his forehead." Nodding, she added, "Perhaps it knocked some sense into the man."

"Doubt it," Laura grumbled, then added, "no offense."

"None taken." Ailish reached out and patted her hand. "I've never seen my son so taken with a woman as he is with our Georgia, and by heaven, if he's too stubborn to see it, then we'll just have to help the situation along."

"What've you got in mind?" Laura watched the older woman warily.

"A few ideas is all," Ailish said, "but we may need a little help..."

At that moment, Ronan walked into the room, cradling his baby daughter in his arms. He took one look at the two women with their heads together and made a quick about-face, trying for a stealthy escape.

"Not one more step, Ronan Connolly," Ailish called out.

He stopped, turned back and looked at each woman in turn. Narrowing his eyes on them, he said, "You're plotting something, aren't you?"

"*Plotting*'s a harsh word," Laura insisted.

He frowned at her.

"None of your glowering now, Ronan," his aunt told him. "This is serious business here."

"I'll not have a part in a scheme against Sean," he warned.

"'Tis *for* Sean," Ailish corrected him. "Not against him. I am his mother, after all."

"Oh, aye, that makes a difference."

Ailish turned a hard look on her nephew and Laura hid a smile.

"We'll be needing your help, and I want no trouble from you on this," Ailish said.

"Oh, now, I think I'd best be off and out of this—"

"Give it up, Ronan," Laura told him with a slow shake of her head. "You're lost against her and you know it." Turning to the older woman, she said with admiration, "You'd have been a great general."

"Isn't that a lovely thing to say?" Ailish beamed at her and then waved Ronan closer. "Come now, it won't be a bit of trouble to you. You'll see."

Ronan glumly walked forward, but bent his head to his daughter and whispered, "When you're grown, you're not allowed to play with your aunt Ailish."

Twelve

"Damn it Georgia, I knew this was going to happen!" Laura dropped onto the sofa and glared at her sister.

"Well, congrats, you must be psychic!" Georgia curled her legs up under her and muttered, "Better than being sensible, anyway."

"So now what?" Laura reached over and turned up the volume on the baby monitor she'd set on the nearby table. Instantly, the soft sound of Beethoven slipped into the room along with the sighs of a sleeping baby.

Georgia listened to the sounds and felt a jab of something sweet and sharp around her heart. If she hadn't loved Sean, she might have gotten married again someday. But now she was stuck. She couldn't marry the one she loved and wouldn't marry anyone else. Which left her playing the part of favorite auntie to Laura and Ronan's kids.

"Now nothing," Georgia told her and couldn't quite stop a sigh. "It's over and that's the end of it."

"Doesn't make sense," Laura muttered. "I've *seen* the way Sean looks at you."

"If I *pay* you, will you let this go?" Georgia asked.

"I don't know why you're mad at me. You should be fighting with Sean."

"I did already."

"Sounds like you should again."

"To what point?" Georgia shook her head. "We said what we had to say and now we're done."

"Yeah," Laura told her wryly. "I can see that."

"I'll get over it and *him,*" Georgia added, remembering Sean's insulting proposal and the look of shock on his face when she told him *thanks, but no, thanks*. Idiot. She dropped her head onto the back of the couch. "Maybe it's like a bad case of the flu. I'll feel like I'm going to die for a few days and then I'll recover." Probably.

"Oh, that's good."

Georgia lifted her head and speared her sister with a dark look. "You could indulge my delusions."

"I'd rather encourage you to go fight for what you want."

"So I can go and beg a man to love me?" Georgia stiffened. "No, thank you. I'll pass on that, thanks."

"I didn't say *beg*. I said *fight*."

"Just leave it alone, okay? Enough already."

She didn't want to keep reliving it all. As it was, her own mind kept turning on her, replaying the scene over and over again. *Why* did she have to tell him she loved him?

Scowling, Laura looked across the room at her husband. "This is your fault."

"And what did I do?"

"Sean's your cousin. You should beat him up or something."

Before Ronan could respond to that, Georgia laughed. "Thanks for the thought, but I don't want him broken and bleeding."

"How about bruised?" Laura asked. "I could settle for bruised."

"No," she said. She was bruised enough for both of them, and she couldn't even blame Sean for it. She was the one who'd fallen in love when she shouldn't have. She was the one who had built up unrealistic dreams and then held them out all nice and shiny for him to splinter. And even now, she loved him. So who was the real idiot? "It's done. It's over. Let's move on."

"Always said you were the sensible one," Ronan piped up from across the room, and then he shivered when Georgia sent him a hard look.

"God, I hate that word."

"I'll make a note of it," Ronan assured her.

"Oh, relax, Ronan," Georgia told him. "I'm not mad at you. I'm mad at *me*."

"For what?" Laura demanded.

"I never should have told him I loved him."

"Why shouldn't you?" her sister argued. "He should know exactly what he's missing out on."

"Yeah," Georgia said, pushing up from the couch, unable to sit still. "I'm sure it's making him crazy, losing me."

"Well, it should!" Laura shot a dark look at her husband and Ronan lifted both hands as if to say, *I had nothing to do with this.*

"Excuse me, Miss Laura."

Patsy Brennan, the housekeeper, walked into the front room. "But Mickey Culhane is here to see Miss Georgia."

Georgia looked to Ronan. "Who's Mickey Culhane?"

"He owns a farm on the other side of Dunley. It was his son Sean drove to hospital during the storm." To Patsy, he added, "Show him in."

"Why would he want to see me?" Georgia wondered.

"How would I know?" Laura asked unconvincingly.

Georgia looked at her sister wish suspicion, then turned to face the man walking into the front parlor.

Mickey was about forty, tall, with thick red hair and weathered cheeks. He nodded to Ronan and Laura, then turned his gaze to Georgia. "I've heard about the troubles you and Sean are having, Miss, and wanted to say that you shouldn't be too hard on him. He's a fine man. Drove thirty kilometers into the teeth of that storm to get my boy to safety."

Georgia felt a flush of heat fill her cheeks. "I know he did, and I'm glad your son's okay."

"He is, yes." Mickey grinned. "Thanks to Sean. Without that Rover of his, we'd never have gotten the boy to help in time. You should probably think more kindly of him, is all I'm saying." He looked to Ronan and nodded. "Well, I've to be off and home for supper."

"G'night, Mickey," Ronan called as the man left.

"What was that all about?" Georgia asked the room in general as she stared after the farmer thoughtfully.

For three days, Sean stayed away from Dunley, from the cottage, giving himself time to settle and giving Georgia time to miss him. And by damn, he thought, she'd better well miss him as he missed her.

During those three days, he threw himself into work. For him, there was no other answer. When his mind was troubled or there was a problem he was trying to solve, work was always the solution.

He had meetings with his engineers, with HR, with contracts and publicity. He worked with pilots and asked for their input on the new planes and tried not to focus on the woman who would be designing their interiors.

He went in to the office early and stayed late. Anything to avoid going home. To Dunley. To the manor. Where the emptiness surrounding him was suffocating. And for three days, despite his best efforts, his mind taunted him with thoughts of Georgia. With the memory of her face as she said *I love you, you boob.*

Had ever a man been both insulted and given such a gift at the same time?

Pushing away from his desk, he walked to the window and stared out over Galway. The city lights shone in the darkness and over the bay, moonlight played on the surface of the water. The world was the same as it had been before Georgia, he thought. And yet…

A cold dark place inside him ached in time with the beat of his heart. He caught his own reflection in the window glass and frowned at the man looking back at him. He knew a fool when he saw one.

Sean Connolly didn't quit. He didn't give up on what he wanted just because he'd hit a hitch in his plans. If he had, Irish Air would be nothing more than a dream rather than being the top private airline in the world.

So a beautiful, strong-willed, infuriating woman wasn't going to stop him either.

But Georgia wasn't his problem and he knew it. The fact was, he'd enjoyed hearing her say she loved him. Had enjoyed knowing that she had said those three words, so fraught with tension and risk, first. It put him more in control, as he'd always preferred being. He hadn't allowed himself to take that step into the unknown. To risk his pride. And yet, he told himself, if there was no risk, there was no reward. He hadn't stepped away from the dare and risk of beginning his airline, had he?

"No, I did not," he told the man in the glass.

Yet, when it had come to laying his heart at the feet of a woman who had looked furious enough to kick it back in his face…he'd balked. Did that make him a coward or a fool?

He knew well that *fool* would be the word Ronan would choose. And his mother. And no doubt Georgia had several apt names for him about now.

But to Sean's way of thinking, what this was, was a matter of control. He would be in charge. He would keep their battle on his turf, so to speak—and since she had up and moved to Ireland she'd helped him in that regard already. What he had to do now was get her to confess her feelings again and then allow that perhaps he might feel the same.

"Perhaps," he sneered. What was the point in lying to himself, he wondered. Of course he loved her. Maybe he always had. Though he hadn't meant to. That certainly hadn't been part of his plan. But there Georgia Page was, with her temper, her wit, her mind. There wasn't a thing about her that didn't tear at him and fire him up all at once. She was the woman for him. Now he'd just to make her see the truth of it.

"And how will you do that when she's no doubt not speaking to you?"

He caught the eye of the man in the glass again and he didn't like what he saw. A man alone. In the dark, with the light beyond, out of reach.

Until and unless he found a way to get Georgia back in his life, he knew the darkness would only grow deeper until it finally swallowed him.

On that thought, he managed a grin as an idea was born. Swiftly, he turned for his desk, grabbed up the phone and made a call.

For the past few days, Georgia had been besieged.

Mickey Culhane had been the first but certainly not the last. Every man, woman and child in Dunley had an opinion on the situation between she and Sean and lined up to share it.

Children brought her flowers and told her how Sean always took the time to play with them. Men stopped in to tell her what a fine man Sean was. He never reneged on a bet and was always willing to help a friend in trouble. Older women regaled her with stories of Sean's childhood. Younger women told of how handsome and charming he was—as if she needed to be convinced of *that*.

In essence, Dunley was circling the wagons, but rather than shutting Georgia out for having turned on one of their own, they were deliberately trying to drag her into the heart of them. To make her see reason and "forgive Sean for whatever little thing he might have done."

The only thing she really had to forgive him for was *not* loving her. Well, okay, that and his terrible proposal. But she wouldn't have accepted a proposal from him even if he'd had violins playing and rose petals at her feet—not if he didn't love her.

But in three days, she hadn't caught even so much as a glimpse of him. Which made her wonder where he was even while telling herself it was none of her business where he was or *who* he was with. That was a lie she couldn't swallow. It ate her up inside wondering if Sean had already moved on. Was he with some gorgeous Irish redhead, already having put the Yank out of his mind?

That was a lowering thought. She was aching for him,

and the bastard had already found someone else? Was she that forgettable, really?

The furniture deliverymen had only just left when the bell over the front door sang out in welcome. Georgia hurried into the main room from the kitchen and stopped dead in her tracks.

"Ailish."

Sean's mother looked beautiful, and even better, *healthy.* She wore black slacks and a rose-colored blouse covered by a black jacket. A small clutch bag was fisted in her right hand.

"Good morning," she said, a wide smile on her face.

Georgia's stomach dropped. First, it was the villagers who'd come to support Sean and now his mother. Georgia seriously didn't know how much more she could take.

"Ailish," she said, "I really like you, but if you've come to tell me all about how wonderful your son is, I'd rather not hear it."

One eyebrow winged up and a smile touched her mouth briefly. "Well, if you already know his good points, we could talk about his flaws."

Georgia laughed shortly. "How much time do you have?"

"Oh, Georgia, I do enjoy you." Ailish chuckled, stepped into the shop and glanced around the room. "Isn't this lovely? Clearly feminine, yet with a strong, clear style that can appeal to a man, as well."

"Thank you." It was the one thing that had gone well this week, Georgia thought. Her furniture was in and she had her shop arranged just as she wanted. Now all she needed were clients. Well, beyond Irish Air. She'd talked to Sean's secretary just the day before and set up an appointment to go into Galway to meet with him.

She was already nervous. She hated that.

"You're in love with him."

"What?" Georgia jolted out of her thoughts to stare at Ailish, making herself comfortable on one of the tufted, blue chairs.

"I said, you're in love with my son."

Awkward. "Well, don't hold that against me. I'm sure I'll get over it."

Ailish only smiled. "Now why would you want to do that?"

Georgia sighed. The woman was Sean's *mother*. How was she supposed to tell the poor woman that her son was a moron? A gorgeous, sexy, funny moron? There was just no polite way to do it, so Georgia only said, "There's no future in it for me, Ailish. Sean's a nice guy—" surely she was scoring Brownie points with the universe here "—but we—I—it just didn't work out."

"Yet." Ailish inspected her impeccable manicure, then folded her hands on her lap. "I've a great fondness for you, Georgia, and I'm sure my son does, as well."

God. Could she just bash her own head against a wall until she passed out? That would be more pleasant than this conversation. "Thank you. I like you, too, really. But Ailish, Sean doesn't love me. There is no happy ending here."

"But if there were, you'd take it?"

Her heart twisted painfully in her chest. A happy ending? Sure, she'd love one. Maybe she should go out into the faery wood and make a wish on the full moon, as Sean had told her.

"Well?" the woman urged. "If my son loved you, then would you have him?"

Oh, she would have him so fast, his head would spin. She would wrap herself around him and let herself drown in the glory of being loved, really loved, by the only man she wanted. Which was about as likely to happen as stumbling across calorie-free chocolate.

"He doesn't, so the question is pointless."

"But I notice you didn't answer it."

"Ailish..." Such a nice woman. Georgia just didn't have the heart to tell her that it had all been a game. A stupid, ridiculous game cooked up by a worried son.

"You've a kind heart, Georgia." Ailish rose, walked to her and gave her a brief, hard hug. Emotion clogged Georgia's throat. She really could have used a hug from her own mother, so Ailish was filling a raw need at the moment. She would have loved this woman as a mother-in-law.

Ailish pulled back then and patted Georgia's cheek. "As I said, you've a kind heart. And a strong spirit. Strong enough, I think, to shake Sean's world up in all the right ways."

Georgia opened her mouth to speak, but Ailish cut her off.

"Don't say anything else, dear. Once spoken, some words are harder to swallow than others." She tucked her purse beneath her arm, touched one hand to her perfect hair and then headed for the door. "I'm glad I came today."

"Me, too," Georgia said. And she was. In spite of everything, these few minutes with Sean's mother had eased a few of the ragged edges inside her heart.

"I'll see you tonight at dinner, dear." Ailish left and the bell over Georgia's door tinkled into the sudden stillness.

It was cold, and the wind blowing in from the ocean was damp. But Laura's house was warm and bright, with a fire burning in the hearth and Beast and Deidre curled up together in front of it. The two dogs were inseparable,

Georgia mused, watching as Beast lay his ugly muzzle down on top of Deidre's head.

Now here was an example of a romance between the Irish and a Yank that had turned out well. So well that, together, the two dogs had made puppies that would be born sometime around Christmas.

Stooping to stroke Beast's head and scratch behind his ears, Georgia told herself that she would adopt one of the pups and she'd have her own Beast junior. She wouldn't be alone then. And she could pour all the love she had stored up to give on a puppy that would love her back.

"Thanks for that," she murmured, and Beast turned his head just far enough to lick her hand.

"Georgia," Laura called, and peeked into the room from the hallway. "Would you do me a favor and go to the wine cellar? Ronan forgot to bring up the red he's picked out for dinner, and I'd like it open and breathing before Ailish gets here."

"Sure," she answered, straightening up. "Where is it?"

"Oh. Um," Laura worried her bottom lip. "He, um, said he set it out, so you should find it easily enough."

"Motherhood's making you a little odd, honey," Georgia said with a smile.

Laura grinned. "Worth every burnt-out brain cell."

"I bet." Georgia was still smiling as she walked down the hall and made the turn to the stairs.

This family dinner idea of Laura's was good, she told herself. Nice to get out of her house. To get away from Dunley and all the well-meaning villagers who continued to sing Sean's praises.

As she opened the heavy oak door and stepped into the dimly lit wine cellar, she thought she heard something behind her. Georgia turned and looked up at Ronan as he stepped out of the shadows. "Ronan?"

He gave her an apologetic look then closed the door.

"Hey!" she called, "Ronan, what're you doing?"

On the other side, the key turned in the lock and she grabbed the doorknob, twisting it uselessly. If this was a joke, it was a bad one. Slapping her hand against the door, she shouted, "Ronan, what's going on here?"

"'Tis for your own good, Georgia," he called back, voice muffled.

"*What* is?"

"I am," Sean said from behind her.

She whirled around so fast, she nearly lost her balance. Sean reached out to steady her but she jumped away from his touch as if he were a leper. He buried the jolt of anger that leaped to the base of his throat and stuffed his hands into his pockets, to keep from reaching for her again only to be rebuffed.

"What're you doing here?" Georgia demanded.

"Waiting for you," he said tightly. Hell, he'd been in the blasted wine cellar for more than an hour, awaiting her arrival for the family dinner he'd had Laura arrange.

The cellar was cool, with what looked like miles of wooden racks filled with every kind of wine you could imagine. Pale lights overhead spilled down on them, creating shadows and the air was scented by the wood, by the wine and, Sean thought…by *her*.

Having Ronan lock her inside with him had been his only choice. Otherwise the stubborn woman would have escaped him and they'd *never* say the things that had to be said.

"I've been waiting awhile for you. Opened a bottle of wine. Would you like some?"

She folded her arms across her middle, pulling at the fabric of her shirt, defining the curve of her breasts in a way that made his mouth water for her. With supreme effort he turned from the view and poured her a glass without waiting for her answer.

He handed it to her and she drank down half of it as if it were medicine instead of a lovely pinot.

"What do you want, Sean?" she said, voice tight, features closed to him.

"Five bloody minutes of your time, if it's all the same to you," he answered, then took a sip of his own wine, telling himself that *he* was supposed to be the cool head here.

But looking at her as she stood in front of him, it took everything in him to stand his ground and not grab her up and kiss her until she forgot how furious she was with him and simply surrendered.

"Fine. Go." She checked the dainty watch on her wrist. "Five minutes."

Unexpectedly, he laughed. A harsh scrape of sound that shot from his throat like a bullet. "By God, you're the woman for me," he said, with a shake of his head. "You'll actually time me, won't you?"

"And am," she assured him. "Four and a half minutes now."

"Right then." He tossed back the rest of his wine and felt a lovely burn of fire in its wake. Setting the glass down, he forgot all about the words he'd practiced and blurted out, "When a man asks a woman to be his wife, he expects better than for her to turn on him like a snake."

She glanced at the watch again. "And when a woman hears a proposal, she sort of expects to hear something about 'love' in there somewhere."

This was the point that had chewed at him for three days. "And did your not-so-lamented Mike, ex-husband and all-around bastard, give you pretty words of love?"

Sean took a step closer and noted with some irritation that she stepped back. "Did he promise to be faithful, to love you always?"

A gleam of tears swamped her eyes and in the pale light, he watched as she ferociously blinked them back. "That was low."

"Aye, it was," he admitted, and cursed himself for the fool Ronan thought him to be. But at the same time, he bristled. "I didn't give you the words, but I gave you the promise. And I *keep* my promises. And if you weren't such a stubborn twit, you'd have realized that I wouldn't propose unless there were feelings there."

"Three and a half minutes," she announced, then added, "Even stubborn twits want to hear about those 'feelings' beyond 'I've a caring for you, Georgia.'"

He winced at the reminder of his own words. She'd given him "love"; he'd given her "caring." Maybe he was a fool. But that wasn't the point. "You should have known what I meant without me having to say it. Let me remind you again that your lying, miserable ex used the word *love* and it meant nothing."

"At least he had the courage to say it, even though his version of love was sadly lacking!"

Her eyes were hot balls of fury and perversely, Sean was as aroused by that as he was by everything else about her.

It tore at him, what she'd said. He *had* lacked the courage to say what he felt. But no more.

Pouring himself more wine, he took a long drink. "I won't be compared to a man who couldn't see you for the treasure you are, Georgia Page. In spite of your miserable temper and your stubbornness that makes a rock look agreeable in comparison."

"And I won't be told what I should do for 'my own

good.' Not by you and not by the villagers you've no doubt *paid* to sing your praises to me for the last three days."

"I didn't pay them!" He took a gulp of wine and set the glass down again. "That was our family's doing. I only found out about it tonight. Ailish and Laura sent Ronan off to do their bidding. He talked to Maeve, who then told every mother's son and daughter for miles to go to you with tales of my wondrousness." He glared at her. "For all the good that seems to have done.

"Besides," he added, "I've no need to bribe anyone because everyone else in my bloody life can plainly see what's in my heart without a bleeding *map!*"

"Yeah?" Georgia snapped with a glance at her watch. "Two minutes. Well, I do need a map. So tell me. Flat out, what *is* in your heart?"

"Love!" He threw both hands high and let them drop again. Irritated, frustrated beyond belief, he shouted it again. "Love! I love you. Have for weeks. Maybe longer," he mused, "but I can't be sure as you're turning me into a crazy man even as we're standing here!"

She smiled at him and his heart turned over.

"Oh, aye," he nodded grimly. "Now she smiles on me with benevolence, now that she's got me just where she wants me. Half mad with love and desire and the crushing worry that she'll walk away from me and leave me to go through the rest of my life without her scent flavoring my every breath. Without the taste of her lingering on my lips. Without the soft brush of her skin against mine. *This* she smiles for."

"Sean..."

"Rather than proposing, I should be committed. What I feel for you has destroyed my control. I feel so much for you, Georgia, it's all I can think of, dream of. I want to *marry* you. Make a family with you. Be your lover, your friend, the father of your children. Because I bloody well *love* you and if you can't see that, then too bloody bad because I won't be walking away from you. Ever."

"Sean…"

"I'm not the bloody clown you once pledged yourself to," he added, stabbing the air with his finger as he jabbed it at her. "You'll not compare me to him ever again."

"No," she said, still smiling.

"How much time have I left?"

"One minute," she said.

"Fine, then." He looked into those twilight eyes, and everything in him rushed toward the only happiness he would ever want or need. "Here it is, all laid out for you. I love you. And you bloody well love me. And you're damn well going to marry me at the first opportunity. And if you don't like that plan, you can spend the next fifty years complaining about it to me. But you *will* be mine. Make no mistake about that."

"You're nuts," Georgia said finally when the silence stretched out, humming with tension, with love, with the fraught emotions tangled up between them.

"I've said as much already, haven't I?"

"You have. And I love it."

He narrowed his gaze on her. "Is that right?"

"I do. I love everything about you, crazy man. I love how you look at me. I love that you think you can tell me what to do."

He scowled but, looking into her eyes, the dregs of his temper drained away, leaving him with only the love that had near choked him since the moment he'd first laid eyes on her.

"And I will marry you," she said, stepping into his arms. "On December twenty-second."

Gathering her up close, he asked, "Why the delay?"

"Because that way, Maeve wins the pool at the pub."

"You're a devious girl, Georgia," he said. "And perfect for me in every way."

"And don't you forget it," she said, grinning up at him.

"How much time have I got left?" he asked.

Never taking her gaze from his, she pulled her wristwatch off and tossed it aside. "We've got all the time in the world."

"That won't be enough," he whispered, and kissed her long and deep, until all the dark places inside him turned to blinding light.

Then he lifted his head and said softly, *"Tá tú an-an croí orm."*

She smiled and smoothed her fingertips across his cheek. "What does that mean?"

He kissed her fingers and told her, "'You're the very heart of me.'"

On a sigh, Georgia whispered, "Back atcha."

* * * * *